What the critics are saying

"A guaranteed winner for Ms Dunne and a fascinating read for every reader." - *Irene Marshall, Escape to Romance*

"An excellent story...you won't want to put down." - *Sensual Romance Reviews*

"Author Jennifer Dunne pens a fantastic tale of erotic romance sure to please and keep readers on their toes. The characters emotions and feelings leap off the pages, pulling the reader into the story. SEX MAGIC is very graphic, and the love scenes, though graphic, are beautifully orchestrated. I look forward to reading more from this talented author." - *Michelle Gann, The Word On Romance*

Discover for yourself why readers can't get enough of the multiple-award-winning publisher Ellora's Cave. Whether you prefer e-books or paperbacks, be sure to visit EC on the web at www.ellorascave.com for an erotic reading experience that will leave you breathless.

www.ellorascave.com

Ellora's Cave Publishing, Inc.
PO Box 787
Hudson, OH 44236-0787

ISBN # 1-84360-567-8

Sex Magic edited by Martha Punches.
Cover art by Darrell King.

Warning: The following material contains strong sexual content meant for mature readers. *SEX MAGIC* has been rated NC-17, erotic, by a minimum of three independent reviewers. We strongly suggest storing this book in a place where young readers not meant to view it are unlikely to happen upon it. That said, enjoy...

SEX MAGIC

Written by

JENNIFER DUNNE

PROLOGUE

Churning darkness filled the room, stabbing Simon with shards of smoke and drowning him in waves of rolling night. A thousand other impossibilities battered his senses as his mind struggled to perceive his opponent, to give form and substance to something that existed outside the realm of physical reality.

Hunger, hatred, and a soul-deep sense of wrongness coalesced into an acid blackness that seared Simon's lungs and burned his skin. Somewhere beyond the darkness, the burning candles still guarded all eight compass points—Simon felt their strength—but the evil entity he battled allowed none of their light to escape.

Simon raised his weary arms. "Attend!"

Power radiated from his hands in a blinding white flash and deafening crack. Spots danced across his vision and his ears rang with echoes, but he glimpsed flickers of candlelight and a hint of cool marble tiles soothed his burning feet. His senses were intact. His physical senses, anyway. He'd lost his good sense when he decided to confront the entity without knowing the extent of its power.

The dark cloud pulled away from him, roiling at the far edge of the circle binding them both. It stilled. His senses reeling, Simon focused on the island of reality at the center of the circle and braced himself for a counterattack.

The entity shrieked, scouring his eardrums with its rage, and poured forth, whipping around Simon until his naked body was coated with a powdery black residue, a sooty manifestation of the entity's malice. But it was unable to hurt him. For now.

"Hear me. Obey me," Simon chanted.

The wind howled with fury, lashing him with icy pellets that stung but did no harm. Realizing the futility of a direct assault, the entity turned its attack on the candles, smothering them with darkness.

Simon hesitated, gripped by cold fear. He'd already used more power than he usually needed, and all he'd done was contain the entity. If the candles died he was lost. Should he protect the candles or finish the banishing spell?

Taking a deep breath, he launched into the final stage of the spell. "I will you to leave this plane. I charge you to — "

The candles guttered and went out. Simon staggered at the sudden loss of power. With a gleeful howl, the entity swarmed over him.

Wrong again, Simon thought. Darkness obscured his vision. The powdered night crawled over his skin, draining the heat of life until his body trembled from the cold. It oozed into his ears and nose and trickled down his throat. He couldn't see. He couldn't breathe. The darkness was going to win.

Drawing on the last vestiges of his personal power, Simon choked out the final words of the spell. "I charge you to leave this plane. I command you to leave this plane. *Begone!*"

The circle vibrated with silence, as painful as the entity's shrieking had been. Simon had given everything he had to this battle, and it hadn't been enough. The entity still remained on the physical plane. He had failed.

Calling up his earliest lessons in magic, Simon banished the negative thoughts and focused his fading willpower on a single truth. The entity must be defeated. He allowed no doubt or question, cutting off the thread of his own power that was fueling the entity with his fear.

The darkness shrieked, roiled, then exploded into nothingness. The battle was over. Simon lay on the cold marble floor, gasping for breath. No sign remained of the entity or their battle, except the thin wisps of smoke rising from the snuffed candle stubs. But he knew he hadn't destroyed the entity. He hadn't even routed it back to its origins, although he'd expelled it from the material plane. The world was safe. Until the next time the entity tried to break through.

CHAPTER ONE

"He's coming in!"

"Who?" Beth Graham put the women's studies books she was shelving onto her cart. She brushed her wayward blonde bangs out of her eyes and craned her neck, but the tall bookcases blocked her view of the small bookstore's front windows. She turned her curious gaze on her coworker behind the counter instead. "Julie?"

"Simon Parkes. You remember, I told you all about him."

"The professor who orders all the weird books?"

"The really *hot* professor," Julie corrected. "I can't possibly wait on him today, not with the books he ordered. I just keep picturing him — well, never mind how I picture him. But he'd know I was thinking it."

A jangle of bells announced the mysterious professor's entry into the bookstore, bringing him into Beth's limited range of sight. She pretended to straighten the books on her cart and surreptitiously examined him.

He wore blue jeans and a faded green T-shirt, like many of the university students that gathered on the store's overstuffed couches to debate politics and philosophy. Older than the students by at least a decade, he radiated a self-confidence that negated any need for their ostentatious self-expression. His black hair was just long enough to show a slight wave, and styled in a traditional cut. He couldn't have made himself more ordinary if he'd tried.

But there was something about the way he moved that captured her attention and refused to let go. He walked with calm deliberation, placing each foot in precise and even intervals on a direct line to the counter. Although his gaze remained focused on his goal, he seemed aware of everything around him, reaching out without looking to push a loose book more securely onto its shelf as he passed, and pausing a fraction of a second before a customer engrossed in a book wandered across his path.

Julie was right. Professor Parkes was definitely hot, hot enough to burn the unwary. The man exuded an air of leashed power, an absolute control of himself and his surroundings. Without conscious volition, she found herself moving toward the counter.

Simon stopped in front of the counter. "Good afternoon, Julie. I had a message that my books were in."

"Yes, Professor Parkes." Julie looked at the professor, flushed a rosy pink, then reached out and pulled Beth the rest of the way behind the counter. "Beth will get your books and ring you out."

Julie fled for the back room, leaving Beth to smile nervously up at Simon Parkes.

Her gaze met his, and the breath caught in her throat. She knew exactly why Julie thought he could read minds.

His eyes, a green so pale they were almost gray, shimmered with intensity. It was as if his eyes were the only things he couldn't control, and they brimmed with all the fire and passion his restrained manner sought to contain.

"Hello, Professor Parkes." Her voice sounded breathy and completely unlike her normal tone. "I'm Beth. I'm new here."

He smiled, a dazzling beam of light that nearly toppled her to the floor. She lifted her hand to fan her suddenly hot face, then realized how revealing the gesture would be, and tucked a short blonde curl behind her ear instead.

His eyes sparkled as he watched her, giving credence to Julie's mind reading theory, and she wondered if he'd seen through her ruse. "A pleasure to meet you. I special ordered some books."

"Of course. I'll get them for you right away."

She turned to the low case filled with paper-wrapped bundles of books, some marked with Julie's neat handwriting, others with David's illegible scrawl. Bending down to see the P's, she felt Simon Parkes's intense gaze on her clinging jeans. Let him look. Two months of hiking cross-country had given her a figure to be proud of, toning the muscles now under his regard. She forced herself to breath deeply. Bending over like this was making her lightheaded.

She read off the names written on each set of books until she reached "Parkes." Grabbing the thick volumes rubber-banded beneath his cover sheet, she stood too quickly, making her head spin. She almost dropped the books. Instead they landed on the counter with a loud bang that echoed through the bookstore.

Beth smiled weakly. "Sounds like you have some weighty reading ahead of you."

He chuckled obligingly, although his eyes still burned with intensity.

She stripped off the paper and the rubber band holding the books together, then pulled them over to the barcode scanner. She hesitated, the scanner in her hand, as she read the first title. *Sex Magic of the Indian People.* Was that what Julie was afraid he'd know she was picturing?

Beth felt the heat of a blush on her cheeks as an image flashed into her mind of the professor shirtless and sweating, his brilliant gray/green eyes blazing with passion as he gazed down at her equally sweaty body beneath him.

The scanner beeped as it translated the barcode. Beth shifted the book aside, dreading what the next cover would reveal. *Modern Mystics and Ancient Teachings.* That wasn't so bad. *Make Money with Psychic Powers!* That was just silly.

She smirked, and dared a glance up. "Thinking of opening your own 900 number?"

His smile was somehow more charming and less devastating the second time around. "I'll keep that in mind if I ever need a second income. But for now, my research grants are sufficient."

"You get paid to read this stuff?"

"I'm an occult researcher." He shrugged. "Some of the most insightful information is found in books with lurid titles."

"Don't judge a book by its cover, huh?"

"Exactly."

His words could have been a warning, but his smile softened them, flooding her with a comforting warmth. He was only a somewhat eccentric professor, not some mystic Svengali. She turned cheerfully to ringing up the rest of his books. *Meditation Gardens. Advance Your Career Through Feng Shui. Nutritious Meals in Thirty Minutes or Less.*

She blinked at the last title, and looked up again. "Occult cooking?"

He cleared his throat and glanced away. "The days of dusty intellectuals being assigned housekeepers are long gone, and I'm really a terrible cook."

The words were out before she knew it. "Let me make dinner for you tomorrow, then. Do you like Mexican?"

* * * * *

Simon spent the next afternoon preparing for and conducting a divination spell. The answer was not what he'd wanted to hear.

He snuffed out the last candle and dispersed the lingering energy surrounding the altar. Sitting back on his heels, he contemplated the patterns of black sand before him.

The entity he'd so recently fought had not been banished to its original plane. As he'd feared, it was lurking at the edge of the ethereal plane, waiting until conditions were right for it to attack again. It didn't even have to breech the material plane to cause trouble. From the ethereal plane, it could easily tamper with the minds of dreamers or people whose connection to the material plane had been weakened by drugs.

He had to warn the other Guardians. But first, he needed to speak to his mentor. At the onset of their struggle, Simon had been fooled by the entity's resemblance to a simple elemental, and no one knew more about elementals than Andrew.

Simon stood and shook out the pale yellow robe he wore to perform divinatory magic, dislodging the grains of sand that had escaped the altar. Reaching out and stirring the sand pattern with his finger, he broke the last tenuous contact with the ethereal plane. What had only moments ago been a window onto another world was now just a pile of dirt and melted puddles of wax.

Turning his back on the remnants of his spell, he walked through the doorway into his study. By habit, he swung the concealing bookshelves back into place as soon as he was through the opening, even though he would need to go back inside to clean up after he made his calls.

The digital clock on his desk caught his attention, blinking 5:07 in glowing blue numbers. It was later than he'd thought. Andrew would already be at his afternoon classes. Simon couldn't count on reaching him until at least seven o'clock California time, or ten East Coast time. Simon would have to finish this later. For now, he needed to prepare for his dinner with Beth, and a different kind of magic.

* * * * *

As six o'clock approached, Beth split her time between glances out of her apartment window toward the street, and last-minute adjustments to dinner. She turned the oven to warm and filled her only two matching glasses with water. After setting the glasses on the round Formica table, she straightened the battered chrome chairs one last time, then darted back to the window.

A dark green Jeep Cherokee had pulled up to the curb since she'd last looked. A moment later, Simon stepped out of the car, a wine bottle in his hand. His dark hair looked delightfully tousled, as if he'd tried to put the wind-blown strands in order, but nothing short of styling gel could completely tame the wildness. Her pulse sped up as she wondered if, now that they were in private, she'd see an equally wild side to him.

He strode up the walkway to her building, his fluid movements reminding her of the leashed power of a prowling jungle cat. She smoothed the fabric of the red cotton leggings clinging to her thighs, and straightened her oversized red and white checked shirt one last time. The loose hem would pose no obstacle if Simon wanted to rest his strong hands at her waist, or glide them up beneath the shirt to caress her breasts.

Beth crossed to her door, and concentrated on breathing deeply. It was just a simple dinner invitation.

When the knock came at her door, she answered it immediately. Simon was just as breathtaking as she remembered. Black chinos hugged his legs, giving him a slightly dangerous air, while his burgundy and gray striped polo shirt brought out the gray in his eyes.

"Right on time." She smiled and stepped away from the door, gesturing for him to enter. Her shirt slid down her shoulder, and Simon's burning gaze locked on the exposed skin. She hadn't imagined his interest back at the bookstore. This evening was going to be much more than just dinner.

She hitched her shirt back into place, and Simon held out the wine. "For you."

"Thank you." Her fingers brushed against his as she took the bottle, and his fingertips trailed an answering caress across her skin as he released it. She looked down at the wine, needing a reprieve from the intensity of his gaze. It was a Merlot.

"This should go nicely with dinner," she told him.

"You said Mexican, so I thought red."

She grinned and waved her free hand at her red leggings and shirt. "So did I. I'm hoping salsa spills won't show on this."

Simon glanced down at his own clothing. "I'll just have to be careful, and hope for the best."

That's what she hoped for, too. Turning, she led him deeper into the apartment.

"Welcome to *Chez Beth*, decorated in what the design books call 'modern eclectic.' I call it 'early garage sale.' This is the living room."

A comfortable old sofa in red, white and blue plaid filled the wall beneath a windowsill covered in plants: African violets, impatiens, and a fuzzy-leafed cactus. More plants hung in baskets above the sofa: lipstick plants and bleeding hearts soaking up the sunshine, with spider plants and aloe filling the shadows.

The scratched wooden coffee table in front of the sofa held neatly piled books that had overflowed the mismatched bookcases against the other wall. She hadn't wasted her salary checks on clothing or furniture, knowing she'd just abandon most of it when she moved on to the next town. Instead, she'd taken full advantage of her employee discount at the bookstore. The knowledge and memories would travel with her, even though the books that had inspired them would be left behind.

The room's only other item was a 1960's pedestal table holding a television set, its antenna cocked at a crazy angle as if it were saluting. Her ex-husband would have been appalled at the display of poverty. Beth glanced at Simon. His reaction would tell her a lot about the professor's true personality.

"It's delightful," Simon told her.

Beth laughed, pleased that her impression of Simon had been correct. "Well, it'll sure beat sleeping trailside in the Adirondacks come winter. But you didn't come here to discuss my tastes in decorating. You came for dinner."

She led Simon through the archway into the tiny kitchen. It was so small that she couldn't open the oven and refrigerator doors at the same time, and couldn't open either if someone was sitting at the table. But instead of being cramped, the room felt cozy. Brightly colored sun catchers hung in the window, and potted herbs filled the windowsill and the small counter between the stove and sink.

Simon stood in the doorway, closed his eyes, and sniffed. "What is that delicious smell?"

She laughed. "Chili. Or marinated steak for the fajitas. Or maybe it's my secret special dessert."

"I can hardly wait."

"Pull up a chair. I'll get a couple of glasses for the wine. Fair warning—the glassware's as eclectic as the furniture."

Beth stretched to reach the cabinet, and felt Simon's hot gaze on her backside where her shirt rode up to show her leggings. She rose onto her toes, stretching for the farthest glasses in the cabinet, and heard his quick intake of breath.

A moment later, she turned and placed two juice glasses on the table beside the already full water glasses, then held out the wine bottle toward him. "Would you like to do the honors?"

"Certainly. Do you have a corkscrew?"

She grinned. "You can't just pull it out with your teeth, like those old pirates in the movies?"

"The pirates didn't have to contend with tamper resistant safety seals." He chuckled as he examined the bottle in his hands. "Perhaps I should just break the bottle against the table, like they do in Westerns?"

"Don't laugh. It may come to that." Disobeying her own order, Beth giggled as she hunted through a drawer. "Although you'd have to say something witty before you broke it. Maybe, this kitchen's not big enough for the both of us?"

He dropped his voice to a fair imitation of Clint Eastwood and asked, "Do you feel lucky, cook? Well, do ya?"

"I don't know. Do I?" She turned to search his expression. Did he want more than just dinner tonight?

Simon cleared his throat. "Did you find the corkscrew? That would be lucky."

"I found it. But I was kind of looking forward to seeing you break the bottle."

"Suit yourself. But I'd hate to spoil your wonderful dinner by having to pick bits of glass out of it."

"You'd better use the corkscrew."

She handed the utensil over to him, watching as Simon freed the cork with a few deft twists of his wrist. It came loose with a loud pop.

"How much?" he asked.

"Half a glass for me."

He nodded, and filled both glasses half way, but left the bottle on the table. While he was busy with the wine, Beth opened the oven door and pulled out a steaming bowl of chili topped with melted cheese, the whole thing surrounded by toasty warm tortilla chips.

She placed it on the table, then circled around to her own seat. They sat and both raised their wine glasses.

Simon touched the edge of his glass to hers. "To new friends."

Beth grinned, then drawled in a bad Bogart impression, "This could be the start of a beautiful friendship."

They sipped their wine. Simon had chosen an excellent brand. She scooped a pile of chili and melted cheese onto a tortilla chip and popped it into her mouth, closing her eyes and sighing in pleasure. Hot, smoky, and with just a hint of brown sugar. Perfect.

"When the cook likes it, it has to be good," Simon said.

She opened her eyes. "There's no place to get real Tex-Mex food here. When I was down in San Antonio, I waitressed at a little hole-in-the-wall dive with the most heavenly food. The cook took pity on a poor Northerner and taught me how to make it right."

Simon hesitated, a loaded chip halfway to his mouth. "What's the right way?"

Copying the cook's thick accent, Beth answered, "Hot enough to bring tears to your eyes, and sweet enough that you'll beg for more."

The chip snapped in Simon's fingers, splattering chili all over the Formica table top.

Beth immediately hopped up and wiped the table clean with her napkin, shattering the mood. Simon scooped up another chipful of chili and stuffed it into his mouth.

His eyes widened, his cheeks flushed, and his mouth opened, gasping for air. He grabbed his water glass, and Beth reached to stop him.

"No, don't drink —"

Simon howled, as the water only increased the jalapenos' potency. He panted for air, fanning his hand in front of his face.

"Simon, are you okay?"

"H-h-hot!" he gasped.

"Well, I did warn you."

He was starting to be able to breath again. "You said hot. You didn't say nuclear meltdown."

She hesitated, suddenly realizing he might not share her adventurous spirit when it came to food. "I hope the rest of the meal won't be too spicy for you to eat."

"I'm sure it'll be fine, now that I know what to expect. It's just..." He patted his mouth with exaggerated movements, clowning around. "I think I burned my lips off. I can't feel them."

She laughed. "It's the jalapeno juice. The feeling fades."

"You're sure?"

Brushing his hand away, she leaned across the table and kissed him lightly on the lips. "Did you feel that?"

Simon stared at her, the fire in his eyes hotter than any chili. "I'm not sure. Maybe you'd better try it again."

Beth leaned forward slowly. She closed her eyes as her lips touched his, savoring the taste and feel of him.

Opening his mouth slightly, he teased her lips apart, then captured her whispered sigh. The tip of his tongue brushed her lower lip, tantalizing her with its soft fire, but she pulled away before he could explore any further.

He definitely wanted more than just dinner.

Her cheeks blazed with as much heat as the chili, anticipating their desert. "I guess you felt it that time."

"Oh, yeah. Definitely sweet enough to have me begging for more."

"You'd better eat up, then. I don't want you fainting from hunger."

He ate another chip. This time he was prepared for the heat, and just smiled. "Delicious."

His gaze swept her lips, and she didn't think he meant the chili. But there was no need to rush. Anticipation heightened her senses, making her aware of the heat of Simon's legs beneath the table, legs he deliberately stretched out and twined with her own. His shining gaze scorched her, and his low voice caressed her as they deliberately lingered over the Tex-Mex feast, drawing out the exquisite torture. Their conversation roamed through favorite movies, places they'd each traveled, and books they'd both read, but their searing glances and brief touches as they reached for the same food only whetted their appetites for what would come after the meal.

Finally, only crumbs were left on their plates. Beth stood.

"I made desert. But I'm not sure if—"

Simon rose fluidly to his feet, a single step bringing him to her side. The silhouette of his chinos clearly showed the strength of his desire for her. "That wasn't the treat I was looking forward to."

Bending his head, he touched his lips to hers, and she swayed forward, closing the gap between them. His mouth devoured hers as she pressed her body against him, trembling beneath his touch. She ran her hands over his shirt, bunching it in her fists as she pulled it free of his waistband.

He groaned, the low sound echoing into her lungs, and slid his hands under the hem of her shirt to cup her bottom, pulling her closer. He was already hard and radiating more heat than the hottest Tex-Mex dish.

And she was already hotter and wetter than the most sultry San Antonio night. She rubbed against him, the thin cotton of her leggings no barrier to the delicious friction of his steely strength against her parted flesh, tender and aching for his touch. She wanted to rip his pants off, wrap her legs around his waist, and let him take her right here in the kitchen. Then she caught her hands moving to his belt and sanity briefly returned.

She tipped her head back, breaking their contact enough to speak. "I bought condoms, just in case. We'd better get one now, or it'll be too late."

He grinned, teasing her, although there was nothing light about the fire burning in his eyes. "Oh, no. I'm a very thorough researcher. Don't you recall the book I bought yesterday?"

Beth moistened her lips. *"Sex Magic of the Indian People?"*

"Mm-hmm." He nuzzled the curve of her neck, making her quiver in his arms. "I have something very special planned. This is going to take hours."

"Really?" she whispered. She couldn't imagine lasting another fifteen minutes without feeling him inside her, let alone hours. But she couldn't remember the last time her body had come alive like it was doing beneath his skilled touch. She was willing to follow his lead.

He scraped his teeth across the sensitive skin covering the pulse at her neck, following it with a deep, openmouthed kiss that set her blood humming. Her legs trembled, and she clung to him for support

"Really," he breathed.

CHAPTER TWO

On shaky legs, Beth led Simon into her bedroom, leaning against him for support. She'd tidied the room earlier, "just in case," so the velvet throw pillows were piled invitingly on the bed instead of being hopelessly scattered around the room as they usually were.

Simon stepped up close behind her, the heat of his body sizzling her skin even through her clothing. Wrapping his arms around her waist, he drew her even closer, until the ridge of his erection pressed into the cleavage of her bottom. One arm holding her tight against him, he slid his other hand down, between her thighs, to cup her dampness. He rocked her gently, pressing her first against his hand and then back against his erection, slowly, forward and back, again and again.

She moaned, low in her throat, forgetting where she was, what she'd been looking for, everything except the feel of his hand and his erection.

His warm breath fanned her ear as he asked, "Are you sure you want this?"

"Yes. Yes. Oh, God. Yes."

He stepped back, turning her so that she faced him before releasing her. "Then get undressed. Slowly."

She blinked. "You want me to undress myself? With you watching?"

He smiled. "It's traditional, according to the ancient rites of sex magic."

"You were just kidding about that, weren't you?" She hesitated, thinking back to the book Conn had brought home once to "liven up" their dying marriage. It had been awkward, uncomfortable, and worst of all, hadn't helped a damn. "I mean, you're not going to ask me to make love with my foot behind my ear or standing on my head or anything, are you?"

The teasing glint in Simon's eyes faded, replaced by an earnest sincerity. "I want to make love to you, Beth. And I know you want me to. The only question is how. We can do it the good old American way, if you'd be more comfortable with that."

He captured her hands and lifted them to his lips, pressing a warm kiss into the center of each palm. Heat flowed outward from the twin points of contact, filling her veins with liquid fire and sparking an inferno deep inside her. She needed this man, now, and she didn't care how.

Simon opened his grasp and stepped away, her fingers sliding through his until she touched only air. Her hands remained stretched toward him, mutely begging for his touch.

"But if you let me," he continued. "I will worship you as the living embodiment of the goddess. Everything I do will be to give you pleasure. You can stop me at any moment with just a word."

"Stop?"

"If you wish."

"I don't wish." A heady sense of adventure filled her. "I've never been considered a goddess before."

Trembling with eagerness, she grabbed the hem of her big shirt and jerked it upward.

"Slowly!" Simon reminded her. "Imagine how I would remove your clothing, teasing you with each brush of fabric against your skin, and let your hands do it for me."

Beth paused, then began inching the fabric upward, gathering it in her fists. She felt the fluttering hem brush her stomach, then slink slowly up her ribs.

She closed her eyes, listening to Simon's deep breathing and feeling the heat of his gaze on her exposed flesh. She imagined his hands were the ones that inched the top slowly higher, revealing the lower edge of her lacy bra. If he was the one undressing her, would he continue to raise the shirt, or would he pause to fondle and caress her breasts through the fabric?

Beth swung the loose hem of her shirt from side to side, arching her back and straining forward as if it was Simon's fingertips ghosting sweet caresses across her breasts. The cotton slid smoothly over the satiny lace of her bra, teasing her nipples into hard pebbles that ached for Simon's lips and teeth to claim them. His breathing grew ragged, a harsh note in the otherwise quiet room.

"Like that?" she whispered.

"Oh, yes." His reply was equal parts sigh and groan.

She pulled the shirt the rest of the way over her head and tossed it away. She reached for the closure of her bra, then changed her mind. Instead, she ran her fingers through her hair, slowly, extending the movement into a long, languorous stretch.

Simon groaned. "You're torturing me."

She hesitated, not quite sure of the rules of their game. "Should I stop?"

"*No!*"

Laughing, she unhooked her bra, then rolled her shoulders to slowly slide the straps down her arms. When it started to fall, she quickly snatched it away, flashing her breasts at him, before lifting the lacy fabric back up to conceal them. She slid the bra back and forth, teasing her nipples until her breath was as ragged as his, and every brush of lace against her sensitive skin seemed to send a wave of fire straight to her core. She tossed the scrap of fabric aside.

Simon sucked in a sharp breath. "You're beautiful."

Beth smiled. She felt beautiful. She felt powerful. But mostly, she felt on fire and aching for his touch.

She kicked off her shoes, then drew down her leggings with a liquid shimmy. That left only her panties.

Hooking her fingers into the waistband, she glanced at Simon. His face was flushed, and his hands flexed and clenched at his sides. His burning gaze was locked on her fingers.

In a husky voice, he whispered, "Please."

His voice spurred her into motion, and she quickly stripped off the last of her clothing.

"You're a goddess."

"Now it's your turn."

Nodding, he slowly lifted his polo shirt, inching it up just the way she'd done. Beth watched, transfixed, as he revealed his rippled abdomen and sculpted ribs. A light arrow of fine black hair drew her attention down, to the tented bulge in his black chinos.

She pulled her attention back with a snap. She already knew he was aroused. The purpose of this little performance was to arouse her, and she didn't intend to miss a moment of it. She watched as he raised his shirt higher, the fluttering hem exposing tantalizing glimpses of dark nipples on his impressive pectorals.

She leaned forward, her fingers aching to play with the light dusting of fine black hairs, and trail seductive patterns over his taut skin.

Simon chuckled. "Not so easy, is it?"

"What?" She blinked, pulled out of her sensual imaginings by his voice.

"It's not easy to stand there without moving."

Beth glanced at his face. His very close face. She was only a foot away from him!

Blushing, she backed up, returning to her previous spot. "No fair. You've had more practice."

Simon shook his head. "Not really. My knowledge of Tantra is theoretical, not practical."

"Oh?" A thrill coursed through her. Given Simon's good looks and the force of his personality, it couldn't have been for lack of offers. "Why?"

"The ritual only works if the man can honestly worship the woman as a goddess. I haven't met many goddesses. In fact, you're the first."

Beth's breath caught. She was his first. The words were an intoxicating aphrodisiac, filling her with a sense of power.

He tossed his shirt aside. Slowly, he unfastened his belt and drew it out of the belt loops. Instead of throwing it onto his crumpled shirt, he ran the thin leather over his stomach. She saw his muscles clench, and hungered to have him respond to her touch that way. She flexed her hands, imagining the feel of his heated skin beneath the pads of her fingers.

Then he slid the belt down and across his erection. Beth gasped, her hands tightening into fists, as he stroked the leather up and down.

"Would you stroke me like this?" Simon whispered, suiting his motions to his words. "Long and slow, wrapping your hands around me until you encompass me, until you are my world?"

Beth whimpered, her hands clenching and unclenching as she trembled with desire, hungering to hold Simon's hot manhood in her grasp, taming and containing all that power for herself.

Simon's eyes were closed, and his head was tilted back, seemingly lost in the sensations as the belt glided up and down. He was getting off without her! Then she noticed the telltale glimmer beneath his lashes. His eyes were slitted open so that he could watch her reaction. Her suspicions raised, she paid more attention to what he was doing with the belt, and noticed the fabric of his pants wasn't moving as the leather slid up and down his erection. The belt wasn't actually touching him. He was teasing her!

"Very funny. It's not nice to fool your goddess."

"Your humble servant begs forgiveness. To prove my dedication, I will worship you for twice as long."

Despite his playful tone, Beth's heart started racing. What would it be like to spend all night being loved by him? Judging from the tension thrumming through her now, she wasn't sure she could survive it.

But Simon took pity on her, and quickly peeled off the rest of his clothing. She caught her breath and stared. He was magnificent.

His legs were firmly muscled, toned and sleek like a Greek sculpture. And the sight of his jutting erection made her all quivery. She could hardly wait to feel his masculine heat pulsing inside her.

She pointed silently to the box of condoms on her dresser. While he took care of that, she admired the view from behind. His shoulders, back and buttocks were as perfectly formed as the rest of him, lean and muscular, although the perfection was marred by a cluster of faded scars nearly three inches across, high on his left shoulder.

He turned back to face her.

Beth's face flamed, but Simon didn't seem bothered by her ogling. He wasn't smug or strutting around like a rooster, either. He just accepted it, willing to wait for her to finish studying him if necessary. But she didn't want to wait.

"Now what?" she breathed.

She watched Simon walk over to the bed and sit down in the middle of her deep purple comforter, folding his legs so that the soles of his feet pressed together and his knees stuck out to the sides. It looked like some kind of yoga posture. Beth's mouth went dry at the proof of Simon's flexibility, and she wondered what he had planned.

He breathed deeply, closing his eyes. Amazingly, he looked completely relaxed and not the least bit hurried. A few moments later, he opened his eyes and smiled at her.

Holding out his hand to her, he said, "Come here."

She clasped his hand and climbed onto the bed beside him. The warmth of his palm soothed and relaxed her hand, turning her arm as limp as a string. "I'm here."

"So you are." He lifted their clasped hands to his lips and brushed a soft kiss across the back of her hand, sending a shiver of delight through her. "Now, sit here, facing me."

She thought she'd feel awkward, but all she felt was a burning desire to be as close to Simon as possible, in every way. She wanted him inside her, filling her, completing her, but sensed that this was something that could not be rushed. Simon promised her more than physical completion, and as much as she hungered for the physical pleasures he could give her, she was starved for the mental and emotional fulfillment she sensed waiting for her. She would do whatever he said, follow wherever he led, and hope it would be enough.

Simon helped Beth settle herself so that she was sitting on top of his feet, cradled by his spread legs, with her feet resting on the bed beside his hips. She could feel the heat rising from him, burning like an inferno where her calves crossed his thighs.

He lifted his right hand and rested it between her breasts. "I feel your heart beating, sending your life force rushing through your veins. I feel your lungs breathing, inhaling the joy and love of a boundless universe, exhaling all fear and anger."

"I'm not angry."

"Not at me. Not right now. But sometime in the past?"

Beth blinked, remembering the last disastrous time she had made love. She had confronted Conn, demanding to know if he was cheating on her, forcing him to admit he still loved and desired her. He'd taken her to bed, but their sex had been angry and strained and solved nothing. Later, he confessed to an affair with one of his associates.

Beth felt a hot tear roll down her cheek. She sniffled, trying to hold it in. She'd be damned if she was going to act like a silly fool and totally humiliate herself in front of Simon.

"Sh," he whispered. "Don't fight it. Let the hurt and anger out. Just breathe."

He lifted her hand and placed her palm against his own chest, mirroring his position. His heart beat steadily beneath her fingers, and his chest moved in and out with his breath. In. Wait. Out. Wait. In.

She closed her eyes, and let herself breathe in time with Simon. Tears rolled down her cheeks, but she ignored them. When they stopped, she felt lighter, freed of a weight she hadn't known she'd been carrying.

Simon's soft voice murmured gentle commands that flowed over her in time with their breathing. She felt radiant, as if her spirit had expanded to fill the whole room, yet at the same time incredibly focused and aware of Simon surrounding her, his knees hugging her hips, his hand on her chest, and the heat building between her legs.

"I'm moving forward now," he said, inching his body closer to her. Her breasts flattened against his chest, capturing his hand and hers between them. His erection pressed against her opening, which was already wet and pulsing with need for him, but there was no sense of urgency. She felt as if she was floating in a sea of warm water that ebbed and flowed around her, lapping against her shore.

Beth relaxed and let the waves wash over her. Simon slid inside her, filling her, but just resting and touching her the way his hand rested on her chest. Listening to his words, she imagined a golden cord stretching between his hand and his erection, stroking and caressing her as it passed through her heart, her lungs, and all her internal organs.

Then, as if he had pulled on the imaginary cord, he flexed inside her. Beth gasped, then released her breath on a shuddering moan.

"Breathe," Simon reminded her. "Breathe. In."

He flexed again, filling her deeper and fuller than before.

"And out."

He relaxed, still inside her, but resting instead of pressing.

"And in."

Beth drew in a ragged breath as he flexed inside her, filling her with his presence, loving her from the inside out.

"And out."

She exhaled, shuddering, unbearably aroused to feel him remaining fully inside her.

"And in."

He flexed, sparking an uncontrollable trembling in all her muscles.

"And out."

When he relaxed, the need to feel him filling her again drove her wild. Her muscles clenched, trying to draw him deeper inside her when he was already completely sheathed by her. Her arms and legs tightened. She had to have him.

"And in."

She screamed, an exultant cry of pure joy, and shattered in a total release. Seconds, minutes or hours later, she became aware of Simon's heartbeat beneath her fingers, of his lungs breathing in time with hers, of his warm hand resting on her chest. Of his erection filling her.

Beth blinked, pulling back slightly so she could focus on his face. Simon's confident smile stopped just short of being smug.

"Did you like that?"

"It was…I can't…Yes! But you didn't…"

"I'm not supposed to."

She frowned, trying to make sense of his words. Her thoughts were still floating, unwilling to rouse themselves to coherency. Simon reached up and lightly stroked her forehead, brushing her frown away.

"My role is to worship you," he reminded her. "My pleasure comes from giving you pleasure."

Her eyes widened. "Oh, God…"

"Oh, goddess," he corrected gently, leaning in to press a soft kiss against her lips. And then he flexed again.

Beth abandoned all rational thought and let him worship her as he willed.

* * * * *

Beth woke to the light caress of Simon's hand stroking slowly up and down her back. The room was midnight black, and she lay tangled with him in the darkness, one leg between his muscular thighs and her palm splayed on his warm and solid chest.

She smiled and snuggled closer. "You want to do it again already?"

"Excellent as that sounds, the reason I woke you is that I have to leave."

"Leave?" Disappointment hit her with an icy fist in the stomach. "You didn't leave when we finished, so I thought you were staying the night."

Simon laughed softly and dropped a light kiss on her hair. "If you'll remember, I couldn't move when we finished."

She remembered. They'd made love for four glorious hours, as Simon alternated long, slow explorations of her entire body with giving her soul-shattering orgasms. He'd kept himself under perfect control while her control exploded again and again, until she'd finally begged him to allow himself to climax. His entire body had shaken with the force of his coming, lasting longer than she'd thought possible for a man, and leaving him so spent he was nearly unconscious. They'd barely had the strength to clean themselves up before crawling beneath the covers and falling fast asleep.

She caressed his chest, sliding her fingertips over his skin. "What time is it, anyway?"

"About two o'clock."

"You were so tired. You can't possibly have had enough rest. Why don't you grab a few more hours sleep? We can set the alarm for five."

"Actually, I feel full of energy," Simon confessed.

"So you *do* want to make love again?"

He laughed. "That would keep us busy until well after five."

Beth's cheeks flared with heat. "I don't have to be at the store until noon."

Simon caught her close in a fierce hug. "You have no idea how tempting that is. But I need to get home soon. I have a telecon with the West Coast."

"At two in the morning?" Beth squeaked. Conn had given her some far-fetched excuses to disguise his infidelity during their marriage, but even he had never tried to make her believe something so outlandish. "Look, if you don't want to stay the night, just say so. You don't have to lie."

"Beth, I wouldn't lie to you." All traces of humor had faded from Simon's voice, and he cupped her face to stare into her eyes. It was too dark to see the nuances of his expression, but she could tell he was intent on convincing her of his sincerity.

Her heart insisted that she trust him. She frowned, dismayed to discover that experience had taught her nothing.

"Beth, I honestly do need to call the West Coast. In another hour, it'll be midnight there. I'm a researcher of the occult. That's an important time for us."

Still not entirely convinced, she grumbled, "I certainly approve of the results of your research. But why do you have to leave? Can't you call from here?"

She felt him stiffen slightly.

"My notes are at my house."

"Oh." They'd learned every inch of each other's bodies, but she had no clue what was going on in Simon's head. She sensed that her reaction now could make or break their relationship.

Beth took a deep breath. She had learned something from her marriage to Connor. If she allowed Con's lying and infidelity to poison all her future relationships, she'd never be free of the jerk. She'd trust Simon.

"When will I see you again?"

Simon frowned slightly, and seemed to be deep in thought. "I'm not sure. It depends how this call goes. I might need to go out of town."

He absent-mindedly rubbed her back in small circles while he spoke, his hand gradually easing down the length of her spine until he reached the small of her back. Increasing the pressure of his strokes slightly, he pulled her hips against his. His heated erection slid up her inner thigh.

She'd teased him earlier about being ready to make love again, but the answering warmth between her legs proved she was equally eager. She shifted her leg from between his thighs to the outside of his leg, opening herself to his loving touch.

The tip of Simon's erection slipped between her damp folds, and she moaned as desire burst over her. Their previous lovemaking had only increased her need to feel Simon's hands and lips and tongue upon her body, to feel his fingers or tongue or pulsing erection deep within her.

Simon caught his breath, then forcefully pulled away from her, separating them, although his hands remained on her hips.

"I have to go, Beth. And if we start now, I won't leave until dawn." Rolling her over, he knelt between her legs. "But we have time for me to give you a proper kiss good-bye."

She swallowed dryly, feeling her liquid heat building, anticipating his touch. Her breasts tingled, nipples tightening, as she lay beneath him, eager for whatever sensual delight he had planned.

"What would a proper kiss be?"

"Let me show you."

Scooting down under the covers, he knelt at her feet. Picking up her left foot and cradling it in his hands, he pressed a warm, openmouthed kiss on her instep.

A path of fire blazed up her leg, connecting Simon's mouth directly with her sex. Beth flexed her hips and moaned his name. He trailed tiny nibbling kisses up the sole of her foot, then took each of her toes one at a time into his mouth, fondling them with his tongue and suckling on them. Every tug seemed to pull at her very core, fanning the fire of passion.

Too soon, he set her foot down. Then he picked up her other foot and repeated the process. She gasped at his hot kiss, and whimpered each time his mouth pulled lightly on her toes.

Setting that foot down, Simon whispered, "Blessed be your feet, that have carried you to this place."

He moved so that his body covered hers, although his weight was braced on his palms, holding him a tantalizing fraction of an inch above her. Before she could arch her back to press herself against him, Simon bent his head and captured her mouth in a fiery kiss.

Beth opened her mouth to him, welcoming his tongue as he explored and then devoured her. He swallowed her whimpered cries as he feasted on her lips, then captured her tongue and drew it into his mouth. He suckled her tongue with his hot, moist mouth, teasing the sensitive flesh with swirling caresses of his own tongue. She moaned, her fingers fisting in the sheets to keep from clutching his taut buttocks and driving his erection inside her where she ached for him to be.

Simon lifted his head, and in a husky whisper said, "Blessed be your lips, that speak sacred words of blessing."

"Simon..."

He knelt between her legs again, near enough that she could feel his heat upon her pulsing core, but agonizingly far from her touch. Then he cupped her breasts, kneading the tender tissue, and she arched upward, thrusting her chest into his hands. He rotated his palms against her aching nipples, the light brush stirring waves of pleasure through her. Then he took one hand away, replacing it with his mouth.

He scraped her aureole lightly with his teeth, his tongue playing round and round her nipple, while he mimicked the action with his fingernails and thumb on her other breast. Beth's hands clenched and unclenched and her head turned frantically from side to side, seeking the release she knew she wouldn't find until Simon was ready to give it to her.

"Please..." she moaned.

He pulled her breast deep into his mouth and suckled her, and her inner dam burst. Hot liquid flowed over her folds, and tears leaked from her eyes.

"More..."

Simon switched his attentions to her other breast, scraping and suckling, while his fingers rolled the damp nipple he'd previously kissed, further arousing her sensitized flesh.

Her hips rose and fell without her conscious volition, instinctively seeking the final touch that would put an end to her glorious suffering.

Simon drew away from her. "Blessed be your breasts, founts of nourishment."

He placed his hands upon her thighs, and she eagerly spread them wider, but he didn't enter her. Instead, he bent her legs, and kissed the back of her knee. His tongue darted out to stroke the pulsing vein, and Beth gasped as each stroke echoed within her. He turned and repeated the kisses and strokes behind her other knee.

"Blessed be your knees, upon which you kneel before the altar of the goddess."

His hands caressed her thighs, slipping on the slick moisture of her desire that had already welled forth. Then his thumbs pressed inside her.

Beth arched upward, needing to feel Simon's touch inside her. "Please, Simon. Please. Now."

He brushed her aching bud once, twice, then a third time, pulling a hoarse cry from her with every touch. Then his thumbs settled firmly between her folds, spreading them wide open, and he pressed his mouth to her opening in an intimate kiss.

Beth bucked and writhed, mindless with need, as Simon's tongue plunged deep within her and he suckled, hard, drawing every drop of moisture from her and demanding more. Her whole body shaking, she begged and pleaded, urging him to kiss her harder, deeper, and faster. He did.

She came in a powerful rush, flooding his mouth with her juices, then collapsed like a boneless rag doll. He swept his tongue around her once last time, ensuring that she was fully satisfied. Lifting his head, he said, "Blessed be your womb, giver of life."

Simon waited a moment, but Beth was too far gone to know whether it was to observe the results of his handiwork or for some other reason. She tried to say something, but her mouth would only form soft kittenish mews. The bed shook and she felt suddenly cold as Simon left her side. He straightened her legs and pulled the covers over her, then brushed the back of his hand against her cheek in a gentle caress.

"That is a proper kiss," he told her.

He dressed and left the apartment before Beth could think of a coherent reply.

* * * * *

The streets were all but deserted, and Simon retraced his route from Beth's apartment to his home far faster than he'd covered it on his way to dinner. Settling himself in the padded desk chair in his study, he called his mentor.

After the usual pleasantries, Simon quickly explained about his battle with the entity. As soon as Andrew reassured himself that Simon had suffered no lasting ill effects from the battle, he launched into a tirade, accusing Simon of disgracing Andrew's teaching as his mentor and recklessly endangering the people they were duty bound to protect. Simon winced and held the phone away from his ear while Andrew lambasted him. When Andrew paused to take a breath, Simon interrupted.

"I know it was foolish of me to confront an unknown elemental without asking you for guidance, but the point is that I did, and the banishing spell didn't work."

Andrew stopped shouting. Simon could picture him twirling a pen between his fingers the way he did whenever he was at a momentary loss for words.

"Are you sure you identified it correctly?"

"Yes. Or I couldn't have banished it to the ethereal plane. But with your help, I'm sure I can dismiss it entirely."

"Simon, Simon, Simon. Have you learned nothing?"

"I learned I was wrong to face this entity alone, and that I need your help."

"You were a better student when you were here in Berkeley. Those cold northern winters must be freezing your brain cells."

"I—"

"What you *should* have learned is that you entered a battle unprepared, without knowing your enemy's full strengths and weaknesses, and were taken by surprise."

"But it's lurking in the ethereal plane where it can reach people's minds."

"I'll help you strengthen your wards, and see what can be done about stirring up the ether. But in the meantime, you need to study this entity. Are you strong enough to do a spell of insight?"

"Yes. I'm almost back up to full power."

"So soon?"

"I...performed a Tantric ritual tonight."

The phone went suddenly silent.

"Andrew?"

"You never mentioned a girl."

"I just met her yesterday."

"And you performed Tantra tonight?"

He hadn't gone to Beth's apartment with that intention, but he wasn't about to apologize for his actions when she'd so clearly welcomed and enjoyed the experience. The rejuvenation of his magical powers had been an unanticipated side benefit of their phenomenal lovemaking.

Anger flushed Simon's face. "Don't preach at me, Andrew. You sleep with anything in a skirt. I've seen you conducting Tantric rituals with women half an hour after meeting them."

Andrew laughed. "That's me, Simon. I love women, all kinds of women. Always have and always will. I can perform Tantra with any woman because I can see the goddess in all of them. But you're not me."

"I had no trouble seeing the goddess in Beth."

"Hmm. This paragon is named Beth. I knew a woman named Beth, once."

"No surprise there," Simon muttered.

"I look forward to meeting her."

"No!"

Andrew chuckled. "Jealous?"

The thought of Andrew meeting Beth, of her becoming another of Andrew's casual conquests, filled Simon with terror, but he'd never admit that. "It's just that I won't be seeing her again for a while, not until this is all over."

"I don't think so."

Simon felt like he'd been kicked in the ribs. Although Andrew's primary expertise was controlling elemental forces, like all of their kind, he worked in all branches of magic. His rare precognitions were legendary for their accuracy. "You don't think I'll see her again?"

"I don't think you'll wait that long. One of the few things you managed to learn about the entity is that even at your full strength, you can barely best it. With all the wards and investigative magics we'll be casting, you'll need her power to buttress yours."

"Ah, well, if it's for the good of my job as Guardian, I suppose I can see her again." For once, his own desires coincided with his duty as a Guardian. Simon's spirits leapt. He wondered if Beth would still be awake when he finished his call to Andrew.

What was he thinking? It was almost dawn. But he'd call her as soon as he could. He could hardly wait to see her again.

CHAPTER THREE

Beth took advantage of the brief afternoon absence of customers to start shelving books, fighting hard to concentrate on each title. Julie joined her in transferring the popular fiction books from the cart to the shelves, but Beth wasn't fooled into thinking she'd been overcome with a sudden urge to be helpful. Julie had been trying to get her alone since she'd come to the store at noon.

"Okay, so dish. How was it?"

"How was what?" Beth hid her smile behind a copy of Oprah's latest book club pick.

"Don't give me that. You know exactly what I'm talking about. Your date with Simon Parkes. How'd it go?"

"He brought a bottle of wine, admired my decorating, nearly choked on the chili, and had me in stitches with some of his stories. I had fun."

Julie made a face. "But did you do it?"

Beth didn't answer. What she'd shared with Simon could hardly be called "doing it," like high school kids getting a quickie in the back seat of a car. She wasn't sure what to call what they'd done, but just the memory was enough to heat her cheeks and make her feel warm inside.

"You did!" Julie crowed.

"We slept together," Beth admitted. And they had, briefly, after the sex, until Simon had to leave for his midnight teleconference.

She frowned, still troubled by Simon's odd excuse. Memories sprang up, of Con's late nights at the office researching briefs—and panties, and thongs.

Dismissing the past, she ruthlessly shoved books onto the shelf, whether there was room for them or not.

Julie grabbed the book from her hands. "You're putting the Stephen King's in the middle of the Danielle Steele's. Was it that bad?"

"No, it was...incredible. He started making love to me after dinner, and didn't stop until well after midnight."

Julie's eyes widened. "When did you finish dinner?"

"About seven-thirty."

"Four and a half hours?" Julie squeaked.

Beth smiled, remembering. She could still feel the heat of Simon's body pressed to hers as he carried her to the stars. "Yeah. And his goodnight kiss knocked me for a loop, too."

"You're going out with him again, right?"

Beth's smile disappeared and she returned to shelving books, careful to get the titles in the right place this time. Her memory of their early morning conversation was somewhat blurry, but she thought he'd promised to call, if he didn't have to leave town. He couldn't have kissed her like he did if she didn't mean something to him, but clearly his work was more important. She remembered all the dinners that went cold while she waited for Conn, the times she'd called his office to remind him that he'd promised to be home an hour earlier. Even when he hadn't been having an affair, he'd always put his work ahead of her. She couldn't go through that again.

She *wouldn't* go through that again. Wasn't that the point of her new footloose lifestyle? She was finally free to go everywhere and do everything she'd been denied all those years as Conn's perfect wife. But did she want to avoid getting involved with Simon because she was embracing her freedom, or was she just afraid?

"I don't know, Julie. Maybe I'll go out with him again and maybe I won't."

"After a night like that?"

"There's more to life than just sex."

"Yeah, there's books and chocolate. And I already know he likes books." Julie hesitated, then dropped her voice to a whisper even though there was no one else in the store. "Is that it? Was the sex, you know, kinky?"

"You have no idea. But I'm just not ready for any kind of commitment."

"Who said anything about commitment?"

Beth laughed. "No one. As long as we keep it simple, and the sex is great, why not?"

She'd just have to make it clear to him that she wasn't interested in a messy emotional entanglement. They were adults. Surely they'd be able to enjoy each other's company without needing to put strings and conditions on their time together. Couldn't they?

She shelved the latest Tom Clancy book and wished she was working in the self-help section. Dr. Ruth or Dr. Joyce Brothers would have something to say about her situation, she was sure. They'd be able to tell her why something that made so much sense felt like such a mistake.

* * * * *

Simon collapsed into his chair, reaching for the phone before he finished sitting. He finally had a chance to call Beth, and he wasn't wasting it.

She answered on the third ring. "Northview Books. How may I help you?"

"Beth, it's Simon."

"Simon." She breathed his name on a sigh, then held an urgent whispered conversation in the background. "I just got rid of Julie, but she won't stay away long."

He chuckled, pleased that she seemed as eager to talk to him as he'd been to talk to her. "I'll make this quick, then. When can I see you again?"

"You don't have to go out of town after all?"

Simon frowned. Had that been a chill he'd heard in Beth's voice? He wished he'd been able to wait and see her in person. So much was lost over a telephone line.

"No, I don't have to go out of town. My teleconference was sufficient." He lowered his voice to a teasing note. "I wanted to phone you when I was done, but didn't think you'd appreciate a call at four in the morning."

"Four in the morning! You must have been asleep on your feet."

"The call was exciting enough to keep me awake. Not as exciting as what happened earlier, of course."

Beth laughed. "Simon!"

He leaned back in his chair and put his feet up on the desk. He must have imagined the coldness in her voice earlier, because she sounded warm and happy now. Simon's pulse sped as he remembered her heated skin pressed to his. He could almost smell the scent of her, a combination of her shampoo and her arousal, like musky gardenias. He smiled, wondering what she'd say if he told her that.

"I slept late," he confided instead. "And almost missed my ten o'clock class. The students were about to invoke the fifteen-minute rule. I think I disappointed a few of them when I actually showed up."

"You've had classes since then?"

"Or meetings. This was my first down time all day. Which gets me back to the reason I called. When can I see you again?"

"How about Saturday? I'm working until two, but I'm free after that."

"Saturday it is. Do you have anything you'd like to do?"

"This is your town. Pick something to show me."

"You've seen it already."

"Simon!" Beth laughed again. "I meant something around town. What do people do around here, besides go to the mall?"

"That's pretty much it. We're a cultural wasteland."

"Then you have between now and Saturday to think something up." She hesitated, then added with a husky tone in her voice, "Although, I wouldn't mind seeing some familiar sights afterwards."

Simon's fingers tightened on the phone. He really wanted to be having this conversation in person, to see the expression on Beth's face.

Door bells jingled faintly across the line, and Beth said, "A customer just walked in. I've gotta go. See you Saturday."

"I'll come meet you at the bookstore."

The phone went dead in his hand. Simon returned it to the cradle with a sigh. Saturday seemed an eternity away. But at the same time, it barely gave him enough time to prepare. If Beth was going to help him with his magic, he had a lot of things to get ready. He'd better stop daydreaming and get to work.

* * * * *

"But Professor Parkes, there's something I just don't understand."

Simon nodded at the gangly senior, one of the few undergraduates allowed in his graduate seminar. "What is it, Carl?"

"Well, if the Eastern tradition says red candles are for joy and happiness, and the Western tradition says red candles are for passion and lust, and the Kabalistic tradition says red candles are for strength, and the Feng Shui tradition says red candles are for fame and fortune..." He shrugged melodramatically and waved his hands. "How can they have any meaning at all?"

Simon smiled. "A good question. Any ideas?"

He scanned the other students seated in the circle, some of whom were frowning as if this was the first time they'd considered the question. Susan glared at Carl, but she glared at everyone she thought was questioning the validity of Wiccan practice. Jon looked bored with the question, again, his usual expression. But a few students nodded.

"Heather? What do you think?"

She tucked a strand of her brown hair behind her ears and sat up straighter in her chair. "The candle has no meaning on its own. The meaning comes from its use by the magician."

"Exactly." Simon pulled his wallet from his back pocket, took out a ten dollar bill, and dropped it onto the floor in the center of the circle. "What is that worth?"

"Ten dollars?" Carl asked.

"Why?"

"It's a ten dollar bill," Jon pointed out.

"Uh, because our society agrees to treat it as a shorthand for ten dollars worth of goods or services?" Alex ventured his opinion.

Simon kept silent, smiling and nodding encouragement, but waiting for all of the students to answer. Most of them were skirting around the correct answer, getting bits and pieces of it.

Then Heather said, "Because we believe that's how much it's worth."

"Exactly." Simon leaned forward and retrieved his money. "So what do the red candles mean?"

"Whatever we believe they do?" Carl guessed.

"Right. Now, is it possible—"

A blinding pain shot through Simon's left temple. He gasped, blinking his eyes until the darkness faded from his vision. His students were all staring at him.

"Excuse me. Migraine. Heather, lead the discussion until I get back."

He hurried from the room, hearing Jon's snide comment to the other students, "Why doesn't he just magic it away?"

"Magic doesn't work like that," Susan snapped.

Simon rubbed his pounding head as he walked to his office. Susan was wrong. Magic did work like that, except it caused headaches more often than it cured them. That's why he was suffering now. The entity had breached Simon's wards on the etheric plane, triggering his warning spell.

Slipping inside his darkened office, he breathed deeply as the pain vanished. His office wards protected him from the effects of the entity's attack just as they'd protect him from a direct attack, freeing Simon to devote his attention to driving the entity back.

He lit a white candle to focus his attention, quickly running through the breathing and visualization exercises needed to bring his body to the proper state for working magic. He increased the power to his wards, knowing that with the bulk of its power contained, any of the entity's extrusions into the material plane would soon wither and collapse. It seemed to be weakening, then a sudden surge of power nearly ruptured Simon's remaining ward.

Pain lanced through his skull. Simon gasped, ignoring his crumbled office defenses to throw his full power into the etheric ward. White light flared behind his eyes. His magical headache disappeared, replaced by a more mundane throbbing of overexertion.

He put his head down on the desk, sucking in gulps of air. Gradually, he realized he was sitting in the dark. When had the candle gone out? More importantly, where had the power for the entity's last attack come from? Had it connected to someone on the material plane and been able to draw energy from the connection? He needed to investigate the disturbances in the ether and trace them back to their source.

But first he had to get back to his class.

The pounding in Simon's temples increased. He sighed as he put his supplies away. He'd love to magically remove the pain, but he had to reserve his strength for the things that mattered. His comfort wasn't one of them.

Simon fumbled for the bottle of aspirin in his top drawer. He tipped two pills into his hand, then pictured the reactions of Susan, Jon, and the others at being left unattended for so long. He shook two more pills into his hand.

* * * * *

A good night's sleep got rid of Simon's headache, but left him no nearer to an answer. He was leafing through one of the research books in his study the following morning when the phone rang.

"Hello?"

"Professor Parkes? This is Detective Freemont."

A chill invaded Simon's heart as he lowered the book to his desk. He'd worked with Thomas Freemont before, and knew the fair but skeptical detective would never call him unless he was faced with a clearly magical crime.

"How can I help you, Detective?"

"I'd like you to take a look at one of my cases. Can you come downtown today?"

Simon didn't feel up to dealing with the atmosphere of the police station today. "Can you come out to the campus?"

"No."

Freemont had files for him to review, then, not just a few questions. Probably crime scene photos. Of an obviously occult crime. The pieces clicked together in Simon's brain. He didn't have to spend his morning following the entity's trail through the ether. The police had already discovered where it had broken through, and he wouldn't be able to relax until he found out what corruption it had caused. "Is eleven o'clock good?"

"I'll tell the duty clerk to expect you."

At the appointed hour, Simon gave his name to the police station duty clerk, and was escorted to Freemont's desk.

"Professor Parkes to see you, Detective."

"Thanks." Freemont clicked on his PC's screen saver, hiding his current case behind a chrome-finned '57 Chevy, and grabbed a file from the stack on his desk. "And thank you for coming down on such short notice, Professor."

"I'm always happy to lend my expertise to the police. You know that."

"I'm happy we so rarely need it."

Freemont shook his head, and adjusted his already crooked tie. It didn't help. The man looked like his ideal of proper police dress had been formed by watching too many episodes of *Columbo*. Simon had never seen him looking anything other than rumpled and disheveled. But like Peter Falk's character, Freemont was an excellent detective with a higher than average ability to end his cases in convictions.

"Let's go to the interview rooms, where you can have some privacy while you look at this. Can I get you a cup of coffee?"

Simon shuddered. "I made the mistake of having some of what you call coffee the last time I was here, and nearly had to have my stomach pumped. How can you drink that poison?"

Freemont laughed. "The antidote is in the jelly doughnuts."

They continued making small talk until they reached the interview room. Simon sat down at the scarred wooden table.

"What have you got?"

Freemont closed the door, and tossed the file onto the table. "The hell if I know. That's why I called you. What I know is I've got two dead college students. Preliminary autopsy says they were high as kites when they died, one from an overdose, the other from blood loss. A knife was found on the scene with both their prints on it. It's all in the file."

The detective paced the confines of the interview room as Simon flipped open the folder and stared at a color photo of a crime scene out of his worst nightmares. A man and woman, both in their late teens or early twenties, naked, and covered in blood, lay tangled amid a pile of pillows in a pool of blood that didn't quite obscure the green-powder pentagram on the hardwood floor. Another photo showed a close-up of the man. He'd been Bobbitized. The location of his missing member was circled on a third photo.

Although painful, the amputation hadn't killed him. Simon's eyes widened at the chemical cocktail found in the boy's blood. With so many drugs in his system, the boy might not have felt a thing. Maybe the amputation *hadn't* been painful.

Simon scanned the police and coroner's reports, determining that the woman had also suffered a sexual injury, which in her case led to the blood loss which killed her. He ignored the other comments about the condition of the bodies and the statement of the hapless roommate who'd found them, and searched for mention of any additional symbols or magical tools. The knife was a simple kitchen utility knife, not an athame or other magical blade.

A line in the report caught his attention. He reread it twice, then looked up at the detective in disbelief. "The pentagram was drawn in *what*?"

"Lime Jell-O."

Simon shook his head. "At least we know they weren't true believers in the occult. Jell-O does not have any known mystical protective qualities. The pentagram was worthless decoration."

"Any ideas on what they were doing?"

"Two naked kids in a pentagram? I don't need a doctorate in occult science to know they were having sex, especially since they had a picture book with various positions bookmarked on the floor beside them."

"But how'd they get from having sex to being dead? That's where I'm stuck. The roommate says the door was locked and the windows were closed when he came home and found them. So either the murderer also had a key, or it was a murder-suicide. But who would kill themselves like that?"

"Double murder is also possible. They'd take a long time to bleed to death from those injuries, and the drugs in their system could have interfered with their natural shock responses."

Simon continued examining the report, forcing himself to peruse it with scholarly disinterest. He'd grieve for the lives he hadn't been able to save later.

Finally, he found the clue he was seeking. On the fourth page of the crime scene report, it mentioned an ashtray containing the butts of hallucinogen-laced marijuana joints and a piece of folded, scorched paper. Simon recognized the symbols on the paper.

"They were trying to summon a demon."

"A demon."

Simon shrugged. "The actual name depends on your religious beliefs, but they were performing a ritual to energize and give form to an entity from another plane of existence, one who does not have humanity's best interests at heart."

Freemont dropped into the chair opposite Simon. "Are you trying to tell me they were killed by a demon?"

"No. I said they were trying to summon one. They were playing with a form of sex magic that gains its power from extending arousal without allowing orgasm. What's the simplest way to prevent an orgasm?"

"Remove the ability to have one." Freemont turned the file around and studied the pictures with a new eye. "High as they were, it's a solution that could have made sense to them. Damn. Just when I think I've seen the depths of human stupidity, people go and surprise me."

"Do you need anything else from me?"

"Not right now. If I have any more questions, I'll give you a call."

Simon nodded, and pushed himself to his feet. He felt suddenly old and brittle, barely able to muster the energy required to stand. His fingers drifted over the pictures of the boy and girl.

"I'm sorry I couldn't help more."

"Hey, Professor, you helped a lot. I missed that orgasm angle." Freemont frowned, and started to come around the table. "Are you okay? You look kind of pale, and a little green."

"I'm fine." Simon smiled tightly. "Now I better get back to campus. I've got a noon class to teach."

Making a hasty retreat, he fled to the comfort of his Jeep, where he rested his forehead on the steering wheel and breathed deeply. The surge of power he'd felt while fighting the entity had been those poor kids giving their lives. As he'd predicted to Andrew, the entity was close enough to affect the minds of those whose defenses were lowered by drugs. Their shields were not strong enough. Something more needed to be done.

* * * * *

"Relax," Julie teased. "You're an adult, remember?"

Beth laughed. "I don't feel like an adult. I feel like a teenager, all giddy and nervous. Do I look okay?"

"For the fifth time, yes. Chinos and a denim shirt will work whether you're going somewhere casual or somewhere dressy. You still have no idea where he's taking you?"

"To the moon and back again, I hope."

"For your date, I mean."

"The only thing he told me is that he wouldn't be cooking, because he can barely boil water."

Beth sprayed the counter and wiped away the day's accumulation of fingerprints. When the door bell jingled, she dropped the spray bottle and cloth, then ducked down and fumbled beneath the counter to retrieve them. She thrust the cleaning supplies into their storage niche beneath the cash register, grabbed her pocketbook, and sprang up to greet Simon.

He'd barely entered the store. Beth hesitated, waiting for him to slowly cross the aisles and reach the counter. He was taking forever to walk the handful of yards. Running out of patience, she slipped out from behind the counter and sprinted across the store, pulling to a breathless halt just before she collided with him.

Simon put out his hands to steady her, and she leaned forward to greet him with a kiss. He didn't respond. For a sickening moment, she feared that she'd misjudged their relationship. Then his hands slid around her back to pull her closer, and he bent his head to explore her lips.

"Hey! Break it up, you two. This is a family bookstore," Julie cautioned.

Beth pulled away from Simon with a breathless laugh. "Before Julie kicks us out, where are we going?"

Reaching into his back pocket, Simon drew out the newspaper's folded up entertainment section. "Art exhibits, shows, movies, and craft fairs. The city's full of activity."

"I thought you said it was a cultural wasteland."

"I never said the art, shows, or crafts were any good."

Beth laughed again, and took the paper from him. It seemed Simon could always make her laugh. She liked that. A lot.

"How about a movie, then? I've heard good things about 'Death by Denial,' the new mystery flick."

"Whatever you want." An odd note colored his voice.

Beth glanced up, to find him staring at her. "Why are you looking at me like that?"

He shook his head. "Nothing. Come on, let's discuss our plans outside. Unless you want to invite Julie?" His teasing tone seemed strained.

"I've got to work," Julie interrupted. "Or I'd love to go with you."

"Oh no you wouldn't," Beth warned. "You don't want to come anywhere near us. So don't get any funny ideas about sneaking over to the theater after the bookstore closes."

"Spoil sport."

Simon chuckled. "Are you sure you two aren't sisters?"

"Come on, Simon. Let's go outside." Beth led the way to one of the wooden benches lining the mall's corridor in front of the bookstore. "It's just the two of us, now. Tell me what's up. The movie was just a suggestion."

"It's not that. It's just..." Simon shrugged, then surreptitiously glanced to either side before continuing. "You heard about the two students that died?"

A rush of compassion filled her, and Beth rested her hand on his knee. "Were they students of yours? I'm so sorry. Of course you wouldn't want to see a murder mystery."

"No, I didn't know them. But the police asked for my help with the case."

Beth frowned. "Why would they ask you? You just said you didn't know them. And the paper said they died of a simple drug overdose."

"The police kept some details from the news media, so as not to embarrass the students' families or provoke copycat incidents."

"It wasn't an overdose?"

"Not entirely. There were occult aspects." Simon looked into the distance, his expression cold and remote as if he could still see the scene before him. Maybe he could. If she'd been asked to help investigate the scene of a death, Beth was pretty sure it would haunt her for days if not weeks.

She sat up straight, her spine stiffening with resolution. She'd take his mind off of his unpleasant memories. Beth flipped through the entertainment section, searching the ads for what she wanted.

"You know what you need? Vigorous physical activity."

Simon's attention snapped back to her. He swallowed, his gaze dipping to her lips, then lower, leaving no question as to what kind of physical activity he'd prefer. "What did you have in mind?"

They'd get to that. But first, she wanted him to relax. She flipped the open paper onto his lap. "Here! Bicycle rentals. And it says there's a bike path."

"You want to go bicycling for our date?"

"Why not? Don't you think you're up to it?" She grinned, already enjoying the sparkle of challenge in his eyes. Her breath caught, anticipating the site of him biking in front of her, laboring up a hill, his khaki pants clinging to his muscular—

Beth reigned in her imagination, although she could feel the heat in her cheeks.

"I'm in excellent shape. But you're already flushed, and you're still sitting on the bench." He slanted her a positively wicked grin. "Perhaps we should put you to bed."

She shook her head, grinning. "Don't you know you're never supposed to go to bed angry or upset? You have to work all those emotions out first. And the best way is to bicycle, fast and hard. Think of it as training."

Simon laughed, and followed her from the mall.

* * * * *

Simon felt awkward and a little silly as the bike shop clerk adjusted the seat for him, especially since he was wearing a plastic helmet that made him look like a blue duck.

"Try it now," the clerk said.

Simon sat on the narrow bike seat and rested one foot on the pedal, as the clerk had shown him previously. "It's fine."

"How about the helmet?" The clerk tugged on the straps beside his ears and under his chin.

Simon fought back the urge to swat the man away. He was just doing his job. "It's fine, too."

He glanced at Beth, waiting patiently on her bike. Part of his irritation was no doubt due to watching the confident way she'd adjusted her own bike and helmet. She obviously knew what she was doing. He hadn't ridden a bicycle since he was a child, and he was terrified that he'd make a fool out of himself. It was only their second date, and he wanted to impress her, not embarrass himself in front of her.

But she was right. He could feel the tension in his neck and shoulders, symptomatic of the guilt and worry caused by the entity's murder of those two college kids. He needed to burn off the tension before if affected his work, and his ability to protect the other people he was responsible for.

"Ready?" Beth asked.

"Let's go." He waved her forward, onto the blacktopped bike path. Letting her go first was partly chivalry, and partly a desire to wobble up to speed unobserved. After a mercifully brief period to adjust to his changed height and weight, his legs were pumping as smoothly as if he'd last ridden a bike twenty minutes ago, not twenty years ago.

The wind caressed his cheeks as he pedaled faster, catching up to Beth. He hung back, watching the smooth rhythm of her cycling as she swept along the path, golden brown leaves swirling behind her to tickle his legs and crunch beneath his tires. She sat up, letting go of the handlebars and riding with her arms outstretched as if she could embrace the wind.

Simon felt something catch in his chest. She looked so free, so happy. She had no idea what evil lurked on the ethereal plane, planning its next assault upon Simon's defenses. He vowed to protect her innocence. And, at least for a few hours, he'd try to forget as well.

She looked over her shoulder and smiled at him. "Feeling better?"

Not completely. If vigorous physical exertion would let him cast his troubles aside, he needed to work much harder. "Race you!"

Bending low over the handlebars, he surged past her in a crackling cloud of leaves. Her laughter sparkled on the breeze.

"You're on!"

Hours later, they returned the bikes, laughing like giddy children. Simon dismounted, then almost fell as the ground swayed beneath him.

"Like a sailor getting his land legs," Beth teased, but she winced as she got off her own bike. "I'm gonna pay for this tomorrow."

He let down the kickstand and carefully balanced his bike. After hanging his helmet on the handlebar, he hobbled over to where she stood beside her own bicycle. "I have one word for you. *Jacuzzi*."

Her eyes widened hopefully. "You have one?"

"And a combination sauna / steam room. We can pick up some Chinese food on our way to my house, and stay there the rest of the night."

She closed her eyes and sighed, a blissful smile lighting her face. "Sounds heavenly."

Unable to resist, he put his arms around her. Her eyes flew open and she jerked back in surprise, before relaxing in his embrace. He pulled her closer, feeling her pounding pulse and the heat of her skin so like his own. He bent his head to nuzzle her neck.

"Perhaps we could be a little wicked, too."

She wrapped her arms around him, twining her fingers through his hair and leaning against him. He closed his eyes, reveling in the pleasure of her touch.

"That sounds even better," she whispered, then kissed him.

The bike shop clerk cleared his throat loudly, and they broke apart guiltily. "That'll be $14.50."

Simon handed him $15. "Keep the change."

Taking Beth by the hand, he led her to his Jeep.

CHAPTER FOUR

Simon juggled the boxes of Chinese take-out and his key ring, managing to fit the key into the lock without dropping any of the food. Behind him on the flagstone porch, and laden with her own collection of boxes, Beth whistled.

"This is practically a mansion. I didn't know the university paid professors so well."

"They don't. It was the gift of an eccentric trustee, and is part of one of my grants. I can live here for free provided I record any paranormal activity that occurs inside the house."

The door swung open. He followed it into the foyer, now struggling to get his key back out of the lock. Turning, he saw Beth hesitating on the wide porch, her eyes vague and confused. She stepped forward, then backed up again.

"It's haunted?"

"Not that I ever noticed." Still, the grant and others like it allowed the Guardians to work out of their traditional strongholds without arousing any suspicion. Not only was it a wonderfully elegant home, but its wards and protective shields freed Simon to devote his power to his magic rather than security.

The shields! No wonder Beth didn't feel like coming inside. The low level magic discouraged casual visitors by generating discomfort and unease, while the stronger spells prevented active magics from crossing the threshold. Reinforced by every new inhabitant of the house, the spells were stronger than any single Guardian could ever hope to be.

It had been so long since he'd invited someone into his home, Simon had forgotten to speak the invocation that would allow her entrance. Damn! He usually did that before his visitor arrived, but he hadn't expected to end up at his own house. So much for not making a fool of himself in front of her.

He yanked the key out of the lock and backed away from the door, deeper into the foyer, until he stood in the center of the black and white marble starburst patterning the floor. With a wrought iron chandelier hanging by a massive chain over his head, and wall sconces converted from the old gas lines casting strange shadows in the dim corners of the room, the setting would be perfect for a scene from a horror movie. An effect the Guardian who initially set the wards had been all too aware of.

"Beth Graham, I give you welcome. Enter freely, go safely, and leave something of the happiness you bring."

She stared at him in disbelief, then burst out laughing. "Dracula?"

Simon winced, inwardly cursing the sense of humor of that former Guardian. Although it was his own fault for failing to anticipate Beth's arrival.

He tried to dismiss the strange greeting.

"Well, I <u>am</u> an occult researcher. And it's a perfectly good traditional welcome blessing."

"In Transylvania, maybe. Not upstate New York." Shaking her head, Beth walked into the house and pushed the heavy wooden door closed with her foot. "Before you start nibbling on my neck, Count, why don't we take this stuff into your kitchen. And don't you dare tell me to 'walk this way.'"

"Frankenstein," he informed her with full professorial dignity, "was early science fiction. Not an occult work."

Beth just laughed. Realizing how pompous he'd sounded, Simon chuckled, too.

"End of lecture. The kitchen is through here."

Beth stopped in the doorway to the vast room, the long counters and glass-fronted cabinets virtually unchanged since the Victorian era. "It's like stepping through a doorway into the past."

"Not quite. Tap water and a gas stove were added sometime in the 20's or 30's, and I updated the wiring and replaced the antique refrigerator shortly after I moved in. But otherwise, yes, this is pretty much how it looked when scores of servants bustled around the kitchen readying the house for a grand entertainment in the ball room."

Beth blinked. "You have a ball room?"

"Had. It's an exercise room now." Simon dropped his boxes of take-out on one of the counters, then helped her unload hers.

He opened three cabinets before he found what he was looking for—a black wooden serving tray with a lacquered picture of cranes in flight. He arranged the boxes on the tray, filled two glasses with ice water, added forks and spoons from the silverware drawer, and then threw on a stack of plain white paper napkins.

Picking up the tray, he nodded toward a door on the far side of the kitchen. "We'll take the back stairs. If you'll follow me, your dinner and a tub of steaming hot water await."

"I'm right behind you. I hope you have everything you need, because I'm not leaving a trail of breadcrumbs to find our way back."

Simon laughed. The house was purposely designed full of strange angles and unusual intersections, partly so that certain rooms would be aligned according to ley lines and celestial influences, and partly so that casual visitors would not notice that there were rooms hidden from them.

"It took me a couple of weeks before I learned my way around, and I didn't discover one linen closet until I'd lived here for almost a year."

He turned his attention to balancing the full tray while navigating the narrow back stairs. When he reached the second floor without incident, he relaxed and checked to make sure Beth was right behind him before leading her to the grand bath at the end of the hall. He nudged the door wide open with his foot, then stepped aside to let her go first. "What do you think?"

Beth gasped. "It's huge!"

"And an antique." Simon set the serving tray on the rim of the six-person marble-tiled tub he'd had refitted as a Jacuzzi, and threw open the hot water tap. "Kind of makes you wonder about those prim and proper Victorians, doesn't it?"

"Well, you know what they say. Cleanliness is next to godliness."

"Then they must have bordered on the divine." He turned and pointed at the two doors on the other side of the tub. "Sauna and toilet, if you'd like to use either before the Jacuzzi fills. It takes about fifteen minutes. I'll go get us some towels."

"Hurry back."

On his way to the linen closet, Simon detoured through his bedroom. He hadn't expected to bring Beth home, thinking they would end the evening at her apartment. He quickly made the room presentable, stuffing yesterday's laundry out of sight and straightening the covers on the bed. Scanning the room one last time, he made sure nothing remained to cause a question. A half-burnt pillar candle sat in a pile of white sand on his dresser, surrounded by carefully arranged meditation stones, but he could explain that if she asked. Nothing more serious was exposed.

After grabbing a pile of fluffy white bath sheets from the linen closet, he added four scented candles and a pack of matches, then returned to the grand bath. It was empty, silent except for the rushing thunder of water filling the tub. The serving tray containing their dinner sat untouched on the marble-tiled wall of the Jacuzzi.

Glancing around, he spotted Beth's neatly folded clothes on the low table beside the glass door to the sauna. Perfect. He could prepare the Jacuzzi as a protective circle without raising her curiosity.

He dumped the towels on top of the table, covering her clothes, and set the candles on the tiled wall of the Jacuzzi at the four compass points. Then he quickly stripped off his own clothing.

Warm steam rose from the half-full tub and misted the room, caressing his skin. A droplet of water formed on his chest, then ran in a wet trail down his body. He shivered, imagining it was Beth's finger sliding over him.

He grabbed the book of matches. Stepping over the Jacuzzi's wall, he waded into the warm water. It lapped around his calves, tickling him and making him hunger to sink beneath the waves with Beth. But he had a job to do. He forced his mind back to business.

Standing in the center of the Jacuzzi, he faced the pine-scented candle to the north. He held the book of matches above his head and struck the first match. Keeping his mind focused, he slowly lowered the match until it touched the wick of the green candle.

"Spirits of the North Wind, dark and cold, nurture my power."

The sweet scent of pine wafted from the lit candle as he turned to his right and faced the yellow candle he'd placed there.

"Spirits of the East Wind, thoughtful and wise, open my eyes."

The spicy fragrance of cloves mingled with the pine, overwhelming the luscious smells rising from the carryout boxes on the serving tray. He turned to the red candle in the south and lit that one, too.

"Spirits of the South Wind, fiery and hot, forge my will."

The wick of the cinnamon-scented candle sputtered. Simon stared at it, wondering what he would do if the protective spirits refused to bless the circle. Especially the one spirit he'd anticipated no problem from. After all, he had plenty of passion already.

He nodded and closed his eyes, concentrating. Visualizing that moment during their bicycle ride when he'd vowed to protect Beth's innocence, he made clear that he was asking for assistance with that, not with seducing her.

The candle wick whooshed into flame, burning brighter than the other two candles. Simon gazed at it. The candle settled down to a normal flame. He watched it a moment longer, then turned to the final, dark blue candle.

"Spirits of the West Wind, deep and fluid, guide the events I set in motion tonight."

The heavy fragrance of patchouli rolled from the flame.

He breathed deeply, inhaling the scented steam. All was ready.

With a minimum of splashing, he climbed out of the Jacuzzi and crossed the slick marble floor to the sauna. He opened the fogged-over door leading into the sauna and stepped inside, the heat from the glowing brazier of rocks quickly baking the moisture from his skin. Beth lay on one of the wooden benches, eyes closed, relaxed, comfortable, and completely naked. He'd never seen anyone so beautiful.

Beth heard the sauna door open and close. She thought Simon had come inside, but when he didn't say anything, she wondered if he'd only looked in on her. "Simon?"

"The Jacuzzi's almost full. Five minutes."

"Mmm. I feel like I could just stay here forever." She turned onto her side, opening her eyes to mere slits. Water clung to his skin, reflecting ruddy light from the brazier and making him appear to have been dipped in bronze. She opened her eyes all the way. The glow highlighted and defined his every muscle. "God, you're gorgeous. You must spend a lot of time in that exercise room."

"That was before I met you. Now I can think of much better uses for that time."

He sat on the edge of the bench. Reaching out, he traced the path of a water droplet over her shoulder and between her breasts.

She closed her eyes and let out a shuddering sigh. "Five minutes, you said?"

"Yes." He retraced the same path with his lips, dusting her skin with kisses.

Beth groaned. "Not long enough."

"Oh, but if you like the sauna, you'll love the Jacuzzi. Warm..." He exhaled softly, blowing heated breath over the skin he'd just kissed. He followed with openmouthed kisses, swirling his tongue over the familiar trail. "Wet..."

"Are you sure... you're talking... about... the Jacuzzi?"

"There's only one way for you to find out." He stood up, then backed slowly to the door. "You'll have to follow me."

Beth sat up slowly, every muscle protesting the effort required to stretch and contract. She watched Simon, not trusting the wicked grin that suddenly lit his face. He was planning something.

He yanked open the door, stepping behind it so that the rush of cold air hit Beth. She squeaked, and jumped to her feet.

"That got you moving!"

"When I catch you, I'm going to dunk you in that Jacuzzi!"

Simon raced out of the sauna. She followed just a few steps behind him, stumbling to a halt on the mist-slicked tiles. He turned and caught her before she could fall.

"Careful. Let me shut off the water, then I'll help you into the tub. All this marble gets pretty slippery."

She nodded, and watched his graceful movements as he bent to turn off the tap, then started the jets. Air sputtered through the valves, then settled into a steady roar as the surface of the water began to roil. Four fragrant candles perfumed the moist air with the faint scent of exotic spices.

Her pulse sped up, remembering their previous lovemaking. She wondered what sensual ritual he had planned for them.

She tried for a light, bantering tone, but her voice came out low and breathy. "Why'd you use marble? Why not carpeting or wooden slats that would give you some traction?"

"Because marble's a natural stone. It represents the element of earth. The jets are the element of air. The water is obvious. And the candles add the element of fire."

She tipped her head and studied him. He was serious. "All that for a tub?"

"Not just any tub." He rejoined her. Taking her hand, he steadied her while she stepped onto the wide rim and then into the bubbling water. Liquid warmth glided over her skin, up to her knees.

Feeling with her toes, she found the edge of the seat and stepped down into the center of the tub. The hot water bubbled and tickled the tops of her thighs.

She let go of Simon's hand and sank onto the tiled seat, letting the water flow up and over her until it lapped at her chin. She inched sideways until she was positioned directly in front of a jet. It pounded her back with a vigorous massage.

Simon slid into the water beside her. It instantly seemed to heat up another few degrees.

"As promised, you've got your tub of steaming hot water. And here's dinner." He grabbed the edge of the serving tray and pulled it along the wall of the tub until it was within her reach.

"I'm not interested in—"

He opened one of the cartons, releasing the spicy scent of Szechuan sauce. Beth's stomach rumbled.

"Okay, maybe I am interested in food. Pass that over."

They soon settled on the most comfortable position, sideways on the bench, their legs tucked under them and their knees just touching, with one arm braced on the wall of the Jacuzzi. The serving tray rested on the wall between them.

"Chopsticks?" Simon held up the paper wrapped bundle the restaurant had included with their order.

"No, I'm hanging on with my right arm. If I try to use chopsticks in my left hand, I'll probably poke my eye out. Unless..." Beth slid her leg through the bubbling water, running her foot up the side of Simon's calf. "You could feed me."

Grinning, he unwrapped the chopsticks. "What would you like to try first?"

"The chicken."

Handling the chopsticks like a pro, he picked up a chunk of Szechuan Chicken and held it before her. "Open wide."

Beth parted her lips. He slid the meat inside her mouth, dropping it on her tongue, and pulled the chopsticks back, gliding the polished wood over her lower lip. She'd never thought of chicken as being particularly sexy before, but having Simon feed her was downright erotic.

"Chew," he reminded her.

She chewed, swallowed, and edged a little closer. "Another piece, please."

This time, Simon fished out a broccoli floret. He pressed it to her lips until she opened them, sliding the spicy tidbit into her mouth. Wrapping her tongue around the broccoli and the chopsticks, she tugged playfully.

Simon swallowed, and inched closer.

Soon, she was sitting on his lap, and they were trading kisses and nibbles in between servings of food. Then the food was forgotten and they were just kissing, their hands busy stroking and caressing beneath the churning water.

Beth arched her back, sighing in pleasure. "Mmm. Being in the Jacuzzi turns the lightest caress into a massage."

Simon stilled, pulling back slightly to look into her eyes. "Would you like a massage? A real one?"

She flushed hotter than the steaming water at the thought of his hands all over her body. "Oh, yeah. Do we have to get out of the Jacuzzi?"

"No. I'll get a couple more towels for you to lean back and rest your head against."

He stood, water sluicing from his naked body, like an ancient god rising from the sea. She wanted to grab him, haul him back beneath the bubbling water, and make love to him until they were both too limp to move. Before she could move, he had stepped out of the tub.

Leaving a dripping trail behind him, he crossed the room to the pile of towels mounded on top of the table where she'd left her clothes. Beth waited, hot and aching, until he returned an eternity later with his arms full of towels.

Beth trembled, remembering how he had worshipped her body for hours on their first date. Her breath caught as she whispered, "Now what?"

First, Simon arranged the pile of towels on the edge of the tub so that she had a comfortable pillow for her head, evenly spaced between the red and yellow candles. To be safe, he moistened the towel edges closest to the flames. When the towels were all arranged, he slid back over the wall into the Jacuzzi and stood by her feet.

Kneeling, so that his chin was barely above the water, he rested her feet on his thighs. Then he picked up her left foot and began slowly massaging her arch.

Beth closed her eyes and surrendered to the feel of the warm water lapping against her skin and Simon's hands kneading her flesh. His fingers moved over her heel and ankle, the pads of her foot, and her toes. Her foot felt suddenly cool. Opening her eyes, she realized he'd lifted it out of the water. Then he bent his head and suckled her big toe.

A jolt of fire shot through her and she gasped in unexpected pleasure. He continued, giving her toe the kind of attention Conn had reserved for her breasts, but without the expectation of an immediate arousal. Simon seemed to have no agenda beyond the thorough and complete loving of her foot. Yet, as he continued, she found her pulse racing and her breathing unsteady, until a wave of pleasure burst over her.

She half expected him to say something snide about her getting so turned on by a foot massage, but he merely shifted her foot back onto his thigh and began massaging her calf muscles. Beth smiled and settled deeper into her pillow of towels. Simon was nothing like Conn. Which was good, because she suspected she was already in love with him.

Beth cast herself adrift on the waves of pleasure Simon's hands provoked as he slowly massaged her entire body. At some point, he'd pulled her into the deeper water with him, so that she sat with her legs around his waist, braced against his muscular chest. She sighed as he lifted his fingers from the back of her neck, then smiled dreamily, content to float in his arms.

"All done. How do you feel?" he asked softly.

"That was magic, all right."

Simon's low chuckle reverberated in his chest, sending echoes through the water. "No, that was just a massage. Would you like to feel some real magic?"

"What did you have in mind?"

"A protection spell."

Beth opened her eyes. "You're serious? Magic as in witches and warlocks and things that go bump in the night?"

A shadow crossed his eyes. Too late, she realized he studied these things for a living, and might not appreciate her making light of his chosen career. But his smile put to rest any fears that she'd insulted him.

"Witchcraft is one form of magic, a type of nature worship, as the Tantric ritual was another form, worshipping its own pantheon of deities."

Beth hesitated. "I thought you had an academic interest. Do you really believe in this stuff?"

He considered her question carefully before answering. "Unlike science or engineering, which produce results regardless of intent, so-called magical spells are no more than ways to focus the will of the caster. So, do I believe reciting a piece of bad poetry while performing certain actions will of themselves cause an event to occur? No. But I think they are useful for producing a state where the will of the caster is aligned with the conditions necessary to bring about a desired event."

"Could you try that again in English instead of professorese?"

"It's like how some people practice the power of positive thinking. Every morning, they recite a statement of what they want to have happen. Because the thought is fresh in their minds, they are able to see how things that occur during the day could help bring about their desired goal, and act on them, where they may not have otherwise."

"Oh. I guess that makes sense." She closed her eyes and nestled against Simon's chest. "So, what would we do for a protection spell?"

"Like I said, witchcraft is a form of nature worship. It uses stylized equipment, such as a cup or chalice to represent the goddess, and a wand or blade to represent the god."

Beth pulled back to look at him. "Is all magic about sex?"

Simon bent his head and feathered her neck with kisses. "For some reason, that's all the magic I seem to think about when I'm with you. I wonder why?"

She laughed. "I wonder. So, I take it you plan on using the obvious substitutions for cup and blade?"

"Mm-hmm."

Pressing close, she slid her hands up and down his velvety smooth back. "Let's make some magic, then."

Shifting slightly, Simon claimed her lips with his. His kiss started gently, no more than a whisper touch, then gradually became more insistent. He cupped the back of her head with his hand, drawing her nearer.

Beth opened her mouth, inviting him to deepen the kiss. He followed her lead, opening his mouth and sweeping his tongue in a gentle caress over her lower lip. She trembled, hungering for a fuller kiss.

Simon's other hand settled onto her hip and nudged her slightly to one side. She felt the length of him press against her, and sighed into his mouth.

The tip of his tongue brushed her lip again, and he moved beneath her, echoing the gesture. A surge of electricity arced through her, and she gasped. She felt rather than heard his low chuckle.

"Like that?"

"Oh, yes."

He did it again, and again, sliding ever so slightly deeper each time. Beth trembled with tension, aching for completion but thrilling to each movement in the slow dance of love, never wanting it to stop.

At last, the ache proved too much to withstand. Wrapping her tongue around his, she pulled him into a full kiss, even as she wrapped her legs around his waist and sheathed him completely. She caught his groan of pleasure in her mouth.

The clung together, locked unmoving, as the waves of passion carried them to the next plateau.

Simon lifted his head, breaking the kiss. "Look at me."

Beth blinked, having trouble focusing. All she could think about was the feel of him inside her and sinking back into the heady delirium of his kiss. Eventually, she stared into his eyes, mesmerized by the light shining within their depths.

He took a deep breath, then recited, "Into your chalice I set my blade, to guard against both shadow and shade. May no foul beings or astral shells disturb the peace where our magic dwells."

A tingle rippled through her as he seemed to swell. She gasped. Closing her eyes, she clung to him. "Simon!"

His mouth found hers, mingling their spirits on a breath of air. She trembled, her muscles shaking uncontrollably as he clutched her to him, straining to make them one.

The candles flared, tiny supernovas she could see even through her closed eyelids, and she joined them, fracturing into millions of glittering splinters that spread throughout the stars. Deep inside, she felt the heated rush of Simon's collapse.

She clung to him, boneless and spent, as their kiss went on and on. She lost track of time, drifting in a hazy realm of warm pleasure, until Simon's gentle shake roused her.

"Hey," he whispered, his breath puffing over her lips. "We need to get out. The water's going cold."

"Mmm." Beth snuggled closer to Simon, wrapping her arms tighter around him. "I hadn't noticed."

"If you don't care about freezing, maybe you'll care about looking like a prune."

She gave him a playful pout. "Why Simon, you know exactly how to flatter a girl."

Beth tried to stand up, only to discover her legs had fallen asleep. She toppled backward, arms splayed in a frantic attempt to keep her balance, and hit the water with a huge splash.

Simon coughed and wiped water from his eyes. "Very graceful."

Warned by her example, he straightened his legs slowly, then held on to the edge of the Jacuzzi's seat until he was standing upright. He circled the Jacuzzi, pinching out the still-burning candles and turning off the jets, then helped Beth to her feet and out of the tub.

She hugged herself against the chill of the air and watched him hunt through the pile of towels until he found two that were still mostly dry. After wrapping one around Beth, he started vigorously drying himself off with the other. She followed suit, but the damp air defeated her efforts. She shivered and huddled inside her towel as her skin turned to goose flesh.

"We need to go someplace dry if we ever want to warm up."

"I know just the place."

Putting his towel-draped arm around her, Simon led Beth out of the grand bath and down the hall to his bedroom.

CHAPTER FIVE

Beth paused in the doorway to Simon's room, admiring the graceful curves and intricate carvings of the antique cherry four-poster bed and dresser. Each of the bed's four posts was topped with a different figure. The one nearest to her had wings and a cruel hooked beak. A hawk, maybe?

Simon tugged her forward. "You can admire the decor later. When we're warm."

He turned back the bedspread decorated with white-on-white candlewick embroidery, as well as the thermal blanket and sheet underneath, and held them up for her. Beth slipped off her towel and darted beneath the covers. The sheets were freezing!

Dropping his own towel, Simon slipped into bed beside her and pulled the covers up around their necks. They curled up together, her back to his front, and he chafed her skin lightly until she stopped shivering. His hand continued roaming gently up and down her body, generating a different kind of heat.

She closed her eyes and relaxed against his warmth. "I like your furniture. It's a long way from my garage sale decorating."

He chuckled, hugging her close. "Not really. It came with the house. I didn't see any reason to replace it when I moved in. Besides, this old stuff weighs a ton! I'm not moving any more of it than I have to."

"I know what you mean!" Beth laughed, turning in his arms to snuggle up against his chest and nuzzle his neck. "Conn wanted our house decorated with real antiques, for the prestige value. When the movers were carrying in the Queen Anne furniture, I thought one poor fellow was going to have a heart attack right on the landing."

Simon's hand stilled. Too late, she realized her new lover might not want to hear about her ex-husband when they were in bed. She pulled back to look at him.

"I'm sorry. I didn't mean to talk about my marriage."

He shook his head. "It's all right. I know you had a life before you met me. It's just..." He resumed stroking her, pulling her close so that her face rested against his chest.

"Just...?" She prompted.

"I know it was just a joke, but I don't want to think about death right now."

"Oh, Simon, I'm sorry I brought it up. My philosophy since my divorce has been to live for the moment. So let's do that, live and celebrate life."

He hesitated just a moment before asking, "So we'll keep this casual? I've got too much going on right now to have a serious relationship."

Beth blinked, stung that Simon was so emphatic about not wanting a relationship with her. Although, on second thought, it showed how considerate he was that he told her his intentions up front, rather than leading her on. And she wasn't looking for a lifetime commitment. She'd done that already, and look how that had turned out. She'd just rather have fun with Simon, and enjoy her time with him for as long as it lasted.

"No commitments," Beth agreed.

* * * * *

Simon slowly pulled his arm out from under Beth's head, carefully inching away from her so that he didn't wake her. He didn't want to leave her. What if she woke up while he was gone? But he needed to perform this divination while the moon's influence was strongest. He'd just have to hope that their lovemaking had tired Beth out enough that she'd sleep soundly until his return.

He slipped out from under the covers, gasping as the chill of the night air hit his bare skin. This old house was impossible to keep warm. Pulling his yellow ceremonial robe out of the closet, he wrapped himself in the light silk. It was better than nothing.

He jogged downstairs to his work room and picked out the supplies he needed, two white candles and a bottle of jasmine scented oil. Then he returned upstairs and entered the grand bath.

The magically charged water still filled the jacuzzi, forming a powerful reflective pool. Simon gathered up the candles they'd used in the earlier ritual and placed them on the serving tray with the remains of dinner. When he was done with his divination, he'd take the tray down to the kitchen and dispose of it.

He set the two candles opposite each other on the jacuzzi wall, then paused to focus his thoughts. Concentrating on his breathing, he reminded himself that the powerfully charged water would ensure success for his normally poor divination skills.

Lighting the candles, he chanted softly, "Lady of Light, Lady of Night, unveil my eyes and grant me your sight." Then he unstopped the bottle and tipped nine drops of the scented oil onto the water, saying as he did so, "As thoughts become images, so the soul becomes a body. The perfect union of body and soul, thought and form, at one with yet apart from the world. You were cast out from the world. I cast away from the world, to travel beyond the visible world into your realm. Make known to me the images that have yet to be born. Reveal the time and circumstances of my next battle."

Kneeling on the cold marble floor, Simon allowed his mind to flow over and around the streamers of oil shimmering on the water's surface. The candles flickered. He felt the gathering of power, the fine hairs on his arms and the back of his neck rising as if he knelt in the center of an electrical storm. But he saw nothing in the glittering reflection.

"Simon!" Beth's cry ripped through the house.

He jerked as if he'd been struck, overbalancing and falling to his side. His elbow slammed against the marble floor. The sudden pain snapped him out of his trance.

He never should have left Beth alone. Simon stumbled to his feet and raced back to his bedroom. Beth was sitting in the middle of his bed, huddled beneath the blanket and bedspread.

"I'm here. What is it?"

As soon as he sat down on the edge of the bed, she launched herself at him, burying her face in his shoulder and wrapping her arms around his neck. Simon held her close, rocking her gently, and rubbed her back.

"It was horrible. Horrible!" Beth shivered.

"Shh. You just had a nightmare. It will be all right. Why don't you tell me about it?"

Another shudder wracked her, but her grip around his neck loosened fractionally.

"I must have been thinking about those poor college students. I dreamt of a boy and a girl. They died..."

A jolt of static electricity crackled over his skin, scorching every nerve ending and leaving him feeling raw and bleeding on the inside. Beth didn't seem to notice anything.

Sickness settled in his stomach. He tightened his arms around her, but for his comfort, not hers. His divination had been interrupted before he saw a vision, but the backlash he'd just felt indicated the spell had completed. His connection to the realm of possibilities had been severed. There would be no vision to guide him.

"But it was so real," Beth moaned.

She trembled, her hands clenching so that her fingers dug into his shoulders. Realizing that she was still frightened by her nightmare, Simon put aside his own worries and rubbed her back with long, soothing strokes.

"It was just a dream," he reassured her. "It wasn't real. What were they wearing?"

"Jeans and sweatshirts."

"See? That proves it wasn't real, because that wasn't how the students who died were dressed. Try to remember the details of the dream, and you'll see that what made sense when you were sleeping seems silly now that you're awake."

She sighed, no longer digging into him with her nails. He nudged her head on to his shoulder and stroked her hair.

"It seemed real enough while I was dreaming it. He looked sick, thin, with circles under his eyes. He was wearing jeans and a rumpled T-shirt with some sort of snake design on it. She was pretty, and seemed to sparkle, the way the sunlight glittered on her beaded headband." Beth frowned, her face tightening with her efforts to remember. "Her sweatshirt had a design of blue and green plaid appliqué. Letters, I think. But I can't remember what they spelled."

Simon forced himself to breathe deeply and steadily, and not betray the sudden fear that sliced through him. Beth's dream didn't sound like a fuzzy nightmare. It sounded like a vision. The vision *he* was supposed to have.

But that wasn't possible. Picking up on an atmosphere of magic was one thing. He could believe that she was sensitive enough to get a nightmare from his efforts to foresee the entity's evil. But actually having an uninvited premonition, especially in a house as warded and protected from magical interference as his, was out of the question.

And yet, Beth's descriptions of the students had been so detailed, especially the unusual beaded headband. It sounded alarmingly like one of his graduate students, Heather. She often wore her sorority sweat shirt to class, and at their first meeting, she'd asked him whether or not the metals and stone beads in her headbands would affect her magic.

"Were they maybe Greek letters?"

"Yes!" Beth's expression cleared. "That was it. One of the letters was a K, but the other two were some squiqqly things."

It was Heather. She and another student were going to die. Beth had received Simon's vision of the entity's next attack, although he had no idea how it had happened. What was important was that instead of protecting her, Simon had pulled her into the middle of his battle. Now he not only had to save Heather and stop the entity, he had to disentangle Beth from the mess he'd involved her in. One thing at a time.

"You said you saw sunlight. Are they outside?"

"Simon, I don't think this is helping. It still feels like I really saw it."

"Just tell me what you saw, Beth. Are they outside?"

She flinched at the sharpness in his tone, but continued describing her dream.

"They're in an apartment. The sun's coming through the window. They're sitting on a ratty old brown couch, stained and full of cigarette burns. There's a thick book, like a text book, open on the scarred coffee table before them. The carpeting is cheap beige industrial stuff, but it's brand new."

It could be any student apartment. But the couch sounded familiar, as did the beige industrial carpet. He'd bet it was the apartment the two students had been murdered in. The blood stains probably couldn't come out of the old carpet, which is why the landlord replaced it. The boy must be the roommate that found the bodies.

Beth started to tremble again. "The carpet scares me. There's something wrong about it."

"It was scary in your dream, but it can't hurt you now." Simon hated himself for putting Beth through the trauma of reliving her nightmare, but he had to know what she'd seen. "What are they doing?"

"The girl started reading out loud, marking her place in the text with her finger. I couldn't hear her, but I could see her lips moving." Beth's breathing quickened, and she fidgeted in Simon's loose embrace.

"Go on."

"She lit some candles. They were on the coffee table, beside the book. She put a key on the table between them."

Beth turned her head from side to side, as if she could keep from seeing what happened next. Perspiration beaded her forehead, and her body shook.

"The key. It started to glow. Then a black cloud came out of it. It rose up from the key and it swallowed them. I could see them fighting to get out of the cloud, fighting to breathe..."

She flung herself against Simon with so much force that she knocked him backward onto the bed.

He held her tightly, whispering words of power into her hair until her shaking stopped. She whimpered softly into his chest. He would do everything he could in the future to ensure Beth remained safe, but first she needed to believe she was safe. Since she didn't believe in magic, that meant he had to lie.

"It's okay. It was only a dream. Now you've talked it out, and it has no more power over you."

"But it was so real."

"It seemed real at the time. But think about it. Keys don't turn into clouds. Clouds are just mists and vapor. They can't eat people."

"I guess you're right. It does seem sort of silly. But it was so much more vivid than most dreams." Beth gave a shaky laugh. "There must have been too much spice in that Szechaun chicken."

Simon hugged her tightly, and felt her finally relax. She pulled away, rubbing her eyes with her fists. When she opened her eyes, she blinked at him, then frowned.

"What are you wearing?"

Damn! Now was not the time to tell her he'd been performing a magic ritual in the other room, and that the ritual had caused her nightmare.

"It's a bathrobe. I didn't want to freeze on my way to the bathroom."

She fingered the fine silk, and traced the delicate gold embroidery. "Looks pretty pricey for a professor. Or did this come with the house, too?"

Simon laughed, certain now that Beth would be okay. "It was a gift. A friend visited China, and brought back a set of robes in all the colors of the spectrum."

"Then you can let me borrow one. I have to make a run down the hall myself."

Simon hesitated only a moment before standing and going to his closet. He pulled out the black robe, the one he wore least. He'd have plenty of time to purify it before he needed it again.

"Here you go. Hurry back and I'll make sure you don't need a robe to stay warm."

Beth smiled, although the shadow of fear still haunted her eyes. "Is that a promise?"

* * * * *

Simon woke in the dim pre-dawn light. Beth, still cradled protectively in his embrace, was turning her head from side to side and whimpering low in her throat. He didn't feel the charged air energy of magic. This was just a normal nightmare.

"Beth," he whispered, shaking her gently. "Wake up."

She gasped, and her eyes flew open. She blinked twice, then smiled as she focused on him. "Simon."

"You were having a bad dream."

They were both naked under the covers, so he felt every inch of her as he pulled her closer into a full body hug. Her breasts pressed against his chest, as the womanly softness of her stomach trapped his hard erection between their bodies, and their legs entwined. His left arm, pinned beneath them, tightened around her shoulders, nudging her closer still, while his right hand roamed freely over her hips and thighs.

She caressed his calf muscles with her foot, the motion stroking the soft skin of her inner thigh over his hip, driving him wild. "Make me forget about my nightmare. Make me forget about everything but you."

He groaned and rolled her beneath him, rising to his knees to stop the torture before he completely lost control. "Think about me, then. Think about this."

Bending down, he kissed her, hard, as his fingers closed upon her nipples. She moaned into his mouth, arching beneath his hands. He plundered her mouth, seizing her tongue and pulling on it as he flicked and tugged on her sensitive nipples. Beth writhed beneath him, alternately arching her back to thrust her breasts against his hands and lifting up her head to deepen their kiss.

Simon inched his knees further apart, spreading her thighs until her legs trembled from the strain. Her musky scent wafted up to him.

With one hand, he reached out from under the covers, fumbling for the protection he'd taken the precaution of placing near the bed before they retired. His other hand reached between Beth's legs.

She was more than ready for him. Her heated flesh pulsed with the blood pounding through her veins, and his fingers were quickly slicked with her fluids.

Simon groaned and abandoned the search for protection, knowing he'd never find it before she came. He'd get his pleasure the second time.

His questing fingers slipped inside her opening, wide and waiting for him. She bucked, forcing his fingers inside her, and gripped tightly.

Using his free hand to hold her hips down, he slid his fingers out far enough that he could move them, and placed his fingertips together. Tucking his thumb into the pyramid of his fingers, he slowly slid them inside her.

Beth threw her head back, arching her body, trembling as his fingers forced their way past the ridge of muscle blocking them. She panted, ragged gasps that mimicked the sharp breaths of labor. Then the widest part of his hand was over the muscle, and his hand slid inside her.

"Oh! Oh, God!"

Her whole body shook, her arms and legs bouncing against the mattress, but Simon kept her hips pinned. Slowly, he spread his fingers, and caressed her inner wall.

She screamed, and wave after wave of rippling muscle pulsed around Simon's hand, forcing his fingers from her body in a heated rush of liquid. Beth cried out at the loss.

"No. No, more."

This time he found the protection, and quickly eased his erection inside her. Ripples of her first orgasm tightened around him, nearly sending him over the edge. This was not the time for gentle caresses and long, slow explorations. He drove into her, as hard and as fast as he could, his sharp kisses landing on her face, neck, and chest, wherever his mouth fell as he reached the top of each thrust.

Beth cried and moaned incoherently, clawing at Simon's back as she urged him to an even greater frenzy. He came in a rush, a shout of pure masculine triumph scouring his throat. But he continued rocking against Beth's ultra-sensitive entrance until she spasmed beneath him, and followed him into the bliss of release.

Simon rolled onto his side and cradled Beth's limp, sweat-covered body against his own.

Later, when she'd recovered the ability to speak, Beth said, "That was awesome. I wish I never had to leave this bed. But I have to open the bookstore on the weekends. I need to go home, change, and get to work."

Simon nuzzled the soft skin of her neck. "Rest a little while first."

She relaxed and closed her eyes. "Maybe just a little while."

They couldn't rest for long. She needed to go, and Simon needed to hunt down his student, Heather, before she started the ritual that would allow the entity to cross over to the material plane. But they could take a short nap, while they recovered from that phenomenal lovemaking.

All too soon, they rose for the day. After a quick cup of coffee and toasted bagels, Simon drove Beth to her apartment. She hesitated before stepping out of his car.

"If you're free, I'll make dinner again on Tuesday."

Simon smiled, then leaned over to kiss her lightly. "I'll be there."

Reassured, she hurried up the walk to her apartment building, shivering in the chill autumn air. Simon grew warm, thinking of the way they'd combated the chill last night. Beth opened the door, then turned to wave. He waved back, then put the Jeep in gear and headed for his office on campus. He could not allow thoughts of Beth to distract him from his work.

As a matter of routine, he collected weekend and evening schedules for the students in his graduate classes. Once at his office, he pulled out the file containing the schedules, then flipped through the pages until he found Heather's information. She worked at the campus coffee bar on Sundays until two o'clock. Like Beth's bookstore, it didn't open until ten o'clock.

Simon glanced at his watch. Quarter after ten. He ran through his arguments in his head one last time as he walked to the student center and descended to the coffee bar in the basement. At one time, it had been a real bar, but it switched to selling coffee when the drinking age had gone up to twenty-one.

Music videos blared on the wide-screen television, ignored by the two students nursing coffees at the tables scattered before the screen. The coffee bar had just opened, and was virtually empty.

Simon interrupted a student who was wiping off tables with a wet rag.

"Is Heather Montcalm working here today?"

"Yeah. She's doing an inventory of the beans." The student gestured toward the back of the coffee bar.

Simon found Heather in the supply area, wrestling twenty pound bags into position on a set of wire shelves. She was wearing her sorority sweatshirt, and a bronze, beaded hair band held back her brown hair, just as Beth had foreseen.

"Good morning, Heather."

She spun around.

"Professor Parkes! Good morning." She glanced at the shelves around them, then said in confusion, "What are you doing on this side of the counter?"

"I was looking for you."

A range of emotions played quickly across her face — nervousness, pleasure, and finally, curiosity. "Me?"

"You're a friend of the boy whose roommate died, aren't you?"

"Yes." She stiffened. "But I never mentioned Keith in class."

Simon hesitated. He needed to tread carefully around the truth. "I've heard a disturbing rumor, that you plan to use information learned in my class to help him find out what happened to his roommate."

Heather's eyes widened, and she took an involuntary step backwards. "How did you...? Who...?"

"I can't tell you who told me. You know that. Is it true?"

Heather ducked her head. "Yeah."

"This boy, Keith, found two people dead because of a ritual. Don't you think asking him to participate in another ritual would be needlessly traumatic?"

"Not if it works!"

"And what do you think the odds of that are?"

Heather flushed, but said nothing.

"Even if, for the sake of argument, we assume the ritual you plan to conduct is a valid magical ritual that will produce the effects it claims to, we've discussed in class how the texts were written in cryptic codes, to prevent their use by the unenlightened. You would most likely accomplish nothing but psychological scarring for your friend."

"But at least we'd be doing something. The police aren't doing anything. They said it was okay for the landlord to replace the carpeting. They wouldn't do that if they were still looking for clues."

Heather paced nervously between the shelves. Simon gentled his voice, seeking to calm and reassure her.

"I saw their file on the case. It has all the information they need to finish their investigation."

"You saw the police file?"

Simon needed to tread carefully indeed. "Yes."

"Why?"

"I consult with the police on matters of the occult."

"What did you tell them?"

"That serious students of the occult would not have drawn a pentagram with Jell-O."

Heather shook her head, and nervously tucked her hair behind her ears. "Keith doesn't believe Brian killed his girlfriend and did…that…to himself. There had to have been someone else in the apartment. The summoning ritual will bring that person back."

Simon closed his eyes for a moment and took a deep breath. "Assuming there was a third party, and assuming the ritual worked, that would put you and your friend Keith in great danger."

"No it won't. Keith borrowed some video equipment and set it up in the apartment. We're going to leave as soon as the spell is finished, and come back later to see who, if anyone, stopped by."

Simon ran a hand through his hair, searching for the words that would convince her that she was in over her head, and she wasn't immortal. "What if the person sees the camera and lays in wait, then kills you and Keith when you come back? Amateurs get killed, Heather. I can't allow you to go through with this. Leave the investigation to the police."

She squared her shoulders and lifted her chin. "I'm sorry, Professor, but I have to do what I think is right. Keith needs my help. If there's even a possibility of the ritual working, I have to try it."

How many times had he said something similar to Andrew? Simon had a sudden sympathy for his mentor. He suspected that Heather would be just as convinced of the rightness of her course as Simon always had been.

He'd been watching Heather carefully since she joined his class, suspecting that her quick grasp of magical concepts and obvious affinity for the occult indicated a budding Guardian, and this attitude of hers clinched it. She needed to be tested for possible apprenticeship. He remembered the rocky beginning of his own apprenticeship, and shook his head. He did not need this complication now.

"We need to have a talk. A long one. Come to my office when you finish working today. And call your friend Keith. Tell him you're not going through with the ritual."

"But—"

"If you don't meet with me, your friend's life could be in danger, as could yours." Simon gestured at the wide-open coffee bar around them, the thin metal mesh of the shelving units doing nothing to stop sound. "I can't tell you more, but I'll explain when you come see me. If you really want to help your friend, meet with me."

He left her standing with her mouth open, staring at him. But she would not summon the entity.

* * * * *

"Do you have any idea what time it is?" Andrew groused.

"Seven-thirty, your time." Simon was sure Andrew could hear his grin over the line. "I don't see what you're complaining about. I was up before the dawn."

"I'd rather sleep."

"No, you wouldn't. I think I've found the next Guardian."

Andrew's voice immediately became alert. "Who? How?"

"One of the students in my class. She sensed the entity's presence, and was trying to perform a ritual to expose the evil influence she felt."

"You stopped her before—"

"Before she even started. Thanks to a divination last night that told me where the entity would strike next."

"You're getting better at divination."

"No, I'm not." Simon leaned back in his chair and put his feet up on his desk. This was going to take a while, and he may as well be comfortable. "I didn't have the vision. Beth did."

Andrew was silent for a long while before saying, "You'd better explain. And start from the beginning."

After relating the events of last night to his mentor, Simon asked, "Have you ever heard of such a thing happening before?"

"Not exactly. I've heard of people sharing visions, especially when they both participated in the raising of power. That might have been what happened in your case. With her asleep, she was more open to the vision, and saw it before you did. Perhaps if she hadn't screamed, you would have had the same vision, only later."

"Might have been? Perhaps? You're not giving me a lot of confidence, Andrew."

"If it had been anything other than divination, I'd know what to tell you. But that's your weakest skill. You might never have seen the vision on your own."

Simon dropped his feet to the floor. "Are you saying I'll need to include Beth in all my future divination work?"

"I don't know what to say. This isn't my field, either. I need to talk to an expert. What time is it in England?"

"Four o'clock, I think. Maybe five. I can never remember if they're five or six hours ahead of us."

"Close enough. I was supposed to call Lydia today anyway. I'd asked her to do a divination about the situation."

Simon forced a smile. "She's probably anticipated your call already."

"Then I shouldn't keep her waiting. I'll let you know when she has anything you can use. In the meantime, get that girl tested and find out if she's really Guardian material. And keep her from trying any more magic!"

"She's coming by my office in three hours. I'll start the test preparations as soon as I get off the phone with you."

CHAPTER SIX

Beth's hands froze in the middle of ringing up a college student's order. A chill crawled down her back, making her skin itch, but she was helpless to move as yesterday's nightmare swallowed her senses. The bookstore disappeared, and she found herself standing in that shabby apartment again, watching the girl read from the book.

It wasn't quite the same as before. This time the girl was alone, and a pentagram had been drawn on the scratched coffee table around the key. But the black cloud still rose from the key. It roiled and billowed in a dark sphere, exactly the size of the pentagram.

Beth dared to hope that it was being somehow contained, that she would not have to witness the girl's death again. The girl stood, eyes wide, and tried to back over the couch, away from the cloud. Then it burst free of its boundary and engulfed her.

Beth's dreamself screamed. The image cleared, and she found herself back in the bookstore. Her finger pressed the Total button on the cash register, the one she'd been reaching for when the dream memory had hit her. Her hand started to shake, then her whole body started to tremble.

The boy she'd been waiting on looked at her strangely. "Are you all right?"

"What?" Beth blinked.

"You got a very strange look on your face all of a sudden," he explained. "Are you all right? You're not having a stroke or something, are you?"

"No. No, I'm not all right. Please excuse me." Beth hurried from the counter, leaving Julie to ring up the confused student. She had to speak to Simon.

Using the phone in the stock room, Beth dialed university information, then asked to be transferred to Simon Parkes. "Please be there. Please be there," she chanted, listening to the interminable ringing of the connection trying to go through.

"Professor Parkes," he answered.

"Simon! Thank God you're there!"

"Beth? What is it? What's wrong?"

She shuddered, wishing he was there to hold her. "I had that dream again. Where the students were killed by the cloud. But I wasn't asleep! I was standing at the cash register and then I wasn't and it was all the same only different and the cloud came out and it killed that girl and I thought I screamed and everyone looked at me and nothing had changed but I saw it I swear I saw it and Simon I'm so scared!"

Beth clutched the phone with both hands, her arms pinned tight to her chest, but couldn't stop the shaking that threatened to tumble the fragile lifeline from her grasp.

Simon bit off a sharp curse, then his voice turned soft and soothing. "Everything's going to be all right. I'll make sure that everything is all right. Just listen to the sound of my voice..."

Beth hung up the phone, not quite certain what Simon had said, but knowing he'd reassured her. Silly of her to let the memory of a dream disturb her, all because the student she'd been waiting on had looked so similar to the boy in her dream.

She shook her head, and went back out to the store. Julie looked up from the counter in concern.

"Are you okay now?"

"I'm fine." Beth shrugged her shoulders. "I didn't get much sleep last night, and it just sort of caught up with me."

Julie handed the last customer her change, waited for the woman to leave the store, then grinned. "Oh, really? The lunchtime crowd has finally cleared out. You've got time to tell me all about it."

* * * * *

Simon floored the accelerator, urging more speed from his Cherokee, as he hurtled toward the apartment where Heather was about to invoke the entity.

"Stupid. Stupid. Stupid. I told her not to do it. Why did I think she'd listen to me? I'm only her teacher."

His anger burned darkly, raging first at Heather for disobeying him, then at himself for not ensuring the girl was protected. It wasn't yet two o'clock. Either Heather had gotten out of work early, or Beth's vision had arrived in time for him to stop the disaster. He hoped Beth's vision had come before the fact.

He reached the apartment building, driving the Jeep up onto the sidewalk in his hurry. He jumped out and raced up the stairs, the rising buildup of magic tingling across his skin. There was no time for subtlety.

Reaching the apartment, he heard Heather speaking words of power. Worse, he felt the first stirrings of dark energy coalescing.

Focusing his will, he kicked the door in. Heather stopped in mid-chant, but the damage had already been done. Two white candles burned on the coffee table in front of her, on either side of a chalk pentagram. Inside it, a door key glowed with a sickly light. Thin wisps of black smoke rose from the key, twining together and forming a dark cloud instead of dispersing as normal smoke should.

"Get away from the pentagram," he ordered.

Wide-eyed and white faced, Heather obeyed, backing away from the entity.

"Shut the door and stay next to the wall," Simon told her. Trusting that this time she would follow his instructions, he focused all of his attention on the piece of the entity that had successfully breached the barrier to the material world. Heather's pentagram bound it now, but she didn't have the kind of power to contain that much magical energy for long. He prayed it would hold long enough for him to complete the banishing spell.

Simon closed his eyes, visualizing the protective white light above him, and drew his athame. Gripping the magical knife, he touched its point to his forehead, beckoning the brilliant white light to fill his thoughts with divine inspiration.

He drew the dagger downward along the length of his torso, until he held it at his waist, pointing at his feet, imagining the shining light following the line into the ground, suspending his body like a bead on a string between Heaven and Earth.

Touching the dagger first to his right shoulder then to his left, he visualized the beam of light crossing his body, crossing the first beam of light, and fixing him in this time and place.

He clasped his hands around the dagger at the point on his chest where the two lines crossed, as a golden glow spread through his fingers, then surrounded him.

Filled with calm and certainty, Simon circled around the growing dark cloud to face toward the east. He traced a pentagram in the air before him, the blade of his knife leaving glowing blue traces of energy. He took a deep, strengthening breath, then stepped forward and thrust both hands into the center of the pentagram.

A surge of energy rocked him.

Holding his dagger blade outward, he traced a glowing white line as he walked to the south, starting to form his circle around Heather's smaller pentagram.

He drew a second pentagram in glowing blue flame, followed by one to the west, then one to the north. He carried the white light to the first pentagram, closing the circle, then returned to his position beside the coffee table where he'd started. Now, even if Heather's pentagram faltered, the entity would be contained.

Simon breathed deeply and confronted the rumbling cloud hovering over the coffee table. The entity was not nearly as dangerous as the last time he had faced it on the material plane. Heather's ritual had been interrupted, and only the barest edge of the entity's true power had been allowed to form. Simon still had enough power to send it back where it had come from.

Spreading his arms wide, he felt the magical wind from the east blowing against his face. "Before me, Rafael. Behind me, Gabriel. On my right hand, Mikael."

Scarlet flames blossomed from the dagger still held in his right hand. Simon tightened his grasp on the painfully hot hilt, and continued his invocation.

"On my left hand, Oriel."

"About me flames the pentagram—"

The entity burst through Heather's pentagram, roaring out to engulf the room. Heather screamed. The entity struck the boundaries of Simon's circle, then focused on him. Darkness gathered around him, filling his eyes and ears, cutting off Heather's frantic shrieks. The powdery black film coated his face like a mask, cutting off his air. His body instinctively gagged, trying to expel the blockage, and his hand reached to claw at his mouth and nose. The charged blade of his athame touched his cheek with a flare of heat, vaporizing the thin skin of evil, and he gulped welcome air. He saw and heard nothing, his eyes and ears still covered by the darkness, but trusted that the glowing protection of his pentacle still burned around him.

"And within me shines the six-rayed star!" he shouted, unable to hear his own voice. The six-pointed star burst into glowing existence, expanding outward from his chest just as the golden ball of light had done earlier. As it swelled, growing brighter, it pressed the darkness out and away. Simon's eyes and ears cleared as the fragment of the entity retreated from his power, although he felt the looming power on the other side of the fragile ethereal barrier, fighting to get through to the material world. He had to banish the fragment before its presence here weakened the barrier enough to let the entity break through. He forced more of his energy into the star of light. Finally, the entity was trapped between the glowing golden radiance of the star and the shining white barrier of the circle. Darkness flared once, then was gone. A crack of sound more felt than heard shook him to his knees.

Simon felt the shadow of the entity's dark presence dissipate, and his strength dissolved with it. He knelt, lacking the power to rise, and whispered the words to seal the rift. "So the circle echoes the whole and the whole world is blessed. Hallelujah. Selah. Aum."

He tucked the athame back into his belt, and drew a shaking hand across his face. That had been too close.

Turning, he looked back at Heather. She stood, plastered against the wall, staring at him out of wild eyes. His earlier fury had burned away in the fires of the ritual he had just performed, and he no longer had any desire to punish her, but he did need to ensure her silence. If she had been any other student exposed to the reality of magic, he would have done her the kindness of wiping her mind of what she had seen. Instead, he climbed slowly to his feet.

"Next time I tell you not to perform a ritual because it's dangerous, you'd better listen to me."

She blinked. "It's real. Magic is real. And you…"

Simon took her by the hand and led her to the couch. "I said we needed to have a long talk, and this is as good a place as any to have it. Yes, magic is real. And I can use it. I'm what's known as a Guardian. Once there were over a hundred of us. Now, there are a dozen, fighting to keep the powers of darkness and chaos from overwhelming the world."

Heather's eyes widened still further. "That many were killed?"

"No. The decline happened over centuries, every generation a few less apprentices to fill the places of the Guardians who died. The world has changed, and there are no longer many who have both the ability and the willingness to devote their lives to the magical arts, for the good of others. But there are some. That's what I wanted to discuss with you. I believe you have the makings of a Guardian."

* * * * *

Simon leaned briefly against the side of his Jeep before straightening and trudging downtown toward Beth's bookstore. The past week had been an unending series of magical rituals as he tried to prepare Heather for her new role as an apprentice Guardian, searched for clues to the entity's next attack, and looked for ways to defeat it. And he'd still managed to carry his usual class load. He was tired and cranky and wanted to lay down and sleep for a week. But mostly he missed Beth.

He'd had to cancel their dinner date Tuesday night to work on Heather's shielding. Judging from her frosty reaction, Beth hadn't quite believed his flimsy excuse that he'd unexpectedly had to work late, but she was too polite to call him an outright liar. He'd wished he could reassure her, but it was impossible when he couldn't reveal any of the details of his work.

He promised himself he'd make it up to her today. They had all of Saturday to spend together. A sliver of guilt needled him, but he forced it away. He couldn't be expected to devote every waking instant to his pursuit of the entity. He needed a little time off to rest and recuperate, or he'd burn himself out completely.

"Andrew had better deliver that help he promised," Simon muttered as he dodged a cluster of chattering university students filling the sidewalk.

Beth was waiting on the bench outside of her bookstore. Her eyes widened when she saw him.

"You look awful!"

Simon winced. That hot shower he'd taken before coming here must not have helped as much as he'd thought it had. "You look lovely."

And she did, too. Pale blue jeans embroidered with tiny flowers around the pockets and cuffs hugged her curves, and a short gray shirt made of some shiny, stretchy material teased him with the possibility of glimpsing the smooth, satiny skin underneath. But mostly he noticed the sparkle in her blue eyes, and the tiny dimple in her cheek when she smiled at him.

Paradoxically, he felt flushed with strength, and so weak he needed to sit down. He settled for putting his arms around her in a loose hug and leaning against her.

Beth locked him in a tight embrace and gave him a deep, soul-stirring kiss, right in the middle of the sidewalk. "That's my apology for being so rude."

She would have stepped away, but Simon had no interest in releasing her. "Give me a moment. I'm sure I can imagine some other slight you need to apologize for."

She laughed. "Later. When we're alone. But for now…what are we doing on our date?"

Reluctantly, he broke their embrace. He considered asking her to forego the date, and just go home with him. Especially after that kiss. He shook his head to clear it. "I'm very tired, so I'm not up to anything too active…at least, not if you want me to do anything other than fall asleep in my dinner."

She laughed again, linking her arm through his. "How 'bout a movie?"

"Mm. You, me, a darkened movie theater. I can see the possibilities."

"Just as long as we see the movie, too."

They strolled hand-in-hand back to his car. Simon needed both hands on the steering wheel to thread the Jeep through the congested streets, but eagerly clasped Beth's hand when they arrived at the multiplex. He consulted the schedule posted above the ticket booths, looking for films starting within the half hour.

"Action adventure, teen comedy, science fiction action adventure, or comedy."

Beth tilted her head as she considered. "Do you feel like watching something blow up?"

He shuddered, reminded of his too close brush with the entity. "No. Let's go for the comedy."

Simon bought tickets, two bottled waters, and a disgustingly large bag of popcorn, then they settled into the plush stadium seats to wait for the movie to begin. He leaned back, resting his head against the cushion that towered over him. Insipid ads touting local car dealers flashed on the screen, interspersed with quotes from movies he'd never seen and actors he'd never heard of.

Beth read one of the quotes aloud and giggled. "That was a hysterical movie." Muffled laughs from the rest of the theater indicated other audience members shared her opinion.

"Never saw it." He closed his eyes, shutting out the images. Did his duties as a Guardian keep him too busy to participate in pop culture, or was he just hopelessly staid and boring? He couldn't remember the last time he'd seen a film in a theater, not counting those dreadful witchcraft films. Those had been research. But when was the last time he'd watched a movie for fun?

Beth's fingertips brushed his cheek. "You really do look exhausted."

"I've been working extra hours on a new project."

"Tell the dean you need another graduate student to assist you."

Simon chuckled dryly. "She is the new project."

Beth pulled her hand away. He opened his eyes and looked up at her.

Her eyes were narrowed slightly and her mouth was pinched in at the corners as she studied the bag of popcorn. She reached into the bag and pulled out a handful, then tipped the bag toward him. Smiling brightly, she asked, "Popcorn?"

"No thanks." Simon closed his eyes again. Lack of sleep was playing havoc with his perceptions. No doubt Beth was having second thoughts about the size of the popcorn. After all, he'd done nothing that could possibly upset her.

Sprightly music announced the nonsmoking policy and location of fire exits. Beth elbowed him in the ribs, and wriggled into a comfortable cocoon in her own seat, her attention focused on the screen before them.

The movie, the slapstick adventures of a goodhearted but inept young man trying to make his fortune and win the girl of his dreams, soon had Simon, Beth, and the rest of the audience convulsed with laughter.

Beth caught herself sneaking glances at Simon. She enjoyed looking at him. She loved the way his face lit up when he laughed. And the sound of his laughter tickled her ears, making her feel all warm inside.

She'd been foolish to distrust him, just because he'd stood her up to work with a female graduate student. He wasn't like Conn, using his power and position to seduce the young women who worked with him. She knew he really did care about the students he taught, and the subjects he taught them.

Beth smiled, relaxing into her seat. All she'd needed to do was look at him to see that he was simply working too hard.

When the movie was over, she slipped her arm through his. "How about stopping at the food court for an early dinner?"

"Great idea. Although I'm amazed you're hungry enough for dinner after all that popcorn."

Beth grinned. "I never said it would be a particularly big dinner."

They ended up getting slices of mushroom pizza and bottles of Snapple, and settled down at a bright red Formica table overlooking one of the mall's entrances. It was too early for the dinner crowd, leaving many of the prime window seats around them empty. They traded favorite quips from the movie while they ate, then leaned back in the spindly wire chairs to finish their drinks.

Simon closed his eyes and sighed in pleasure. "This is nice, just being with you."

It was the perfect opening. Beth leaned forward and asked, "What are you doing at work that's got you so busy?"

"Well, there's the project I was working on before. You remember, the midnight telecon with the west coast? And on top of that, I'm training a new assistant. I could always just tell her what I want her to do, but if she's going to be any use at all, I have to explain why I want it done, and why it needs to be done the way I asked her to do it. I'd never realized how much explaining a teenager requires."

"You were a teenager once," Beth teased.

"Ah, but all of my questions were insightful and to the point. I couldn't possibly have been this annoying." Simon tried to look self-righteous, but his grin spoiled the effect. He probably had been just as bothersome as his new assistant, if not more so.

"I have a question for you, if you can stand to answer another one."

"What?"

"Are you ready to go?"

Simon stood, gathering their empty paper plates and napkins. "Where to? My place?"

Beth carried the bottles to the recyclable bin while Simon disposed of their trays. "Your place. If you're so tired, maybe you should take a nap."

"You're right. The best place for me is in bed." He grinned as he took her hand. "That's the best place for you, too."

Beth studied Simon as they drove back to his house. He seemed happier and more relaxed than he had been. And his weariness had been replaced by a sense of eagerness.

She was pretty eager herself. It had been a week since they'd made love so spectacularly in his Jacuzzi. She couldn't wait to see what he had planned for tonight.

Simon parked the car and hurried around to help her out of the Jeep. He continued holding her hand as they walked up to the front door, only letting go to pull his keys out of his pocket. He fit the key into the lock, then frowned as he turned it.

He pushed the door open. "It wasn't locked. I must have been more tired than I thought."

Beth followed him into the foyer, bumping into him when he stopped suddenly. A woman's voice, deep and sultry, with a British accent, made the reason for his abrupt stop clear.

"Simon! Where have you been? I've been waiting hours for you!"

Beth moved to the side so that she could see. The woman was slim, with short dark hair and classically beautiful features. Her black spandex catsuit, clinging to her body as if it had been painted onto her, proved that the rest of the woman was equally perfect.

Beth risked a glance at Simon's face. His broad grin and glowing eyes indicated he was thrilled to see this woman, more so than he should be for a casual acquaintance. And no casual acquaintance would have keys to his house. Beth's heart sank.

"Lydia! Why didn't you let me know you were coming?"

Lydia shrugged, a graceful rotation of shoulders worthy of a ballerina. "You know how it is, darling. I decided this morning, far too early to call across the pond. And I refuse to use those air phones." She smiled at Beth. "You must be Heather."

"No, this is Beth," Simon corrected her.

Lydia's expression hardened, all the warmth evaporating as she said in a chill tone, "I don't believe you mentioned her on our telephone call."

"No, I didn't," Simon said, equally coldly. His voice and expression warmed as he turned to Beth. "Lydia is one of the researchers working on that big project. I'm sorry, but I'm going to have to cancel our date."

Beth forced a semblance of a smile onto her face. She'd already jumped to conclusions once tonight. She wasn't going to do it again. Even if Simon had never mentioned his late night calls included ones to a beautiful woman in England.

The woman on the stairs exuded a sense of smug confidence. Was she that sure of her welcome? Yet, while Simon had been initially pleased to see her, his behavior after that opening exchange had given no further clues as to his relationship with Lydia.

Hoping for more information, as well as trying to salvage her date, Beth asked, "You just flew across the Atlantic? You must be tired after such a long trip."

"Not too tired to work," Lydia purred. "I know what's important."

Simon caught his breath as if she'd struck him. His eyes glittered but his voice was gentle as he told Beth, "I'm sorry, but I have to work. Come on, I'll drive you home."

"Don't be too long," Lydia warned him.

"I get the idea, Lydia. Enough already. I'll be as quick as I can."

Turning his back on the woman, Simon smiled apologetically at Beth. "It's not how I wanted the date to end, but what can I do? I'll make it up to you."

Over his shoulder, Beth saw Lydia stiffen, her eyes widening and color rushing to her face. Simon apparently sensed the coming tirade as well, because he hurried Beth out the door before Lydia could say anything else. Beth was nearly running to keep up with him. He bundled her into the Jeep and started the engine before she had a chance to gather her scattered wits.

Beth studied Simon's profile as the Jeep crunched down the gravel driveway. His face was pale, his lips were taut, and his fingers clenched the steering wheel so hard the knuckles were white. The tension she'd sensed in him when he met her at the bookstore was back with a vengeance, far more than could be justified by an unexpected house guest, no matter how abrasive.

Beth thought back over what had been said. Simon had seemed surprised to see Lydia, but had otherwise acted normally, until she'd said that she knew what was important. Was it some sort of cryptic code phrase? Or an oblique way of reminding him that she knew something about him? Maybe she was blackmailing him!

Certain that she'd read too many mysteries, Beth asked, "So what is it you and Lydia are working on?"

"She's one of the people working on that big project."

"Yes, I gathered that. But what exactly is the project about?"

Simon darted a glance toward her, then turned his attention back to the road. "I'm not at liberty to say."

She blinked. How secret could his project be? He was a philosophy professor, for Heaven's sake, not a nuclear scientist.

Feeling like she'd stepped into the pages of a spy thriller, Beth tried another tack. "Then let's discuss something else. When can I see you again?"

"I don't know."

"Will Lydia be here all weekend? For the whole week?"

"You heard everything she said to me. She didn't tell me her travel plans."

"Well, how long will your project take?"

"I don't know, Beth!" he snapped.

"You don't have to yell at me. I'm not the one who canceled our date for a better offer."

"She's not a—" Simon shook his head. "I can't believe we're having this argument. Look, I don't know how long she'll be in town, or how busy we'll be. I'll call you when I get a chance, but don't be surprised if you don't hear from me for a few days."

Simon pulled up in front of her apartment. He must have been driving well above the speed limit to get there so quickly. That wasn't like him at all. None of this was like him.

She tried one last time to find out what was going on. "You won't have any free time for days? I hadn't realized academic research was so grueling."

"Please, Beth, I can't tell you any more. I'll call you when I can."

He sat there, eyes forward and hands clenched on the wheel as the Jeep idled hungrily. Beth unsnapped her seat belt and opened her door.

Simon turned to her, his expression filled with such misery that she longed to gather him in her arms and kiss his troubles away. "Beth—"

He bit off whatever he was going to say, and bent his head. "I'm sorry."

Beth forced herself to smile brightly. "Your work comes first. I understand. Just don't make a habit out of it. And call me."

He nodded, but made no move to lean forward and kiss her. She waited a moment longer, then slid out the open door.

"Call me," she repeated.

She slammed the door shut, almost muffling Simon's soft, "Good-bye. Be safe."

He threw the Jeep into gear and squealed away from the curb, leaving her staring after the rapidly disappearing car. "Good-bye," not "I'll call" or "Be seeing you." It sounded so final. And what had he wanted her to be safe against?

Beth hugged herself against a sudden chill, remembering Lydia's cold eyes as she told him not to be gone long. She'd clearly been warning Simon. But why? And about what? What kind of trouble had Simon gotten himself into?

CHAPTER SEVEN

Simon spent the entire drive back to his house cursing himself for his foolishness. He'd known that taking time away from his work to be with Beth was a selfish indulgence, yet he'd convinced himself that it was not only acceptable but necessary that he see her today. What kind of a Guardian was he, when he couldn't even guard his own thoughts and feelings?

At least Beth was safe. After the cold way in which they'd just parted, no doubt she'd want nothing to do with him for quite a while, if ever. She'd told him about her divorce, and her philandering husband. Simon knew she'd been suspicious about Lydia, yet there had been nothing he could say. He needed to explain the situation if he hoped to win her trust, but the secrets of the Guardians were not his to reveal. He hoped he could find a way to make it up to her after everything was over. But if she couldn't accept a man who had to keep one aspect of his life shrouded in secrecy, perhaps it was better if he learned that now.

That thought stung, distracting him temporarily from his self-flagellation. He didn't want Beth to leave him, even if it would keep her safe.

Simon sighed, and pulled the Jeep into his driveway. Lydia was waiting for him in the foyer when he pushed open the front door.

"You're making a habit of meeting me at the door." He couldn't quite keep the bitterness out of his voice as he added, "Don't you think you're taking this happy homemaker routine a little too far?"

"I was listening for your car from the kitchen while I had a cup of tea. I haven't been waiting in the hall the entire time you were gone."

"I got back as quickly as I could. Now, what really brings you to America?"

"It's going to take a while, and my tea is getting cold."

"After you."

Simon followed her to the kitchen. Ignoring the second cup she'd set out, he waited impatiently while she topped off her cup from the teapot, added milk and stirred. She sipped the liquid, smiled, and leaned back in her chair with a sigh.

"There are very few things that can't be cured with a proper cup of tea."

"I don't think you came all this way just to show me how to make tea."

Lydia's expression turned serious. "I came because of a vision. Andrew asked me to see what I could about your entity, and I saw you dying."

"What?" An icy fist slammed into Simon's chest, and struggled to breathe normally. "When? How?"

"There's no need to panic, at least not yet. You know these things aren't precise."

He sat, taking the time to bring himself under control by pouring a cup of tea. His hand didn't shake too badly, only spilling a little tea onto the table top. He didn't trust himself to actually pick up the cup, though. "So is this one of the things that a cup of tea can fix?"

"Possibly."

Simon stared at her. "You're joking."

Lydia sighed again, and ran her fingers through her hair. "At this point, I don't know. The divination was clear that you would not succeed against the entity on your own, and that I could be of some assistance. I called Andrew this morning and he agreed that I needed to come in case my being here would make the difference. So I came."

Unwilling to dwell on the possibility of his imminent demise, Simon focused on the trivial details in her recitation. "I thought you said it was too early to call this morning."

"It was too early to call you, darling. It was only eleven o'clock at night for Andrew." She frowned. "He was certain you'd be here when I arrived, as he said you've been working around the clock on the problem. Neither of us expected you to be out on a date."

Simon flushed. "It won't happen again. After today, I'm sure Beth never wants to see me again. Your presence here, and our obvious familiarity, led her to draw the wrong conclusion, as I'm sure you intended. You knew I couldn't correct her, since I can't tell her anything about the Guardians."

"I hadn't intended that, but I'm glad it happened. You'll need all your concentration on the task at hand if you're going to survive your battle with the entity. I don't want you distracted by thoughts of your personal life."

Simon struggled to control his temper at Lydia's high-handed reorganization of his life. She was always infuriatingly certain that she knew best for everyone around her. The problem was, she usually did. And she had put herself to great inconvenience in order to help him.

Reminding himself that she'd probably been traveling for something like eighteen hours with all the time changes, he smiled at her, and picked up his teacup in a steady hand. "Thank you for flying all the way out here. If there's a way to defeat the entity, I'm certain together we will find it."

"You and me against the world? Darling, you know I'll do everything I can for you." Lydia set her teacup down firmly on the table. "Finish your tea, and we'll see how my being here has affected the probability currents."

The tea had been standing long enough that it was merely warm, and Simon gulped it down. "A full divination?"

"I think it's best. I set everything up while I was waiting for you."

"If you'd only let me know you were coming—"

"Tut." Lydia cut him off with a wave of her hand. "What's done is done. It's the future that concerns us now."

He nodded. "I'll change into my robes and meet you in the workroom."

"Take the time to do a ritual cleansing, first. I don't want anything interfering with your participation. And you know I love you dearly, Simon, but you couldn't divine your way out of a paper bag."

He laughed weakly to let her know he appreciated her attempt to lighten the mood, but not even a well worn joke could ease the tension coiling within him now. He'd never tried to divine the manner of his own death before. It was something he'd prefer not to know.

"All right," he agreed. "Shower first. But don't worry. I'll be quick about it."

"Good." She started cleaning up the tea things. "But you'll be quicker if you start now."

* * * * *

Beth tidied her house, using her unexpected free time to put away the pile of books that seemed to spontaneously grow on her coffee table. She slammed a stack onto the bookshelf.

What had Simon gotten himself into? All sorts of farfetched scenarios spun through her mind. Blackmail? Cults?

She remembered his reticence to discuss the police investigation. Was his current trouble involved with that? But then why was the woman from England involved? And what was she doing making herself at home in his house?

Glancing down, Beth noted the book beneath her fingers. *Good Night, Mr. Holmes* by Carole Nelson Douglas, about the unsung woman who helped Sherlock Holmes solve his cases. Maybe this mystery woman consulted for Scotland Yard, the same way Simon worked with the local police.

A cold weight settled on the back of Beth's neck. She shrugged her shoulders, trying to dislodge the feeling, but it didn't work. Instead, the tingling chill spread down her back.

Simon was in danger. She just knew it.

She'd picked up the phone and dialed his number before she was even aware of crossing the room. "Come on, come on, answer it already!"

The phone continued to bleat in her ear, as Beth imagined the rings echoing through Simon's home. He'd had plenty of time to get back there after dropping her off. Why wasn't he answering the phone?

Beth shivered. Maybe he couldn't.

She hung up the phone and paced her apartment, trying to convince herself that she was letting her imagination run away with her. After all, look at how freaked she'd gotten the other day, thinking that boy in the store looked like the boy in her dream. If she could reach Simon, no doubt he'd be able to quickly reassure her that there was nothing at all to worry about.

But she couldn't reach Simon. That was the problem.

Beth gnawed on her thumbnail. Then, noticing what she was doing, she clasped her hands behind her back and started pacing again. The chill was getting worse, and a sick feeling started to grow in her stomach.

She snatched up the phone again and punched in Simon's number.

Filled with nervous energy, she drummed her fingertips on the table while she listened to the endless rings. He wasn't going to answer the phone. She refused to think that maybe he couldn't answer it.

She dropped the handset into the cradle. Never mind. She'd just have to go over to his house and see for herself that he was all right. It was a stupid thing to do, and her old self would never have considered it—but her old self had been married to a philanderer for years without learning about his true nature because she only did what everyone expected her to do. She wasn't going to be the last one to find out what was going on this time. If Simon was in trouble, she wanted to know about it while she still had time to help him. And if there was something else going on, well, it was better that she learn it now.

Her newly purchased secondhand bicycle made quick work of the miles to Simon's house. Too quick. By the time she rode up his driveway in the early twilight, she still hadn't decided on a plan.

His Jeep was parked in front of the house, and light spilled around the edges of a curtain covering one of the downstairs windows. Barely perceived shadows shifted across its surface. The lights were on in that room, and people were moving about.

Beth strode to the front door, fighting the stomach cramps and shivers that threatened to knock her to the ground. Maybe there was nothing wrong with Simon. Maybe she'd just eaten popcorn popped in rancid oil at the movie theater that afternoon. But the sense of dread propelling her forward had nothing to do with food poisoning.

She rang the bell, listening as the merry peals echoed through the house. She waited another five minutes after all the sounds had died away, then rang again. And a third time.

Backing up, she glanced at the curtained room again. The light was still on, but she saw no movement. Had she imagined it? Or were the people in there frozen in place, hoping to escape detection?

She tried the door. It was unlocked.

Swallowing, she pushed the door open. "Simon? Hello? Is anybody home?"

No answer. She hadn't expected one.

She glanced around the gleaming black and white foyer, but saw nothing she could use as a weapon. A sturdy fireplace poker would have done much to steady her nerves.

Turning in the direction of the lighted room, she made her way in that general direction, although the house's twisting corridors confused her a bit.

A scent teased her nostrils. She sniffed. Heavy and floral, with an undercurrent of smoke. Incense.

She followed the fragrance down a short hallway that doubled back at an angle to where she'd thought she was going, and found light spilling from an open door. "Simon? Hello?"

Tentatively, she crept around the door and into Simon's study. No one sat at the desk, or stood before the bookshelves.

She frowned. Something was wrong with the position of the bookshelves against the inner wall.

The scent of incense grew stronger as she approached, as did the flickering light coming from behind the shelves.

She blinked. Flickers of light still licked at the edges of the shelving unit. Reaching out, she gave the shelf a light tug. The entire unit pulled silently away from the wall, pivoting on a hidden axis.

"I don't believe it. He's got a secret room," she whispered to herself. The chill shuddered through her again. Why did he need a hidden room? Was he hiding from someone or something? Or was he doing something he wanted no one to see?

Beth took a deep breath, and stepped around the shielding bookshelf to the room on the other side.

Simon and Lydia were both dressed in yellow silk robes. They stood inside a pentagram formed of marble tiles on the floor, chanting in a foreign language. Yellow candles burned at the points of the pentagram's star, and dark purple candles were centered in the places between the star and the circle surrounding it. Lydia bent to toss a handful of powder on the glowing brazier between their feet, and a fragrant cloud rose up. It hung in the air between them, stirred by their movements but not enough to dissipate.

Beth stared in shock. Simon really believed in this magic stuff. He thought he was some kind of sorcerer!

"Simon! What do you think—"

Simon whipped around to see her, the hem of his robe flaring out and passing through the cloud of smoke. There was a crack of sound. What broke? And the heat of a roaring inferno of flames. Surely that tiny brazier couldn't put off that much heat.

Terror chilled Beth's soul. Simon's robe hadn't brushed across the coals, had it?

Simon fell to his knees. No! She stepped toward him, despite the heat and the smoke.

He started coughing, deep wracking coughs that shook his whole body, interspersed with raspy gasps for air. He wasn't on fire, but he must have breathed in a lot of the smoke.

Billowing clouds of incense filled the room. Beth took a step back, away from the encroaching smoke. Her eyes stung, reflexively tearing up to combat the floating ash. She blinked rapidly, trying to focus. Her blurred vision made it look as if the smoke was filled with shifting shapes, when she knew only Simon and Lydia were in the room.

Lydia! Simon continued to cough and struggle for air, but Beth hadn't heard anything from the woman. Had Lydia been overcome by the smoke?

Beth took a deep breath, and braced herself to enter the swirling cloud to look for Simon's guest.

An errant breeze swept past Beth's cheek, into the smoky room, and parted the haze. She saw Simon, on his knees with his head bent, still coughing, but not as hard or as often. She could barely make out the yellow silk of his robe under the streaks and smears of ash.

Beside him, the brazier glowed red hot, but no more smoke rose from it. Thankfully, the incense seemed to have burned itself out.

Behind the brazier, her yellow robe untouched by ash, Lydia glared through the swirling smoke at Beth. "Get out!"

Beth hesitated, her gaze going to Simon's hunched figure on the floor. He'd stopped coughing, and the smoke was slowly rising. Soon he'd be able to breathe with no difficulty. He didn't need any help.

"Out! Now!" Lydia pointed to the door. The glowing light of the coals reflected off the blade of a knife in her hand.

Beth turned and ran from the hidden room, dashing through the study and pelting down the house's twisting corridors until she reached the foyer. She yanked wide the partially open door and darted outside. Her bicycle gleamed in the sunlight, offering her a means of escape.

She kicked it forward as she jumped onto the pedals, rolling down the drive before she'd even mounted.

* * * * *

Beth couldn't leave! Not like this. Simon gulped a deep breath of air to shout her name, forgetting until too late that the hot air was full of ash. Another paroxysm of coughing seized him, and Beth fled the room.

He watched helplessly as Lydia banished the lingering magical energy. Finally, she bent down to help Simon to his feet.

After leading him through the study and back to the kitchen, she sat him at the table with a large glass of water. "Drink. Slowly. I'll make you some tea."

Simon sipped at the blessedly cool water, soothing his ravaged throat. Lydia bustled around the room as she filled the kettle, put it on to boil, and got out mugs and tea bags. Her faith in the power of tea was endearing, but tea couldn't fix a ruined divination. Tea couldn't fix his relationship with Beth, which had been strained enough by Lydia's unexpected arrival. Having Beth discover him performing ritual magic had probably destroyed it. He knew he should go to her and try to explain what she'd seen, if he hoped to salvage things between them. But he lacked the energy to do anything more than just sit there.

He sighed, which sparked another round of coughing. After his lungs calmed down, he wondered what Beth would do with the knowledge. His speculations were pointless. What made him think he could predict her next move when he'd failed to anticipate her return this afternoon? She could have been badly injured by his oversight, just as Heather had nearly been killed by his failure to correctly predict her reaction to his warning.

A wave of desolation crushed him beneath its weight. Closing his eyes, he rested his head in his hands. So far, luck and fast reflexes had kept tragedy at bay, but he shuddered to think that his skills were all that stood between the entity and its material incarnation.

Lydia poured two mugs of tea and carried them to the table. Sitting down, she asked, "Did you see anything this afternoon?"

He shook his head. He'd failed at that, too. "Not clearly."

He'd caught a glimpse of a figure with an unnaturally pale face wearing a black cloak. But unless the entity planned to incarnate as Bela Lagosi, the image made no sense.

Lydia sighed. "Honestly, darling, sometimes I wonder how Andrew ever let you out of your apprenticeship. Fortunately for you, I did see something."

"What?"

"Halloween. We have three weeks before the entity breaches your defenses and crosses onto the material plane."

"So soon?" he rasped. "What else did you see?"

"If you try to fight it alone, you'll die."

He sucked in a quick gasp of air. Trust Lydia to cut straight to the point. "But will I succeed?"

"Possibly. That was unclear."

Simon groaned. Death would be a high price to pay for success, but the ultimate failure if the entity still broke through. And given how things were going lately, he was sure he'd end up failing on his own. There had to be another way.

"What if you help me?"

"I'm not sure." Lydia fidgeted with her mug, turning it around and around in her hands. "I believe we will be successful. The divination was vague, as if there was another element I hadn't taken into account. It was just starting to sharpen up when your girlfriend burst into the room and destroyed your concentration."

"It's not Beth's fault—"

"That you left the door open when you were planning on working magic? That you must have keyed the house's wards to allow her entry? That you didn't explicitly tell her to stay away?"

Simon's anger flared as hot as the coals they'd used for the divination spell. "So this is all my fault?"

Lydia quirked an eyebrow at him. "Isn't it?"

He glared at her. He hadn't created the entity, or called it across the barrier to the material plane. But he could have made the break with Beth cleaner. The truth was, he'd wanted her to return. He just hadn't wanted her to return while he was in the middle of a ritual.

"I warned you about getting involved with a mundane. She distracted you."

Simon took a swallow of his tea. It was good, much better than he made, even though she'd used his tea bags. He'd accused her once of possessing tea magic, although her mundane occupation as the owner of a small tea shop in London probably had more to do with her skill.

He forced his mind away from such comforting trivialities, and made himself consider her words. Twice Beth had interrupted his rituals and ruined his focus. The first time was helpful. This time she'd at least caused no harm, although the backlash of broken energy had thrown him for a loop. But the power he was working with was growing. The next time, the sundered energies could really injure him. Or her. There couldn't be a next time.

"My attention was divided. That won't happen again. From now on, I'll focus completely upon the task at hand."

Lydia tipped her head and studied him, seeming to both look at him and through him at the same time. He shifted uncomfortably in his chair. Finally, her eyes cleared.

She shook her head. "There are too many variables."

"You said that before. Could one of the additional elements you weren't sure of be my apprentice, Heather? In three weeks, she might be trained enough to be of some help."

Lydia sipped her tea while she considered his suggestion. "Possibly. I got the sense that you would be doing some teaching. But I wasn't sure if that referred to training your apprentice, or your work at the university."

"My poor class. They were really looking forward to their Halloween field trip."

"What field trip?"

"We were supposed to be the guests of a Wiccan circle, then spend the hours around midnight in a cemetery reputed to be haunted." He smiled wryly. "I doubt any of the other professors will be willing to take over for me."

"You'll have to cancel."

"I know. But how do I explain it to them?"

Lydia shrugged. "You'll think of something, darling. You always do."

He wished he shared her confidence. "How do I explain to Beth?"

"She was going on your field trip?"

Simon glared at Lydia. She was being purposefully obtuse. He could tell, because she was terrible at looking innocent. "I meant, how do I explain what she saw this afternoon? You realize she probably thought you were coming after her with a knife."

Lydia's eyes widened in honest innocence. "Why would she—? Oh."

"Right. You were holding the athame."

"No wonder she ran so quickly. I'm sorry, darling. I didn't think. I was worried that she'd try to run to you and break the circle. We had enough things going wrong with the spell without that happening."

Simon grimaced. They had been lucky that Beth only interrupted a divination. Breaking off in mid-spell had caused a magical backlash, stronger than the minor backlash he'd felt when her nightmare interrupted his last divination. But a divination was primarily an information spell. The worst breaking it could do was give him a headache and sap his magical energies. If they'd been performing a protective magic, or worse, an offensive magic, Beth's innocent interruption could have unleashed forces capable of killing one or all of them.

He gulped the last of his tea, wetting his suddenly dry throat. Flecks of tea clung to the bottom of the mug. He studied it intently, hoping to make some sense out of the arrangement, but it just looked like specks and clumps.

"Reading tea leaves now? You're getting desperate, darling."

He set the mug on the table. "Yes, I am. I haven't made such a stupid mistake since I was an apprentice. I lost my concentration in the middle of a ritual. We're lucky it was such an innocuous spell, or I'd have suffered more than a singed robe and a sore throat. I'll take reassurance anywhere I can get it."

Lydia placed her palms on the kitchen table and studied her fingers for a moment before looking up at him. "I'm sorry, Simon, but I can't offer you any. If you lose your concentration again, you'll lose your life. And quite possibly, loose the entity onto the material plane."

* * * * *

Beth rode blindly, only gradually realizing she'd steered her bicycle to the main commons of the town. Students and shoppers enjoyed the Indian Summer warmth, putting off the long winter nights for as long as possible.

She parked her bike and sat down on one of the decorative cement benches. It was still warm from the heat of the day, although it would get too cold to sit on as soon as the sun set, which would be in half an hour or so. But that gave her plenty of time to surround herself with the nice, normal sights of people shopping and laughing with friends while she tried to figure out what she'd seen at Simon's house.

He and Lydia were acting out some magical spell. That much was obvious. And Lydia had been carrying a knife.

Why? They hadn't planned on some sort of sacrifice, had they?

Were Simon and Lydia witches?

If they were, then Beth had interrupted them in a religious ritual. That could explain Lydia's extreme reaction. There might be some sort of prohibition against nonbelievers witnessing their rites.

Beth shrugged and settled more comfortably against the bench. She could understand if Simon was a witch. Or a Wiccan. Whatever they were called. Religious prejudice was alive and well in this country, and he was probably justified in keeping his religious beliefs a secret.

If the university learned that he was a Wiccan, would that affect his job? Would they be afraid that he might be converting some of the students, and fire him?

Beth shivered. What about his research assistant, Heather? Lydia had seemed to expect Simon would bring Heather. Was that why Lydia was really here? To turn Heather into a witch?

The sun dipped below a building. She needed to get back to her apartment. It was still a ten minute ride from the downtown area.

As she raced through the encroaching darkness, Beth's thoughts turned increasingly dark and dismal. What if her suspicions proved correct? Was she obligated to tell the university?

Worse yet, what if Simon's occult activities were less than benign? The police had questioned him about those two students who died. Were their deaths really accidents? Or were they sacrifices? Were they members of a coven? Magical rivals?

Scenes from every late-night movie she'd ever seen about magic tumbled through her mind. She forced the fear down. Simon was a good man. She had to believe that. She'd spent enough time with him to know that he cared about his students, that he was considerate of others, that he was a giving and attentive lover. He would never condone the sort of magic that required violence or sacrifices.

She pulled up in front of her apartment building and locked her bike into the rack beside the parking area. She fumbled for her keys, opened the door, and trudged up the stairs to her apartment.

But what kind of magic had Simon been practicing? If it wasn't witchcraft, then he really believed he was some kind of sorcerer. He might not mean to hurt anyone, but that sort of delusion was bound to be dangerous in the long run. And he certainly shouldn't be teaching impressionable teenagers.

Beth took a pint of ice cream out of the freezer and collapsed on the couch to think. She needed to learn more about what he'd been doing.

She'd go into work a little early and check out some of the books in the store's New Age section. They had a fairly wide variety, from all the respected pagan presses as well as some of the fringe publishers. She'd find what she needed there. And then she could decide what to do next.

CHAPTER EIGHT

Simon's students stopped talking as he walked into the classroom with Lydia. Eight pairs of curious eyes focused on the stranger in their midst.

"I'd like you to meet Lydia Hammond-Jarrar, from England. She's going to be a guest lecturer for the next few weeks."

Jon sat up straighter in his chair, showing signs of interest for the first time ever in Simon's class.

"Thank you, Simon." Lydia turned to the class. "My specialty is divination. How many forms of divination are you familiar with? How many different ways to tell the future?"

"Reading tarot cards," Jon offered. So the boy had been paying attention after all. Simon hid a smile.

"Scrying in a mirror," Susan said.

Tiffany piped up, "Astrology."

"Reading the lines on your hand," Carl said.

"Palmistry," Lydia corrected, then glanced around the room. "What else?"

"Talking to spirits?" Heather suggested.

Lydia nodded. "Yes, various cultures seek guidance from both spirits of the dead and from guardian spirits. But you've mentioned mostly eastern European divination methods. What about other cultures?"

Alex grinned. "Fortune cookies."

"What about those Viking rune stones?" Rich asked.

"Good. Good." Lydia looked at Kim, who usually let Tiffany speak for her in class. She was the only one who hadn't offered a suggestion. "What about you? Can you think of any ways to tell the future?"

"Everyone else mentioned all the ones I know."

"Try."

"Well, my mom used to bake charms inside our birthday cakes, and whichever charm we got in our slice was supposed to tell about the coming year, like a horseshoe for good luck, or a coin for money."

The rest of the class smirked and giggled, and Kim's face flared bright red. Lydia silenced them with a deadly lift of her eyebrow.

"Actually, that sounds like Sortilege, which is any divination where you pick from a collection of items."

"Way to go, Kim," Tiffany murmured to her friend.

Lydia turned to Simon. No doubt the class missed the way that her lips twitched up at the corners, but he knew she was setting him up. "What about you, Simon? Can you think of a form of divination we haven't mentioned already?"

"Capnomancy. Divination using the patterns in smoke."

"Very good." Lydia turned back to the class. "Also very old. Most of you no doubt think of divination as a party game. But to our ancestors, it was a vitally important method of survival. They used it to predict weather for their crops, migratory patterns for the animals they hunted, and even such things as whether or not marriages would be fertile."

Her comment provoked another round of smirks and giggles, as even the most oblique references by a professor to sex usually did. They probably thought the ancients who made up the faculty had long since forgotten the passions of their youth. He wondered what they'd think if they knew of his and Beth's wild lovemaking.

Simon lost the thread of Lydia's lecture as he turned his thoughts to Beth. He'd caught himself time after time yesterday making an excuse to call her. Only the knowledge that it was safer for her not to get involved prevented him from breaking his resolution to Lydia.

The need to see Beth again was like an insatiable hunger, gnawing at his spirit. He couldn't stop thinking about what she might be doing, or how she might be feeling. The worst of it was at night, alone in his bed, remembering Beth sharing it with him.

Unable to sleep, he'd gotten up and paced the halls, until at last Lydia had come out of her own room to ask him what was the matter. She'd suggested that he relax with a hot bath or a session in the sauna, and he'd been too embarrassed to explain why neither of those would be particularly relaxing. He'd ended up falling asleep on a mat in the exercise room, one of the few rooms in the house that contained no memories of Beth.

Stifling a yawn, he turned his attention back to Lydia's lecture. The class was entranced by her description of the particularly gruesome divination method of Haruspicy, the reading of animal entrails. He watched the students' faces, shifting rapidly between disbelief and horror. But they'd certainly remember her lecture. Lydia always did know how to make an impression on people.

She finished with a bright smile. "Any questions?"

"I'm gonna have nightmares for a week," Tiffany moaned.

The other students shook their heads.

"Then here's your homework assignment. I want each of you to choose a method of divination, and try to make a prediction about something that will happen between now and, oh, Halloween." She fixed the students with a stern glare. "Even if you think it's all a bunch of flibbertigibbet, give it your best effort. Don't think that you can just make something up. I *will* know the difference."

Heather raised her hand. "Is this assignment in addition to the individual projects we're working on already?"

"Yes," Simon answered. "But anyone who would like to work this assignment into your overall semester project should see me after class and we can discuss it."

"Will you be in your office during normal office hours?"

Simon caught Heather's gaze, waiting until she acknowledged his attention with a brief nod. "It would be best if you scheduled a time to see me, so that I can devote the proper time and attention to each of your situations. See me after class and we can set something up."

* * * * *

Julie looked up as Beth entered the store Monday morning. "Another hot date, huh? You look like you didn't get any sleep at all this weekend."

"Our date was a disaster. But you're right that I didn't sleep well."

"Oh, Beth, I'm sorry. You seemed so happy together the few times he came into the store. What happened?"

Beth sighed, wondering what she could possibly tell her friend. That the gorgeous woman staying at Simon's house had brandished a knife at her? That Simon had a secret room in his house where he conducted who knew what kind of magical rituals? That she'd trespassed in Simon's home and nearly set him on fire?

"You don't want to talk about it," Julie sympathized. "I understand."

"No, that's not it. It's just…I don't know where to start."

Julie leaned forward, eager to hear anything Beth had to offer. Too late, Beth remembered Julie's fondness for gossip. If Simon was trying to hide his beliefs to protect his career, Beth would have to tread carefully, since telling Julie would be tantamount to taking an ad in the university newspaper.

"Was it something Simon said? Something he did?"

Beth shrugged. "He's more serious about the whole magic thing than I'd realized."

"More serious, how? You mean, he drones on and on about it? Or do you mean he's, like, a Wiccan?"

Wicca. Why hadn't she thought of that? She'd shelved enough books on the subject. But she'd never read any of them.

"What do you know about Wicca?" she asked Julie.

"Me personally? Not much." Julie giggled. "But there's a circle that meets locally. The head priestess stops in from time to time. She's very nice."

"Isn't witchcraft just for women, though?"

Julie shook her head, and led the way to the New Age shelves. "I know just the book for you. It covers all the basics, in a straightforward tone. It's very popular with people who think they might be interested, but aren't yet convinced. Or do you need something more specific?"

Beth hesitated, not sure how much to reveal. But she needed Julie's help or else she'd spend all morning looking through books and still might not find an answer.

"Simon ended our date early to go home and do some sort of ritual. I'm not sure if it was research, or religion. We didn't exactly talk about it." Beth shook her head. "There was more shouting than talking."

Julie nodded sympathetically. "He didn't bother to tell you what he was planning in advance? Men are so like that."

Beth bit her lip to keep from smiling at the girl's tone of world-weary wisdom. Julie wasn't old enough to know anything about men, only teenaged boys. As Beth knew from experience, they got much more complex and devious as they got older.

After glancing at the titles, Julie plucked a slim volume from the shelf and flipped through it. "The next big ritual should be Halloween, but let me see if there was a small one this past weekend. No, the last one was September 21st."

"But that doesn't mean it couldn't have been a Wiccan ritual, right?" Beth was surprised by how strongly she wanted Simon to be a Wiccan. He'd lied to her, or at least misled her, kept a huge secret from her, and worst of all hadn't answered the phone or called since Saturday, but deep in her heart she wanted to find a rational explanation for his behavior and a way to restore their relationship.

Julie tipped her head to the side and studied Beth intently. "What other kind of a ritual do you think it was?"

"I'm not sure."

The bells on the door jangled, announcing their first customer. Beth waved Julie toward the door.

"Look, you go wait on the customer. I'll just poke around in these books and see if I find anything to match what I saw."

Julie hesitated. "If you're sure..."

"I'm sure. Go, help the customer."

Julie reluctantly headed to the front of the store. Facing her fears, Beth picked up a book about devil worship. She was relieved to learn that the ritual she'd observed bore no resemblance to a Black Mass or any other Satanic rite.

She picked up the book Julie had looked at, an overview of Wiccan practices. The first chapter described the components of a ceremonial altar, including a decorative knife called an athame that was used to make magical gestures. To highlight its ritual significance, it was usually kept dulled.

Beth felt her cheeks burning. That had probably been the knife Lydia was holding. No doubt she'd been as unwilling to drop it on the floor as Beth would have been to drop a Bible. She hadn't been threatening Beth at all.

And Beth had run away like a scared child confronted by a bogey monster. What must Simon think of her? She practically broke into his house, interrupted a private religious ceremony, and then instead of helping to clear the smoke or getting him out of the room, she'd turned and bolted.

She'd been upset that he hadn't trusted her, but really, what had she done to show him she deserved his trust? She hadn't even waited around to give him an opportunity to explain.

Remembering their lovemaking in the Jacuzzi, she groaned out loud. Hadn't she as much as told him that she didn't believe in witchcraft or any other kind of magic? She'd been so self-confident and superior. What had he said in reply?

She struggled to recall his exact words, as she pictured the scene in her mind. She could almost smell the fragrant candles, and feel the warm water lapping at her skin as Simon moved inside her.

Blinking rapidly to dismiss the memory, she glanced up and down the aisle. No one had seen her. Thank goodness. She wasn't sure what her expression had been like, but suspected it wasn't anything she wanted to explain.

She'd remembered Simon's words. *I don't believe reciting a piece of bad poetry while performing certain actions will of themselves cause an event to occur.* More importantly, she remembered what he hadn't said. He hadn't said if there were other things that he did believe would cause events to occur. He hadn't denied his belief in magic and witchcraft.

Beth took a deep breath. Her boyfriend was a witch. If he was still her boyfriend.

She could deal with that. She'd prove to him that he could trust her with his secrets. But first she had to get him to talk to her. He could start by letting her apologize.

* * * * *

Simon signaled Lydia to close the office door while he turned off the ringer on his phone. He didn't want anything disturbing this session with Heather. Too much depended on it.

Lydia closed her eyes and concentrated for a moment, then announced, "All clear."

Heather stared at her with wide eyes. "Are you...?"

"A Guardian," Lydia confirmed.

Heather glanced back at Simon, a question in her brown eyes.

"I've explained about the Guardians, and how each of us has our own specialty. Lydia's is divination." He hesitated, needing to tell the girl enough to explain why they were rushing her training, but not wanting to frighten her. "Lydia saw that I would need her assistance to fight the entity."

Heather paused, thinking through the implications of his words.

"Is it that serious? I know you've been pushing me to get my basic training completed quickly, so it can't attack me again, but I always figured you could handle it. I mean, you kicked its butt at Keith's apartment."

Lydia shot a questioning glance at him. "Do tell, darling."

Her words practically froze in the air. Simon winced. The last thing he needed was to get Lydia mad at him, and he knew how much she hated not being told all the details of a situation. He'd honestly forgotten that he hadn't discussed Heather's near disaster with her. It was just another example of how his preoccupation with Beth had caused him to lose focus on what really mattered.

"It was trying to manifest as a result of Heather's summoning spell. I broke the spell, and banished the small portion of the entity that slipped onto our plane," he explained, then turned to Heather. "But that was just the edge of the entity's power, a bridge to its natural state. Come Halloween, we're going to be facing a full incarnation on the material plane, with all its powers intact. Or that's what we're going to face, if we can't stop it from incarnating."

He hoped he sounded serious yet optimistic about their chances. It wouldn't do to have his apprentice realize that he was terrified of the coming confrontation.

Heather collapsed in one of the guest chairs. "So what do I have to do?"

Her naive self-confidence was a refreshing counter to his own self doubts.

Lydia smiled gently at her. "Your most important task, darling, is to complete your training. The entity can manifest a physical form if it needs to. But it will probably prefer to absorb an existing physical form, as that requires less effort. Ideally, it will look for someone young, with lots of energy, and a high level of magical potential. In short, an untrained and unprotected future Guardian would be its first choice."

"Oh." Heather shrank in upon herself, finally realizing that she could be at risk. She turned her mute, appealing gaze on Simon. He wished he could reassure her that it wasn't as bad as it seemed. Unfortunately, it was worse.

"We had to tell you, so you'd understand the seriousness of the situation. And the timetable. Normally, you'd have two to six months to prepare for your dedication. We can give you two weeks to get ready. It will be hard, but you can do it."

The tests he'd given her had shown that she had an above average level of natural power, which would both help her prepare faster and necessitate that she be dedicated before the entity attempted to incarnate. Channeling her power would make her harder to locate and less appealing to the entity.

"I don't understand. What's a dedication? How is that different from the oath I already swore?"

"Simon, what have you been teaching the child?" Lydia crossed the room to sit next to Heather. "The dedication ceremony is where a Guardian initiate is dedicated to his or her future area of service, channeling his or her power into the aspect most needed for the guardianship. For example, I am dedicated to divination. Simon is dedicated to wards and other defensive magics."

"What are the other Guardians' specialties?"

Simon answered, "Andrew, the Guardian I apprenticed under, works with elemental powers, with an affinity for fire magic. Rashid does charms, talismans, and amulets. Ling works with spirit guides and animals. Moira is an herbalist, and is dedicated to potions and brews."

"It isn't important what the rest of their dedications are," Lydia interrupted. "The list would tell you twelve forms of magic other Guardians are dedicated to, but because of the nature of Guardians, you would not be able to repeat any of those twelve. The possibilities of what you could be dedicated to are endless."

Simon paused to study Heather's reactions. She was taking the information very well, with none of the challenging questions that had marked their earlier discussions. Or perhaps the novelty of meeting another Guardian hadn't quite worn off yet.

"We'll perform the dedication ceremony next Saturday. There are a few rules you need to abide by before the ceremony."

Heather sat up straighter, and muttered, "Aren't there always?"

Simon traded looks with Lydia, remembering their first attempts to work pair magic. Frustrated by the lengthy list of rules, far more excessive than the magic he was used to, Simon had asked Andrew why he and Lydia couldn't just get started with a simple spell, and learn the rest of the rules as they needed them. 'Because I'm too old to be picking up all the pieces of you if you try it that way,' Andrew had answered.

"The rules are for your protection, darling," Lydia told Heather. "Magic flows through currents in specific ways. If the current is blocked, the magic finds another outlet. Usually, an unpleasant outlet."

"The rather graphic example my mentor used was that if you try to direct magical power out your fingers, but your hand is closed in a fist, you're liable to blow your arm off."

Heather shivered. "I liked her explanation better."

"But you'll remember mine," Simon countered.

"I'll remember. So what are these rules that I need to obey?"

"They're quite simple, really. For one week before your dedication, you should eat no meat, no fish, and no fried grains. You should not drink any alcohol. And you should not have sex."

Heather blinked. "For a week? I'll starve!"

"No, you won't." Simon grinned, remembering his own dedication ceremony. "It will only feel that way."

"Darling, you are not helping."

Simon nodded an apology to Lydia. "It's actually a very healthy diet. You can have boiled rice. All the fruit and vegetables you want. And you can still eat proteins like cheese or peanut butter."

"So if anyone asks why I'm eating such healthy food, I can just tell them I'm on the magic diet?"

Lydia laughed. "Exactly."

"What about the ceremony itself?"

"It's a lot like tossing a dart at a dart board," Simon offered. "I can't tell you more than that."

"You don't have anything to worry about," Lydia added. "There's nothing difficult about it."

"Nothing difficult? I'll only be committing the rest of my life to serving a single dedication. I thought picking a major was hard, and that's only for four years!"

Simon laughed. "That's one advantage of magic over mundane life. You don't have to choose a dedication. It chooses you."

Heather studied him, as if she wasn't quite sure whether or not he was teasing her. Then she shook her head. "And that's supposed to make me feel better?"

"I know something that will cheer you up, darling."

Heather looked over at Lydia.

"This is a form of divination, so you don't have to do any additional assignment for class."

Heather grinned. "It's not much, but I'll take it."

* * * * *

Beth slammed the bookstore's phone down. She'd reached Simon's voice mail. Again. Where was he? He was supposed to be in his office during scheduled office hours, yet she'd been calling every fifteen minutes for the past three hours and he'd never picked up.

Sighing, she dialed his number again. She'd just have to leave a message, and hope he was too busy to answer his phone, not that he was purposefully ignoring her.

She smiled as she listened to the recording of his melodious voice. The beep caught her by surprise.

"Uh, hi, Simon. It's Beth. Please don't hang up or delete this message. Listen, I just wanted to say that I'm sorry for going into your house uninvited and interrupting your uh...for interrupting you. I know I overreacted. It's just...I was worried about you. I still am. Why aren't you answering your phone? Please call me."

Beth hung up the handset and stared at the phone, as if it were still connected to Simon. "Whatever it is you're in the middle of, I'm sure I can help, if you'll only talk to me and tell me what's going on."

David came in to take the afternoon shift, and the process of turning things over to him kept her mind off of Simon for at least five minutes. Then she picked up her bag of employee discounted books, and all her questions returned.

Julie had helped her pick out two good books on Wicca, which she planned to study before she met Simon or Lydia again. She wasn't going to make another foolish mistake born of ignorance.

She'd also purchased two of the books Simon used in his classes, *The Shaman and the Magician* and *The Rebirth of Magic*. The first compared different types of magic, and the second was a history of magic from the middle ages to the mid-1980's. She still wasn't quite sure how magic, or magick, however it was spelled, was different from Wicca. There seemed to be a lot of overlap. But she'd know what she was talking about by the next time she saw Simon. More importantly, she'd know what he was talking about if he tried to explain what he'd been doing.

As she walked toward her apartment, she imagined meeting her old friends at one of their interminable cocktail parties, and explaining what she'd been doing since she'd left Conn.

"I've been traveling the countryside, taking odd jobs and learning odd things. Why, recently, I learned the difference between magic and Wicca."

They'd be horrified.

Beth laughed out loud, not caring who saw her. She was her own person now. She wanted to get back together with Simon, but she didn't need him. She wasn't going to need a man ever again.

CHAPTER NINE

Detective Thomas Freemont took another close-up photograph of the gutted and decomposing sheep while the irate farmer rambled on. Why would someone slaughter a sheep then leave it to rot in a field? He shook his head, and turned to the farmer, hoping to get useful information from him.

"When did you notice the sheep was missing?"

"We usually don't count the herd unless it's shearing or lambing season. I noticed it was missing when I found its body. We counted the rest quick enough. This is the only one missing."

"When did you find the body, then?"

"'Bout two hours before I called you. I wanted to take a count first, in case any more were missing."

"Have any of the other farmers around here had attacks on their animals that they haven't reported to the police?"

"No. Well, Arnold Pendleton lost a few chickens a week ago. But he said he thought it was foxes or coyotes." The farmer waved a hand at the dead sheep. "Foxes or coyotes didn't do this."

Detective Freemont looked down at the sheep again. Its throat had been cut, a neat flap cut in its hide, and the intestines and other organs removed and placed on the ground beside it. It reminded him of the way deer hunters field-dressed the carcasses to keep them from spoiling.

He put on his latex gloves and ran his fingers through the sheep's fur, searching for bullet holes. There were none on the exposed side. He searched the grass around the sheep, but found no footprints or physical evidence. Then he turned the carcass over and searched the other side for bullet wounds.

No other injuries. It had bled to death from the throat wound. Although the delay in finding the body made the scene virtually useless for gathering evidence, there was no torn grass or other sign of the sheep struggling or thrashing. It had died quickly, most likely before it had been gutted.

Whoever had killed the sheep hadn't wanted the animal to suffer, which ruled out the usual sort of sicko who preyed on animals. That brought the detective back to his original question. Who would slaughter a sheep then leave it to rot?

"Did you see anything suspicious in this field over the last few days or nights?"

"No."

"Have you or any of your workers been in the field? Or near enough to scare someone off?"

"Not 'til today." The farmer studied the stubbly cornfields and pastures surrounding them. "The corn's harvested. But we put goats out to graze the next field over. One of the boys usually rounds them up in the evening. He could've spooked someone, I suppose."

"Do you have any enemies? Anyone who might be trying to get back at you by killing one of your sheep?"

The farmer thought carefully. "Not as I know of. And if someone did, they'd go after a ram, as those are more expensive."

Detective Freemont studied what he could see of the white wooden fence surrounding the two-acre field. It would be easy enough to climb over, meant only to keep sheep in, not to keep people out. He couldn't dust the whole fence for fingerprints.

"We came in the gate by the barn. Is there another gate on the far side?"

"No. If anyone needs to get in from the road, they just hop the fence."

The detective's ears pricked up. "The field meets a road?"

"Just a dirt service road, between the cornfields."

Better and better. There could be tire tracks in the dirt road, or at least a depression showing where a car had been parked on the shoulder. That would narrow down the likely point of entry to something he could search.

"I'd like to check that out."

The farmer nodded and led him toward the distant service road. Detective Freemont studied the path they were taking, checking to see if it was visible from either the barn or the house. He could just see the top floor of the barn, which held hay and would have been empty of people.

He smiled, remembering his own youth. It was possible that there could have been a couple of people up there during the time the crime was committed, but if so, they would have noticed nothing besides each other.

As he and the farmer walked slowly down the length of the wheel ruts called a road, Detective Freemont examined the strip of grass and dirt between the ruts, as well as between the near rut and the fence. Paydirt! A single narrow tire tread veered out of the rut and ran parallel with the fence.

Waving the farmer back so that he wouldn't accidentally step on the tread, the detective knelt and examined it. Too much time had passed for the tire's tread pattern to still be evident, but he could measure the width of the tire. He could tell that it was from a bicycle tire, but touring bikes, off-road bikes, and racing bikes all took slightly different size tires. With so many students unable to afford cars or dedicating themselves with teenaged abandon to environmental causes, the town was filled with new and used bicycles of every possible make and model. Being able to narrow the field of suspects however slightly would make his search easier. And the depth of the tread could help establish the perpetrator's weight.

He photographed the clearest tire track and noted the various measurements in his notebook. Then he stood and slowly followed the trail, keeping an eye out for anywhere the bicyclist might have stepped onto the ground. He found where the bicyclist had stopped and leaned the bike against the fence. A black scuff mark marred the white fence, and dry, brown blades indicated where the grass had been torn up and trampled.

After snapping another photo, he bent to search the grass for clues. Nothing. He moved to the next segment of fence and hopped over it into the field, then circled back to the entry point. A mark on the lowest board caught his attention.

A broken splinter had caught a bit of blue thread, probably denim. More importantly, it looked like the sheep killer had jerked his or her leg to free it from the splinter, hitting the board and staining it with a hint of red. Sheep's blood, no doubt. Detective Freemont photographed it and scraped off a sample of the bloodied paint.

He tested the fence for fingerprints, although it seemed likely the perpetrator had worn gloves to slaughter the sheep, since there were no bloody fingerprints. The only prints on the fence were fragments too old to be any use.

"Thanks. I think I've got everything I need for now. I'll give you a call if anything comes up. In the meantime, you probably want to bring your livestock in at night."

The farmer nodded. "I'll tell other folks to be careful, too. This is more serious than the usual Halloween stunts of spray-painting the sheep or tipping the cows."

"Halloween's not for another two weeks."

"Someone might be getting an early start this year."

Detective Freemont grunted noncommittally. Privately, he wondered if something had been added to the air or water to make people behave strangely of late. All summer long, the police department had nothing more serious than bar fights, car accidents and a few domestic disputes. This fall, they had that grisly murder/suicide of the college students, and now someone was mutilating farm animals. Preying on the detective's mind was the fear that the mutilations would follow the traditional escalating pattern of animal abusers, and the perpetrator would eventually turn to a human victim. He vowed that there would be no more murders in his town.

* * * * *

Simon handed the student's paper to Lydia. "You think Tiffany deserves better than a C?"

She grinned. "Don't you think inventiveness should count for something?"

Snatching back the paper, Simon read from the opening paragraph. "Rhapsodomancy is divination by poetry. Since songs are poems set to music, my divination device was the radio."

"She's right, darling."

"She claimed that an oldies station playing 'Jive Talking' indicated her professors would give incomprehensible lectures during the next week!"

Lydia laughed. "Are you upset because you don't think she worked hard enough on the assignment, or because she is insulting your teaching skills?"

Simon picked up his pencil and erased the C, replacing it with a B. "Satisfied?"

"Oh, dear." Lydia's expression of good humor faded as she read the next paper. "Your Susan may have an attitude problem, but she appears to be a competent witch. She used a mirror to scry for her assignment. 'My vision of the future was dark and turbulent, growing darker and more chaotic as Halloween approached. I think it means there will be a very bad storm, or the outbreak of a new war that could affect the students here.'"

"An A for the paper. And it confirms what we knew."

She handed the paper to Simon for him to grade, and studied the next paper intently, a furrow appearing between her eyebrows. "There's something…"

"Who's paper is it?"

"Rick's. He says he borrowed a set of tarot cards, and pulled three to indicate past, present and future. The ten of cups, showing a happy home life, followed by the six of rods, indicating unity against adversity, ending with the five of pentacles, which he claims to mean failure. He predicts a member of his study group will fail a coming exam. But he's looking at the surface."

Simon waited patiently while Lydia gathered her thoughts from whatever distant realm they traveled to. When her eyes cleared, he asked, "What's your interpretation?"

"The five of pentacles predicts failure, true. But it is a failure due to a flaw, like a stress fracture causing a bridge to collapse, not failure of a venture. We're overlooking something. Something important."

The telephone rang before Simon could reply. He picked it up. "Professor Parkes."

"Professor, this is Detective Freemont. I've got a case for you."

Simon felt the blood drain out of his face as he clenched the phone. "Another one?"

"Not another murder, thank God. But someone's been attacking livestock on the farms around town. First chickens, then a sheep. Last night whoever it was got a cow."

Simon resumed breathing. No one else had been killed.

"What makes you think these are occult attacks?"

"I don't know what else they could be. The animals are killed quickly, I might almost say mercifully. Then they're gutted, and their internal organs are spread out on the ground beside them."

Although disturbing, the situation the detective described was not necessarily occult. It could have been any run of the mill psychopath doing midnight vivisections. Especially since the detective didn't mention anything about any of the animals' organs being harvested. Spreading the organs out on the ground sounded more like they were being examined.

Simon blanched. A mundane examination was possible. But it could also have been a magical examination. Divination by animal entrails. Exactly what Lydia had described to his class. Had one of them done this? Simon couldn't picture any of his students murdering livestock, but he couldn't afford to be wrong. Not now.

"I need to see the crime scenes."

"The first one was cleaned up before we learned of it, but I've got photos and a report from the second. And I'm going back to the latest crime scene in an hour. Are you free then?"

"I can be."

"Meet me at the station. I'm picking up another officer to handle some of the interviews."

Simon scratched the basic information down on a note pad, startled when Lydia leaned over his shoulder to read what he'd written. Picking up another pen from his cluttered desk, she wrote, "Ask if I can go."

Simon hesitated, strangely reluctant to involve her. Knowing from experience when to trust his intuition, he shook his head, and quickly ended the call.

Lydia frowned at him. "Why didn't you ask if I could go?"

"I got a bad feeling about it."

"A premonition? You?"

He blew out his breath in annoyance. "No, not a premonition. More likely I brushed against one of my protective wards."

"You'd better explain, darling." She reclaimed her seat on the other side of his desk, and studied him intently, her manner once again coolly professional. After all, he was as much an expert on protective wards as she was on divination.

"I don't know how things work in England, but over here, the police don't let just anyone visit a crime scene. You need to be approved as an expert consultant. Even then, most cops don't like turning to outsiders. I'm lucky in that Detective Freemont is more open minded than most, and more interested in solving cases than in his standing with his fellow detectives."

"But darling, I am an expert."

The sense of danger crystallized in a single word. Suspect. "You're a visiting expert. And these attacks just happen to coincide with your arrival."

Lydia's eyes widened. "You think they'd believe I did these things?"

"I don't think you can help me from inside a jail."

"They'd have to let me out as soon as the real person killed another animal." Her gaze grew distant, as she walked the pathways of possibility. When she focused on Simon again, her features were molded into an expression of horror. "If I am arrested, there will be no other crimes."

Simon nodded, her words confirming his own fears. "This is a ploy by the entity. It has found another weak mind to influence. The divinations will serve it, one way or another, either by telling it how to remove us, or by being the reason we are removed."

"It's not just powerful, it's cunning."

He nodded, not at all encouraged by the revelation.

She essayed a tentative smile. "Then we must be cunning as well. We will use its own divinations against it. You must tell me everything you see and hear. Enhance your senses and your recall, so that you can repeat everything to me."

"Wouldn't it be easier for you to shadow me, and observe through my eyes?"

"No. That's too powerful a magic to use around a site that has been contaminated by darkness. The chance of my shadow picking up a shadow of its own is too great."

Simon shuddered. They couldn't use any magic that might open a pathway the entity could use to slip back into the astral plane. That would bring it far too close for comfort.

* * * * *

Beth paused on her way to the bookstore to eye the crowd growing outside the rent-to-own store. They were watching one of the large screen TV's in the window.

She caught her breath as a chill fear settled in the pit of her stomach. Edging closer, she felt the anger and outrage of the crowd as they muttered to each other.

"I can't believe that would happen in America."

"Is no place safe any more?"

"How could someone do such a thing?"

"It's those video games, corrupting children."

Her pulse quickened. Oh, God, not another Oklahoma City or Columbine.

Prepared for scenes of mass destruction, Beth didn't understand what she was seeing at first. The television showed a field, with a farm house and barn in the distance. What was so upsetting about a farm? Then she saw the remains of the cow.

The carcass lay in the center of a blackened pool of dried blood. One side had been cut away, and the animal's liver, stomach, kidneys, and other organs were laid in a neat row beside it. The intestines had been removed, then coiled beneath the rest of the parts. There was a lot of intestine.

She swallowed hard, hoping she wouldn't be sick. As she struggled to regain her composure, the picture on the screen shifted to a close up of a concerned reporter. One of the local reporters. It must have happened on one of the farms outside of town.

The cries of outrage grew louder, as did demands that something needed to be done. Some people were calling for police action, and others wanted to take matters into their own hands.

"When they find the sicko who did this, I hope they cut him up like that Holstein!"

Suddenly unable to stand the press of people around her, Beth turned and shoved her way out of the crowd. She staggered a short way down the street, until she reached the corner, then leaned against the sturdy pole of the street light.

Who could have done such a thing? And why?

The traffic paused in front of her, momentarily halted by a red light. Beth's gaze was captured by the red, white and blue markings of a police car. Two police officers sat in front, with someone in the back.

Then she recognized the man in the back of the police car. Simon.

Beth clutched the light pole for support.

She forced her numb brain to think the situation through logically. Just because he was in a police car didn't mean he'd been arrested.

She faced the harder question, next. Could Simon be involved in the crime? A suspect? Or was he a police consultant?

If he was a Wiccan, slaughtering that farmer's animal would be as against his beliefs as murder was to a Christian. Although, since a depressingly large number of people still managed to murder other people even knowing it was wrong, his religious beliefs didn't automatically rule him out. And that was assuming he was a Wiccan. According to her reading, magicians also cast spells, but were not bound by the Wiccan law of harming no one by their use of magic.

She knew from things he'd said about his work that he was familiar with a wide range of magical beliefs and practices. The first time they'd made love, he'd teased her by saying that he'd lifted some of the practices from a book on Indian magic. She hadn't been able to find the exact lovemaking style in any of the research books she'd devoured in the last few days, but there were enough similarities to concern her. The second time, they'd actually performed a Wiccan protection spell. So was Simon a magician who dabbled in Wicca, or a Wiccan who dabbled in other forms of magic?

Stepping away from the light pole that had supported her, Beth started walking toward the bookstore. She rubbed her throbbing temples. She needed to speak to Simon. She had to find out what was going on. All this second-guessing of the situation was driving her crazy.

A wave of nausea struck her, doubling her over. She reached blindly to the side. Her fingertips brushed the wall of a building, and she gratefully moved over and leaned against its comforting bulk.

Breathing shallowly, she slowly straightened. Fever flushes and chills chased each other across her skin, cresting over her in waves of heat and cold. The rough brick of the wall behind her alternately scraped her sensitive skin and faded from her awareness. The roar of the traffic and the babble of pedestrian voices rose to an incomprehensible assault of sound. She covered her ears, but a moment later, the painful noise was gone, the city inexplicably silent.

She started to shiver. What was going on?

Normal sound resumed around her. Beth pushed herself away from the wall and staggered the remaining block to the bookstore. The cacophony of discordant bells as she pushed through the door set her teeth on edge.

Concentrating on her breathing as a way to keep her rebellious stomach in line, she crossed the store to the counter. David was working the register today.

"David, I can't work today. Something—"

Another wave of nausea gripped her. With a sharp cry, she bent over the counter, her fingers clutching the glass. Panting, she waiting for the spasm to pass.

"Beth? What's wrong?"

She straightened slowly, testing her stomach's acceptance of each slight change of position before continuing. She stared blankly at David for a moment, watching as his image faded in and out. It was really quite a pretty effect, like the transporter beams in the old Star Trek series.

Blinking, she realized he was speaking to her.

"...you to the hospital."

Terror flooded her with adrenaline, temporarily clearing her head. She couldn't go to the hospital. Instinctively, she knew that she needed to get to Simon. This instant stomach flu was somehow related to him, and the cattle mutilation. She wasn't sure how she knew that. She just did.

"I'll be all right. I just need to go home and lie down."

"You're sure? You looked like you were going to pass out."

"A touch of the stomach flu. I'll be fine."

"Okay. I'll cover your shift." He grinned. "I can use the extra money, anyway."

"Thanks."

"You go straight home."

"I can't wait to lie down," she answered, making it sound like she agreed with him. Instead, she staggered from the store, and headed immediately for Simon's house. She'd wait on his front porch until he returned from wherever the police had taken him. But she had to see him. She could no longer afford to wait for him to come to her.

She managed to go only two blocks before another wave of pain struck her. When she could see again, she turned back to the bookstore.

David looked up in surprise. "Weren't you going home?"

"I didn't take my bike today, and I can't walk the whole way. I'm going to call a cab."

"I'll call for you." David pulled the phone book out from the cabinet beneath the register, and flipped through it until he found the listings for cab companies. "Any preference?"

"Whichever one is cheap and fast."

He selected one, dialed, and gave the bookstore's location. Hanging up the phone, he said, "They'll be here in five minutes."

"Great. I'll wait out front on the bench."

Two more of the strange nausea attacks hit her before the cab arrived. She gave the driver Simon's address, and settled back against the seat, wondering what she'd do when she got there.

Simon was with the police. She couldn't sneak into his house a second time, even if by some fluke he'd left the door unlocked again. She either had to hope that Lydia woman was there, or wait on the porch until Simon came home. Although waiting inside would be more comfortable, Beth hoped she had to wait on the porch.

As the cab pulled into Simon's empty driveway, the front door of his house opened. Beth counted out the fare, along with a generous tip.

"You sure you're going to be all right, ma'am?" the cabby asked.

Why did everyone keep asking her that? "I'll be fine." She glanced at the open door of the house. "I'm expected."

Beth carefully climbed out of the cab and closed the door, resting against the reassuring metal bulk for a moment before turning and heading for the house. She stepped onto the flagstone porch and paused. Behind her, the cab's tires crunched on gravel as the cabbie drove away. She had no escape. She had to enter the house, and confront Simon and Lydia.

Another wave of nausea drove her to her knees. The solid stones beneath her wobbled alarmingly, and she shut her eyes to hide the sight. Instead of helping, that made the sensation worse. Swallowing a choking gulp, she opened her eyes.

A pair of black ankle boots and legs wearing dark blue leggings stood right in front of her. She blinked. They were still there.

Lydia knelt on the stone porch in front of Beth, her features swimming in and out of clarity. "If I help you stand, can you walk?"

Beth nodded, then gulped again as the motion did terrible things to her stomach. "Yes. But...slowly."

"Right you are." Lydia wrapped one of Beth's arms around her shoulders, and curled her own arm around Beth's waist. "On three. One. Two. Three."

Lydia stood, dragging Beth up with her. Beth's stomach surged, and she gagged. She would not vomit on Lydia. That would be just too humiliating.

Of course, as soon as she thought of it, her body responded by trying to do exactly that. Frantically, Beth forced herself to think of something, anything, else.

She pictured Simon as he'd been the first time they'd made love, gloriously naked, telling her calmly how to breathe. In and out, slowly, deeply.

Her queasy stomach stabilized, and with Lydia's support, Beth staggered to the door. Lydia stepped through the opening, pulling Beth behind her.

Pain filled her arm, as if a hundred nails had been driven into her flesh and then dragged along the bones. The rest of her body passed through the doorway, and Beth's world darkened to molten agony. She felt as if that creature from Alien was trying to claw its way out of her chest, while heated spikes pinned her body in place. Lydia pulled on her arm, nearly tearing it off.

What was the woman doing? What kind of evil spell had she cast over her? Crazed with pain, Beth ripped herself out of Lydia's grasp, turned, and tried to flee out the still open door.

Steel bands encircled her waist, trapping her, and she kicked out. She had to escape. She had to break free.

Lydia hauled on Beth's flailing body and pulled her fully into the house, sprawling them both on the black and white marble floor.

Beth blinked. The pain was gone. She sat up and ran a shaky hand over her face.

"What…?"

Lydia curled herself into a graceful kneeling position, wincing as she rotated her shoulders. "I was about to ask you the same thing. Or do you always attack people who attempt to help you?"

Beth shook her head, struggling to make sense of the fragmented memories. "I attacked you?"

"Most emphatically."

"I didn't mean to. I just—The pain was so bad."

"Pain? What pain?" Lydia's voice sharpened.

"As I came into the house. It felt like thousands of red hot nails dragging through me. I couldn't think. I just wanted to get away, to make the pain stop."

The beautiful British woman's face turned a deathly shade of white. "Oh, dear."

Judging from Lydia's expression, Beth suspected that was an example of the British gift for understatement. "What is it?"

"Nothing you need to be concerned about. Let's get you up to bed. There's a guest room all prepared for you. And then, I'll bring you a nice hot cup of tea."

CHAPTER TEN

"Simon, we need to talk," Lydia said as she entered the house.

He closed the door, then sealed and reinforced the protective wards. "You look pale. Are you all right? I felt the echo of an attack while I was at the crime scene."

"I'm fine. But we have a problem."

"The wards held."

Lydia shook her head. "It wasn't a direct attack. It used some form of possession."

"Possession?" Simon leaned forward eagerly. "If we know who the entity is influencing, we can go to the police. They want a profile for the person mutilating these animals. If I know who it is, I can slant the details so they're sure to investigate him."

Lydia rested her hands on his shoulders, simultaneously comforting and restraining him. "It's Beth."

"What?" He jerked free of Lydia's grasp.

"She's upstairs now, resting. I didn't realize she had a connection to the entity, and pulled her through the wards. They acted like a cleansing."

"Is she all right?"

"For now. She's tired and weak, but otherwise unharmed."

"Why did she come here? And what did you tell her about the wards?" This was all his fault. He'd opened Beth to the entity's influence by involving her in the divination spell. He should have left such a tricky divination to the experts. But then, Heather and her friend would be dead, and the entity would be loosed on the world. No, he'd done what he'd had to do, and would do it again. But he didn't have to like it.

Lydia shrugged and started walking toward the kitchen. No doubt she intended to make tea. It would take more than a cup of flavored water to soothe Simon's anxieties, but he wasn't allowing her to end the conversation so easily. He trotted after her.

"Lydia? Did you explain about the house's protective wards?"

"She doesn't believe in magic."

That stopped him in his tracks. "I know she didn't before. But surely after she felt—"

"She felt the cramps and fever of a stomach flu. Anything else she might have thought she felt was a result of the fever. High temperatures can bring on hallucinations, you know."

Simon frowned. "You lied to her."

"I allowed her to continue believing what she thought was the truth."

"I need to see her." He turned away and headed for the stairs. "Which guest room is she in?"

"Simon, be careful. She's not ready to hear the truth."

He'd worked hard not to lie to Beth, but he would, if he had no other choice. Their whole relationship had been a cautious dance around the facts of his reality, when he should have saved himself the effort. He could never have a future with her, not when he needed to subjugate everything and everyone in his life to the needs of his calling. He was a Guardian. Beth was just another person to guard. That was all he could afford to ever let her be to him.

"I'll tell her no more than I have to, to keep her safe."

"Can you?"

Simon frowned again, or maybe he'd never stopped frowning. There was nothing about this situation to make him smile. "Can I what?"

"Keep her safe, once she leaves the protective wards around this house."

A chill ghosted across his flesh. "Why? Do you have a premonition?"

"No." Lydia shook her head, diffusing her warning with a somewhat strained smile. "I'm just worried. I don't like mixing mundanes in magical business."

"I don't want her involved, either. The sooner I can get her safely out of the picture, the better. You concentrate on untangling what the entity wanted with her, and I'll make sure it can't get its hooks into her again."

"Be quick about it. I need to review what you saw at the scene of the cattle mutilation."

Simon nodded, and resumed climbing the stairs. He'd rather not go through that grisly scene again, especially in the detail Lydia was certain to demand. But he would. It was a small price to pay to ensure it never happened again.

"Oh, and Simon," Lydia called after him. "She's in the guest room next to mine."

Lydia had been taking no chances, putting Beth as far from Simon's room as she could. But she wouldn't be staying long enough to warrant the extra protection.

Simon tapped lightly on the guest room door. When there was no answer, he edged the door open, and peeked inside.

Beth was asleep, her arms wrapped tightly around the second pillow. Simon remembered waking to that same determined embrace. He ruthlessly forced the memories away. He was here to protect her. That was all.

The covers had fallen down to her waist, revealing the baggy green T-shirt she slept in. Too big for her, the neckline had shifted to allow a glimpse of one smooth shoulder. Simon blinked. She was wearing one of his shirts. And she looked good in it.

He shook his head, pulling his attention back to the problem at hand. Taking advantage of her slumber, he cast a few of the most basic wards over her, and contemplated the results.

The wards would protect her from an external force attempting to invade her psychic or physical space. But because he'd combined his earlier protection spell with the divination, she'd somehow internalized a connection to the entity. The thought of the noxious presence he'd battled spreading its filth over Beth made Simon feel physically ill. Worse, because he'd opened the pathway for it. If she left the greater protection of this warded house, she'd be an open target.

Simon took a deep breath. He had no other choice. She would have to stay here until they had defeated the entity, or until he could get another Guardian who could help sever the connection. Carlos, perhaps.

Protective feelings surged within him, and Simon had a sudden vision of himself barring the door of the house, allowing no one to come near Beth, even if they meant to help her. She was his, and he would take care of her.

He ran a shaky hand through his hair. A Guardian couldn't afford to be overconfident. Look where his arrogant assumption that he could handle the entity had landed them. But the situation with Beth was different. He needed to protect her, and none of the other Guardians was as skilled at defensive magics as he was. No one else needed to be involved.

As if aware of his scrutiny, Beth stirred restlessly, mumbling into her pillow, then blinking and lifting her head. "Simon?"

"I'm here." He stepped around the foot of the bed and sat down on the edge so that she could see him clearly. Suddenly, he knew what he had to say to keep her here, to keep her safe. "How are you feeling?"

"Embarrassed." She laughed weakly. "I all but collapsed on top of your house guest. The fever came on so suddenly."

"Fevers will do that." He paused. "Beth, why did you come to the house?"

Her gaze slid out of focus as she concentrated on her memories. "I...don't really know. I had to see you. I remember that. But I don't remember why."

"Well, even if you hadn't, I would have gone looking for you."

"You would have?"

Simon hated to crush her hopeful expression, but it was necessary. "Yes. To warn you. You know I work with the police department, as a consultant. I've been called in to work on a series of escalating attacks. For now, they're contained to animals —"

"The cattle mutilation! I saw that on TV." Beth shuddered.

"Yes, the cattle mutilation. But before that, chickens and a sheep. The police fear that this will follow the standard pattern of escalating abuse, and that a human will be next."

Beth's eyes widened.

"They also think that the perpetrator is positioned to watch the results of his actions, either watching it on television or perhaps working at a farm near where these attacks have taken place. So we have to assume he'll know I'm involved."

The entity knew Simon was involved, all right. He'd fought it three times now, successfully enough that it was attacking the people around him rather than directly attacking Simon. That put Beth at more risk than him. But Simon couldn't explain his reasoning without explaining about the entity, and the magical situation.

Beth gasped. "Are you in danger?"

"I can take care of myself. But I'm worried about you."

"Me?"

"We've been seen together enough that you're at risk. The perpetrator might try to attack you to get to me."

She paled, and clutched her pillow to her chest. "No."

"I'm afraid so. I'd like you to stay here, where I can watch over you."

"But what can you do?"

Most of what he could do to protect her, she'd never believe. "The house has a full security system. I don't normally use it. That's why you were able to walk in that time. But I'm taking all possible precautions, now."

"I can't stay locked up in here. I have to go to work."

"Not for a while. You've been ill. Stay here while you recover, and when you're well, we'll figure out what to do about getting you safely to and from work, and protecting the bookstore." He smiled. "Who knows? Maybe the police will have caught the person responsible by then."

Beth favored him with an answering smile, then dropped her gaze and traced the pattern of the bedspread with one finger. "Simon, is that the only reason you're asking me to stay? Because some crazy might be out to get me?"

"I don't want you to be hurt."

"But you also don't want to be lovers, do you?"

Simon sucked in a quick breath. Faced with her direct question, he wasn't sure how to respond. Finally, he settled on the truth. "I want it more than you could imagine. But I can't. I have to be completely focused on my work. Too much is at risk for me to chance being distracted by anything or anyone."

When she didn't answer, he added, "I'm sorry."

"Well, at least you're honest about it. Now, if you'll excuse me, I'm very tired. I'd like to go back to sleep."

"Rest well." Simon quietly rose and left the room.

* * * * *

Beth glared at the closing door, and the man on the other side of it. How dare Simon order her around as if she was one of his students? She wasn't about to stay here, an unwanted guest, while he devoted himself to his work with Lydia. Something the perfectly proper Lydia would be certain to remind Beth of at every opportunity.

Lydia. Everything had been going so well until she arrived. Now Simon had no time for Beth, no time for anything except the mysterious project he and Lydia were working on. As far as he was concerned, Beth could have just ceased to exist.

Shaking her head, Beth admitted that wasn't quite true. She'd seen the pain in his eyes when he admitted he wanted to be her lover, but couldn't. And why couldn't he? Because Lydia demanded his complete attention on her project.

Beth settled more deeply into her pillows, and contemplated the situation. Lydia didn't want her here. She'd made that much plain, even while she was installing Beth in the guest room and bringing her tea to settle her stomach. Lydia wouldn't care if there was some slight possibility that the crazy man Simon was chasing might try to attack Beth. So the invitation to stay must have come from Simon.

Now that she thought about it, his excuse was pathetically thin. Not only would the criminal have to know who was investigating his crime scenes, and recognize that Simon had been brought in as a consultant, but unless he'd been stalking Simon beforehand, anticipating his involvement, the criminal would never have seen Simon with Beth. And the idea of kidnapping Beth or otherwise placing her in danger in order to prevent Simon from executing justice was something out of a Victorian novel. Modern police had all sorts of electronic surveillance and indirect methods of backup, and could still track and arrest the man, even without Simon's involvement. Attacking her would do nothing to protect the criminal, and would actually increase the police effort to bring him in. Even insane, as the man had to be to do those terrible things, he would recognize that mutilation of livestock was legally a minor charge, much less severe than an attack upon a human.

No, she was in no real danger. Simon had made up the excuse to keep her here. An excuse that Lydia, being from a foreign country, might not recognize. The police forces might work completely differently in England, and Simon's theory of a vindictive criminal out to silence his pursuers could be more plausible there.

Beth smiled. He wasn't willing to say so out loud, but Simon wanted her here. Lydia hadn't managed to get her hooks into him completely. And Beth would make sure she didn't get the chance. She'd fight for Simon, using the excuse he'd provided to stay close and discover what kind of hold Lydia had over him and how to break it.

Closing her eyes, Beth pictured Lydia's face when Simon told her that Beth was going to be staying at the house indefinitely. She wished she could be there to see it.

Her sudden illness had weakened Beth, and she found herself drifting back to sleep. As her mind fuzzed and faded, her last thoughts were of her plan.

First, she would regain her health. Then, she would tease Simon with her body, offering lingering glimpses and stolen touches that she would refuse to follow through on. For his own good, of course. She didn't want to distract him from his work. Unless he could explain what that work was, and why making love to her wouldn't really be a distraction.

When she returned to work, she'd ask Simon to drive her back and forth to the book store. With detours down secluded roads for lengthy "discussions" in the back seat.

Beth sighed in contentment. Lydia didn't stand a chance.

* * * * *

"What did you put in her tea?" Simon asked as soon as he entered the kitchen. He was proud of his calm and reasonable tone, when what he really wanted was to do was leap across the room, grab Lydia, and shake her until she confessed to hurting Beth.

Lydia glanced up from the legal tablet she was writing on. "I gave her herbal tea, darling. I put herbs in it."

"Which ones?"

"Chamomile. Feverfew. Catmint. Things to settle and soothe her." She waved her hand, dismissing the question as unimportant. "Now you've seen her, can we get to work on what you saw at the crime scene?"

"No." Simon slammed into the chair opposite her. "She's exhausted, completely wiped out. My wards didn't do that."

"She was under the entity's influence—"

"Then she'd have been prevented from entering. Passing through the wards might have hurt like hell, if the entity fought the protective spells while still linked to her. But once she broke free, she'd be fine. She's not. So you must have done something to her."

Lydia threw her pen onto the tablet. "You see? I told you having her here would affect your reasoning. You need to focus your attention on what's truly important."

"Beth is important!"

Lydia stared at him with glacial patience, waiting until her icy expression cooled his anger. Then softly, she asked, "More important than all the other people on this planet?"

Simon glared at her silently, knowing the truth but not wanting to admit it, then finally sighed and gave in to her argument. He was a Guardian. He could never allow his personal feelings to distract him from his duty.

"Of course she isn't more important than the whole world." He put all of his strength of will into his words, so Lydia would know that on this, he wouldn't be moved. "But that doesn't mean she's less important. I won't just ignore her condition."

Lydia sighed. "Very well. I was concerned that the entity might have left behind a channel that it could use to reach your friend again. So I transformed the tea into a purification tisane."

Her words seemed to strike Simon in the chest, a sharp blow that made him unable to catch his breath. "Then she's so ill because—"

"I was right."

His breath came back in a rush, quick gasps that did nothing to stop the buzzing in his ears.

"Simon?"

"It reached her through the house's wards once before. It can reach her again."

Lydia frowned. "What do you mean? You said the wards would keep it out."

"Yes. The entity can't enter the physical plane. But when Beth is sleeping, she's open to attack on the astral plane."

"Then it's good that I—"

Simon shoved his chair away from the table and stood up.

"Simon? Where are you going?"

"She's falling asleep even as we speak. I have to get up there and protect her!"

"Simon, she'll be fine. Your duty—"

"My duty can wait." Five minutes wouldn't mean anything to their ability to make sense of the augury he'd seen at the crime scene, and it could mean the world to Beth. Simon raced from the room, Lydia's shrill voice following him.

"Simon! Come back here!"

The pounding of his feet up the stairs drowned out the rest of her demands. He'd stay by Beth's side until she was safe. If Lydia wanted to talk to him, she could talk there.

CHAPTER ELEVEN

Beth stepped out of the shower Saturday morning, luxuriating in finally feeling clean, and briskly toweled herself off. It felt good to be able to do anything briskly, after the days she'd spent lying in bed.

Pulling on her freshly laundered clothes, she smiled at her exaggeration. It had only seemed like days. She'd collapsed in Simon's foyer Thursday afternoon, and had drifted in and out of consciousness for the rest of that day and night, always aware of Simon's reassuring presence. Although perhaps she'd dreamt some of that. She thought she remembered him speaking loudly in something that only vaguely sounded like English, and gesturing to someone who wasn't there.

She'd used Friday morning and early afternoon for further rest and recuperation. As soon as Simon had come home from the university and looked in on her, she'd insisted that she was well enough to get up. He'd insisted that she needed more rest. They'd finally compromised. He had carried her down to the kitchen to join him and Lydia for dinner, then carried her back up to bed. Beth wasn't sure which had felt better, being cradled in Simon's arms, or seeing Lydia look like she'd sucked on a lemon.

Beth finished toweling off her hair, and started dragging a comb through the snarls. No doubt the small guest bathroom near her and Lydia's rooms was fully stocked with toiletries, but Beth preferred to share the grand bath at the other end of the hall with Simon, and it contained only the basic shampoo he used. If she was going to be taking many showers here, he was going to have to stock up on conditioner.

She paused. How long was she going to stay? True, Simon had held her in his arms last night, carrying her up and down the stairs, and settling her in bed. But he'd been a perfect gentleman, his touch solicitous and completely unromantic.

Glancing at the darkened sauna and empty Jacuzzi, she remembered the way he'd touched her the first night she'd stayed here, bringing her entire body to quivering excitation.

She sat on the tiled wall of the Jacuzzi, overcome with a sudden weakness that had nothing to do with her illness. No one else had ever made her feel so complete, so totally adored. She'd never guessed lovemaking could be like that.

Snapping upright, she made a decision. She would stay as long as she needed to stay in order to free Simon from Lydia's clutches, until he recognized that they belonged together. He could be stubborn, but she'd just have to wear him down. After all, they were meant for each other. Sooner or later, he'd have to admit that fact.

Tugging the comb through the last remaining tangles in her hair, Beth walked out of the bathroom. Lydia was in the hall by the linen closet, a towel-covered basket at her feet.

Lydia closed the closet door. "Did you leave any hot water?"

"Yes." Beth bit off the rest of her response, knowing that the other woman was trying to provoke her. Instead, she smiled sweetly, and asked, "Did you forget to wash something earlier?"

"It's not for me," Lydia snapped. "I've been up and dressed for hours."

Beth blinked, her attention called to Lydia's outfit. She wore an ankle-length white dress, and white ribbons and sprigs of baby's breath were twined in her upswept dark hair. The innocent and flowery look was completely contrary to Lydia's domineering personality. What was she up to?

Lydia picked up her basket and headed down the hallway, calling over her shoulder, "Simon wants to speak to you. In the kitchen."

She disappeared into the guest bathroom, shutting the door before Beth could reply. Fighting a pitched battle against the churning in her stomach, Beth hurried down the stairs. Simon was leaning against the kitchen counter, drinking coffee.

The normalcy of the scene soothed her nerves, and she smiled. Then she noticed what he was wearing.

Flowing white pants loosely encased his long legs, belling around his ankles, and revealing his bare feet. The matching top had side buttons of polished stone. He'd left the shoulder buttons undone, letting the thin white fabric flop over so that it looked like a cross between a robe and a fencing jacket.

"Simon? Lydia said you wanted to see me."

He turned and smiled at her. When he set down his coffee cup, Beth could see that the liquid had a strange greenish tinge. It wasn't coffee.

"Good morning. How are you feeling today?"

"Much better, thank you. Now, what's this all about?"

"Lydia and I will be working in the study today, for a few hours, and can't be disturbed. For any reason."

Beth frowned. "Working? On what? And why the funny clothes?"

Simon held up his arm, scrutinizing the sleeve that fluttered around it. "You think it's funny looking? I thought it was exotic and maybe even dashing. Can't you imagine Errol Flynn in an outfit like this, fending off pirates or the villainous Sheriff of Nottingham?"

Beth snorted. "No. You look more like Luke Skywalker, if his Jedi robes were furnished by a Arabian harem."

"Well, at least I got the exotic part right."

She chuckled at his plaintive tone, then quickly sobered. "Don't try to get me off track, Simon. You didn't answer my question. What sort of work are you and Lydia going to be doing?"

The doorbell rang, sparing him from answering. Beth followed him to the foyer.

Simon opened the door, revealing an attractive young woman. Beth stared at her, her mouth hanging open. This was the girl she'd seen in her dreams!

The memory vanished almost as soon as she recognized it. Beth struggled to recall what she'd dreamed about this girl. It wasn't pleasant, she knew that much. But what exactly had it been?

"Heather, come in. Lydia is waiting for you upstairs."

The girl darted a curious look at Beth, but seemed to accept that Simon wasn't planning to introduce her. "Sure thing. I've got all my stuff in my backpack. I'll be ready in five minutes."

Simon chuckled. "Not with Lydia in charge of your preparations. I'll expect you downstairs in twenty minutes."

Heather grinned, and pounded up the stairs, calling out, "Hey, Lydia! I'm here!"

Simon watched her go, shaking his head. "I'm always surprised by how loud my students can be."

Beth shoved the front door closed, the sudden slam making Simon jump. She stared at him.

"Okay, Simon. Level with me, here. What is going on? Who's that girl, and what are you three doing?"

Simon hesitated, then gestured toward the kitchen. "Come on. I have to finish that repulsive concoction Lydia brewed for me. Then I'll explain what I can."

Beth followed him back to the kitchen. He picked up his discarded coffee cup, grimaced, then swallowed a mouthful of the liquid. She leaned against the door frame, watching him.

"Well?"

"Heather is my assistant. She's here to help me and Lydia with our work."

"Which is...?"

Simon choked down another swallow of his drink. He studied the liquid intently for a long minute, then came to a decision. His posture stiffened, and he met Beth's gaze straight on.

"Heather is not just any graduate assistant. She's also my apprentice. Today is her initiation ceremony."

Beth blinked. She wasn't sure what she'd been expecting, but that hadn't been it.

"Her initiation…?"

"Yes. To practice magic."

Beth blinked again. She must have washed away her wits in the shower, because she had none left.

"You're saying you believe in magic. You think you can do magic."

Simon's lips softened in a smile, but sadness haunted his eyes. "I know what I believe. The question is, what are you going to do?"

"I don't do magic!"

"I meant, what are you going to do with this knowledge? You must realize the university would not look kindly on a professor who claims to actually perform magic, as opposed to studying other people who believe in it."

She nodded. He was confirming her own suspicions from when she'd interrupted his ceremony with Lydia. Although the ceremony hadn't seemed to match any of the Wiccan rituals she'd read about later, she'd managed to convince herself that Simon must have been acting out a mystical ceremony for his research when she'd discovered them. He seemed so normal.

"Why are you telling me this? You could have lied. You could have told me you were trying to reenact some ceremony you'd read about in your studies, to see if you could duplicate their claims using scientific methods or trickery."

"I could have." He shrugged, and gulped the last of the brew. "But this is who I am."

Beth's heart quickened. Even though a lie would be safer for him, Simon was telling her the truth. He trusted her. And her opinion of him mattered. There was only one reason she could think of why that would be. "And you wanted to see if I could accept you as you are?"

"Can you?"

Was this what had kept Simon from her? Had Lydia convinced him that Beth would never be able to accept someone who believed he could do magic? The way they made love was certainly magical. She'd consider the jury still out on the rest of his claims.

Besides, did it really matter if he thought he was some kind of sorcerer? Normalcy was overrated. Playing it safe had gotten her a boring, lifeless marriage that had drained her soul. So what if Simon wasn't completely normal? That was part of what made him so exciting.

Beth took a deep breath. Instinctively, she sensed that their relationship would be saved or destroyed by her answer. Now was not the time for safe prevarications and tentative half-truths. She had to go for broke, and risk as much as he had.

"Simon, I love you. I may not understand why you feel that way, but those beliefs are a part of you. They're part of the man I love."

She took a step toward him. He placed his coffee cup in the sink and moved toward her, his gaze locked on her face. He searched her eyes. Apparently, he found whatever truth he was looking for, because his attention shifted down to focus on her lips.

Beth's lips turned suddenly dry beneath his regard. She moistened them, nervously, and Simon sucked in a harsh breath. They stopped, just over a foot apart from each other, staring at each other. The pulse leapt in his throat. She longed to press her lips to the spot, simultaneously soothing him and inflaming him.

Simon stepped abruptly away from her, turning and grabbing the counter. He bent his head, obviously struggling for composure.

"Simon?"

A moment later, he turned to face her. His expression was once again cool and composed, although a smoldering fire lingered in his eyes.

"You have no idea how much I've wanted to hear you say that. But your timing couldn't be worse. Heather and Lydia are going to be coming downstairs in just a few minutes, and when they do, my attention has to be entirely on Heather's initiation ceremony. I can't afford any distractions. I'm sorry, Beth, but when you finish your breakfast, would you mind going up to your room for the next few hours?"

She smiled. "I don't mind at all, as long as you join me there later."

Simon closed his eyes and groaned. Laughing softly, Beth left the kitchen, a mug of coffee and a bagel in hand. She'd go to her room, as she'd promised. But she didn't plan to stay there long. While Simon and Lydia were occupied with Heather's initiation ceremony, Beth could examine Lydia's room. Lydia may have told Simon that Beth would never accept his beliefs, but Beth doubted the woman had done so out of friendship. She seemed far more interested in having Simon obey her than in his happiness. And for some reason, Simon couldn't see how she was manipulating him.

No, there was still a piece to this puzzle that Beth didn't understand. Lydia wanted something, and if Beth ever hoped to have a lasting relationship with Simon, she had two hours to try and find out what Lydia was really after.

* * * * *

Simon poured the last of the yellow rice powder onto the design Lydia had drawn in grease pencil on the marble floor of the work room. Stepping back, he examined the intricately patterned mandala made of red, blue, white, and yellow. He'd also mixed some of the powders, allowing him to color sections of the drawing in purple, green, orange and brown.

No marble floor showed through the dense powder. It was ready for Heather's dedication ceremony.

Ordinarily, the house's protections would be enough to protect such a simple ritual. But since the entity had already tried to breach their defenses at least twice, Simon was taking no chances. He put the jars of rice powder away in the study, and took out four white candles and a jar of sanctified salt. As soon as Heather was ready, he'd cast a protective circle around her.

A moment later, Lydia led Heather into the study. She was wearing Lydia's white silk robe, and a white cotton headband held back her brown hair. With a last whispered admonition to relax, Lydia stepped aside, delivering Simon's apprentice into his keeping.

He smiled at the nervous girl. "Today's your big day, Heather. After your dedication, you'll join the ranks of the Guardians."

"I'm ready. I think."

"Have you abstained from alcohol?"

"Yes."

"Meat and fish?"

"Yes." Her expression turned wistful. "I made excuses for the past two weeks to avoid meeting Rick and Keith for pepperoni pizza night."

Simon chuckled. "That's why it's called a sacrifice, Heather. Have you avoided fried grains?"

"Yes. I convinced the girls in my apartment that I was on a new diet—boiled potatoes and fruit. Two of them joined me in the diet, and between the three of us, we've lost thirteen pounds in the last two weeks."

He'd known Heather was clever, but this proved she'd be able to handle the double life of a Guardian with ease. Better than he'd handled things with Beth.

Focusing his mind on the task at hand, he asked Heather the final question. "Have you abstained from sex?"

"Yes." She sighed. "Although I think Rick thinks I'm cheating on him."

"Because you wouldn't sleep with him?"

"Because I've been dodging him. I knew if I saw him, I'd want to drag him off to bed. Not being able to do it just made me think about it even more." She shook her head. "You wouldn't understand."

Simon suspected Heather would be shocked to learn how well he understood her problem. He felt the same way around Beth. He didn't know how he was going to live in the same house with her and still keep his thoughts focused on his magic rather than on making long, luxurious love to Beth.

He brought his attention back to Heather. "You showed much wisdom. It will be needed in the years to come as you perform your duties as a Guardian. Pluck the flower of wisdom, and let it guide you on your path."

Heather followed his gaze to the bowl on his desk where a lotus blossom floated. She lifted the full white flower out of the bowl, and reverently shook the droplets of water from its petals. Cupping the flower in her hands, she followed Lydia through the concealed door into the work room. Simon stepped through behind them.

"Heather, you stand at the east point. Lydia, you'll be in the south."

While they moved to their positions, Simon set the candles in the four cardinal points and poured out the salt in a protective circle. He and Lydia joined their voices to sanctify and protect their ritual space.

When the protective spells were completed, Simon took his position opposite Heather. "We come today to dedicate this Guardian, Heather, to her field of magic. We beseech the powers that she will serve to reveal themselves."

They began the longest part of the ceremony, Simon and Lydia taking turns naming the aspects of the inner and outer worlds reflected in the mandala, then giving Heather a visualization image to attune her thoughts to that aspect. She closed her eyes and concentrated on each, then nodded for them to continue.

At last Lydia named the final aspect. When Heather nodded for them to continue, Simon announced, "You have presented yourself to all of the forces of the universe, both inner and outer worlds. Now it is time to learn which you will serve."

Heather stepped forward and recited her short invocation. "I open myself to learn your mysteries. Reveal your nature to me."

Closing her eyes, she tossed the lotus blossom into the air. It tumbled end over end as it arced over the mandala drawn on the floor. The flower hit, bounced, and skidded to a stop, its trail clearly marked in the rice powder.

"You can open your eyes now, Heather."

She stared at the pattern before her.

"Read it," Simon prompted. This was the first test of any new Guardian's skill. He'd reviewed all of the components of the mandala with Heather. He knew she could identify the segments her flower had touched. But she had to demonstrate the ability to interpret that knowledge.

He held his breath. Heather frowned, studying the design.

"The flower struck the realm of the outer universe, in the area of thought. It bounced into comprehension, and settled in the area of control." She considered for a moment, then her eyes widened. "I'm going to understand and control other people's thoughts."

Heather took a step backward, shaking her head. "No. I don't want to become some sort of psychic puppet master."

Simon released his pent up breath, and traded a grin with Lydia. Close enough. More importantly, her first concern had been for the misuse of power, proving she had the right attitude for a Guardian.

"Forget what you've seen in horror movies," he cautioned her. "And think through what the pattern is telling you."

Heather studied the design on the floor, then shook her head in frustration. "I don't know."

"Your first skill is understanding. Your secondary skill is control. So you will first have to attune your mind to another person's, experiencing their thoughts and feelings, before you can influence those thoughts."

Heather beamed. "So I wouldn't hurt them, because I'd be hurting myself."

Simon nodded. "Guardians tend to dedicate themselves to areas of magic similar to the non-magical aspects of life most important to them. I was always interested in protecting and safeguarding people and things, so I naturally wound up working with wards and protections."

"I was studying probability and statistics," Lydia added. "Not so different from picking a likely path through the future."

"So you're saying this magical skill to understand and influence people's thoughts is just the occult version of the psychology I was already studying? I doubt my psych professors would see it that way. But I can handle that." She stepped forward, returning to her previous position.

Intellectually, she'd accepted her path. Now, they'd see if she could accept the reality. Simon had tried to prepare her, but without knowing what her dedication would be, he'd been limited to general recommendations. His own reaction had been mild, his vision merely seeming to sharpen and become more acute, but his mentor, Andrew, had nearly been burned alive when a fire elemental welcomed him. Hopefully Heather's reaction wouldn't be that extreme.

He paused, and mentally tested his wards. If the entity planned on attacking them, this would be the best time to try. But the defenses were sound.

Simon bent down and picked up the flower. He carried it to Heather, formally presenting it to her on his outstretched palms.

"You stand now at the entrance to that pathway. If this is a path you are willing to walk, take the knowledge you will need, and step forth."

Heather lifted the flower from his hands and cupped it in her own. After a moment, she looked up at him in confusion. "I don't feel any—"

She cried out, dropping the flower, and clasping her hands to her temples. With a low moan, she fell to her knees.

Lydia stepped forward, but Simon motioned her back. Nothing had broken through his protective wards. Heather was not being attacked. This was just a dedication reaction.

He knelt beside the girl and gently pulled her hands away from her head. Heather's arms quivered with tension, her hands balling into fists. Her eyes were screwed tightly shut, and her face contorted with pain.

Softly, Simon began reciting the instructions for centering the spirit and building a protective mental wall around the self. Heather's tension lessened slightly. He recited the instructions a second, then a third time.

Heather's shoulders slumped, and her arms went limp in his grasp. Her chin dropped down to her chest. Her breathing deepened and steadied. Eventually, she lifted her head and met his gaze. Tears glimmered in her eyes.

"I know you taught me the spells to ward and protect my thoughts, but I'm not strong enough. I can feel both of you, like burning hot spotlights, blinding me."

"You'll get the hang of it eventually." Simon turned his will to strengthening her delicate wards. "How's that?"

A tremulous smile hovered on her lips. "Better. It doesn't hurt now."

Simon stood, then lifted Heather to her feet. "Welcome to the Guardians."

* * * * *

Beth waited five minutes after Lydia and Heather trooped down the stairs, to make sure they hadn't forgotten something and were coming back. They stayed downstairs.

Reminding herself that she was doing this for Simon's sake, Beth slipped into Lydia's room and looked around. The beige bedspread on the twin bed was folded with a precision that would have done an army drill sergeant proud. A paperback rested face down on the night stand, beside the digital alarm clock.

Beth picked up the book. *Murder at the Musicale*. The cover featured blood spattered sheet music.

She quickly replaced the book as she'd found it. Lots of people read mysteries, and would never think of raising a hand in violence. But in the current situation, Lydia's choice of reading material seemed sinister.

The room's only other furnishings were a chest of drawers, desk and chair. Predictably, the desk was bare, with the chair tucked neatly beneath it. Beth pulled out the chair, and discovered a waste basket, filled with crumpled paper.

"Of course," she muttered. "The clues are always in the trash."

Kneeling on the floor, she pulled out the first sheet of yellow legal paper and smoothed it on her leg. It held row after row of neat pencil sketches, each of four or five similar squiggly things, with one circled in each row. She set the paper aside, and pulled out two more that were equally confusing. The fourth paper had a sketch she recognized, of a roughly oval object with tubes coming out the sides and connecting the two halves of the top. She'd seen the likeness in enough advertisements and public service announcements. It was a heart.

Swallowing her revulsion, Beth forced herself to study the paper in more depth. The four drawings in that row were all of hearts, but the proportions differed, ranging from an almost round one to a grotesquely elongated design.

She flipped through the other pages, spotting something with the distinctive shape of kidneys, and on another paper, lungs, with the right lung on one row and the left lung on the row below. A chill rolled down her back, as she realized what she was looking at. These were all drawings of internal organs. And someone had selected one drawing of each organ. The ones that most closely matched a set of real organs, like the ones spread out on the grass around that dead cow?

The waste basket yielded no more surprises. Beth crumpled the pages and threw them back in. She'd seen all she needed to see. There was no reason to keep the papers.

She turned her attention to the drawers of the desk. The center drawer contained a legal pad, no doubt the one the discarded pages had come from, covered in precise writing. Quietly, she read the first few lines.

"Normal color. Slight distortion—outward bulge—in the upper left section. White mark—a line, not a circle—in the middle right."

A two-toned chime interrupted her reading. Beth's head jerked up, her ears straining to place the sound. It repeated a moment later, and she identified it. An old-fashioned door bell.

She recalled Simon's warning. Their ceremony was not to be disturbed. The chime sounded again.

Stuffing the pages back into the desk and slamming the drawer closed, Beth hurried out of Lydia's room. She raced downstairs to the foyer, and fumbled with the heavy latches on the door. "Hang on. Just a minute."

Finally, she mastered the trick of turning the spring latch and door knob together then pulling, and the door swung open. A young man in jeans and a flannel shirt was just stepping off the edge of the flagstone porch toward the bicycle parked in the gravel driveway. At the sound of the door opening, he turned around.

"Oh. So someone is home. I wasn't sure..."

"Can I help you?"

He crossed the porch and hesitated before the door, glancing nervously at the house, and the foyer beyond Beth.

"I shouldn't have come. Never mind."

"Well, then, have—"

"I'm looking for Heather. Her roommate said she was coming here."

"Yes, she's helping Professor Parkes and his colleague with their research. Is there a problem? Something she needs to be notified of?"

The boy looked away, digging his hands into his pockets and scuffing one sneaker on the stone. "No."

Beth blinked. "Then I'm afraid I don't understand why you came out here."

"Neither do I." He shook his head. "I was just so desperate to see her, and she wouldn't return any of my calls. When I went over to her apartment this morning, they said she was already gone. All I knew was I had to see her, and find out what was going on."

Beth nodded in sudden understanding. This must be Rick, Heather's boyfriend.

Rick hunched his shoulders, looking as completely miserable as only an angst-ridden 20-something could. "She'll probably think I'm a stalker, now."

Beth smiled. "Only if I tell her you came by."

The boy's eyes shone with sudden hope that was immediately extinguished. "She'll have heard the doorbell."

"The professor's study is at the other end of the house. I doubt they heard anything."

"Then she doesn't need to know."

"I won't tell Heather anything. But if you're so worried that you'd bike all the way out here, you do need to talk to her. Would you like to wait?"

"No. That would look pathetic. And the only thing worse than a boyfriend who's a stalker is a boyfriend who's a pathetic stalker. I'll try to catch her later. She'll be finished by dinner, right?"

"Definitely. Simon said he'd be free in a few hours."

"Simon?"

Beth's cheeks heated. "Professor Parkes, I mean." Hopefully Rick couldn't guess why she was so interested in when Simon would be free. Maybe she could convince Lydia to drive Heather home, so she and Simon could be alone. Now that he knew she could accept his belief that he could perform magic, there was nothing to keep them apart anymore, something she intended to demonstrate quite clearly.

"Thanks for your help," Rick said.

Beth pulled her thoughts back to the boy before her. "No problem. But be sure you do talk to Heather. Love is too important to lose because of a misunderstanding."

He grinned. "Sure thing!"

Beth watched Rick turn and walk back to his bicycle, whistling, then softly closed the door. That was one misunderstanding that could be cleared up simply. But what about Lydia, and those drawings?

CHAPTER TWELVE

Simon tapped lightly on Beth's door.

"Come in."

He stepped inside, then stopped. Beth was sitting on her bed, wrapped in the black silk robe he'd loaned her.

"Close the door." She smiled. "And your mouth."

"I see you were expecting me." What else had she been expecting? He'd come up here to talk to her, to explain why they couldn't make love until after the entity had been defeated. But right now, he couldn't remember why. All he could remember was the feel of her skin against his, the way she smelled, like vanilla ice cream in the rain, and how much he loved her. What had Heather's phrase been? He couldn't see Beth without wanting to drag her off to bed. And when she was in, or at least on, the bed already, his willpower was tested to its maximum.

"Come. Sit." She patted the bed next to her.

His common sense screamed that he should open the door and walk out, or at least stand as far away from her as he could. Simon crossed the room and sat down beside her.

She smelled like shampoo. His shampoo. The scent heated his blood, as if it was a brand of possession. His scent. His robe. His woman.

Simon drew in a shaky breath. What was wrong with him? He was getting positively Neanderthal.

"So, you're all done with your magic for today?"

"Yes." He would have said more, but his mouth was too dry to speak.

Beth walked her fingers up his tunic. "Then you don't need this anymore, do you?"

He shook his head, no. Beth undid the first two buttons, at his collar and at the middle of his shoulder.

Reaching up, he caught her hand. "No. We can't—"

"Why not?" Before he knew what she was doing, she'd turned and thrown one leg over him, so that she was straddling his waist. It was impossible for her to miss how badly he wanted her.

She settled more comfortably against him, and Simon groaned. She felt so good, and he wanted her so much, he couldn't think of anything else.

"Simon? Why can't we?"

"Why?" He forced his foggy brain to think, even as he wrapped his arms around Beth and bent his head to nuzzle the side of her neck, beneath her jaw and behind her ear. She quivered, enflaming him even further. "You smell so good."

He pushed her loose robe open, sliding the sleeves down her arms so that he could kiss her shoulders. He felt her fumbling with the unfamiliar buttons on his tunic, then the brush of cool air as the fabric parted. The brief chill was replaced by heat as she pressed her bare breasts against his chest.

Pulling his arms from the sleeves, he shrugged out of his tunic, then slid his hands under her robe, glorying in the touch of skin on skin. She leaned into him, and they fell backward across the bed.

She rose up on her knees, and he tried to pull her back down on top of him where she belonged. Then he realized she was untying the drawstring waist of his pants, and eagerly helped her strip them away. She settled over him again, her moist heat welcoming him, and he trembled.

His hands on her hips, he held her close as he rubbed against her. She shifted her position slightly, and he slid inside her.

He whispered her name on a ragged breath. Then even that much thought was too great for him, and he gave himself up completely to the feelings surging through him.

Later, Simon managed to resurrect just enough rationality to get himself and Beth lengthwise on the bed, under the covers, before falling into a contented doze beside her.

* * * * *

Beth leaned on her elbow, admiring how a band of sunlight snuck between the curtains to highlight Simon's face. He looked relaxed and peaceful. It was only in contrast that she realized how common lately the slight furrow between his eyebrows and the lines at the corner of his mouth had become.

Lately, it seemed that whenever she saw him, he was worried about something. Even this morning, on what she assumed was a joyous occasion, he had seemed tense and concerned.

His eyes opened, and he smiled at her. Then, his smile faded, and the furrow reappeared between his eyebrows. His contentment had been so brief.

"Beth, we have to talk."

"I know. What's the deal with you and Lydia?"

Simon blinked. "I told you. She's a colleague."

"But why is she here? Why now?"

"She's here to help me. And now is when I need the help."

Beth walked her fingers up Simon's blanket-covered torso until she reached the hem, then slipped her hand beneath the blanket and started stroking his chest. "What's she helping you with? This police case?"

"Yes." Simon turned toward Beth, freeing one hand from the covers and tumbling the blanket to his waist. Snuggling closer, he tucked her head against his shoulder and began caressing her back.

Beth smiled, enjoying the leisurely pace of their lovemaking. She'd missed it, as she'd missed so many things about Simon. No one else had ever held her like this, touching her just to make a physical connection, because it was almost painful to be separated, yet without any immediate expectation that it would lead to more heated passion.

She almost subsided into silence, floating on a cloud of pleasant sensation. But this was likely to be her one chance to question Simon about Lydia when he was in a receptive mood. Beth had to press on.

"She arrived before the police asked for your help on this latest case, didn't she?"

"I'd asked for help on the previous one."

"You asked her to come here?"

"Not directly. I called my mentor, Andrew. He's the one that called Lydia."

"I haven't met him."

"No, he's in California."

A sudden chill rolled through Beth at Simon's words. The mentor he'd called for assistance was in California. He'd left her bed after their first date because he had to make an important call to California. But that had been days before the students died.

Beth kissed the curve of Simon's neck. His skin tasted salty, a testament to their earlier, more energetic coupling.

Simon sighed and shifted position slightly, stretching his neck to expose more of it to her mouth. His hand drifted down to the base of her back, nudging her hips closer to his.

Beth snuggled nearer still, her legs pressed against his and his erection captured between them. She swirled her tongue up the column of his neck, drawing a ragged, breathy sound from him. Simon cupped her backside, then began kneading the soft muscles.

Shivering with pleasure, Beth forced herself to focus on their conversation. She stopped kissing Simon, and went back to simply stroking his chest. After a moment, he accepted the change of pace and returned to caressing her back, although his hand remained at the base of her spine.

"Do you call your friend in California often?"

"It depends. Sometimes I go for months without talking to him, sometimes I talk to him every day."

That was reassuring. Beth dropped a brief kiss on Simon's chest. "And Lydia?"

"Lydia is Lydia." Simon kneaded Beth's backside again. When she did not continue kissing him, he sighed and went back to caressing her, although this time his hand roamed over her hip and along her leg. "I don't call her. She calls me. Or anyone else that needs to speak to her."

Beth's fingers hesitated. That definitely sounded like a one-sided relationship. What sort of hold did Lydia have over people that they jumped to do her bidding like that?

Simon inhaled deeply, pressing his chest into the palm of Beth's hand. She smiled, reminded of the way her Golden Retriever used to thump his head against her hand when he wanted to be petted.

Splaying her fingers against Simon's strong chest, Beth reassured herself that he was just as loyal as Sunshine had been. He wasn't cheating on her. But she still needed to know what was going on.

"So Lydia came to help with the first crime, and stayed to help solve the second. How do the police feel about involving a foreigner?"

"They don't know." Simon's hand glided down Beth's thigh, tugging her leg up over his. His shaft slid between her opened thighs, resting its full length against her dampened skin. "They can't know."

Beth shimmied closer, gasping at the sudden cloud of sparkles that filled her vision when the base of Simon's shaft pressed against the cluster of nerves waiting for his penetration. But she couldn't allow herself to be distracted.

"Why can't the police know?"

"Because then the attacks will stop, and they'll arrest Lydia."

Beth froze.

Simon rotated his hips, at the same time kneading her backside. Her flesh parted, slicking his shaft with moisture. He rocked against her, once, twice, then found her entrance and slid inside.

Beth shuddered, locking her leg around Simon's waist to keep him buried within her. He cupped her backside and squeezed gently, then squeezed her again. Her vision dimmed, all of her attention focusing on the heated length of him, hard and pulsing inside her. Then he rotated his palm, moving her around his rigid shaft. She gasped.

"Simon!"

Another wave of sparkles darkened her vision.

"You like that?"

"*Like's* not the word."

He chuckled softly. "Then I guess I'd better do it again."

He did. The pleasure was even stronger the second time. When he did it a third time, Beth went wild with need. She pressed hungry kisses up and down his shoulder and throat, clawed his back to pull him even closer, and ground her hips against him with animal abandon.

Simon rolled onto his back, carrying her on top of him. He continued kneading and rotating her, while he slid his newly freed hand between their bodies. His fingertips brushed her cluster of nerves, then pressed, hard, while he pulled her all the way down his shaft with his other hand.

Wave after wave of ecstasy shuddered through her. Arching her back to drive him even deeper within her, Beth's every muscle clenched, desperate to share her fulfillment with him. Simon's steady breathing turned ragged and hoarse.

"Beth, I can't hold —"

"I don't want you to."

"But—"

"Come now. With me. In me."

"Oh, yes!"

Simon's hips lifted from the bed with the force of his thrust, then he was exploding inside her and she was exploding around him and nothing existed but their shared pleasure.

Later, when time began to have meaning again, Simon sighed and reluctantly separated himself from Beth.

"We should get dressed. Lydia was going to be working with Heather for a few hours, but they'll come looking for me if I don't show up soon."

Beth glanced at the window, expecting it to be dark, but the beam of sunlight striping the floor had hardly moved. Reaching over, she touched Simon lightly on the shoulder.

"Before you go running off, I want to finish our conversation."

Simon frowned. "I've already told you more than I should have."

But his answers had only led to more questions, from which he had so delightfully distracted her. The questions remained, though. He couldn't mention Lydia's imminent arrest without explaining. Unfortunately, his sex-induced talkativeness seemed over. She remembered all too well how close-mouthed he'd been about Lydia and his mysterious project when she'd pressed for details after Lydia's arrival. But that had been before Simon confided his belief in magic to her. Maybe now he'd be more forthcoming, as long as she didn't scare him off by asking too much.

"You don't have to tell me anything you don't want to. But I have to ask. How is Lydia involved?"

"You don't have any reason to be jealous."

Beth blinked, thrown by his answer until she realized he'd misunderstood her question. "I know that. I meant how is she involved with your work for the police, not if she's involved with you."

"Good, because she's just an old friend."

Beth refused to be sidetracked down that conversational trail. Simon was sidestepping her question. She was going to have to provoke an answer.

"I saw her drawings of animal parts. The same internal organs that had been removed from that mutilated cow."

Simon sucked in a quick breath. "Where did you—"

"I looked through her room."

"You did what?"

"Looked through her room. I admit it." Beth shrugged, determined not to feel guilt for fully justified snooping. "I know she's a guest in your home, but I don't trust her. I'm worried about you, and you won't tell me anything, so I had to see what I could find out for myself."

Pulling Beth into a tight embrace, Simon buried his face against her shoulder and stroked her hair. She wasn't sure if the gesture was supposed to comfort her or him.

When he spoke, his voice was muffled. "Promise me you won't do anything like that again. It's too dangerous."

"Are you afraid Lydia will find out?"

"Not if she doesn't already know. But you were lucky. She could have laid all kinds of traps to protect her work."

Traps? Beth shivered, envisioning poisoned arrows flying from the walls or the ceiling collapsing, like an Indiana Jones movie. Maybe James Bond types of traps, razor blades on the drawer handles or capsules that would break and release a deadly gas.

No, Beth was allowing her imagination to run away with her. First of all, those things were impractical anywhere but a Hollywood sound stage. Second, Lydia couldn't possibly be that paranoid, or Simon would never work with her. Simon must mean a more prosaic kind of trap, like misleading information planted in her papers to confuse anyone reading them. But what could be so sensitive that Lydia would feel a need to protect it even in the security of Simon's home?

"Is that the work she's afraid the police will learn about?" Beth asked.

"She hasn't done anything illegal. The police arresting her would be a mistake."

"But if she didn't do anything wrong, they'd let her go again once they realized they had the wrong person."

"The crimes would stop, so they'd think they had arrested the right person."

Beth blinked, and shook her head. She was trying, but she just couldn't get this conversation to make sense. Every time she thought she'd figured out what Simon was talking about, he spun her in a different direction. "What makes you think the crimes would stop?"

"Lydia said so."

"And you believed her?"

"Of course."

Beth snorted. Couldn't Simon hear himself? If Lydia wasn't involved in the animal mutilations, how would she know they would stop? And why would Simon trust someone who was acting so irrationally?

Unless...perhaps Simon had a vested interest in believing Lydia? After all, he'd been the one to raise the jealousy issue. Beth didn't doubt that Simon loved her. Now. But had he been in love with Lydia in the past? That could blind him to Lydia's true agenda, whatever it was.

"Simon, I'm trying to understand. Really I am. But why do you think Lydia has any idea what the criminal will do?"

Beth heard him take a deep breath, and thought for a moment he wouldn't answer. But then he said softly, "That's her gift. She is the most accomplished divinatory magician currently alive."

"She tells the future."

"Yes."

Beth was glad he couldn't see her face, because there was no way she could hide her opinion of that idea. It was one thing to perform magical rituals and believe in forces outside the physical. That was just another kind of religion, of faith in a greater power. But fortune tellers dealt in vague generalities, allowing people to discover the "truth" of their predictions later, fitting circumstances to the prediction, and forgetting the predictions that didn't come true.

Simon believed what he was telling her. That much was obvious. And since he was an otherwise intelligent man, Lydia must have done something to convince him of her power. But why? What did Lydia have to gain by convincing Simon she could foresee the future?

Suddenly Simon's reaction when Beth had first met Lydia made sense. Beth had taken Lydia's cryptic comments as veiled threats. Simon must have thought they were a prediction. No wonder he'd been so reluctant to explain his sudden change in attitude.

"What did she say? When she saw me for the first time?"

"What does that have to do with anything?"

"She tried to scare you away from me, by saying something would happen. If she can tell the future, I want to know what she said."

"She said I was spending too much time with you, and that I was being distracted from my work when I needed to be at my most focused." Simon shoved himself away from Beth and scrambled out of the bed, then hastily dragged on his clothes. "Both of which I've just amply proved. Heather just had her dedication ceremony. I should have been with her, not whiling away the afternoon in bed with you. No, this isn't going to work."

He stalked across the room to the door, flinging it open.

"Simon, wait! You can't just walk out!"

"I'm sorry, Beth. But Lydia was right. I can't think when I'm around you. I love you, but I can't be with you."

Beth stared at the empty doorway that Simon had just stepped through. What had just happened? She'd been trying to discredit Lydia's fortune telling skills, and had ended up playing right into the woman's hands.

Flopping back down onto the bed, Beth pulled the pillow over her head. It smelled like Simon. Remembering the long, lonely nights during her divorce when she'd cried herself to sleep, Beth resolved that she would not give up without a fight. What she shared with Simon was worth holding on to. He'd said he loved her. Somehow, she'd find out what Lydia's game was, and make the woman stop meddling in Simon's life. Whatever Lydia had done to drive them apart, Beth was sure she and Simon could fix it, if he just gave them the chance.

* * * * *

Beth avoided the unlabeled tins filled with herbs that lined the kitchen counter, and dug around in Simon's pantry until she found a bottle of Coke Classic. By the time she'd showered and dressed, the house had been quiet, and Simon's Jeep had been gone. She assumed he'd taken Lydia and Heather with him. No doubt he'd left while she was in the shower so that he wouldn't have to see her again until he'd had time to think. Beth planned on using the unexpected solitude to do some thinking herself. But it would have been nice if he'd at least left her a note.

She dumped ice into a tall glass and poured the soda over it, enjoying the cheerful fizz of carbonation and crackle of ice.

Her encounters today with Simon had given her emotional whiplash. First there was that meeting in the kitchen, when he finally revealed his big secret. Then there were the two times they'd made love, that she thought proved how well suited for each other they were, and that they'd successfully overcome their differences. The final conversation, however, put the lie to that impression. No, they still had a lot to figure out. But how could she make sense out of any of it, when Simon refused to tell her what was going on, saying nothing or dropping cryptic remarks that only added to her confusion?

Beth set down her glass, a strategy taking shape in her mind. First, she'd find out how Lydia had convinced Simon she could tell the future. Then, she'd trick Lydia into saying or doing something that would prove Simon and Beth had a future together. Faced with contradictory predictions, Simon would have to admit that Lydia's fortune telling was a hoax. Once free of Lydia's influence, they could chart their own destiny.

"Hi."

Beth turned around. Heather was standing in the doorway to the kitchen, wearing the same jeans and T-shirt she'd worn when she arrived this morning.

"Hello, Heather. I must've been wool gathering. I didn't hear Simon's Jeep pull up."

"Professor Parkes and Lydia aren't back yet. I had a pretty bad headache, so I was lying down."

"I hope you're feeling better."

"Yes, thank you."

Heather hesitated in the doorway, then took a few steps in and leaned against the counter. "Beth, isn't it?"

"That's right. I was just getting myself a Coke. Would you like some? Caffeine usually helps when I have a headache."

"No, thanks."

The pleasantries completed, they watched each other in awkward silence. Recalling Rick's visit earlier in the day, Beth asked, "Will you be going home for dinner?"

"Professor Parkes is picking up pizza. Pepperoni." Heather closed her eyes, smiling in an expression of pure bliss. "Extra pepperoni."

So that's where they'd gone. It didn't take two people to pick up a pizza, but maybe Simon had wanted the opportunity to talk to Lydia alone.

Heather edged closer, then nervously joined Beth at the table. "Can I ask you something?"

"Sure."

"How do you make it work?"

"Make what work?"

"You and Professor Parkes. Lydia said we could really only have relationships with people who were, you know, one of us. But you're not. So how do you do it?"

Beth snorted. At the moment, she wasn't sure their relationship was working. But she owed the girl some kind of an answer. "Trust, I guess. I know there are things Simon can't or won't tell me. But if he trusts me enough to tell me the rest of it, I'll trust that he has good reasons for his secrecy and not press him."

Heather listened intently, and Beth felt like a fraud. She and Simon wanted to trust each other, but it was a new and fragile emotion. She didn't know why Simon believed Lydia, or how they were involved, and her pressing to discover that had led to their current situation. Still, Beth was confident that if they could just get everything out in the open, they could find a way out of their difficulties. He could be as secretive as he liked about his magical beliefs, as long as he was honest with her about his relationships with the other people who believed as he did.

Beth pulled herself away from contemplating her own situation, and focused on Heather.

"Are you thinking about your friend, Rick?"

"Yeah." Heather slumped in her chair. "He thinks I'm cheating on him, I'm sure of it. He's started coming to my apartment at all sorts of weird times, hoping to surprise me. And when I'm not there, it only makes him more suspicious."

"He seems a nice enough—"

Heather bolted upright. "He was here!"

"What gives you that idea?" Damn. She'd promised Rick that she wouldn't tell Heather about his visit. Did it count as breaking her promise if the girl guessed?

"He was checking up on me!"

"He was just concerned—"

"Oh, I'll give him something to be concerned about!" Heather rose and started pacing the kitchen floor. "I've had it. I've got my own life, not just an extension of his. He's got to respect that, or he's history. And this time, the cute puppy expression won't get him out of it."

Beth pictured the boy she'd seen this morning, but with his eyes wide and soft, a half-smile on his lips, and, for some reason, wearing a tilted baseball cap and sitting backwards on a wooden desk chair. No doubt her imagination was reinforcing his relative youth, although she was surprised at the depth of detail in the mental picture. She could almost read the titles of the books on the desk behind him.

Heather cried out, and clapped her palms to her temples, squeezing her eyes shut.

"Are you all right?" Beth jumped up and started to circle the table.

"Don't touch me!" The girl staggered backward, bumping the counter, then blindly following the curve of the counter to the door. "Stay away."

"I'm not touching you. I'm staying right here. Now, calm down. What's wrong?"

"I need to lie down. Alone. And be quiet. When Professor Parkes and Lydia get back, ask them to save some pizza for me."

Still keeping her eyes closed, she felt her way out the door and into the hallway. Beth watched her go. As the only adult in the house, she felt like she should be doing something. But Heather's sudden, debilitating headache, along with a need for darkness and quiet, sounded like a migraine, and there was really nothing that Beth could do to treat one of those other than giving Heather the solitude she'd requested.

Then Beth realized that Heather's absence from dinner meant she'd be sharing the entire meal with Lydia and Simon. The prospect was enough to give her a headache, too.

CHAPTER THIRTEEN

Simon followed Lydia into the kitchen, carrying the two boxes of pizza. Beth was sitting at the table, looking miserable. He ached to go to her and reassure her, but he knew it would be futile. He was the one who'd upset her in the first place.

On the ride to pick up dinner, after he'd asked Lydia to repeat herself for the second time, she had archly pointed out that deciding not to sleep with Beth seemed to distract him nearly as much as actually sleeping with her had. Then she'd offered to do a divination for him to try and find a path through the morass of his romantic entanglements. He'd turned her down. The last thing he needed was another conflicting compass to guide his behavior. Besides, he knew what he needed to do. He had to make it through Halloween without screwing things up even worse with Beth than they already were. Once the entity was dealt with, he'd make the time to work on his relationship with Beth.

"Heather's lying down," Beth announced. "She was up for a bit, then her migraine came back with a vengeance. She asked if you'd save some pizza for her."

"I'll do better than that." Lydia took the top box out of Simon's arms. "I'll bring it to her."

Beth frowned at Lydia's retreating back. "Doesn't food make migraines worse?"

"Don't worry about it." Simon set the remaining box on the table, and gathered plates and cutlery. "Back at Berkeley, Lydia had the same problem. She knows how to treat it."

"Oh. So you two went to school together?"

"Briefly."

"How briefly?"

Simon handed Beth her place setting, and turned to the refrigerator. "Does it matter? What do you want to drink?"

"Water's fine. And I was wondering if you met her while you were still an impressionable young student."

"I met her when I was an obnoxious, self-important know-it-all. Otherwise known as a first-year graduate student."

"Did she also get a doctorate in occult studies?"

"No, she got expelled and sent back to England. And if you want to know why, you'll have to ask her." He set a glass full of water beside Beth's plate, and took a swig out of his own before sitting down across the table from her. "Dig in."

Dinner was an agonizing affair of stilted conversation and awkward silences, as Beth probed for answers Simon was unwilling to offer. When he compared this meal to the easy, laughing camaraderie of past meals they'd shared, Simon wanted to bellow like a bull and shatter the nearest breakable object. He had to keep reminding himself he'd chosen this course. It was for the best. Nothing good was ever accomplished without cost. And dozens of other platitudes that did nothing to ease the ache in his heart.

Lydia's return near the end of the meal was a welcome relief, forcing him and Beth to retreat behind shields of polite civility.

"How's Heather?" he asked.

"Better. As soon as you finish your dinner, you can drive her back to her apartment."

"Wouldn't you rather take her?"

Lydia patted his hand as if he was a small boy. He hated it when she did that. "You don't want me driving your car. I'm liable to forget to stay on the wrong side of the road."

"You can drive me back to my apartment at the same time," Beth added.

"What?"

Beth shrugged. "I've got to get back to work tomorrow, anyway."

"Absolutely not," Simon answered. "It's not safe."

He glanced over at Lydia for confirmation, only to see her nodding at Beth.

"Of course you want to return to your own home. There's no reason for you stay here any longer," Lydia told her.

Beth stiffened, but had no chance to respond before Simon blurted, "Of course there's a reason to stay here. I can keep you safe here."

"I'm not a child, Simon."

"I didn't say you were."

"Then stop treating me like one!"

"She doesn't need your protection," Lydia added. "No more than anyone else. Turn your attention back to protecting them, and you'll protect her."

"I'm not neglecting my duties! I know my damn duties!"

"Of course you do, darling." Lydia's tone said clearly that he didn't, but she didn't come right out and accuse him of neglecting his new apprentice to make love to Beth.

"Besides," Beth added. "I'm not completely naive. I'll be careful. There are always at least two people at the store. And I'll make sure someone escorts me home if I'm closing."

Simon stared at her in impotent frustration. She still thought she had a human enemy to be concerned about. There was no way he could explain the danger she was in without revealing the full extent of the power they battled. That would needlessly terrorize her.

"But you'll still be alone at night, and walking to work."

"She'll be fine."

Simon glanced at Lydia. "Are you sure of that?"

Lydia hesitated. "I wasn't speaking professionally."

"Then she's not leaving this house."

"Simon, you're overreacting." Beth threw her napkin onto her plate and pushed her chair away from the table. "This isn't the middle ages, and I'm not a damsel in distress. You can't imprison me for my own protection."

He scrubbed at his face, torn between the need to protect Beth and the desire to make her happy. "What if you slept here, and I gave you a ride back and forth to work every day? Would that be an acceptable compromise?"

Lydia glared at him. "You can't afford to spend that much time escorting her. We have a very tight schedule."

Beth sat down again, smiling smugly at Lydia. "I accept."

"Darling, it's out of the question. You can't—"

"Lydia, shut up."

Lydia's eyes widened. Her mouth opened and closed but no sound came out, making her look like nothing so much as a fish struggling to breathe.

Simon leaned across the table and took Beth's hand before she could retreat again. "If you have to go back to work and resume your life, I understand. But I'll worry about you every minute that you're not someplace I know is safe. Let me cast a protection spell around your bookstore."

Lydia began lecturing him. "You can't afford to squander your—"

"Lydia. Shut. Up." Simon kept his gaze locked on Beth. "I know you don't believe in magic, but it would make me feel better. Please?"

Beth's expression softened and she smiled at him. "Of course, Simon. I'm scheduled to close the store tomorrow. You can do it then."

Simon tightened his fingers around Beth's. She trusted him enough to allow him to protect her. That would be enough, for now.

Lydia snapped, "This isn't finished, Simon. Since you're so concerned with safety, I'll let you see Heather safely home first."

Simon started, stung by the reminder that he'd once again forgotten about his apprentice.

Beth nodded, slipping her fingers from his. "Go."

* * * * *

As soon as Beth entered the bookstore, Julie rushed to her side.

"Beth! How are you feeling? David said how sick you were on Thursday. I tried calling you over the weekend, and when you didn't answer, I didn't know what to think."

"Oh, Julie, I'm so sorry. It didn't occur to me to let you know how I was doing. It was just a 24-hour stomach bug."

"Then why didn't you answer your phone?"

Beth's cheeks heated. "I wasn't home."

"Simon was nursing you back to health? How sweet!"

"Something like that."

Julie tipped her head and studied Beth. "You don't look like someone who's spent the whole weekend making mad, passionate love. Except for the shadows under the eyes."

"Julie!" Beth laughed, no doubt exactly what her friend had intended. "I was sick, remember?"

Beth spent the next few hours trying to subtly and not so subtly distract Julie from prying into the details of her love life with Simon. The situation was too uncertain for Beth to describe, and too bizarre to explain. She began wondering how much of Simon's reticence regarding his magic was simple inability to explain his beliefs without sounding like a crackpot.

Beth breathed a sigh of relief when Julie finally gave up and headed back to the stockroom to unpack a carton of books. The welcome respite from questions ended when a customer walked in. The young man looked the right age to be one of the university students, but his lank, tangled hair, dirty clothes, and pinched expression were more suited to a street person.

He walked up to the counter. "Are you Beth?"

Her first instinct was to deny it, but there didn't seem to be any point. If he hadn't noticed her name tag already, he would soon enough. Still, she wasn't willing to give him her name.

"May I help you?"

"I hope so. Rick said that you might know where Heather was. I'm trying to find her."

Beth blinked. The young man really was a student, then. But one who'd taken the "grunge" look to an obsessive extreme. "I haven't seen Heather since yesterday."

"I tried her apartment, the library, the student union, and all the labs in the psych building." His head bobbed in time to his words, punctuating each location with a jut of his chin.

Beth frowned, wondering why the boy was asking her. Shouldn't he be asking one of Heather's friends? Maybe they wouldn't tell him anything. The boy might be some sort of a stalker. Hadn't Rick mentioned Heather being worried that he was stalking her? Perhaps Heather had a reason to be concerned.

"I'm afraid I can't help you. But if I do see her, I'll tell her you're looking for her. What's your name?"

"Keith. Keith Whitehall."

"All right, Keith."

A wisp of memory teased the edges of Beth's recall. Something about this boy. Something unpleasant.

The memory clicked into place.

"Your roommate was the one who—"

"Yeah." He shuddered. "That's why I have to find Heather. I can't sleep. She said she'd listen any time I needed to talk."

Beth felt guilty that she'd misjudged the boy so badly. She'd look like a wreck if there had been a murder/suicide in her apartment, too. "Maybe you could talk to one of the school's counselors?"

He jerked backward. "No way! And have them put it on my record?"

"But if the choice is between that and not sleeping—"

"One more day won't make much difference." He reached into his jeans pocket and pulled out a battered roll of candies. After he popped one into his mouth, he seemed to relax briefly.

Beth wished she could do something to help him. Perhaps he didn't need to talk his troubles out right away. A good night's sleep might help him deal with his problems on his own. The solution might be as simple as a sleeping pill and a glass of warm milk.

"Maybe you could go to the infirmary."

"No! I'll be fine. I just need to talk to Heather." Keith's eyes narrowed. "Why are you so insistent? Why do you want me to go to the infirmary?"

His earlier jitters returned in full force, and Beth wondered if what she'd thought was a candy had really been some kind of stimulant. Perhaps his problem was not so much being unable to sleep, as being afraid to sleep.

"Keith, please, I'm just trying to help. You don't have to go see anyone if you don't want to. I'll give Heather your message if I see her. And if you don't find her, please, come back and let me know. Simon might know how to find her."

"Simon?"

"Professor Parkes. Heather is his research assistant."

"Parkes...got it."

Beth's shoulders chilled as if someone had placed an ice cube at the back of her neck. She felt the tiny hairs at her nape standing on end. She didn't want this boy to know anything about Simon. Which was silly of her, overreacting simply because he looked unsavory. Beth had always thought of herself as a reasonably kind and compassionate person, but her every instinct urged her to hurry Keith out of the store as soon as she could. He looked vaguely familiar. And while she couldn't place the exact circumstances of their previous meeting, she sensed that it hadn't been pleasant. Still, it wasn't right to turn her back on someone in need, just because he gave her the creeps.

"I'll call Simon as soon as I go on break," she promised, assuaging her guilt. "He's teaching this afternoon, so I'll probably get his machine, but he'll get the message eventually."

If he didn't pick up the message before he left the university, she'd tell him tonight when he came to cast the protection spell on the bookstore. But she didn't want Keith knowing any more about Simon's schedule than she'd already let slip.

"If Simon knows where Heather is, he'll tell her to call you."

"Maybe I should go to his office —"

"No!" Beth flushed at her vehemence, but she couldn't stand the thought of Keith lying in wait for Simon. "You should go home or wherever Heather would expect to find you. Or you'll just switch places, and she'll be hunting all over for you."

Keith bobbed and weaved, swaying in place as he mulled this over. "Yeah, okay. I'll be at my new place."

"I'll pass that along."

They stared at each other, then Keith looked away. "Right. I'd better be going."

Beth watched as he shuffled out of the bookstore. She felt her tension drain away as the door closed behind him. Her fingertips tingled, and she realized that she'd been clutching the counter so hard that they'd turned numb.

"Too bad magic isn't real. Because I've never seen anyone more in need of a magic wand to make their troubles disappear." She sighed, and picked up the phone to call Simon.

* * * * *

Beth shut and locked the bookstore door, flipping the sign in the window to display, "Closed." She rested her forehead against the cool glass of the door, gathering her nerve for what she was about to do. Despite the chill in their relationship, she still trusted Simon. She didn't think he'd do anything to jeopardize her position. Whatever ritual he planned to conduct would simply reassure him about her safety while at work. Still, she couldn't quite believe she was letting him cast a magic spell in the store. She'd have to double check to make sure all traces of his activities were cleaned up before they left.

She turned to Simon, waiting in the shadows of the stacks where he couldn't be seen from the street. She caught her breath. While she'd been busy closing the store, he'd gone into the back room to change. He was now wearing a scarlet robe, one of the silk robes in a rainbow of colors that she'd seen in his closet. It was loosely belted around his waist, revealing a sliver of bare chest, and hinting that he wore nothing else beneath the robe.

Swallowing against the sudden dryness in her throat, she lowered her gaze. Simon's toned and muscled calves reminded her of the first time they'd made love, when she'd sat, cradled and protected, on his crossed legs. A powerful longing filled her, and she ached to once again feel connected and completed.

"Store's locked," she whispered, strangely unwilling to disturb the mood with her voice.

"Then we're ready to begin. I've set everything up on a folding table in the Self Help section." He flashed her a grin. "It seemed appropriate."

She nodded. That was in the center of the store, where the tall bookcases would hide their actions from any curious late night passersby.

He held out his hand to lead her to the ritual space. Beth placed her palm against his, feeling a thrill of electric desire when her skin touched his. His fingers closed around hers, tightening briefly, reminding her of their gentle union on Saturday before everything had gone wrong, their bodies entwined with no sense of urgency, only an overwhelming joy that seemed to go on forever.

The memory reassured her, reminding her that she and Simon were bound on a level too deep to ignore.

His fingers tightened on hers again, a wordless echo of the rhythms of their lovemaking. Drawing her close, he escorted her to the center of the store.

The large wooden reading table and heavy chairs that usually filled this space were gone, replaced by the small folding table from the store room covered with a length of crimson silk. A white candle burned at each end of the table, with a collection of mystical paraphernalia arranged neatly between them. She recognized a red and yellow wand, an enameled chalice, a dagger, and a small brass bell. Simon had also included what looked like four drink coasters and a piece of pottery that was either a deep dish or a shallow bowl. A string on the floor formed an almost complete circle around the table, enclosing most of the open space.

Beth hesitated, suddenly unwilling to take the irrevocable step and participate in his ritual. So long as magic remained something Simon did in secret, behind the hidden door in his study, she could ignore it. But once she faced it, she'd have to admit that the man she loved was delusional. A tiny voice deep within her whispered that another possibility existed. His elaborate rituals and spells might be no more than a complex outward sign of his unusual but perfectly understandable religious faith. She dismissed that possibility as wishful thinking.

Feeling her hesitation, Simon squeezed her fingers again. "Let me protect you."

His words triggered more recollections, of the protection spell she'd thought was a game. Of him placing his "dagger" in her "chalice." Her body remembered, warming and accepting. She nodded.

He led her through the opening in the string circle, to the other side of the makeshift altar, where he'd placed a pillow for her to sit on. "This will take a while. I don't want your legs falling asleep."

He grinned, gently teasing, and Beth's breath quickened at the reminder of their lovemaking in the Jacuzzi. Remembered desire bubbled up, flooding her veins with fire. She wanted him to make love to her, right here and now.

Somehow, she found the strength to let go of his hand and seat herself on the cushion. "Let's get on with it, then."

Simon nodded, then his expression turned inward. Beth stared, transfixed, as he chanted softly. This was the first time she had seen him openly work magic. He seemed to glow with an inner radiance, as if only now was he fully alive.

Finished with his preparations, Simon lifted the bell to reveal a lump of incense. He touched it to one of the candle flames, blew on it softly until it glowed orange, then set it down in front of the painted bowl. A thin wisp of smoke rose from the altar and wafted toward Beth.

She sniffed. It smelled like pipe tobacco, the kind that reminded her of Santa Claus. Despite her nerves, she smiled.

Simon rang the bell three times, soft chimes that seemed to hang in the air. He waited a moment, then rang it four times. Another moment, and he rang it three more times. The sound pressed against her ears, setting them ringing in harmony so that she almost didn't hear his words.

"This ritual is about to begin. All those present, both physically and non-physically, who are not entitled to witness our ritual must depart!" He rang the bell one last time.

Putting down the bell, he proceeded to make a series of sharply defined gestures, most of which Beth couldn't see because of the intervening table. He walked slowly around the circumference of the circle, carefully staying inside the string, stopping at every quarter to draw pentagrams in the air with his finger.

Returning to the altar, he rang the bell twice more. Chanting in a guttural language, he held his arms straight out to either side. A trick of the flickering candles and reflected headlights from passing cars made it seem as if the air before his chest glimmered with blue light. He paused, then said, "Osiris is slain. Isis mourns."

Beth gave a start, stirring on her soft cushion. She recognized those names. They were ancient Egyptian gods. That made three different traditions he'd used — the Indian Tantra, the Pagan Wicca, and now something from Egypt. She wondered if all magicians were so well versed, or if perhaps the magic that Simon believed in was even more ancient than the religions that had sprung up to explain it.

He lifted his right arm straight up and bent his head. A moment later, he held both arms above his head, slightly spread. Beth was reminded of her cheerleading days, and "V" for "Valley" when they spelled the name of their school.

"Typhon and Apophis," Simon intoned, staring at the ceiling. Beth's gaze instinctively followed his, but there was nothing there. Nothing she could see, at any rate.

Folding his arms across his chest, he sighed. "Osiris has risen. The light shines forth."

He repeated the same gestures, this time chanting, "Mother. Destroyer. Slain and risen. Isis. Apophis. Osiris."

Finishing with a wordless howl, or perhaps a word in some strange language with no consonants, he shouted, "Let the Divine Light descend!"

He waited, breathing deeply, as if he'd just run a race. Or as if he was spent from making love. Beth found herself breathing in time with him, her body matching itself to his rhythms.

Simon walked around the circle again, drawing more invisible pentagrams. When he passed behind her, sealing her within the safety of the ritual space, the small hairs on her arms and the back of her neck lifted, charged with static electricity. Her pulse pounded strongly in her veins, each of his softly spoken words echoing in the beat of her heart. She felt alive, vibrant, and desperate to do something to use the energy filling her. But she knew she needed to remain quiet and still, and not disturb Simon's concentration. When his ritual was over, then she'd be free to act on these feelings. Her body sang with the joy of that promise.

She watched his slow, sinuous movements as he glided back to the altar, picked up the bell, and rang it nine times. She gasped with each sharp snap of his wrist, as if his fingers reached out and flicked her sensitized flesh. Ignoring her reaction, if he'd even noticed it at all, Simon lifted the red and yellow wand.

"The phantoms have vanished. See, now, the holy fire, darting and flashing through the hidden depths of the universe. Hear the voice of Fire. Angels of the southern watchtower, I invoke you!"

Mesmerized by the sight and sound of Simon's recitation, Beth felt herself losing her grip on the world around her. She fancied she heard the crackling of flames. Or maybe it was the sound of her blood rushing in her ears. Her skin was alive, hot and burning for Simon's touch.

He traded the wand for the chalice, reminding her again of their interlude in the Jacuzzi. Sprinkling water from the enameled cup, he said, "He who would rule the flames must be cooled by the loud, resounding sea. Angels of the western watchtower, I invoke you!"

Beth licked her lips, remembering the foaming water lapping at her sensitive core, beating and pulsing until Simon rode the wave to pulse inside her. She struggled for breath in the humid air, aching for him to fill her again.

With effort, she focused her gaze on Simon. He now held the gleaming dagger. "The fire burns with a great rushing of air. The formless fire, speaking in a loud voice. A flashing light, abounding, revolving, whirling, crying aloud."

As he spoke, her senses whirled and revolved, the circle enclosing them spinning like a midway ride. All was chaos, except for Simon. He shone with a bright golden light, anchoring her amid the darkness. She cried out, but her small voice was lost beneath the force of his shout.

"Angels of the eastern watchtower, I invoke you!"

Holding the bowl up to expose the gleaming pentacle painted within, Simon faced her, and said softly, "Do not enter the darkly splendid world of faithless depths. Images, sensed but not understood, delight with ceaseless windings. The black abyss, roiling forever, shining luminous on a body that is formless and void."

As he spoke, his voice seemed to fade, quieting as the room dimmed. Beth felt as if she was made of Silly Putty, alternately flattened and stretched. She gripped the edge of the pillow she sat on to try and anchor herself to reality, but her hands closed on nothingness. There was no pillow. There was no reality.

She strained her eyes, desperate to see some glimpse of Simon and what he was doing, but the store was completely black. If she was still in the store.

In the distance, something glimmered silver, reflecting wetly like light on water. It was moving toward her, undulating through the darkness. Beth tried to get up and run away, and found herself paralyzed. She tried to scream, and found herself mute. All she could do was watch as the thing, whatever it was, moved closer and closer.

A strange desire filled her, to get up and approach the thing, to run toward it and offer herself to it. Horror filled her as she rose to her feet and took a single step forward. She didn't want to go nearer to it, she wanted to run away! Her other foot slid forward. Screaming silently, Beth fought with all her will to keep her feet where they were. Yet slowly, inexorably, one foot crept forward.

Simon's voice boomed through the darkness. "Angels of the northern watchtower, I invoke you!"

Beth was back in the bookstore, sitting on her cushion, while candles bathed Simon in flickering light. Her body trembled as if she'd just experienced a sexual release. Her heart hammered as she struggled to remember the images from her vision. They fragmented, crumbling into meaningless ash before she could capture them. She had a sense that she'd been pulled back from some edge, a hidden precipice over which she would have tumbled to her doom. While Simon chanted more nonsense syllables, she slowed her breathing. Resting her palms on her thighs, she concentrated on calming herself until they no longer trembled.

"Angels of the celestial spheres, dwellers in the invisible, I invoke you. You are the guardians of the gates of the universe. Guard also this mystic sphere, and the room that encompasses it. Keep far removed the evil and the unbalanced. Strengthen and inspire those that work here. Let this sphere be pure and holy, a chamber reflecting the invisible sun of the spirit shining from above."

More chanting and gesturing followed, which Beth watched with a dispassionate air. She felt grounded, safe and secure, and confident of Simon's protection.

He finished his final walk around the edge of the circle and returned to the altar. He rang the bell ten times. "I release any spirits held witness by this ceremony. Depart in peace and blessing to your homes."

"This ritual is over. The gateways to this space are closed." He rang the bell once more.

The vibrant force he'd contained during the magical ceremony suddenly drained out of him, and he sagged, nearly dropping the bell. Head bent, he braced himself against the altar.

Beth started to rise to her feet, instinctively wanting to go to him, although she had no idea what she could offer him. Simon lifted one hand to forestall her, shaking his head.

"No, don't get up. I'll be all right. I just need a moment."

She waited in silence until he gathered himself and straightened. Beth sucked in a sharp breath. He looked exhausted, lines of weariness etched into his face. Then he smiled, as bright as ever.

"What did you think?"

"It was...incredible." She didn't know what else to say. But after having been caught up in whatever he'd done, she couldn't doubt the reality of magic. She'd felt the power running through her.

That meant the danger he wanted to protect her from was real, too.

She gulped. "Simon? Did it work?"

"The store will be safe. I'll place the four wards at the compass points of the store, and leave the blade here."

"Not where any of the customers can reach it!"

He chuckled weakly. "I'll wrap it, and you can hide it under the counter. I've seen the junk you and Julie keep under there. No one will ever notice one more bundle."

She laughed, allowing him to diffuse the tense moment. She needed time to think through the implications of all that happened this evening. This marked a turning point in their relationship, but she had no idea where they would go from here.

Retreating to comforting normalcy, she told him, "You look about ready to collapse. Finish doing whatever you have to do, then let's get your stuff gathered up, and go home."

CHAPTER FOURTEEN

Simon wasn't sure what he'd expected Beth's reaction to the magical ritual to be, but he hadn't anticipated icy silence. He'd been prepared for fear, and had hoped for acceptance. But her silence unnerved him. He tried to draw her into conversation during the drive home, telling her that he'd passed on her message to Heather and asking if Keith had returned to the bookstore. Beth remained turned away from him, staring out the window. Finally, just as he was about to pull onto his street, she spoke.

"Can you keep driving? I'm not ready to go in yet."

"Sure." He continued down the main road. In about half a mile, it ended in a T intersection, giving him two choices, right in a loop back towards downtown, or left out through subdivisions and eventually farmland. "Do you have any particular destination in mind?"

"Someplace quiet. Where we can talk."

He darted a quick look at her, but her expression gave nothing away. "Can't we talk at home?"

"No. I want to talk just to you, not Lydia."

He turned right. "We'll go to my office, then. No one will interrupt us there."

The campus was still active when they drove into the faculty parking lot. The evening labs had just let out from the chemistry building two doors down, and students spread across the lawns heading for the library, the computer center, campus parties or back to their dorms. Simon led Beth up to his office, muttering the key to his protective ward while he unlocked the door.

He reached around the door frame to flick on the lights, then held the door open for Beth to proceed him into the office. "After you."

Beth walked around the cluttered room, examining the books and paraphernalia that filled the shelves and overflowed across the desk and tiny table. The whole time, she kept her hands clasped behind her, as if she was afraid to touch anything.

Simon closed the door, reactivating the ward, and took one of the two chairs at the table. "Well? What did you want to talk about?"

Even after she sat down beside him, Beth avoided his gaze, toying with the stack of papers on the table in front of her. Finally, she said softly, "It's real."

"Yes." He wondered what she'd experienced during the cleansing ceremony to convince her. She shouldn't have felt anything. If she did, it meant that the cleansing had included her, too. Lydia's purification tea had removed the entity's taint from Beth, but somehow during the course of the day, it had reestablished contact with her.

This vindicated his earlier concern for Beth's safety, but he'd have been far happier if Lydia had been proven right. Still, the bookstore was protected, as was Simon's house. As long as she stayed in those two places when he wasn't with her, she would be safe.

Beth nodded, fidgeting in her chair. "I thought it was like a religion. You know, rites and ceremonies and belief in a higher power. But it's more than that. There's a power out there, and you can actually control it."

"What changed your mind?"

"When you did magic before, like that spell you did in the Jacuzzi, I didn't feel anything." She blushed. "I mean, I didn't feel anything that felt like magic."

"But tonight you did?"

"Yes. It felt like I was getting sucked out of my body, spinning through the darkness, until you pulled me back."

Simon hoped she couldn't see how white his face turned. It was worse than he'd feared. The entity was directly targeting Beth. The time for blissful ignorance was past. Beth needed to know what she was up against. He didn't care that Guardian tradition forbade telling her the details of the situation. She needed to know.

"I have something else I need to tell you," he said.

"There's more?"

He nodded. "Lydia and I are Guardians. It's our job to use our magical skills to protect normal people from occult dangers."

Simon paused, waiting for an outburst of disbelief that never came. Instead, Beth greeted his statement with calm acceptance. Perhaps, now that she had first hand experience of magic, she was willing to reconsider all of her previous beliefs regarding what was or wasn't possible. That would make his explanation much easier.

"And Heather?" Beth asked.

"She just passed her first test, and was accepted for training as a Guardian." Simon took a deep breath. "About a week before I first met you, I faced one of those occult dangers. It was an entity, intent on invading this plane."

"Can you explain that in English?"

"An evil, nasty monster from another dimension that thinks the people of Earth are tasty snacks."

Beth's smile was strained. "Godzilla? Mothra?"

"More like the Blob." Actually, that wasn't a bad analogy. Simon leaned forward, instinctively going into teaching mode. "This entity doesn't have a corporeal body, like we do. So it can't act directly in this plane. Instead, it gets as close as it can, in the ethereal plane where people's consciousnesses go when they sleep or when they're mentally disturbed, and it attacks their minds."

"Why do I think you're going to say it does more than just give them nightmares?"

"Because it does. A strong mind capable of resisting the entity would probably just suffer bad dreams. But a weak mind will fall under the entity's control. The entity could use the bodies connected to those minds to perform ritual magic enabling it to gain entrance to this plane."

"The animal mutilations?"

Simon blinked, amazed at how quickly she'd made the connection. He was glad he'd broken his silence and confided in her. Even though she knew little about magic, he sensed Beth could be of great help analyzing the entity's movements.

"Also those students who died in the murder/suicide," he added.

Beth's eyes widened. "I forgot all about Keith! Were you able to locate Heather for him?"

"Yes. But she's not up to dealing with someone who's under so much stress right now. I suggested she call him, and talk over the phone, rather than risk meeting him in person."

"Because of her headaches? Are those related to magic?"

"Part of the dedication ceremony opens channels to the apprentice's powers. Heather's skill is a mental power, and she's going to be overwhelmed for a while until she can adjust to all the new input. Lydia can help her deaden the effects, but it's only enough so that Heather can function in normal classroom situations. A one-on-one meeting with an emotionally distraught individual is beyond her capabilities."

Beth nodded. "Okay. So, to get back to this monster —"

Simon winced. "Please, call it an entity."

"Whatever. This entity, the one that wants to belly up to the Earth buffet. You're fighting it?"

"Yes. With Lydia's help. I fought it once on my own, which is how it was banished to the ethereal plane."

"Why are only two of you fighting it? There are more Guardians, aren't there?"

"Part of it is the nature of Guardian magics. Since we all have different specialties, the more of us that work together, the more complex an undertaking it is. And if we wanted to fight the entity on the ethereal plane, it would probably take at least five of us. But we're going to let it take material form, weakening it and cutting it off from the source of its powers, so that we can banish it completely. That will only take two of us." He sighed. "Unfortunately, it's a Catch-22. The entity can't be banished until it takes a material form, but it will need to break through our defenses and invade this plane before it can take a material form."

"You're going to fake a retreat, and when it comes to finish you up, attack with your reserves and kick it back where it belongs?"

Once again, she'd surprised him with her quick grasp of the situation. "Pretty much. How'd you know?"

She shrugged. "You may have a degree in philosophy, but you obviously don't know much about history. That strategy has been around since before the Romans."

* * * * *

The next day, Simon's office was once again preempted for Guardian business. This time, the wards offered Heather an oasis of calm. Although Lydia's concoction muffled the mental cacophony surrounding her, the effort of maintaining her shields against the constant onslaught of thoughts and emotions was exhausting Heather. As soon as she entered the peace and quiet of his office, she'd put her head down on the table and fallen asleep.

Simon worked quietly at his desk, although he suspected he could chant and beat a gong without disturbing Heather's deep sleep. About fifteen minutes before the evening class began, he neatly stacked his notes regarding the banishing spell, and slid the pages into his desk drawer. Time to switch roles, from Guardian back to professor.

He picked up his class notes, then walked over to the tiny table and shook Heather awake. She needed to get settled in the classroom before the other students started arriving. It would be easier for her to add one or two people at a time to her mental screens, than to walk into a room already full of people.

"What? Huh?"

She lifted her head and blinked sleepily at him. A line scored her cheek where it had rested against the edge of a stack of paper.

"Time for class, Heather."

She rubbed her eyes, and brushed a stray sticky note off of her sweatshirt. "I'm sorry, Professor. It's just that stuff Lydia gave me makes me so tired."

"How are the headaches?"

"Better. But I really appreciate your letting me nap in your office while you work. This is the only place on campus that's quiet."

Simon smiled. "If you can arrange for your roommates to be out, we can ward your apartment. That will give you another quiet space."

"Good. Because I'm sick of hearing their voices in my head." She grinned. "And I thought they never shut up before."

He watched Heather's reactions as she left the office, ready to intervene if she became overwhelmed. She paused and sucked in a quick breath, her shoulders tensing, then forced herself to continue walking.

"It's getting easier," she reassured him.

"You're getting stronger."

Heather seemed to be handling the rush of students' thoughts as they walked through the halls of the Philosophy building, so Simon turned his attention to mentally arranging the evening's lecture. With Halloween just around the corner, he had the perfect opening to discuss the darker side of magical beliefs, and to review some basic protections the students could take. The simplest self-defense was the arcane version of "don't look like an easy target," but it required little magical power or skill. Combined with the unrelieved ordinariness of their magical auras, that should be sufficient to protect them from the entity's attentions.

Distracted as he was, he didn't see Heather's boyfriend Rick waiting in the hallway outside the classroom until it was too late to avoid him.

"Hey, Heather. You've been hard to find lately."

Heather looked away, putting one hand to her temple. Rick's emotions must be very strong, although he hid them well.

Simon started to step between the two, but Heather stopped him with a quick shake of her head. "I have to talk to him, Professor."

"I'll be in the classroom. Come inside when you're ready." He nodded to both her and Rick, knowing Heather would pick up his unspoken message that he would be listening and could come to her aid if she needed help.

He positioned himself just inside the doorway, where he could hear their conversation without obviously eavesdropping.

Heather spoke first. "I've been busy."

"I know. I was expecting you back at your apartment for dinner on Saturday. I was going to surprise you with a meal at The Castaways."

Simon nodded to himself. Dinner at the trendy restaurant would make a significant dent in a graduate student's budget. No wonder Rick was upset at Heather's apparent disregard for his gesture.

"I'm sorry, Rick. If I'd known you were waiting, I'd have tried to get back in time. But I'd have been lousy company. I've had the worst headaches for the past few days."

"Your roommate said you'd been sick. But you still went out to work on your research project."

"I had to."

"Not if you were sick."

"I wasn't that sick."

"You were too sick to talk to Keith."

Simon risked a peek around the door frame. Heather was rubbing her temples again, but she didn't seem to need his help.

She sighed. "I did talk to Keith."

"Over the phone. The guy's a mess, Heather. He's popping No-Doz like they're candy. When I tried to talk to him, he nearly took my head off, then started babbling all sorts of chemical names, side effects and symptoms, to prove he knew what he was doing."

"Well, he is pre-med."

"He found his roommate dead in their living room! They don't cover that in basic medicine."

"They don't cover it in basic psych, either," Heather snapped. "So what do you think I can do for him?"

"Talk to him. You're the only one who can, the only one he'll let close enough to talk to." Rick stuck out his jaw in a belligerent pose. "That is, if you care enough to help him."

"Rick! Of course I care."

"Uh-huh. You said you cared about me, too. But you've been avoiding me for weeks now. There's someone else, isn't there?"

"Rick, please—"

"Another graduate student?"

"There isn't—"

"A professor?"

Heather stiffened. "I'm going to say this once, and once only. I have been busy, and I've been sick. You are the only one I'm involved with. But if you're going to be an idiot, we can call it quits right now. I don't need hassles from you on top of everything else right now."

"What else?"

"Just stuff."

"Tell me."

"No."

"Why?"

"It's personal, all right?"

Rick paled. "You're pregnant?"

Heather burst out laughing. "I'm not pregnant. You don't have to marry me, or learn how to change diapers. I just need some time to work some things out. I'll tell you what I can, when I can, but not now."

Simon shook his head, and stepped back into the concealment of the classroom. For Heather's sake, he hoped Rick accepted the restriction more easily than Beth had.

Rick started to protest, "But—"

"Your turn. If you really care about me, you'll give me some space. Can you do that?"

"You're really not interested in anyone else?"

"I swear."

Rick took an audible breath. "Okay. I won't bother you. But when you figure out whatever it is that's got you all turned around, I'll be here."

His declaration was followed by a moment of silence that Simon suspected marked an embrace. Then Heather said softly, "I love you, too."

Simon crossed to the other side of the classroom, searching for chalk he wouldn't use, and giving them their privacy. The other students would be arriving soon enough, and Heather deserved what few moments of peace and happiness she could get. As a Guardian, she'd find few enough of them.

* * * * *

In his study with Lydia the following afternoon, Simon shoved the book he'd been consulting back into its place on the shelf, and turned to face her. He waited for her to finish copying a line from one of the books spread out across the top of his desk.

"We're agreed that one of us must contain the entity, while the other one attacks it," he said.

"Yes."

"Then it only makes sense for me to do the containment, and you to do the combat."

"No, it doesn't." She shook her head. "You're the only one who has ever fought this entity before. As the one with more experience, you should take that role."

"I fought it, but I wasn't able to defeat it. That's not the kind of experience we should be seeking to repeat."

"Darling, don't be melodramatic. The conditions were entirely different. We'll be fighting it together now."

Simon leaned one hip against the desk, crossed his arms, and looked out the window of his study. Through the partially bare screen of trees surrounding his house, he glimpsed a woman taking her Black Lab for a walk. Life continued in its accustomed patterns, with no one realizing that it could all end in little more than a week.

He sighed. Every so often, he thought about how nice it must be to live in blissful ignorance like the vast majority of people. But he had a talent. It was his duty to see and understand the darker side of the universe, to protect all of those ignorant people.

It wasn't always pleasant, but at least he had the reward of being able to make a difference. How much worse must it be to know what was going on, like Beth or Heather, and be unable to do anything about it?

Although that wasn't strictly true. Beth was doing as much as she could. She was following without argument all of his instructions for remaining safely within the protective wards he had set around her bookstore. She was being civil to Lydia, rather than circling around her like a spitting cat. Most importantly, she understood the reason why he couldn't make love to her right now, why he couldn't have any sort of a relationship. And she accepted it. For now.

He dragged his thoughts back to his argument with Lydia, the same argument they'd been having all afternoon. "No, the circumstances are distressingly similar. We're under strict time constraints. We're fighting an entity we don't really understand. All we know is that previous spells did not have as much of an effect on it as they should have."

"Still, the exact circumstances of the battle will be different."

"How could I forget? Instead of combating the entity safely on another plane, facing only a shadow of its power, we're going to throw open the dimensional doors and invite it into the material plane so we can square off against its full power."

It frustrated him that the only way they could effectively attack the entity was to drop their defenses. A master of combat magics could take the battle to the entity's home plane, but the Guardians hadn't had one of those since Ingmar's death nearly twenty years ago. Andrew had thought he'd found a replacement last year, but the boy didn't survive his initiation ceremony. Now it was too late. Even if a new Guardian was dedicated tomorrow to battle magic, he'd be like Heather, like all new Guardians, more in need of assistance than capable of providing any. Simon and Lydia would have to make do with Ingmar's notes and journals.

Lydia had no comment, so Simon pressed his point, leaning across the desk to confront her.

"That's why it's crucial that I perform the containment spell. Neither of us is a specialist in attack magics, but I am the recognized master of protective magics. It's more important that the entity not be let loose on the material plane, than it is to completely destroy it."

Lydia stood up and started pacing, chafing her arms as if she suffered a chill. "What do we do if we don't defeat it?"

"Get it the hell out of Dodge."

She stared at him blankly. "We're doing the ritual here."

"That's not what I meant." Obviously western movies and the associated lingo didn't form an integral part of British children's formative years. "I mean we have to at least banish it from the material plane. That puts us no worse off than we are now, and we've ruined it's window of opportunity."

"No worse?" Lydia lifted a questioning eyebrow. "You do realize — "

"The remaining Guardians will be faced with no worse a situation than we're facing now."

She nodded solemnly. Neither of them wanted to voice the likely reason for failing to defeat the entity, that one or both of them would have died in the attempt.

Simon shifted the subject away from that possible outcome. "Anyway, I don't see why you're protesting. You did a divination this morning. More than one, judging by how long it took. You haven't said it indicated you needed to be the one containing the entity. So I must be the one that performs the containment."

Lydia slammed one of books on his desk. "The divination said nothing of the sort."

Simon frowned. Then why hadn't she said so, instead of letting him argue in circles? "So, you have to contain the entity for our best chance of success?"

"No. Yes. I don't know." Lydia ran her hands through her hair. "The signs were contradictory and unclear."

Her failure to interpret the divination clearly troubled her. It troubled Simon as well. He'd been counting on her skill to provide the guidance they sorely needed. They only had one opportunity, and had to make sure they did everything right.

"Could the entity have been interfering?" It was obviously aware of them and their efforts to defeat it. But so far, it had not directly interfered. Simon realized he'd made the mistake of equating "had not" with "could not."

"It's possible. Anything is possible. I know that better than most. But I don't think so. I think I just wasn't asking the right questions."

"What did you ask?"

"Which of us should perform the containment and which the attack. And the answer was murky."

Simon struggled to swallow with a suddenly dry throat. "No path led to success?"

"There was at least one possible path. I checked that first. The possibility of success exists. But I couldn't find any set of circumstances that seemed to favor it."

He let out his breath. They still had a chance. If they could figure out the puzzle.

He considered the situation, but saw no immediate solution. Not that he expected to. Lydia was the expert at interpreting divinatory messages, and she'd been contemplating the problem far longer than he had.

"So what do you suggest?" he asked.

"Well, I was thinking. We've assumed that because there are two of us, and two spells that need to be cast, that each of us would cast one of the spells. What if we work together?"

"Both cast both spells?"

"Yes."

Simon thought about it. "Combining talents like that is harder than having a single Guardian doing the work."

"But stronger. Maybe there will come a point in the battle where we will need to stop attacking and both turn our full efforts to defense in order to contain the entity."

"I think you're on to something. We'll structure the spells so that our attentions are split, but leave it so we can easily shift our power between defense and attack."

Lydia nodded and flashed a tentative smile. "It feels right to me, too. But just to be on the safe side, I'm going to conduct another divination."

"How long?"

"Not very. An hour, maybe. Will you keep working here?"

Simon glanced out the study window again. The red and gold stretch of woods behind the house seemed to call to him. "No. I'm going to take a break, and make sure the house's far perimeter wards are still secure."

"Do you suspect they might not be?"

"No. But this is too important to take any chances. I'll set them to automatically invoke at full force if the worst happens. It wouldn't help us with the battle, but the wards will keep the entity contained for the few hours necessary for another team of Guardians to get here."

She nodded. "I'll see what I can uncover to keep that from happening."

"You do that." Simon grinned. "In which case, I'll just be going for a walk in the woods on a crisp fall afternoon."

CHAPTER FIFTEEN

After dropping Beth off at the bookstore Saturday morning, Simon drove to Heather's apartment. Her roommates were planning to be out all day, allowing plenty of time for Simon and Heather to place wards and psychic dampening fields around the house.

He circled the block twice before he found a parking space. It was three houses down from Heather's apartment, further than he wanted, but the best he was likely to do in this area where six to twelve students lived in each subdivided two-story house originally designed for a single family.

Aside from the abundance of parked cars, the quiet side street was deserted. He'd timed his arrival perfectly. The early risers were already gone on the day's errands, and those students who had been partying heavily Friday night had yet to awaken. There were no pedestrians or other drivers who might see him and wonder why a professor was going to a student's apartment.

Simon reached into the back seat and grabbed the black leather gym bag that contained all of his supplies for the rituals. Checking one last time to ensure the street was still empty, he got out and walked to Heather's house. Two entry doors flanked the rickety porch. The left-hand door was unlocked, and opened directly onto the flight of stairs up to Heather's second floor apartment. She answered the doorbell immediately.

"Hi, Professor. You're right on time."

"Are you ready?"

"As I'll ever be."

"Then let's get started."

She locked the door behind him, and he cautioned her, "You know, you really should keep the first floor entry door locked. Anyone could come in off the street and be hiding in there."

Heather rolled her eyes. "You sound like my parents. I left it open because I was expecting you."

"It's one of the conditions of being an adult. You have to lecture kids who do the same stupid things you did when you were their age. Preferably, with the exact same lecture that was used on you." He wouldn't push her, since even if she dutifully locked the door every time, her roommates would probably leave it open. He'd put a protective spell on it before he left, in addition to the wards meant to protect Heather from psychic interference.

Heather grinned. "It's hard to imagine you being my age."

"I'm that ancient?"

"No, I didn't mean that." She turned abruptly serious. "It's more how you're so calm and in control all the time. Is that because of the magic?"

Simon thought of Andrew's extravagant lifestyle. "No. Guardians are more focused and aware than most people. But it magnifies existing personality traits, not replaces them."

She breathed a sigh of relief. "Good."

"Worried about becoming dull and boring?"

"I've been worrying about a lot, lately. My own worries, and everything my roommates are worried about, too."

"We'll get your apartment warded, and that will free you from listening in on your roommates' worries. Protecting you from unwanted psychic impressions will be the first step of the warding. Then, once your thoughts aren't distracted by other people's thoughts, we'll add the more difficult general protections."

Simon glanced around the living room, noting locations for physical anchors in the overstuffed book case, crystal-bedecked windows, and on top of the elaborate moldings framing the tall doorways.

"You said we should do the rooms where I spend most of my time first, then a general ward around the entire floor. I spend most of my time in my room, or here in the living room."

"Which is more open?"

"Well, the living room is bigger, but it has more furniture."

"We'll start with your room, then. It'll be easier for you to do a smaller space first."

She led the way to one of the small bedrooms flanking the bathroom. Simon stayed in the doorway. There wasn't room for him inside. The room couldn't be more than six feet across. Heather's twin bed, adorned with a pink and purple ruffled bedspread and with a large stuffed hippopotamus sitting in the middle of it, filled one wall. On the wall opposite the door, a narrow highboy crowded against the window. A matching pink and purple daisy-shaped throw rug occupied the scrap of open floor space.

Simon edged around Heather and put his bag on the bed, next to the hippopotamus. Heather peered over his shoulder as he took things out and laid them on the bedspread.

"Do you remember the spell I did when I rescued you at your friend Keith's apartment?" Simon asked.

"Uh-huh."

"Well, you'll be doing something similar to that."

"But that spell totally wiped you out, and you're an expert at this!"

Simon smiled. "I also rushed into it with no preparation and no tools. For example, I used my hand to draw the pentagrams instead of an athame."

He rested the blunt blade of the white handled knife across his palms, and held it out toward Heather. Tentatively, she reached for it, then drew her hand back with a sharp cry.

"It's all tingly!"

Simon set the knife on the bedspread and continued emptying his bag. "That's because it's charged with magical energy. The more energy provided by your tools, the less required from you, although you still have to control and shape that energy."

Heather wrapped her arms around herself. "I'm not sure I can do this, Professor."

"Of course you can. We'll take it one step at a time. And I'll be right here in case anything goes wrong."

"Like the last time?"

He wasn't sure if she meant the last time she'd tried to cast a spell, when the entity had attacked her, or if she referred to being overwhelmed at the end of her dedication ritual.

"I misspoke. I meant, I can correct you if you're doing something improperly. So that your spell will be successful."

Heather nodded, but didn't look entirely convinced. "So, what do I do next?"

"First, we review the tools you'll be using, what each is for, and how you'll be using it."

"We covered that in my lessons."

"That's why this is a review, not a lecture." He held up the chalice. "Let's start with this."

After Heather reassured him of her mastery of their lessons, he led her through the basic purification spell, demonstrating the Kabalistic Cross, the different pentagrams used for the elements, and the invocation words and gestures. Twice he reprimanded her for losing focus.

"I'm sorry, Professor. I'm trying, really I am. But the girl downstairs is entertaining her boyfriend, and it's really hard to shield against their thoughts when there's so much emotion behind them."

A muffled cry of passion could be heard through the thin floor.

Heather nodded. "Okay. They're done."

Simon could only guess what it must be like, having other people's thoughts filling your head. His own gifts led to a clarity of seeing, making the energy patterns that flowed around and through the material plane visible. But as Lydia had so often teased him, he was too certain of his own rigid existence. He lacked the flexibility that allowed her to float among the various paths of possibility, the same flexibility that allowed Heather's consciousness to drift among thoughts not her own.

A standard protective circle took the definition of self and other one step further, defining the space in which a magician existed as an extension of the magician's own identity, and refusing entry to anything not of the magician's self. His rigid certainty was the very reason he was so adept at protective wards, like the one he'd cast over Beth's bookstore. But that wasn't what Heather needed. A ward powerful enough to block all psychic thought would create a dangerous dead zone in her powers.

Instead, Simon planned for her to create a temporary ward that would allow her to concentrate on the more elaborate secondary spell. Then, he would lead her through a ritual of psychic integration. That would turn this space into a haven for her, where she could still access others' thoughts if the need arose, but allow them to pass harmlessly through her consciousness without affecting her if she so wished.

Freed from the distractions of the pair below, Heather quickly memorized the simple ritual. At last, Simon pronounced himself satisfied, and let her conduct it for real.

As Heather recited the Kabalistic Cross, Simon opened his magical senses and watched the flow of energy around her stabilize into two solid lines, one vertical and one horizontal, stretching into eternity. Her pentagrams hung, glowing with a reassuring blue light, at the eastern, southern, western and northern points of her circle.

Simon felt a pressure building in his mind, and suspected they had attracted the entity's attention. As close as it was, only a week away from breaking through to the material plane, any magical working must shine like a beacon. He resisted the urge to hurry Heather along.

She recited the symbolic names of the archangels, calling forth their powers to protect her and sanctify the space within her circle. The pressure in Simon's mind dissipated and he relaxed, returning his attention to Heather's efforts.

When she finished, she stood with her head down, breathing heavily, before lifting a shining face to him. "It worked! I could feel it!"

"Well done. What did you think of your first spell?"

"It was…it was…I can't describe it. All that power and energy flowing through me. It was better than sex!"

Simon choked, caught off balance by Heather's gleeful comparison. Unbidden, his thoughts returned to last Saturday, and his visit with Beth. Magic might be better than sex, but making love to Beth was even better than magic.

"Um, er, yes."

"Professor Parkes, you're turning pink around the ears!"

"Let's concentrate on the second part of the ritual, shall we?"

Again, they reviewed everything Heather needed to know, and Simon coached her on the proper responses to make in answer to the ritual questions. The room was cramped, but if Heather took very small steps, she'd be able to make the three circuits of the room required for her spiral into the center of the circle.

"You're ready," Simon told her. "Begin when you want."

Heather nodded, took a deep breath to compose herself, and then launched into the integration ceremony. She stood at the northern point of the circle and raised her arms.

"Arianrhod, goddess of transformation, of birth and initiation, I beseech you. Open my heart and mind to understanding, part the veils of mystery, and unite the magic of the earth with the stars in the sky."

Keeping careful watch on the position of her feet, Heather walked around the very edge of her circle, passing just to the inside of where she had stood for the opening invocation, and stopping at the western point. She bent her head, and folded her hands together at her chest.

"I am afraid," she said.

"Tell me child, of what are you afraid?" Simon asked the first of the ritual questions.

"Of Darkness. Of Death. Of all that is unknown."

"Without these things, there can be no life. Tell me child, what do you choose?"

Heather lifted her head, straightening her shoulders, and said in a clear voice, "I choose death. I choose darkness. I choose mystery. I choose life."

"Then continue your travels, child."

Simon smiled. She had successfully passed the first barrier to integration, recognizing the inherent duality of nature. There could be no self without others, and no others without a strong sense of self.

Heather walked another circuit around the room, slightly inside her first path. She again passed to the inside of the point where she had begun the circuit, this time stopping in the south.

She stretched out a hand, as if in greeting, then let it fall. "I have no name. Without a name I am nothing."

Simon posed the second ritual question. "Tell me child, why do you not ask the goddess for your name?"

"I am still afraid. I am afraid of her."

"You must face your fear, or remain nameless and nothing."

"I face my fear. What is my name?"

"The goddess will reveal it when you see her. Continue your travels, child."

Heather had successfully mastered the second barrier, defining herself by her true self, rather than allowing herself to be defined by those around her.

On her next circuit, Heather's foot caught in one of the petals of the daisy rug, and she stumbled. She steadied herself before falling outside of the circle, and quickly returned to her position. She finished the circuit, completing one circle and continuing on to stand in the east.

Simon frowned, unsure whether or not to stop the ritual. But Heather had not broken the protective circle. He let her continue.

She crossed her right hand to her left hip, then held out her hand palm upward. "I have no weapons."

"Tell me, child. Why do you not ask the goddess for weapons to defend yourself?" Simon posed the third ritual question, that granted the initiate the power to separate self from others.

"I am still afraid of her."

Simon hesitated. Had he just seen a flicker of the energies surrounding Heather? He looked, but all appeared in order. She'd probably just had a brief lapse of concentration, thrown by her near accident. He waited a moment longer, but the energy surrounding her remained strong and regular.

He posed the third challenge. "With no weapons, you are defenseless, a victim of the darkness."

He knew as soon as he said the words that he'd made a mistake. Heather shrieked, falling to the floor, and the entity's foul power polluted the clean lines of her magic.

Simon snatched the athame from the piece of black velvet on which it rested in the center of the circle, and slashed at the lines of force binding Heather. Chanting a frantic litany of protective spells and invocations beneath his breath, he quickly severed the entity's pathway to Heather's power. Then he wrapped her in a protective cocoon of purifying light for good measure.

Kneeling beside her on the absurdly cheerful rug, he held her in his arms like the child he'd named her while she shivered and sobbed into his shoulder. When she could finally breathe enough to speak, she choked out, "I don't want to be a Guardian anymore."

Simon patted her head, comforting her as best he could. "I'm afraid you've already made your choice, Heather. You can't go back now."

"No. I'm never getting near that...that *thing* again!"

"That's the entity Lydia and I are going to fight. After next Saturday, it will be gone for good."

Heather sniffled, her composure returning. Simon released her, and she sat up straight, wiping at her eyes. "How did it get through the protective circle? Did I break it when I tripped?"

"No. It must have made enough of a connection with you when you first summoned it at your friend Keith's apartment, that it was able to pass through your protections, posing as the darkness of your fears."

"It can do that?"

Simon sighed. "Apparently, it can. The more elaborate wards at my house and office must have kept it bay during the other times you were open to magic."

"So, what am I supposed to do? Be like Beth and hide in your house until you're done fighting?"

That had been Simon's first idea. But he quickly realized it wouldn't work. Beth's attraction for the entity lay in her connection to Simon. She was in no danger in her own right, and would not need to be protected once the entity substantiated on the material plane. But Heather was a blazing light of unschooled magical power that the entity could bend to its own desires. She'd be an irresistible target, and Simon couldn't afford to fragment his power by protecting her and still fighting the entity.

"No. I'm afraid that won't work. We have to get you out of here, and send you someplace where you'll be safe."

"You're sending me away?"

"Only for a week." If they were successful, she could come back. If they failed, she'd go wherever her new mentor lived.

"But where will I go?"

Simon thought quickly. She needed to be someplace with strong, well-established wards. Someplace where a Guardian could watch over her.

"Have you ever been to California?"

* * * * *

Half an hour later, Simon led Heather into his house. Letting out her breath, she finally relaxed. She shrugged off the back pack she'd hastily filled with the jeans, T-shirts, underwear, socks, and books she deemed necessary for a week-long stay.

Lydia strolled out of the kitchen. "Simon, how did...Heather? What are you doing here?"

"The spell went wrong. Horribly, horribly wrong," Heather answered. Then her face crumpled, and she looked like she might start crying again.

Lydia hurried over and put a consoling arm around the girl's shoulders. "There now. What you need is a good cup of tea. That will put everything to rights."

Simon shook his head in disbelief, amused despite the seriousness of the situation by Lydia's devotion to the near-mystical restorative powers of tea.

She shot him a look over Heather's head, and glanced to the kitchen. He nodded. Message received. They'd discuss this further while Heather had her tea.

Lydia seated Heather at the table then busied herself with brewing up a pot, calling out directions to Simon as she worked. "Get down the tea things. There's an extra cup on the board. Why don't you open the package of biscuits for Heather?"

The last request threw him, until he realized Lydia was talking about the bag of Pepperidge Farm cookies on the counter. He dutifully opened the bag and dumped the cookies onto a plate, snatching one for himself and setting the rest down in front of Heather.

In short order, the tea was served, and they all sat around the table drinking it. Lydia watched Heather carefully until, satisfied that the tea's soothing properties had taken effect, she turned to Simon.

"So, what happened?"

"The entity attacked Heather. She's fine, but it isn't safe for her to be here. Her danger will only increase as the entity grows stronger."

They both glanced at Heather, who was ignoring them in favor of the cookies.

"I assume you have a plan?" Lydia asked.

"I want to send her to Andrew."

Lydia nodded. "The Guardian House in Berkeley is well warded, and he can help Heather with her control. That's why I was sent to him, when I was a new Guardian."

"Let's hope he has more luck with Heather."

Lydia grimaced. "He taught me control of my magic. I'm afraid only time and hard experience taught me to control my temper."

"So, is this Andrew a professor at Berkeley, like you are here?" Heather asked, proving that she'd been listening to their conversation after all.

"Yes. He was my mentor, as well as, briefly, Lydia's."

"A real Merlin type, huh?"

Simon and Lydia both burst out laughing.

"Andrew is no wise and reclusive old man," Lydia said.

Simon added, "But he'd be happy to buy Merlin a beer if the old wizard showed up at one of his parties."

Heather's eyes widened.

"Well, darling, he is from California," Lydia said. "Some allowances must be made."

"You remember how I said the study of magic intensified Guardians' existing personalities?" Simon asked. When Heather nodded, he continued, "Andrew is a very energetic, very outgoing person, constantly looking for new sources of fun and excitement. Not surprisingly, his talent is communion with and control of fire elementals."

Heather frowned in confusion. "How old is he?"

"Chronologically, he's in his early fifties," Lydia answered. "But his students tend to think of him as a boy whose hair is touched with gray."

"If you're choosing fictional archetypes, he's closer to Peter Pan," Simon added.

"He sounds kind of neat. I guess it won't be too bad staying there for a week. Although won't people wonder why I'm taking off in the middle of the semester?"

Simon shrugged. "You'll enjoy yourself and have fun. In the meantime, I'll clear up your absence with the university on Monday. I'll tell them you had a family emergency, and weren't able to reach the administration since it was Sunday."

Heather pushed one of the cookies around on the plate. "I hadn't thought that far. I'll have to call my parents and let them know where I am. And tell Rick."

"I don't think that's wise," Lydia said.

"But what if they call looking for me?"

Simon thought for a moment. "I don't want to suggest you lie to your parents, but the truth is, they're probably better off never knowing you're a Guardian. Very few people can accept our reality."

"I suppose I can tell them it's part of an exchange. Students from our school visiting Berkeley and students from Berkeley visiting here."

Simon got up and located a scrap of paper and a pen. He wrote down Andrew's address and phone number, then handed the paper to Heather.

"You can give them this address and phone number. That should reassure them."

Heather pocketed the paper. "But how am I actually going to get to California?"

"You need to be accompanied by a Guardian, in case the entity tries to reach you again," Lydia said. "I'll take you out, introduce you to Andrew and make sure you're settled, then fly back."

Simon frowned. He didn't like the idea of Lydia being gone so long, not with Halloween coming up so quickly. But it made more sense for Lydia to fly out with Heather than for them to summon Andrew to come pick her up. This way, they could get Heather away from the entity's primary area of activity as quickly as possible. The added safety was surely worth a lost day or two.

"I'll make the reservations," he said.

Lydia smiled. "Lovely. As soon as we have all the details, Heather can call her parents."

"And Rick," Heather added.

✻ ✻ ✻ ✻ ✻

The 9:45 am jet flight to La Guardia was sold out, so Simon had to settle for buying tickets on the 11:00 am Turboprop. After the first short leg, Heather and Lydia would be on jets for the longer flights to Texas and on to Oakland. They'd spend most of the day traveling, meeting Andrew at the Oakland airport at 7:00 pm California time. If everything went well.

He suggested that Lydia might want to do a divination for their trip, but she just shrugged.

"What's the point? I've been on enough long flights to know something will go wrong. It always does. The only question is how inconvenient the problem will be, and a divination wouldn't be able to tell me that."

She gave Heather a soothing tea to help her sleep that night, in case her experience with the entity troubled her dreams. But Heather slept like a rock, waking bright and chipper the next morning. The breakfast table was more crowded than Simon could ever remember it being, with Beth, Lydia and Heather all there. He felt distinctly outnumbered.

Beth and Heather traded quips from some movie or television show he was unfamiliar with, and Simon smiled at their easy camaraderie. He enjoyed the chance to see this side of Beth's personality. A sudden longing struck him, to spend every morning at this table with Beth, to hear her talking and laughing with her own daughter. With their daughter.

He shook his head, banishing the thought. He couldn't allow himself to think beyond this coming Saturday. He certainly couldn't afford to indulge in the fantasy of a future with Beth as if they were any mundane couple. Guardians didn't have family lives. Perhaps it had been different when there were more Guardians, but in recent history, the few that had married always married other Guardians, and were often stationed in distant locations, seeing each other only on holidays or vacations.

Simon knew he was brusque and uncommunicative when he drove Beth to the bookstore. He expected her to leap out of the Jeep when he pulled to a stop in front of the store, but instead she turned to him and smiled.

Beth ran her fingers lightly through his hair. "Poor Simon. You're so worried about Heather. She's in good hands. Lydia and your friend Andrew will keep her safe."

Simon wanted to scream at Beth's gentle understanding. He also wanted to pull her across the seat into his lap and kiss her senseless.

He settled for growling, "I'm supposed to worry. It's my job."

"And you take your job so very seriously."

She sighed, and pulled her hand away. He didn't reach for her. Mostly because he wrapped his fingers around the steering wheel and clenched the molded plastic until he was afraid he'd snap it.

Beth opened the door and stepped out, then turned back to say, "You don't have to do it alone, though. If you want someone to lean on, I'm here."

His mind went completely blank, unable to formulate a response. Beth's reaction went against everything the Guardians were trained to believe. By all rights she should be running in terror from the little of the occult menace he'd allowed her to see, not volunteering to help shoulder the burden.

She shook her head, and walked into the bookstore. Simon stayed frozen until the blare of a car horn behind him jolted him into motion. As he drove back home, his thoughts chased each other in chaotic confusion. Could he possibly have a future with Beth? Could he allow himself the distraction of contemplating that question?

He hid from Lydia's probing scrutiny by claiming urgent professorial paperwork and locking himself in his office. An hour later, he'd recovered his equanimity enough to drive Heather and Lydia to the airport.

"If I ever decide to give up teaching," he joked, "I can always get a job as a chauffeur. I'm getting lots of practice lately."

Lydia smiled. "Nonsense. Everyone knows proper chauffeurs are named James."

"There's no hope for it, then. I'll have to stay a professor." His theatrical sigh sent Heather into convulsive giggles.

He dropped Lydia and Heather at the airport entrance, and promised to meet them at the ticket counter as soon as he'd parked the car.

"No need, darling," Lydia told him. "You paid with a credit card. The new ticketless tickets are all electronic. Skip the queue entirely and pick up your boarding pass at the gate."

She turned and frowned at Heather. "You do have a driver's license, don't you?"

"In my wallet."

"Good. We'll meet you at the gate, then."

Simon nodded, bowing to her greater travel knowledge, and left to park the car. He checked the departure schedule as he entered the airport lobby. Locating their flight, he headed for the assigned gate.

Lydia was standing, watching the travelers streaming down the hall. There was no sign of Heather.

He ran the rest of the way to Lydia's side. "Where's Heather?"

She laughed. "Calm down, darling. She's in the ladies'. I think she's old enough to go on her own."

"Are you sure she's safe?"

All humor faded from Lydia's face. "Simon, you protected her to the best of your ability before we left the house. She's not using any of her magic. She's in no danger. I'm more concerned about you."

"Me?"

"Yes. I suggested to Heather that she make a preflight stop, so that I could talk to you. Your paperwork kept you so busy this morning that I didn't have a chance."

Cold dread pooled in Simon's stomach. "What is it?"

"I did a divination last night, a number of divinations. Much was still clouded, but one thing was clear. You must not attempt to confront the entity alone. If you do, you will fail. Utterly."

He'd die. "And the entity?"

"Free."

An image of his peaceful little college town swallowed in a firestorm of rage and insanity filled his thoughts. He couldn't allow that to happen.

"You'll be back Wednesday. I won't face it alone."

Lydia bit her lip. "That's the plan."

"Did your divination say anything about you not coming back?"

"It wasn't clear. I'm not sure what I should do."

Simon frowned. Lydia's precognitive gifts rarely failed her, but divination was notoriously unreliable when the diviner's own actions were being considered. The mere act of reading a future changed the possible outcomes.

"Concentrate on the path that leads to the entity's defeat, not on your specific actions. That might let you see the choices more clearly."

"Then I'll be back in plenty of time," she said. "You need me to win the battle."

Simon glanced at the door to the ladies' room just in time to see Heather bound out. "Get Heather to safety. Then worry about how you'll get back to me."

CHAPTER SIXTEEN

Beth held the steaming take-out containers of Szechwan Chicken and rice while Simon unlocked the door to the house. With Lydia escorting Heather to California, it would be just the two of them, alone in the house. The similarity to her first visit to Simon's home wasn't lost on Beth, and she hoped that the evening would end the same way.

Simon seemed determined to douse those hopes. As soon as they entered the kitchen, he said, "I'll just take mine into the study. I've got research to do."

"No."

Her sharp protest took them both by surprise. But it had been instinctive. She finally had him all to herself. She wanted to make mad, passionate love to him all night. The new rules of their relationship made that unlikely, but he could still have dinner with her. If Simon truly had research that couldn't wait, that was one thing. But judging from his inability to meet her gaze, the research was just an excuse.

"If Lydia were here, would you be having dinner with us, or would you still closet yourself in your study?"

He hesitated. Beth suspected he was searching for a way to sugarcoat his answer without either lying or insulting her.

"The three of us would have dinner together," he admitted. "But Lydia and I would be discussing our research, so it's not the same."

"You can discuss it with me."

Beth made the offer, although she didn't have much hope that he'd take her up on it. After all, she knew very little about magic, other than the general books she'd read and the bits and pieces she'd picked up overhearing the others' discussions.

Simon tilted his head and considered her. "Actually, you might be able to help."

A warm glow filled her at his words. "How?"

"You were very quick to pick up the connections between apparently isolated events. Maybe you can spot other connections that we've missed."

"I'd be happy to try. Just promise me one thing."

"What?"

"Save any discussion of gross things until after we finish eating."

Simon laughed. "I promise."

He laid out tableware, and they sat down to eat. After a few minutes dedicated to shoveling food into his mouth as quickly as possible, Simon settled back in his chair and started talking, pausing every so often to scoop up another forkful of chicken and rice.

Starting from the first occult event, the murder/suicide of those two students, he described all of the things leading to the current crisis, both those he had witnessed directly and those he and Lydia inferred from the evidence. Beth found his explanations so fascinating, Simon had to remind her to keep eating. It was as if, now that she knew and accepted that he worked magic, he was free to tell her all the things he had kept secret before. At the time, she'd thought he looked tired and worried. Now she understood.

"Wait a minute," she interrupted. "How did you know Heather was going to cast a summoning spell?"

"A precognitive dream."

"But you said you were no good at telling the future."

Simon glanced away. "I didn't say it was my dream."

"Whose was it then?" When he didn't answer, she prodded again, "Simon?"

He pushed the grains of rice around on his plate, drank half of his glass of water, and started gathering up the empty take-out containers. His obvious discomfort puzzled her, considering how open he'd been about so many other things.

Forcing her voice to remain steady, Beth asked, "Whose dream was it, Simon? Lydia's?"

Finally, he looked up and met her gaze. "Yours."

"Mine?" She jumped backward, instinctively putting distance between herself and his assertion. "That's impossible."

"No, it's not." He slumped in his chair, looking completely miserable. "That first night you stayed here, when I got up in the middle of the night, I was trying to do a divinatory scrying. I needed a large, flat surface of water, so I cast it upon the water in the Jacuzzi. Somehow, it was still magically connected to you, and because your mind was more open, the image I was searching for showed up in your dreams."

Beth shivered. The details of her nightmare had faded, but Simon's words brought back the terror of that night. The harder she tried to not think about it, the more she remembered.

An image from her dream burst vividly into her mind, and she gasped.

"What is it?" Simon jumped out of his chair and circled the table to reach her side.

"I remember the dream. That's why Heather looked so familiar when we met."

He nodded.

"But there was someone else in the dream with Heather, someone I just met. Now I know why I disliked him. It was Keith."

Simon blinked. Slowly, as if he was considering all of the possible ramifications of her statement, he said, "I'd forgotten that you originally saw Keith in your vision."

"You said my mind was open. Is that because I was asleep?"

"Yes. And because of your connection to me and the water I was using for the spell."

"Then does Keith have some connection to the things Heather used in her spell? He told me he's terrified of falling asleep. That would make sense if his mind was also open."

Simon shook his head in quick negation. "That sort of a connection is ephemeral, quickly dissipating unless it's constantly reinforced. Even if a link was established during Heather's summoning spell, it would be long gone by now. And such links don't just spring up from casual circumstances. It usually requires a significant magical working to create in the first place."

Beth frowned, her attention snared by his first comment. "If the connections fade so quickly, why are you still worried that the entity might be able to affect me?"

"That's my fault." Simon turned away, and seemed suddenly consumed by a need to inventory the contents of one of the cabinets by counting all the plates visible through the etched glass door.

"You'd better explain."

"We mingled essences, which strengthened the force of the connection. When I continued seeing you, continued thinking about you, and continued making love to you, the bridge between us strengthened even further. By the time I realized the entity had forged a link to you as well, it was well established, if weak."

She swallowed, and leaned back against the comforting solidity of the kitchen counter. "You couldn't have known."

"I should have." He shoved a hand through his hair. "But you see why I doubt Keith has a similar connection. In his case, he's probably just afraid of nightmares. That seems natural, since he was the one who discovered the dead bodies of his roommate and his girlfriend."

Accepting Simon's redirection of the conversation, Beth considered his argument, then shook her head. "I think it's more than just nightmares. You didn't see him. He was past being on the ragged edge. He'd already started down the slippery slope into full scale psychosis. He said that he hadn't slept in days. I think he was taking caffeine pills to stay awake."

Simon drummed his fingers against the table top as he thought. "You may be right. Heather's boyfriend, Rick, said something to that effect last Tuesday when he cornered Heather outside my classroom."

"What should we do about it?" Beth didn't question that something needed to be done. No one else would recognize the occult influence in Keith's problem, and standard psychiatric treatments might do more harm than good.

"He must have slept by now. Those pills don't work forever. The human body just can't cope with staying awake longer than four days in row." Simon shrugged. Without apparent conscious volition, he put his arm around Beth's shoulders. She held her breath, unwilling to draw his attention to his gesture with even the slightest movement.

Despite the danger that Simon had revealed, his touch still turned her blood to liquid flame. She ached to take him upstairs and make passionate love to him, even if that risked reenacting the spell that had gotten her involved in this whole thing.

"He must have fallen asleep at least once since you saw him," Simon continued. "Probably two or three times. Since nothing happened to him, we can assume his fears were of the mundane sort."

"How do you know nothing happened to him?"

"I would have sensed if the entity made an attack on a person within my sphere of protection, even if I couldn't pinpoint where the attack was aimed. The entity did not break through my wards anywhere in this city. Heather's friend is safe."

"Oh," Beth breathed. Her gaze locked on Simon's mouth. He suddenly stilled, but did not move away.

She kissed him. And he kissed back.

As soon as he realized what he was doing, Simon broke off the kiss and stepped back. "No. We can't do this."

Beth growled. The incongruity of her sweet, soft appearance and the deep-throated noise almost made Simon smile, but he knew she would not appreciate the observation. And since she looked about ready to tear his hair out by the roots, he didn't want to give her any additional provocation.

"Why?" She demanded. "Why can't we?"

"Because the stronger my physical connection to you, the stronger the entity's connection will be."

Beth's face paled. "Are you sure?"

"Not one hundred percent." He hesitated, wanting desperately to take that small chance, but he forced himself to turn away from the comfort to be found in each other's arms. "The exact percentages don't matter. I'm not willing to take that risk."

She nodded. Taking a deep breath, she stepped back, placing herself out of the range of temptation.

The tension drained out of Simon's shoulders. It was so much easier to have a relationship with her now that the truth of his magic was in the open. He wasn't going to have to fight Beth on this point, or hurt her feelings with plausible excuses to camouflage the occult rationale for his actions.

Beth twisted a curl of hair around her finger. "Is there anything I can do to help you?"

He considered. He needed to do more research, and having her near him but being unable to touch her was a constant source of frustration. But knowing she was in the house and not near him was equally frustrating. At least if she was in the study with him, he could see her, talk to her, and feel her presence.

His mind made up, he said, "I have to read through a stack of books and journals. You can help by copying and organizing the bits of information I find."

Beth beamed. "I'd love to."

They quickly settled into a routine. Simon continued reading the bound copies of Ingmar's journals that he and Lydia had been researching, looking for anything that could apply to their current situation. When he found something, he passed the book to Beth, and she carefully copied the information, as well as noting the volume and the page it appeared on.

After nearly two hours of reading, Simon set his current book down and rubbed his eyes. The accumulated dust from all of the ancient volumes seemed to have collected beneath his eyelids.

"Tired?" Beth asked.

"I just need to rest my eyes for a bit."

"This print is very hard to read. But I gather, from the bits you wanted copied, that your plan is to force the entity to put all or most of its energy here, then send it packing to its home dimension." She grinned. "And I can't believe I just said that. I sound like a bad fifties sci-fi film."

Once again, Simon was amazed at her perception. He'd located six different references to dimensional transfers, including one warning of the dangers to astral and ethereal travelers who pulled too much energy from their bodies back on the material plane, the error that had cost Andrew's apprentice his life. Yet she'd instinctively grasped the overall structure of his research.

"That's the plan," Simon agreed. "We lure it through the weakened barrier between dimensions, I contain it, and when enough of it makes it through the barrier, Lydia blasts it."

"What if it knows what you're planning?"

Simon's breath froze, and he turned to face her. "What do you mean?"

"Well, you said the entity seemed to know enough about you and Lydia to frame her for the animal mutilations. That seems to imply a level of cunning and manipulation. Twice it nearly got Heather, in very straightforward attacks. Both times you were there to save her. What if the entity never wanted to possess Heather? What if it was testing you to find out how you'd react?"

A rushing filled Simon's ears. His senses spun, and he heard clearly in memory Lydia's voice puzzling over one of his student's tarot divination. Their structure had a flaw that would cause it to fail.

He blinked, focusing on Beth. "I used the same basic containment and banishing spells we plan on using on Saturday."

"Can it develop counter spells?"

"We have to assume it can." He wondered if his face was as pale as Beth's. This changed everything. Not only did they need to develop attack spells, they needed to develop a new method to contain the entity while they attacked it. He couldn't believe he'd been so blind not to have anticipated this possibility.

"Do you want to call Lydia?" Beth suggested. "She and Heather should be there by now. It's eight o'clock on the West Coast."

"Yes." Simon dug his desk phone out from under the pile of paper that had engulfed it, and quickly punched in Andrew's number. His mentor answered on the second ring.

"Simon, we were expecting you to call. Heather's settled in comfortably. No trouble on the flight at all."

"I'm glad to hear it. But I didn't call to find out about Heather. We have a problem. Get Lydia on the line."

When both Guardians were listening, Simon outlined Beth's deduction. Secretly, he'd been hoping they'd find a flaw in the reasoning, but they both agreed. And Andrew added yet another twist to the already complex situation.

"I've been reviewing your assumptions with Lydia. You've been treating this thing as if it's an elemental. But it isn't behaving like any of the elementals I'm aware of."

Simon closed his eyes and breathed deeply, visualizing a protective sphere of light. He needed all the help he could get right now. "You're the elemental expert," he reminded Andrew. "If it's not an elemental, what is it?"

"I didn't say it wasn't an elemental. Just that if it is, it's acting strangely."

"Maybe it never read your treatise on elementals, and doesn't know the proper etiquette," Simon snapped.

Lydia broke in, "There's no reason to be rude, Simon. Andrew's doing the best he can. We've been combing his library for information ever since we got Heather settled."

"Have you found anything?"

"Not yet," she said. "Even with two of us looking, we'd need a whole day to get through everything."

"Do you really think you can find something that will help?"

"If this thing is an elemental, I've got material on it," Andrew answered. "More importantly, if it's not, the suggestions I gave you to incorporate into your attack spells won't work."

"We can't take that chance," Lydia said. "I'm going to have to stay here another day. I'll come back on the first flight Thursday. That will still give us Thursday night and all of Friday to prepare."

Simon hesitated, not liking to cut their timing so close. "What about Carlos or Esperanza? They could fly from Mexico City or Rio de Janeiro to California to help out Andrew, so you can come back as scheduled."

"Carlos is master of the dead," Andrew pointed out. "He's got his own problems at Halloween."

"Esperanza then."

"By the time she gets here, it will be too late to incorporate anything she finds in the spell," Lydia said.

"Besides," Andrew added. "Most Guardians work alone, with no advance notice, or only general warnings."

"And they die alone, too," Lydia snapped, before Simon could respond. He wished she'd stop mentioning his imminent death.

"If it comes to that, having another Guardian present is no guarantee of survival," Andrew said. "I was standing only a few feet away from Scott when his spell went bad, and he was dead before I could reach him."

All three were silent for a moment, then Lydia sighed. "None of that changes anything. The only sensible course is for me to stay in California and do the research. I'd suggest asking Esperanza to go to New York, but she's adept at candle magic. We'd have to rewrite all the spells we've already done. You need to devote your time to finding new information, not rewriting the old."

"You're sure you'll be back on Thursday?"

Andrew answered, "Regardless of what we find, I'll put her on that plane first thing Thursday morning. She'll be there in plenty of time for the big day."

"Okay. Keep in touch about what you find."

Simon hung up the phone, and met Beth's worried gaze.

"Lydia's staying an extra day? Is anything wrong?"

Simon shrugged, not able to put his feeling of unease into words. "They're going to try and find some additional material we can use, since our initial line of defense may be compromised."

She nodded, accepting his version of the conversation. "Who are Carlos and Esperanza?"

"Two other Guardians. They'll be available as backup, just in case."

"In case of what?"

"I wish I knew."

Simon ran his hands through his hair and sighed deeply, his whole body seeming to sag for a moment before he stiffened his shoulders and put on a patently false smile. "There's nothing more we can do tonight. I'll get a fresh start in the morning, when my mind is clearer."

Beth longed to find a way to ease his burden, to help him relax and forget the immense pressure he was under. Stepping behind him, she reached up and started massaging his shoulders.

He twitched at the unexpected touch, then groaned and let his head droop. She could feel the knotted muscles beneath her fingers slowly begin to unclench. But as Simon started to relax, a different kind of tension began filling Beth.

Her fingers stroked his warm skin, her thumbs digging rhythmically into his flesh, and her own skin heated as her pulse and breathing took on the rhythm of her massage. Unable to stop herself, she slid her hands off of his shoulders and around to the front of his chest. His nipples were as hard as pebbles beneath the thin cotton of his shirt.

He sucked in a sharp breath, but didn't tell her to stop. Emboldened, Beth let one hand drift downward, and found his equally hard erection.

Simon placed his hand over hers, stopping her exploration, yet trapping her fingers around his shaft. "Beth, we can't. I explained the dangers."

"You can't make love to me. But what if I make love to you?"

"No. It's still too dangerous. Although…"

As Simon's thoughts turned inward, he seemed to forget about their clasped hands, still cradling his erection. Slowly, as if moving without his conscious volition, his hand slid up the length of his shaft, pulling Beth's hand beneath his along the same path. Her fingers tightened around him, caressing him through his clothing, as their joined hands reached the head of his shaft, paused a moment, then started the journey downward.

Simon muttered beneath his increasingly ragged breath, occasionally stressing a phrase enough that Beth could hear it, such as "break the connection" and "no direct link." She ignored his words, focusing instead on the feel of him beneath her hand, trembling at her touch and thrusting against her palm with every upstroke. And still his hand rested on hers, guiding her up and down his length, so that she almost felt that her hand was being caressed by his erection rather than the other way around.

She rested her cheek against his shoulder and wrapped her free arm more tightly around his chest for balance. Her legs were beginning to get as unsteady as her pulse and breathing. Sliding her fingers down his erection, she imagined it driving into her, and felt the answering wetness between her thighs.

When Simon lifted their clasped hands away from him, she cried out at the sudden loss and unfulfilled ache.

He turned and faced her. "It's too dangerous for me to make love to you, or for you to make love to me. But I have an idea. Come on."

She eagerly followed him up to his bedroom.

"Take your clothes off," he ordered, as he stripped naked. The sight of his erection, freed of his pants and thrusting proudly forward, made her knees weak with anticipation. She quickly followed suit, dropping her clothing to the floor.

"Now what?"

"The mirror." He turned her so that she faced the full-length mirror. "It's an antique, made with real silver on the back, protective silver that will prevent a connection if we make love to our mirror images."

Beth frowned. "If we do what?"

He stepped in front of her, also facing the mirror, and twined his fingers with hers. Then he guided her hand around his erection. "Look into the mirror. See the man in the mirror's expression as you touch him. Let his hands guide yours."

Startled, and unable to see his face any other way, Beth did as Simon requested. Their gazes locked, reflected in the mirror. Simon's eyes shone with fevered passion as he guided her fingers to resume their caresses of his erection. In the mirror, Beth could see him moving with her touch, swelling in response to her motions. She saw a tell-tale glimmer of wetness at his tip, and confirmed his readiness with a brush of her thumb at the end of her next caress.

Simon groaned, his hips pumping as he tightened his fingers around hers and increased the speed of her strokes. Beth's breathing turned as ragged as his as she watched his reflection bobbing and pumping, slicking in and out of the circle of her fingers, imagining his rock hard erection thrusting in and out of her aching flesh instead.

Their gazes met again in the mirror and locked.

"God, Beth. Now," Simon panted. "I'm going to—"

His words ended in an inarticulate cry as he came, the thick white stream arcing toward the mirror.

They stood that way for long minutes, hands clasped, staring into each other's reflected eyes. Simon looked as dazed as she felt. But at least he'd had a release.

He smiled into the mirror, and let go of her hand. "Now it's your turn."

Circling behind her, he rested his chin on her shoulder and met her mirrored gaze. His hands reached down and twined their fingers with hers.

"Guide me."

She swallowed, nervous yet incredibly turned on by the challenge. Watching in the mirror, she lifted Simon's hands and placed them on her breasts. His palms pressed against her nipples, and she rotated their joined hands, teasing herself with his touch.

Her breath quickened. Making love to his mirror image had already aroused her, and she had no patience left for teasing. Bringing her left thumb and index finger together, she guided Simon's fingers to roll the sensitive nipple in his grasp.

She moaned, feeling the pinch all the way to her core. Then Beth guided his other hand down between her legs.

The image in the mirror appeared as if she was touching herself, her hand clearly visible dipping between folds of skin.

Yet it was Simon's fingers she felt sliding along her cleft, back and forth, then slipping inside her.

Her vision hazed, and Beth was no longer certain who was touching what as their joined fingers slid in and out of her wet opening, and their thumbs found and stroked the swollen bud of her desire. Her hips rocked, urging him onward as she guided his hand harder and faster, swirling his fingers around and around inside her. Gasping for breath, she whimpered, softly at first, then louder and louder, rising in pitch as their hands moved faster and faster.

She came in a furious rush, screaming her release as the liquid of her passion washed over their joined hands.

Still shuddering with the aftershocks, Beth lifted her head and met Simon's triumphant gaze in the mirror.

She smiled shakily. "So that's the occult version of safe sex, huh? I like it."

＊ ＊ ＊ ＊ ＊

They had no more time to make love, even through the medium of the mirror, as Simon spent every waking hour of the next two days formulating magical attacks and defenses. He was glad of Beth's assistance and insights, but most of the work only he could do. Wednesday night, he finally convinced her to go to sleep around midnight, while he stayed up putting the finishing touches on the ritual he and Lydia would use against the entity. Exhausted but satisfied, he finally crawled into his solitary bed around three in the morning, knowing that for once, he had no faculty meetings or other campus business to fill his morning. He counted on sleeping late. Instead, a phone call roused him out of bed shortly after eight.

"Hello?"

"This is Detective Freemont. I've got another case you might be interested in."

Simon was instantly awake. "Another mutilation?"

"Thank God, no. But until we get this thing solved, I'm the department's own Fox Mulder. Anything weird, they give to me."

"But you think the newest crime is related to the others?"

"I think it's not like anything I've ever seen before. Can you come down to the station?"

"Can you give me about an hour?"

"Sure. There's no hurry on this one."

Despite the detective's reassurances, Simon hurried through his shower. When he walked into the kitchen, he found Beth savoring a leisurely mug of tea at the table, reading one of his reference books.

"Good morning, Simon. Who was on the phone?"

"The police."

Beth dropped the book. "Not another mutilation?"

"No. But Detective Freemont wouldn't tell me about the crime over the phone. Just that it's something strange."

"Did you feel anything last night?"

Simon shook his head as he plugged in the coffee maker. "All quiet. Of course, that just means the entity wasn't trying to get through to the material plane. It could have influenced someone's dreams, convincing them to do who knows what when they awoke. Or it might be totally unrelated to the entity."

"So what are you going to do?"

"I'm headed for the police station, to talk to Detective Freemont and find out what the police know. If I can help, I will."

"Even if it's related to the entity?"

Simon smiled. "Yes. I've had years of practice phrasing descriptions of occult events so that the police can accept them as something strange but mundane, and to find ways of rationalizing unconventional courses of action they can take to solve their crimes."

He poured a cup of coffee, closing his eyes and inhaling the fragrant steam before taking a sip. Leaning against the counter, he asked, "What are you doing today?"

"I'm closing at the store tonight, so I don't have to be there for a couple of hours yet. Will you be back in time to give me a ride?"

"I should be. If not, I'll call and you can get a taxi."

"Maybe I should take advantage of the weather and bike. According to the newscaster on the radio this morning, we're due for a cold snap in the next few days."

"The first cold weather of the season always hits on Halloween, just in time to freeze all the little kids out trick-or-treating."

Beth's eyes widened. "Simon, what are you going to do about trick-or-treaters? You can't have them ringing your doorbell while you and Lydia are fighting the entity!"

"I'll do what I usually do. Get a huge bowl of candy, and leave it on a chair at the bottom of the driveway with a sign saying to help themselves. Every year, some of the kids dare each other to come up to the house and ring the bell, but the wards always deter them."

"I guess you would normally be working on Halloween, wouldn't you?"

"Yes. There are many spells that are easier to perform on that day." His mind immediately skipped to some of the more interesting rituals, Tantric meditations that took advantage of the lowering of the veil between worlds. If it wasn't for the entity, Simon would gladly spend the day transporting Beth to other worlds of lovemaking.

He shook his head, dislodging the fanciful notion, and quickly gulped the last of his coffee. "I'll see you later."

He made a less than graceful escape, eager to get away from the temptation of Beth's presence. He would be glad when Lydia arrived tonight to provide a buffer between them. He'd be even gladder when he and Lydia defeated the entity so that he could resume his relationship with Beth.

Detective Freemont was waiting for him when he arrived at the station. Simon had stopped at Dunkin Donuts on his way downtown, and handed the detective one of the extra large cups.

"Thanks, Professor. I've got the case file at my desk."

Simon nodded and followed the detective back into the open room filled with desks. They stopped at a desk two thirds of the way down the side wall. A familiar '57 Chevy sailed across the computer's screen.

The detective pointed to the battered plastic chair beside his desk, then sank into his own chair with a squeak of protesting castors.

"All the meeting rooms are in use. But there's nothing hush hush about this case." He handed a manilla file folder to Simon. "Young woman, waitress at Dirty Jack's, left work around one in the morning, and was assaulted in the parking lot."

"Sounds straight forward enough."

The detective shook his head. "Read the file. It doesn't match any profile I've ever seen."

Simon flipped open the folder and scanned the contents. The woman hadn't been able to describe her attacker, who had come up on her from behind. He'd knocked her unconscious by reaching around her and holding a cloth soaked in some chemical over her nose and mouth. She'd come to three hours later, laying on a park bench, with no obvious injuries other than a neatly bandaged wrist. When she tried to get up, she'd fainted, but had eventually found her purse—nothing stolen—under the bench, and called 9-1-1 on her cell phone.

The rest of the police report contained no useful information, being mainly a list of all the things that hadn't happened. There were no fingerprints on the woman's clothing or purse, but one partial and two full prints were found on the surgical tape binding the woman's wound. The prints did not match any in the database. There was no theft, no sexual assault, and no physical assault other than the initial drugging. The woman had lost a significant amount of blood, from the incision —

Simon glanced up at Detective Freemont. "Incision? Not a cut or slash?"

"No. It was very precise, perpendicular to the veins in the wrist, just deep enough to open the veins without severing them."

"The same precise way those animals were dissected?"

The detective nodded. "Made with the same type of blade."

Simon read the rest of the report, but saw little else of interest. The woman's wrist had been bound in a manner the emergency room doctor termed "professional," which, coupled with the neat incision, explained why she hadn't bled to death. To Simon, that detail raised more questions than it explained.

He handed the folder back to Detective Freemont. "You called me because you think it might be a ritual use of her blood?"

"And because it might be the same guy. Same sort of knife, knows anatomy, makes sure his victim doesn't suffer. But it's that last bit that's throwing me. The profiles all say if an animal mutilator moves to humans, the mutilations get more violent, not less. And they don't patch their victim up when they're done."

"That's what's got me, too," Simon admitted. "Traditionally, there are two schools of thought regarding blood magic. The first believes that a blood sacrifice gains its power from the life force in the blood. Someone who ascribed to that theory would have killed this woman."

"What's the second school?"

"The second school also believes the life force empowers a blood sacrifice, but they think it is the willing gift of life energy that provides the power, not the life itself. Someone from that school would take only what blood was necessary for a ritual sacrifice, and ensure the wound was treated properly. But they'd insist upon a willing sacrifice. A victim kidnapped off the street and bled while unconscious would be a useless sacrifice, because it wouldn't be a willing gift of energy."

The detective glared at the unforthcoming file folder. "So this doesn't match any of your profiles, either."

"It's possible that it's unrelated to the mutilations. Maybe it's someone with a vampire fetish, trying to consummate a relationship with this woman."

"Huh. Exchange of blood, she has to become his eternal bride or some such hogwash?"

"Something like that. If it really is someone with a vampire complex, he'll probably return in the next few nights, to 'claim' his new 'bride.' You might want to make sure this woman has some protection."

"Yeah, that hangs together. He wouldn't want her to die, because he wants to make her his love slave." Detective Freemont rubbed his face. "God, I hate Halloween. All the nut cases come out of the woodwork."

"I have some books back at my office about people who suffer delusions of vampirism. I can work up a more complete profile for you, but in general, these people had traumatic childhoods, suffering abuse, neglect and/or abandonment, and lack the ability to form interpersonal relationships. Acting as a vampire can also camouflage a man's inability for normal sexual activity."

"You mean he can't get it up?"

"Yes."

"Okay." Detective Freemont slapped the file folder. "I'll turn this one over to the sex crimes department, and let them handle it from here."

CHAPTER SEVENTEEN

When Simon picked up Beth to take her to the bookstore, she told him Andrew had called while he'd been out.

"Did he say why he called?"

"He wanted to let you know Lydia boarded the 6:20 plane out of Oakland this morning."

Simon let out a relieved sigh. "Good. I'm glad something's going right."

"Not necessarily. He also said the plane's takeoff was delayed. You should call the airport before you go to pick her up."

"I will, although her connecting flight will probably still be on time. I'm just glad she's finally on her way."

Lydia left a message on his voice mail at work that afternoon, correcting his assumptions. Her flight had never left Oakland, but she might be able to get a later flight as far as Chicago. If not, she'd try again Friday morning.

He got the full story when Lydia called the house shortly after 11 PM.

"Where are you calling from?"

"Oakland. The blasted plane never got off the ground."

"Why didn't you catch another flight?"

Lydia growled. "Don't you think I would have if I'd been able to? They should have canceled the flight to begin with, but they thought it was just a glitch in the control systems. The radio and intercom were not working. The Captain announced that they just needed to replace one part, and we should be airborne in half an hour. Except that part didn't fix the problem. So they decided another part was needed. It took half an hour to get that part over to the plane, and another hour to do the repair. And it still didn't work."

"Two hours? And you were stuck on the plane the whole time?"

"It gets worse. The next piece they decided to try replacing was a big one. The airline had takeoff and landing rights at the Oakland airport, but it's not one of their hubs, so they didn't have a full scale maintenance facility. They didn't have the part."

"Someone must have had the part."

"It was specific to this model plane, and only one other airline flew that model from the Oakland airport. There was apparently bad blood between the airlines, because the other airline, who had a spare part, didn't want to let them have it. Of course, it took even more time for them to try negotiating for the part first."

Simon shook his head in disbelief. "But they still didn't let you off the plane?"

"Of course not. We might have tried getting a seat on the competitor's flight! Instead, they flew the part in from one of their hubs."

"How long did that take?"

"An hour and a half to get the part, and another half an hour to install it. But, of course, the problem was still not fixed."

Simon smothered an urge to laugh. The situation was serious, but the antics of the repair crew sounded like the Keystone Cops had been hired as mechanics.

"It gets worse," Lydia continued. "The mechanics kept tinkering until after noon. The Captain made *another* announcement. Since the flight crew had officially been on duty this whole time, even if the plane was fixed, they wouldn't be able to take off. Your FAA has rules about how many consecutive hours a flight crew can work, and if they did take off, they'd be obliged to stop the plane in midair for a bit of a rest."

Simon disguised his snort of laughter as a cough.

"You'd better not be laughing," Lydia warned.

"No. That was a cough." He cleared his throat loudly. "Go on. So they finally let you off the plane at noon."

"Yes. They reassured us that the plane would take off as soon as a replacement crew could be found. Most of the passengers didn't want to wait, and rushed the other airlines' ticket counters. The other major carrier, the one that had refused to give our airline the part, had been forced to cancel some of their own flights due to weather problems at the destination airport. All the eastbound flights were overbooked. I bought standby tickets for every flight, but couldn't get onto any of them."

"Well, rest up tonight. You won't be getting much sleep tomorrow night. It'll take you a couple of hours to learn your part of the ritual, and the earlier we can perform it on Saturday, the better."

The phone line was ominously silent, before Lydia said softly, "I may not be arriving on Friday."

"What?"

"Don't you think my being stranded in Oakland was the result of a rather lengthy chain of coincidences? An extremely unlikely chain? I'm not sure, but I think the entity may have been behind it."

"Are you saying the entity understands how to cause airline delays? That seems pretty far-fetched."

"Andrew told you it wasn't behaving according to the normal patterns. I tried to confirm my suspicions with another divination. I still can't get a clear reading. I think we'll have to assume it may be successful in blocking my return."

Simon breathed deeply, clutching the phone. He needed to remain calm. "You might still make it. But just to be on the safe side, I'll give Esperanza a call."

"Do that. Remember, you must not fight the entity alone. If you have to wait until Saturday evening for someone to get there, wait. In the meantime, I'm going to fax you what Andrew and I found. I was bringing the papers with me, but you need to read them before Saturday."

Simon hung up, and waited for the pages to come through on the fax before he called Esperanza, or rather, tried to call. The phone lines were out. He wasted fifteen minutes trying to locate his address book with her cell phone number, cursing South American telecom companies the entire time. He finally reached her just before midnight.

"Esperanza, it's Simon. Can you come up to New York? It's urgent."

"Sí, Simon. I can be there on Sunday."

"Sunday's no good. I need someone here by Saturday."

"Was not Lydia with you?"

"She was. She went out to California to see Andrew, and we're afraid she won't be able to get east in time."

"In time for what?"

"A paradimensional entity is going to try to breech the barrier of the material plane Saturday, on Halloween."

"I am sorry, Simon. But we've had a terrible storm here. Power, phone lines, even some gas and water lines, all are disrupted. Regular passenger flights will not resume before late Saturday."

"There's no way you can get here?"

"I am sorry, but no."

"Thanks anyway."

Simon hung up the phone and stared at it. So much for backup. In a little more than twenty-four hours, he was going to die.

He hurried upstairs, and tapped lightly on the door to Beth's bedroom. If she was already asleep, the soft sound wouldn't wake her. But if not—

The door opened. Beth blinked at him, one of his reference books tucked in the crook of her arm. Her "I don't do mornings" sleep shirt had slid down one shoulder, giving her a delightfully rumpled look.

"Simon? It's after midnight."

"I know it's late. But, I thought, if you weren't asleep yet..." He trailed off, not sure what he'd thought, only knowing he'd had to be with her.

"Come in." She stepped away from the door, and retreated to her bed. From the way the covers were turned down and the pillows were mounded against the headboard, he guessed that she'd been reading in bed when he disturbed her.

Simon grabbed the spindly chair from in front of the vanity and drew it over beside the bed, then sat down in it. He didn't dare trust himself to share those rumpled covers with Beth.

"So what was so urgent that it couldn't wait until morning?" she asked.

"I heard from Lydia."

"Was that who called? But the phone rang an hour ago. Have you been talking to her all this time?"

"No. Our conversation was fairly short. She's still in California."

Beth put the reference book on the nightstand, and pulled the covers over her legs, settling into her pile of pillows. "I sense this explanation is going to take a while."

"She had airplane trouble."

"Okay, so maybe it won't take that long." Beth flashed a grin. "What time is her plane arriving tomorrow?"

"She's not sure if she'll be able to make it tomorrow."

Beth's eyes widened. "But tomorrow's Friday. She has to get back tomorrow. Doesn't she?"

"She doesn't know when she'll be able to get here. We have to assume she won't make it in time, and plan accordingly." Simon closed his eyes, unwilling to look at Beth's reaction as he said, "I have to prepare to do the ritual alone."

"What about Carlos and Esperanza, your back ups?"

"Can't make it. There was a huge storm in South America, and the airports won't be open for commercial traffic until Saturday evening."

"Isn't there anyone else?"

"No. Andrew can't get here any faster than Lydia can. That's it for people in this hemisphere. Even if I called one of the other Guardians now, they'd have to travel nonstop to get here from Europe or Asia. And when they did arrive, they'd be so jet lagged, they'd be worthless."

"But the ritual you created requires two people."

Simon sighed, a soul-deep weariness at the thought of all the work and long nights that had gone into creating the first ritual, and knowing he had to do it all again. "I'll just have to rewrite it for one."

When Beth didn't answer, he opened his eyes. She was staring into the distance with a slight frown of concentration.

"Can you?" she asked softly. "You told me that the binding magic and the attack magic come from completely different bases. Can you really do both at once?"

He didn't want to admit it, but the answer was no. The death of Andrew's apprentice, Scott, had proved that. Although Andrew would never know exactly what had gone wrong, he'd been moving to intercept and disperse a second elemental that had been attracted by the energy of his apprentice's astral battle. He surmised that his apprentice had also seen the second elemental and tried to defend himself before he'd completely released his attack spell against the first elemental. The apprentice had severed his spirit's connection to his body, killing him instantly. But Beth was worried enough. Simon didn't want to upset her further.

"A single magician can't do both at the same time, no. The power of the magic rests on the strength of the magician's will, and trying to do multiple things at the same time fragments the will. But the magic can be layered. Create a strong, lasting containment spell. Then switch to battle magic."

"You make it sound easy."

"In concept, it is." Simon shrugged, and noticed the building tension in his neck and shoulders. He breathed deeply, focusing his attention on relaxing the muscles and releasing the tension.

"In concept?" Beth prodded. "What about in execution?"

"The trick is getting the percentages right. Some of the magician's power is used up to perform the protection spells, and the remainder is directed into the battle magic. Too little, and the protection will fail. Too much, and the attack will fail."

In either case, the magician would die. But Simon would rather err on the side of protection. That way, even if the entity was not driven back to its home dimension, it would be prevented from entering the material plane. If done correctly, the restraint would last long enough for another Guardian to arrive. Simon would be sure to leave detailed notes regarding both rituals he had crafted, so that the replacement Guardian could finish the job.

"Simon?" A note of fear trembled in Beth's voice. "Why are you looking at me like that?"

He blinked. "Like what?"

"Like you were never going to..." Beth's face paled. Her eyes grew large, and she clutched the coverlet with white fingers. "You don't think you can do it."

Simon bit his lip. He wouldn't lie to her. But he couldn't say the words out loud. He didn't dare. Words had power, and this was one thought that didn't need any more strength than it already possessed.

"Beth, I—" He swallowed. What could he say except the truth? "I don't want to be alone right now."

She folded back the bedclothes in mute invitation. He pulled off his shoes and stood, hesitating with one hand at his belt. He longed to lose himself inside Beth, burning away his fears and worries in a blaze of passion. He wanted to be as close to her as physically, emotionally, and mentally possible. But the entity could use that very closeness to attack her.

"I won't risk your life," he insisted. "But I don't have the strength to stay away from you unless you help me."

She nodded. "No sex. I understand. But I can still hold you."

"Yes." Simon's voice was a husky whisper. He quickly stripped to his shorts and crawled into Beth's bed.

She pulled the covers over them to form a cocoon of darkness, and wrapped herself around Simon in a gentle embrace. He shivered, like a frostbite victim returning to warmth. Isolated terrors popped and fizzled in his brain like pinpricks of pain. He clutched her, and buried his face against her neck.

Beth stroked his back and ran her fingers through his hair, crooning low, soothing noises that he felt more than heard. Slowly, his shivers abated.

She sensed the change, and rubbed her cheek against his head, whispering into his ear, "You're not alone. I'll do anything I can to help you. We'll find the right spell, and you will succeed. I believe in you."

Simon let out his breath in a ragged sigh, and felt the tension drain from his body. Words had power. Beth believed in him. Somehow, he'd find a way to defeat the entity.

* * * * *

The next morning, Simon woke to the delightful sensation of cuddling a sleeping Beth in his arms. He snuggled closer, fitting his body to hers, and nuzzled the soft skin of her neck below her ear.

"Good morning," he whispered. She answered with an inarticulate noise that could have meant anything or nothing at all. But she turned her head, exposing more of her neck to his lips, and wriggled her hips in clear invitation.

Simon caught her around the waist with his free arm, and pulled her tight against his hardening erection. He wouldn't endanger her with sex, but that didn't mean he couldn't give her pleasure. His other arm was mostly pinned by her weight, but he shifted it enough to be able to brush his thumb over her breast in a light caress.

Beth moaned and arched into his touch.

Stroking, rubbing and tweaking her breast and sensitive nipple with his one hand, Simon slid his other hand beneath the hem of her sleep shirt and inside her panties. Cupping her heat, he rocked his hand against her. He licked and kissed her neck, then used his teeth to pull Beth's sleep shirt over her shoulder, exploring the newly exposed territory with wet, openmouthed kisses.

She twined the fingers of one hand over his, pressing his palm more firmly against her breast as she arched her chest into his touch. She reached up and buried her other hand in his hair, urging him to even more daring explorations with his mouth, all the time rocking her hips in time with the motion of his hand between her legs.

Simon's fingertips brushed wet flesh, and Beth whimpered. He thrust two fingers inside her. She gasped, clutching him, her hands fisting until he feared she'd rip a chunk of hair out of his head. Then she started moving again, rocking faster. He had no time for subtlety or finesse, his panting breath as rough and ragged as hers as he plundered her eager flesh with striving fingers, rubbing his hard length against the soft cleavage bucking against him. She started to tremble, her escalating cries building from a soft gasp to a full-throated shout.

Simon gasped as his own release left him breathless. He held her, pressed close, as their breathing returned to normal.

Beth sighed in contentment and stretched. "Much better than an alarm clock."

"Much."

She rolled to face him, her face contorting in an expression of disgust as she encountered the results of his passion. "I guess I'm doing laundry while you're at work today."

Simon shook his head. "I'm not going to the university today. I have too much to do to prepare for tomorrow's ritual."

"But what about your classes?"

"I'll call in sick. I've got the quizzes on file for the undergraduate survey of religions class. Any TA can give them. And the graduate classes can have discussion groups about their reading assignments, with a joint class report."

Although he stated the plans with confidence for Beth's sake, forcing himself to act as if he believed the weekend held no danger, he took comfort from the ordinary concerns of class assignments and quiz grading. They gave him a simple, straightforward focus for the nervous doubts about the future churning through his mind. Yet, while he spoke with surety of reviewing the graduate students' report at the next class, his imagination pictured his students gathered in somber knots around his closed casket.

Simon tightened his hold on Beth, and banished the negative image from his thoughts. He didn't want to die. That meant the ritual had to succeed. He had to have faith in himself and his abilities. Beth was counting on him.

Regretfully, he released her and got out of bed. He had a lot of research to do, to prepare for Saturday's showdown.

After a brief delay to shower, dress, and call the university, Simon closeted himself in his study and reviewed the notes Lydia had faxed him the night before. They raised more questions than they answered.

Andrew had categorized their foe as an elemental symbiote, a new categorization that was based mainly on hypothesis and interpolation. According to Andrew's theories, the original elemental had combined its power and desires with a human's thoughts and memories, so that it was able to understand the workings of human society at a much greater level of detail than any previous elemental had achieved. Normally, they weren't interested in such things, and in fact lacked the capabilities to interact with the material world in any way that would allow them to gain that knowledge.

Andrew's assumptions had some traditional basis. Malicious elementals, at least the ones that did not immediately attack and destroy their victims, often made promises regarding future events and outcomes. The knowledge used to bargain for power and control was taken directly from the person with whom they were negotiating, as the elemental read the person's deepest fears and desires.

What was unusual in this instance was the level of detail that appeared to have nothing to do with a prospective victim's fears and desires. The entity was clearly aware of the Guardians' efforts to combat it, and was taking intricate, elaborate steps to negate those efforts. It was more like playing chess against a grand master than fighting a traditionally straightforward enemy. Whereas traditional battle magic called for weakening an opponent until it fled or could be destroyed completely, in the coming conflict, Simon was going to have to be alert for feints, bluffs and countermeasures completely outside the realm of his experience.

A tap on the door of his study broke Simon's circling thoughts. Beth poked her head inside.

"Simon? I thought you'd like to know. The Weather Channel is predicting that a huge storm will hit the Great Lakes this afternoon."

"It's going to hit Chicago?"

"It's going to hit everything. If Lydia's plane is delayed again, she's not getting through."

"Maybe they'll reroute her through another city." Simon glanced at his watch. He'd been lost in thought for hours. It was after ten, East coast time, which meant Lydia's 6AM flight should have left California.

He called Andrew, who confirmed that Lydia's plane had already departed. She should make it to Chicago before the storm.

Simon didn't believe it. Too much had already gone wrong.

* * * * *

Beth was distracting herself by making sandwiches when Simon came into the kitchen, looking for lunch. Her heart ached to see how tired and drawn he looked.

He stopped and stared at the pile beside her.

"How many people were you expecting to feed?" he asked.

"Just us."

Simon raised an eyebrow at the five sandwiches already on the plate, and the one in her hands. "You must be very hungry."

"I figured I'd save some time, and make sandwiches for dinner in advance." She sliced the sandwich before her into quarters, then added it to the pile. "I thought maybe you could use my help with the research."

"No, I told you this morning—"

"Eat, then talk." She waved him to the table, and set the plate piled with sandwiches in front of him.

He devoured a sandwich quarter in three bites, then quickly polished off a second while she filled glasses with water and got a second plate for herself.

Nibbling on a quarter of turkey and Swiss on whole wheat, she asked, "What have you found so far?"

"Andrew came through with a categorization for me to work with, so hopefully I know what to expect."

He turned his attention to another sandwich quarter, and Beth realized that was all he planned to say. She took a deep breath, and launched into her carefully rehearsed argument.

"I helped you with the original research. You said then that I'd saved you a lot of time, handling the copying and collating so you could do the in-depth study. Now more than ever, what you don't have is time."

Simon tossed his half-eaten sandwich to the table. It bounced, shedding bits of lettuce as it tumbled. "Never mind the time. More research won't help. What I need is more power."

She blinked, dismayed by the note of bitter defeat in his voice. "What do you mean?"

He closed his eyes, sighed, and scrubbed his hands over his face. Beth thought again how exhausted he looked. She was certain he hadn't looked like that when he woke her this morning. He'd learned something during his studies that had drained him of his earlier optimism.

"Forget it," he said, then picked up his discarded sandwich and resumed eating. His methodical chewing looked like the effort made by someone who knows he must eat, and who is forcing himself to do so with no pleasure or desire for food.

"Simon." Beth used the I-will-have-an-answer-and-it-will-be-the-truth voice she'd perfected during her divorce. "What did you learn this morning?"

From the rigid set of his shoulders, she thought at first that he'd insist it was nothing, or retreat behind the time honored defense of "you wouldn't understand." Then his shoulders bent, and he looked at her through eyes flat with no expression.

"I can't do this alone. I don't have the power. I thought I could, using tools that were already charged to supplement my own energy. But Andrew's information changes everything. It will take most of my skill just to handle the protections. I'll have to use all my remaining energy to launch an attack."

Beth frowned in confusion. He'd said he couldn't do it. But it sounded like he could, as long as he got the entity with his first attack. After that, he wouldn't have any energy left for a second attack.

Then she remembered one of the passages she'd transcribed, that explained the source of magical power.

She clutched the table and stared at him in horror. "When you said 'all' did you mean —"

"I meant all."

All his magical energy. His life energy. She realized he was planning on a suicide attack.

Outrage replaced horror. "You can't be sure of that."

"Actually, I can. Lydia warned me, repeatedly, of the consequences if I fought the entity alone."

Beth hated Lydia in that moment. If not for her negativity, Simon might still be searching for an answer, instead of giving up. Well, she didn't believe Lydia, and she wouldn't allow Simon to quit while there was still a chance. They'd find a way, together.

"Then don't fight it alone. Let me help." The suggestion was out of her mouth before she consciously thought it, but as soon as she heard the words, she knew they were true.

"Out of the question."

"Why?"

"I refuse to allow —"

Beth shoved herself away from the table. "You don't have that right. I'm the only one who decides what I do with my life. And I've decided to help you. Your only choice is to accept that help and possibly defeat this thing, or waste my help, possibly killing us both."

He shook his head. "You don't understand."

"Then make me understand."

They glared at each other across the vast divide of the kitchen table. Then Simon's expression softened, and his voice dropped to a husky whisper.

"The only thing getting me through this is knowing you'll be safe. Despite the mistakes I've made so far, I can shield and protect you from the entity, and hold it off long enough for the other Guardians to get here."

A cold chill wrapped itself around Beth's heart. "But how much will that protection cost? If you didn't have to protect me, would you still have enough energy to survive attacking this thing?"

"Probably not."

"Probably?"

"It doesn't matter, because I won't abandon you. What good is my survival, if I give you to the entity to achieve it?"

Beth blinked, caught off guard by his unusual phrasing, and instinctively sensing the importance. "Give me to the entity?"

"It's trying to instantiate. If it can find a ready made host, that makes its task much easier."

"That's why you needed two people. Lydia was supposed to be the bait."

"Actually, I was supposed to be the bait, since I've got the better defensive magic. She was going to attack it."

Beth breathed deeply, stiffened her shoulders, clenched her fists, and did everything else she could think of to anchor her courage. Even so, she had to force her words out of fear numbed lips. "I can be the bait. That way you'll have enough energy to attack and defeat it."

"No. It's too risky."

"Damn it, Simon. Shut up and think!"

His eyes widened, and he jerked back from the table in surprise. Beth took advantage of the brief moment to compose her thoughts, then launched her argument. If there was one thing she'd learned from marriage to a lawyer, it was how to craft a compelling argument.

"Henry Ford once said that if you think you can or you think you can't, either way, you're right. You yourself have told me numerous times that magic isn't so much about words and gestures, as it is about focusing your will, harnessing your belief. I believe you can succeed. We can succeed. But you're the trained magician. You're the one who has to find a way to harness that belief and create magic out of it."

A spark of hope kindled in his eyes, although his expression remained bleak. "You have no idea what we're up against."

Beth grinned. He'd said "we."

"Then tell me. Make me understand. Together, we'll find a way to beat it."

CHAPTER EIGHTEEN

Simon couldn't believe how foolish he'd been, wasting the morning in solitary study. With Beth's help, the afternoon passed quickly, and they soon had the rudiments of a plan sketched out. Saturday morning, he'd fill a magically prepared vessel with power he could call upon to attack the entity during their confrontation. That way, he'd have time to recover his strength, with Beth's help, before casting his protective spells and engaging the entity in the afternoon.

He traded a grin with Beth. "I think it will work. But I need to run this by Andrew. He's the expert."

"But you said before he specialized in fire elementals."

"He also knows more about...uh...I wanted his advice about the energy restoration."

"I'd think you'd be an expert by now. Don't you usually restore your power after you do magic?"

"Not this quickly. I meditate, and do other rituals to focus my energy. It takes anywhere from a week to a month to build myself back up to full strength."

Beth's stared at him. "But you'll only have a few hours."

Simon felt his face heating, and glanced away. "There have been occasions when I've gotten my strength back faster."

"How?"

"Once, actually. The first time we made love."

He risked a look at her. A soft smile floated on her lips, and her eyes were vague and out of focus. Her memory of that night appeared to be a happy one. Then her mouth turned down in a frown and her eyes narrowed. Did she think he'd slept with her only to use her as a magical battery recharger?

"I didn't intend for that to happen," Simon rushed to reassure her. "I just wanted to make you happy. The energy restoration was an unexpected side effect."

"It's only happened that once?"

"We only did a Tantric ritual that once. That's what I'm checking with Andrew."

Beth nodded. "Call him."

Simon studied Beth surreptitiously while he punched in Andrew's phone number. She didn't seem as upset as he'd first feared. He'd avoided Tantric rituals since that night, not wanting to take mystical advantage of her, but in retrospect, perhaps he'd been overly cautious. Despite the gravity of their current situation, his body reacted to the memory of being held at the center of a flood of energy as Beth had experienced wave after wave of pleasure.

The phone rang, and he cleared his suddenly dry throat.

"Hello?" Andrew answered.

"Andrew, it's Simon."

"You got Lydia's message?"

A sudden chill drove all pleasant memories out of his mind. "What message?"

"She left it on your phone mail."

"I called in sick today."

Andrew's voice sharpened. "You're sick?"

"No. I used the time to put together a backup plan, in case she can't get here. Beth and I have been so busy, I completely forgot to check the Weather Channel for updates on the storm."

"Well, it hit. Hard. They had to close the airport for a few hours. Her plane landed before they closed it, but when they reopened it, only the big jets were cleared to take off. Her connecting flight was on one of those little prop planes, and the weather was still too rough for those. They couldn't tell her whether or not tomorrow's flights would be canceled, too, so she decided not to wait. She rented a car, and is driving."

"From Chicago?" he yelped.

Beth half-rose from her chair, no doubt alarmed by his tone, and Simon forced himself not to shout.

"Does she have any idea how far that is?"

"About twelve hours, I believe she said. Allowing for the time change, reduced speed because of weather, and a brief overnight rest stop, she expects to arrive at your doorstep by three o'clock tomorrow afternoon."

Simon's fingers tightened around the phone. Lydia had put her own backup plans in place. He hoped her plans were more successful than any of their other efforts had been, and that she would get here in time to fight the entity. Then Beth could remain safely away from the battle.

"But if you didn't call about Lydia's message, why did you call?" Andrew asked.

"I had a question about Tantra."

"Yes?" Andrew infused the single word with a richness of anticipation.

"I just wondered if it always restores a magician's magical energies."

"Done correctly, and with the right person, yes. As long as you don't rely on the technique too frequently."

"Thanks. But I hope I won't need it, now."

Simon smiled as he hung up the phone.

"Good news?" Beth asked.

"Yes and no. Lydia's plane made it to Chicago. She rented a car, and is on her way now."

"Why'd she leave a message with Andrew? She should have had the decency to call you herself."

"She did. She left a message on my office phone mail."

"Really?" Beth tried but couldn't quite achieve a look of wide eyed innocence. "You'd think a great fortune teller like her would know you were home today."

He shrugged. "She's probably conserving her power, like I am, and wouldn't waste her energy on something so trivial as finding out whether I was at home or at work."

Surely she would have tried to read the future regarding her flight, though. Yet Andrew had made it sound like she'd relied on the airline personnel for information rather than an arcane source. The entity might still be interfering with her divinatory ability. In which case, she might not know for sure that she'd get here by three o'clock tomorrow. That might be no more than the same sort of estimate anyone could put together before embarking upon a trip.

"I'd better check her message." He dialed into the University's voice mail system, and retrieved his messages. Skipping to the end of one about a department meeting next week, and the rambling comments of the TA they'd found to administer the quiz to his undergrads, he located Lydia's message.

"Simon, I'm calling from Chicago. My connecting flight is grounded, and no one knows if the little planes will be allowed out tomorrow, least of all me. The interference in my readings has gotten to the point where I'm almost as inept as you."

"Low blow, Lydia," he muttered.

"The attendants at the airline counter informed me that I can replace the two hour plane trip with a twelve hour car ride. Given the weather, and my need to sleep if I'm to be in any shape to work magic when I arrive, I'm doubling that estimate. Rather than wait to see what tomorrow holds, I'm leaving now. Mostly because if I wait, all the cars will be rented. I'll see you tomorrow. Remember, do not, under any circumstances, try to fight the entity alone. Wait for me."

He played the message a second time, just in case he'd missed something. Then he hung up.

Beth was watching him, her face lined with concern. "Bad news, this time?"

"The entity is messing with her ability to read the future. She's guessing, just like we are. She expects to be here tomorrow afternoon, but she isn't sure. We can't take that chance." Simon sighed, and picked up his pen and the pad already filled with his notes. "We have to assume we'll be on our own."

"Then we'd better get to bed early and rest up. We've got a big day ahead of us tomorrow." She tilted her head, flashing him a look he could only describe as coy. "Unless you need to build up your magical powers before you cast your first spell."

His pulse sped up just thinking about her offer, but he forced himself to remember the danger to her if the connection between them grew too strong too early. "No. I'm already at full strength."

He hesitated, then added, "But we could still share a bed tonight."

Her teasing manner instantly disappeared. "Because the entity's also almost at full strength, and might attack first thing in the morning?"

"There's a slim chance of that." Simon stepped around the desk and folded Beth in his arms. "But it's a certainty that I'd be lonely without you."

Beth leaned back in his embrace so that she could smile up at him. "We can't have that. Never that."

Bending his head, Simon kissed her. A chaste kiss, that risked no mingling of essences. He wanted so much more, but he could wait. It looked like he was going to survive tomorrow's battle. He'd have plenty of time with Beth.

* * * * *

The telephone shrilled, shattering the pre-dawn quiet. Simon groaned and fumbled for the receiver, while Beth pulled a pillow over her head.

"H'lo," he mumbled.

"Am I speaking to Simon Parkes?" a man asked.

"Yes."

"This is Robert Forester from the Emergency Room at Portside Hospital. I'm calling on behalf of Ms. Lydia Hammond-Jarrar."

Simon bolted upright. "Is she all right?"

"She's in stable condition."

"Then why isn't she calling?"

"A few hours ago, Ms. Hammond-Jarrar's car went off the road into a ditch. When the ambulance brought her in, she kept repeating this number, insisting that we contact you."

"But she's okay?"

"She experienced loss of consciousness and blurred vision. The doctors suspect a concussion, but they're doing a CAT scan now to rule out more serious injury. She'll need to stay in the hospital for at least the next twenty-four hours."

"Can I speak with her?"

"Not while she's having the CAT scan. When she gets out, she'll be transferred to a private room, where she'll have a phone. I don't show a room assigned to her yet, so I can't give you the number. You can call information in a while and they'll be able to help you."

"What's their phone number?" Simon located the pen and paper he kept beside the phone. He copied down the number and repeated it, to make sure he had it written correctly. Then he asked, "When will she be in her room?"

The man hesitated. "It's hard to say. At least another half an hour, maybe as long as two hours. Do you have any other questions?"

"Just one. Where's Portside?"

"Ohio, a little over half an hour east of Cleveland."

"Thanks."

Simon hung up, then stared at the phone, lost in thought. Thank God Lydia had only suffered a concussion. The combination of a storm, late night, unfamiliar roads, and driving on the wrong side could have proven fatal.

But it also meant there was no way she could help him fight the entity. Even if the doctors released her early and she managed to find some way of getting here, she couldn't work magic with a concussion.

He had no choice. He'd have to use Beth as his bait. Nothing else could be allowed to go wrong.

Slipping quietly out of bed, so as not to disturb Beth's sleep, he headed downstairs to his study. He could use the phone there to call Andrew.

He dialed Andrew on the secure line, then stared at the pale gray square of window until his mentor finally answered the phone.

"Do you have any idea what time it is?" Andrew snarled.

"No. I left my watch by my bed," Simon answered truthfully.

As he expected, the quiet answer derailed Andrew's wrath. "Simon? What are you doing calling at this hour?"

"I just got a call from a hospital in Ohio. Lydia was in a car accident. She's okay. But she hit her head. They think it's just a concussion, but they're giving her a CAT scan to be sure."

Andrew absorbed this news in silence, then said, "You've called Esperanza for help?"

"They also had a storm, but theirs did more damage. She'll be here Sunday."

"One day too late."

"But soon enough to finish what I start if I can't."

"Damn it all, Simon. If I didn't have to watch over Heather, I'd be there to help you."

"Thanks. But considering your gift helps elementals cross the boundary into our world, and we're trying to keep this one out..." Simon's attempt at lightheartedness fizzled. "Besides, I won't be doing this alone. Beth is helping me."

"Beth? She's less of a Guardian than Heather!"

"But she loves me."

Andrew's voice turned cold. "What are you planning, Simon?"

"Blood magic," he whispered.

Andrew's quick inhalation carried clearly across the phone line.

"We've worked it all out," Simon hurried to explain. "I'm going to channel most of my power into a vessel, storing it to use in my attack against the entity."

"That's why you asked about Tantra."

"Yes. Beth will help me recharge my energy, then I'll cast the best protection spell I can, keeping it focused and specific to the entity so that I don't waste power needlessly. My remaining power and the previously stored power will be enough to fuel the attack against the entity."

"And how are you planning on getting the entity to show up inside your circle so you can attack it?"

Simon hesitated, not wanting to speak his plan out loud. It terrified him. He feared that if he thought about it too much, he'd never go through with it. Then the entity would win. Once it burst through onto the material plane, many Guardians' lives would be forfeit to chain it again. And who knew how many innocents it would destroy before they succeeded. He had no choice.

"That's where the blood magic comes in. By mixing her blood and mine, in the vessel holding my banked power, I'll draw her life force out of her body, and encourage the entity to step into the waiting host."

"So you'll attack Beth."

Simon bit his lip. Bowing his head, he struggled to breathe. Yes. He planned to attack Beth with deadly force. There was no other way.

* * * * *

Beth ripped open the bag of Halloween candy, sending fun-sized Snickers bars exploding through the kitchen like tiny missiles. One struck a pot behind her with a sharp gong, and she jumped at the unexpected noise, spinning to see what was behind her.

It was only candy, the brown and gold wrappers stark against the white kitchen counters, table and floor. So many candies. She glanced down, and noticed that she clutched the two halves of the bag in white-knuckled fists.

Bending her head, she began to laugh, a strangled noise that sounded as much like tears as it did like merriment. She couldn't even help Simon get the candy ready for the trick-or-treaters. How could she possibly help him defeat the evil and far too powerful creature he faced?

His soft voice rose up in memory, replaying the conversation they'd had this morning. She'd woken to find him missing from the bed they'd shared, and discovered him in the kitchen, drinking another of his vile brews.

"Good morning," she had greeted him.

"Not particularly. And I suspect the day will only get worse."

Simon had set his mug on the counter, and gestured to the table. When Beth hesitantly took a seat, he'd told her of Lydia's accident. They would have to use the backup plan. That's when he explained the details of the magic involved.

"You need to be certain, in your heart, that you are willing to do this," he'd warned her. "More, you need to be willing to fail. Your conviction must be strong enough so that, even if there were ninety-nine chances out of a hundred that you would die, you would still make the attempt."

Beth had gazed at him in horror. "Are our chances really that bad?"

He'd folded her hands in his, and gently kissed her trapped fingers. "Would it matter?"

She'd considered what she knew of the entity. Even with its power restrained to just a fraction of its native force, there were two students dead, another psychologically scarred, and who knew how many injured or killed by the storm. Not to mention the hideously mutilated animals that could all too easily lead to hideously mutilated people if the entity had its way. It could not be allowed to succeed.

"One chance in a hundred or one chance in a million, if there's any chance at all, we've got to try," she'd told Simon.

But now, staring at the candy scattered around the kitchen, Beth wondered if, when the time came, she'd have the courage to go through with it. Could she really slit open her own flesh with Simon's knife, and watch as her life drained away into an enchanted cup? What if her hands shook, as they were shaking now? She might slash her veins so deeply that, even if the magic succeeded, she could not be healed. Or she might knock over the cup, depriving Simon of the power he needed to defeat the entity.

Beth braced her palms on the table and breathed deeply. She had to trust Simon. He would not let her fail.

Feeling once more composed, she began picking up candies and putting them in the large glass bowl. The door bell rang, and she dropped the bowl with a gasp. The heavy glass dented the wooden table, but did not break.

Picking up the candy bowl, she went to the front door and opened it, expecting to see a concerned parent leading a costumed toddler. Instead, a painfully thin college student stood on the flagstone porch.

"Is Heather here?" he asked.

Beth blinked, recognizing the student's voice but temporarily unable to place his face. A wave of shock drove her a full step backwards, into the foyer. It was Heather's friend

Keith, but at least ten, maybe twenty pounds thinner than he had been when she'd seen him last week.

His skin stretched over his chin and cheekbones so tightly, she feared his bones would poke right through. The skin itself was pale and papery looking, with deep indigo shadows beneath his eyes. His jeans were cinched around his waist in a mass of folded denim, and his belt showed three new holes inexpertly punched through the leather.

"My God, Keith!"

The boy shook his head, wavering on unsteady legs. "I've looked everywhere for her. But no one knows where she is. This was my last hope."

Beth hesitated, wondering what Keith would do if she admitted that Heather was in California. He'd been irrational before. He might try to follow Heather across the country, when he looked like he'd barely make it as far as the airport. Beth didn't dare risk him running. The boy needed help. Now.

Reaching through the open doorway, she grabbed Keith's wrist. Her fingers closed completely around the bones with plenty of room to spare. She pulled him forward.

"Come inside."

Keith stumbled into the foyer. He swayed for a moment on unsteady feet, then his eyes rolled back and he crumpled to the floor.

Beth stared at the student sprawled limply across the black and white marble. Simon would know what to do, but he was engaged in the first part of his ritual, and couldn't be disturbed.

She bit her lip. Common sense said that she should call an ambulance, and have Keith taken to the hospital. But while Simon had reassured her that the sound of the doorbell could not penetrate his workroom, surely an ambulance siren would. That would be a disaster.

Maybe she could drag Keith out to Simon's car, and drive him to the hospital herself? But they'd have all sorts of questions she couldn't answer. She didn't even know what Keith's last name was. And who knew how long it would take before she could escape the hospital administration's red tape. She couldn't risk not being here when Simon needed her.

She closed the door and set the bowl of candy on the floor beside it. Keith's main problem, at least it had been when she'd spoken to him in the bookstore, was that he was afraid to go to sleep. Perhaps the best thing would simply be to let his exhausted body get the rest it needed. When he woke up, she would try to convince him to go to the hospital, or at least to call some of his friends to look after him.

The room Simon called the front parlor, and that Beth thought of as the music room because it contained Simon's stereo system, was the first room off the foyer in the house's public wing. She'd have to drag Keith maybe fifteen feet to the music room, and another ten to the couch. He was light. She could do that.

Grabbing Keith under the arms, she pulled him up and staggered backwards, dragging him after her, across the foyer and down the hall. She used her hip to swing the partially open door wide open, then dragged him into the music room. The thick fringe of an oriental carpet nearly tripped her, but she recovered her balance and staggered onward, the carpet bunching in front of Keith's dragging heels.

Finally, the back of her calves hit the sofa and she collapsed onto the cushions, Keith sprawled bonelessly on top of her. She wriggled her way out from underneath him, then swung his legs up and arranged him lengthwise on the sofa, one of the plump throw pillows beneath his head.

Alarmed by his complete lack of movement, she leaned down and checked to make sure he was still breathing. He was. She'd learned the rudiments of first aid during her crisscrossing travels across the countryside, and did her best to check him over. He didn't appear sick so much as exhausted.

"Sleep," she whispered. "That's what you need."

She closed the door softly on her way out, although if being dragged through the house hadn't wakened him, she doubted the click of a door would.

Retrieving her candy bowl from the foyer, she went back to the kitchen. First, she'd gather up the rest of the spilled candies, and set the bowl out for the trick-or-treaters. Then she'd make a pile of sandwiches for Keith to eat when he finally awoke.

Beth gave a rueful smile. As she'd learned yesterday, sandwich making was a wonderful way to distract yourself from things you'd rather not think about. Like the end of the world.

CHAPTER NINETEEN

Simon banished the protective circle, gasping as the grounded energy returned to him. In his weakened state, even that small amount made a tremendous difference. But he'd done it. Virtually all of his free power was contained in the glowing silver cup sitting in the center of the room, waiting for the moment when it could be used against the entity.

He staggered to the wall, where he'd left a pile of supplies. First, he glanced at the watch. Just past noon, right on schedule. Then he uncapped the thermos bottle full of Gatorade and chugged half of it. Closing his eyes, he sighed in satisfaction, half convinced that he could feel all the dehydrated and depleted cells in his body plumping up with nutrients.

More slowly, he drank from a second thermos of plain water, then alternated sips until he had finished the contents of both thermoses. He felt almost human. If that human had been run over by a truck, that is.

Leaning against the false wall, he allowed his weight to slowly open the concealed door to his study. The bookcase swung into the room, revealing Beth sitting at his desk, reading, a stack of books open before her. She sprang to her feet and rushed toward him.

"Simon! How are you? Did it work?"

He smiled, wrapping one arm around her shoulders. "Beth. Tired. Yes."

He held her a moment longer in what was half loving embrace and half desperate need for support. Her arm settled around his waist, the plush cotton of her shirt sleeve rasping over the sweaty silk of his robe.

"I need a shower before the next ritual," he said softly. "Will you join me?"

"Absolutely!"

"Good, because I don't think I can make it upstairs without your help."

As they made their slow, laborious way upstairs to the bathroom, Simon asked, "What were you reading?"

"I went back through all the cross-references we used, and read the material around the quoted parts. I wanted to get a better picture of what we're doing."

"I doubt that was very helpful."

"No." They climbed another few steps in silence, then she asked, "Has anyone ever tried this before?"

"Exactly what we're doing? Not among the Guardians. That doesn't mean it hasn't been done."

"But the Guardians are the experts on magic, aren't they?"

Simon sighed, idly wondering when the staircase had grown so long, then turned his attention back to Beth. "That's precisely why this has never been tried. Traditionally, Guardians do not reveal the secret of their existence to others. You're the first mundane to consciously assist in a ritual. But since you lack the occult discipline to focus your energy, or combine your energy with mine in a working, we're forced to rely on brute strength."

He smiled at her, and with his fingertips, brushed away her trace of a frown. "You'll do fine. We both will."

Beth nodded, then focused on getting him down the hall to the grand bathroom. His obvious weakness terrified her. He'd said that making love to her on their first date had restored his energy, but he hadn't started off in such poor condition. What if making love only restored a limited amount of strength? He might not be able to finish the fight against the entity.

She opened the door to the bathroom, then blocked the doorway with her arm. Turning to confront Simon, she said, "I want you to promise me something. When the time comes for the big magic, if you're not strong enough, don't try to fight the entity. Throw everything into your defense and wait for reinforcements."

"That was always my intent." His smile seemed sad, and not at all encouraging. It was the same sort of look he'd had when he'd planned on a suicide attack.

She caught her breath. Not a suicide attack, but a suicide defense. Too late, she realized she should not have said to throw "everything" into his defense. Before she could correct herself, he reached out and pressed a clove-scented fingertip lightly against her lips.

"Words and thoughts have power. Let us speak as if we shall succeed, so that we believe we shall succeed."

Mutely, she nodded.

"Good. Our shower awaits."

She followed him into the bathroom, memory teasing her with sense impressions of that first time they'd made love in the moist heat of the sauna and Jacuzzi. By contrast, the air today was cool and dry.

Simon reached inside the shower stall and started the flow of water. Needles of water struck the tiled walls with audible pings.

He shrugged off his robe, letting it fall to the floor in a puddle of blue silk. He pointed at a stack of towels on the small table. "I set aside towels and robes for us both this morning, so we wouldn't waste time this afternoon."

Recalled to the urgency of their task, Beth quickly stripped off her clothes, and followed Simon into the shower. When the first icy stream hit her, she yelped in surprise.

Before she could protest the temperature, Simon had rinsed his hair, face, and body, then turned off the taps.

He grinned, some of his normal bounce restored. "Well, if it was warm, we might spend too long in the shower, and waste some of our sexual energies."

She blushed, wondering if her reaction to their remembered lovemaking had been obvious. "Never a waste, Simon. Not with you."

He leaned forward and kissed her, the lightest of brushes against her lips, then opened the shower door. "After you."

They dressed in matching silk robes, hers a deep emerald green, and his an orange gold. Beth breathed deeply, and followed him from the room.

Simon's energy flagged before they reached the study, and Beth wrapped his arm around her shoulders again to support him the rest of the way. Once inside Simon's secret workroom, she let go of him to wrestle the book case into position. It wasn't perfectly closed, but he nodded that it was good enough.

Taking her hands in his, he kissed the fingers of each, then clasped them in front of his heart while he looked into her eyes. "Beth, I'm not doing this just because it will help me recover my energy. If one of us doesn't make it—"

"You said not to speak like that!"

He nodded, accepting her chastisement, then continued with what he'd started to say. "But if that happens, I want this to be our last, beautiful memory."

Beth blinked the mist out of her eyes. "Okay. We'll make a beautiful memory. Then we'll make another one tomorrow."

Simon smiled, and gestured to where two rounded pillows, one green and one gold, waited on a length of red silk. "I was afraid the marble floor would be too hard for you."

A strangled laugh escaped her. The comfort of the floor was the least of their concerns. That he'd troubled to think of it at all just proved his love for her.

She sat down cross-legged on the green pillow, and waited while he cast a basic circle of protection around them.

"The house is warded, as is this room, but so close to Halloween, we don't dare take chances."

Worry spiked through her. Gently, she said, "Simon, today is Halloween."

"According to the calendar, yes. But the actual parting of the veils won't happen until after sundown."

He joined her, taking his seat on the golden pillow. "Are you ready?"

Beth took a deep breath, stilled the inner voice that insisted she had no business getting involved in something like this and should run as far and fast as she could, and looked into his serious gray/green eyes. They shone with dedication, but also with love.

"I'm ready."

"Okay. We're going to start on the floor." Simon undid the belt of his robe, pulling the sides apart so that his shower-dampened body was exposed to her. He sat on the red silk, his legs spread wide apart, with his hands braced behind himself.

Beth fumbled with her belt, then pulled open her own robe. She flipped the silk behind her like a tail to get it out of the way as she sat between Simon's legs, her calves bracketing his hips. Leaning back on her hands, she tilted her hips, pressing Simon's warmth against the very edge of her opening.

Their gazes locked.

"I love you," he whispered.

"I love you, too."

He waited a moment longer, staring into her eyes, then began speaking softly. "You are woman, the power of the universe. All life, all energy, flows from you. You are the sun, whose light guides trees and flowers to grow."

As he spoke, and their bodies remained immobile, she felt a growing warmth where he rested against her. She wanted to move forward, closer, so that he could slide inside her. But instead she waited, motionless, and allowed the energy to build.

"Feel the energy pulsing within you," he told her. "Feel it reaching, strong and powerful."

Her nipples tightened, her breasts jutting forward. Inside her, the tiny bud that longed for his caress swelled to aching tenderness. Each pulse seemed to inflame it further, demanding satisfaction.

"Oh, yes. I feel it," she whispered.

"Fill yourself with the power. Stretch yourself with it."

She focused on the sensations building within her. Waves of heat radiated from her sensitized flesh, aching and insisting on satisfaction.

Then she became aware of Simon, a point of cold in the midst of her heat, suprisingly soft contrasted with her swollen rigidity.

His voice took on a husky quality. "Fill me with your power. Let your strength flow into me."

He moved, ever so slightly, slipping his tip between her heated folds. Her muscles clenched, drawing him in, filling him with her heat. Slowly, her power filled him, and he swelled as she swelled, pressing outward against her as she pressed inward against him.

They were perfectly balanced, neither needing to move as their energies pulsed in harmony. The room, the floor, even the robe she wore faded into the gray mists obscuring everything but Simon's voice, and the feel of their deep embrace.

"We are one," he said. "Our bodies and power joined. Our feet have tread the first step. Now, let us rise higher."

She sensed his gaze upon her, and with effort, opened her eyes. It was something of a shock to see the marble walls and floor surrounding her, instead of billowing mists and clouds.

Simon leaned forward, lifting his arms and reaching toward her. Instinctively, she echoed his movement, and his hands clasped her upper arms. Her fingers closed around his biceps.

They held the position a moment longer, then Simon arched backward, pulling her toward him. The angle of her hips shifted, pressing her down onto his strength. She gasped, and Simon immediately bent forward, reversing his movement.

"No, it's okay," she blurted, afraid he'd thought he'd hurt her. Then she realized he was bending her backwards, and she clutched his arms for support, while his strength pressed deeper inside of her.

"I know," he whispered, once again leaning backwards and pulling her after him. This time, she followed eagerly, then leaned back herself and pulled him on top of her. They swayed, back and forth, each gentle movement driving her harder onto him or driving him deeper into her.

Beth's blood pounded in her ears, her harsh breathing scraping her throat, as she rocked forward and back, faster and faster, until her body trembled out of her control. With a final gasp, she burst apart, lost to the brilliant colors shooting through the mist. Gradually, she realized Simon still held her, and they were still rocking, but slower, softer, more gently, until finally they came to rest.

"The second stair," he said. His voice sounded stronger.

She forced her eyes open, and blinked until she could focus on Simon's face. He was smiling, and seemed filled with a soft radiance.

"How are you feeling?" he asked, something in his tone telling her that this was just Simon asking Beth a question, not part of the ritual.

"Relaxed. Fabulous."

He chuckled softly. "I'm glad. But this next part gets a little tricky. You need to open your eyes."

Startled, she did, realizing she'd let her lids drift shut.

"Good. Now, first I'm going to pull you up so you're sitting on me. Then we're going to twist around, so that you're sitting across my lap."

Beth thought about this for a moment. It seemed like their arms and legs were too tangled for that to work, but she nodded agreement and hoped it would become clear.

Simon dropped his hands to her waist. Lifting her slightly, he scissored his legs closed, so she was sitting on his thighs.

That's when she realized that he was still inside her, although more relaxed than he had been.

"Can I really turn sideways?" she asked. "Won't that…um…hurt you?"

"Just follow my lead."

Slowly, he leaned back, until he was laying flat on the floor. Careful to move with equal patience, she swung her leg up and across his prone body, then continued turning, until she was sitting across him. Simon sat up again, and braced one hand against the floor.

"Put your hand by mine," he told her. She did, and he wrapped his other hand firmly around her waist. "Now, we lay down."

Like a tower of blocks toppling in slow motion, they gradually fell toward their braced hands, until she was flat on her back, and he lay on his side, facing her. The hands they'd used to control their descent were now linked together, fingers intertwined. Her legs bent at the knees, forming an arch for his legs to pass under. And still, miraculously, they remained joined.

"Now, you can close your eyes," he said softly.

With his free hand, Simon adjusted his robe, covering Beth's legs so that she would not catch a chill. When he had arranged them to his satisfaction, he slipped his hand through the opening at the front of her robe.

She expected him to cup and caress her breast, but instead he curled his fingers around her waist and let his arm rest across her stomach. She waited a moment, but he didn't move any further.

"Aren't you going to do something?" she asked.

"I am."

She waited. Just when she'd given up on his ever elaborating, and was opening her mouth to ask another question, the hand holding hers tightened in a reassuring squeeze.

She heard the smile in his voice as he answered, "Don't think about 'making' love. The love already exists. Think about receiving it. Just close your eyes, relax, and feel how much I love you."

Obediently, she relaxed, letting her breathing slow, and focused on what she was feeling. Simon cocooned her with his body, radiating warmth and security along her side, around her waist, and under her thighs. The fine hairs on Simon's legs brushed the backs of her thighs, so different from his thick hair where they were still joined, or the soft fur along his arm where it rested across her middle. Soft layers of silk, warmed by the heat of their bodies, cushioned her back and floated against her legs.

She felt all of these things, but nothing that she could point to and call "love." Eyes closed, she listened to Simon's gentle breathing, and felt the steady beat of his heart through the pulse point at his wrist. Her lungs moved in and out in time with his breath, and her heart matched the rhythm thudding softly against her sensitized palm. They were one.

Her heart swelled with emotion, the recognition that here at last she had found her other half. A montage of memories cascaded over her, images of Simon and her working as a team, images of Simon caring for her, images of her caring for Simon, images of the thousand and one gestures and moments born of his feelings, bits and pieces that created a mosaic of love.

Beth trembled, overwhelmed with the joy and fulfillment surging through her. She needed to share these feelings with Simon, to flow into him as she knew he was flowing into her. If she didn't, she would burst!

Her fingers tightened their clasp around Simon's hand, fusing her palm to his. With her free hand, she reached down to stroke his thigh, needing to touch him and complete the circuit of awareness burning through her.

Simon squeezed her waist lightly, with his other hand returning the pressure of her entwined fingers.

"The third step is attained," he announced, his voice husky and not entirely steady. She wondered what revelation he'd experienced.

He seemed to consider their position for a moment, then released her hand and tightened his grip on her waist.

"Straighten your legs," he instructed. As soon as she lifted her feet from the floor, he pulled them back up to a seated position. He held her a moment longer, cradled against his chest, then smiled gently and kissed her.

The kiss ended before it could be more than just a promise of future happiness.

"As you first contemplated then experienced your strength, you have contemplated your receptivity. I ask you now to experience it, and let me gift you with the power you have gifted to me."

Beth barely let him finish speaking before answering, "Yes."

Simon smiled. "Then you will have to stand up."

"I don't want to lose my connection to you."

"I will be with you again in just a moment. And the more important connection, of heart to heart and soul to soul, remains as strong as ever."

The truth of his words resonated within her. She brushed a kiss across his lips, and stood. A moment later, he stood as well.

"Kneel down," he instructed. "Then cross your forearms on the floor and lean forward to rest your head on them."

She tried to follow his directions. It was like a game of Twister, where the red circle she was supposed to put her hand on hovered just out of reach. Trusting that he wanted her to feel safe and loved, not stretched and overbalanced, she warned "This is incredibly awkward."

Simon's robe whispered past her bowed head, then he was pressing the green pillow beneath her folded arms. "Try this."

"Better. But still strange."

He considered a moment, then nudged her knees further apart, dropping her hips another few inches.

She sighed, settling into the position as if she'd been doing it all her life. Which she had. "If you'd called it the 'time to get up no just another five minutes' stretch, I'd have known exactly what you meant."

He chuckled softly, and knelt behind her, between her legs. "Then let me be your alarm clock."

Reaching under her robe, his hands found her hips. He pressed the heels of his palms into the flesh of her buttocks, rotating gently. She sighed again, relaxing into his touch.

He slid his hands down, to the very top of her thighs, and, using his fingertips, rubbed in tiny circles, from her hip bones around to her inner thighs. Beth was no longer interested in sleeping.

Simon's hands drifted upward, kneading her firmly. She wrapped her arms around her pillow and clutched it tightly. Simon's fingers continued their relentless drive north, until he reached the base of her spine.

He pressed one thumb on either side of her vertebrae. She groaned. Inching his thumbs upward, he pressed again, driving her head into the pillow and her buttocks back against him. The whisper light contact teased her, and with the next firm press of his thumbs, she was certain of what other part of Simon brushed against her. Twice more, he pressed downward with his thumbs, driving her back against him.

The heat between her legs that had never really dissipated grew to an inferno. Beth panted, the slightly inverted position making her lightheaded. Silk danced over her sensitized skin as Simon lifted the back of her robe. She could the feel the heat of him behind her. Her insides melted in liquid welcome, but he waited, his hands on her hips holding her just out of reach.

Slowly, ever so gently, he entered her, barely more than the tip of his length sliding inside her. She gasped, clutching, trying to pull him further in, but instead, he slipped out.

"Simon…"

"Hush, my love. Feel my strength, filling you."

He slipped his tip inside her again, the damp skin sliding easily over her hyper aware folds. Once more he pulled out, and slid his tip inside.

She whimpered. "But you're *not* filling me."

He pulled out again, but the tightening of his hands upon her hips alerted her that he was doing something different. He thrust deeply, pulling her hips back as he thrust.

She sighed. Yes. That was what she wanted. Before she could say so, he pulled out, then plunged back in.

"Simon!"

Gently, he teased her with another of the barely-there thrusts. "Yes, my love?"

He slipped out and again slid his tip within, his strong hands holding her where he wanted her to be. She trembled, every sense focused on that tender point of entry. He dipped inside her a third time.

She cried out. "Fill me, Simon. Please."

With aching slowness, he slid into her, inch by ravenous inch. Her whole body shook, wordlessly begging him to take up the familiar driving rhythm. His breathing was hoarse and ragged, but his movements never faltered as he slid equally slowly out of her.

She clenched her pillow, gripping the solid length of him as once again he edged slowly, deeply into her. With every gasp of her breath, she urged him, "Now. Now. Now."

He pulled out again. "Now," he agreed, as he slid inside, harder, hotter, and fuller than ever before. He paused, and she thought he'd begin pulling out again. The thought drove her over the edge, and she strained to not only keep him from leaving, but to draw him deeper inside.

"I give you my strength," he whispered. Then, pulling her back against him, he somehow stretched inside her, reaching deeper and deeper until he touched her where she'd never been touched before.

Beth screamed his name as she shattered.

When she regained her senses, he was still kneeling behind her, but she was vertical, her back against his chest and her head resting on his shoulder. And he still filled her.

"The fourth step is achieved," he whispered, his voice shaking with strain.

She let him guide her limp body backward as he shifted from kneeling, to kneeling on one knee, to sitting, then lying stretched out on the floor. Her calves flush against the red silk carpet, she straddled his hips, holding his strength deep inside her, while her upper body sprawled along his chest and her head and arms flowed over his shoulders to rest on the floor. His hands wrapped around her stomach, holding her securely.

They lay there, quietly breathing. Beth became aware of Simon's chest moving slowly up and down as his exhalations drifted across her shoulder, their moist warmth penetrating the thin silk of her robe.

The strength of his desire gradually faded, but that was as it should be. Everything was as it should be. They were one, sharing passion, strength and love.

When it seemed they had lain together long enough to impress this closeness forever upon their bodies and spirits, Simon tightened his hold on her in a gentle hug.

"The fifth stair is attained. You have gifted me with your strength. I have gifted you in return. We are one, sharing our gift. We come together even when we move apart."

Simon helped her to stand. "How are your legs feeling? No cramps?"

She closed her eyes and smiled as she breathed a sigh. "I feel wonderful."

"Good, because you're in charge for the last part."

Her eyes flew open. "But I don't know what to do!"

Simon gazed at her with complete faith and trust. "Love me."

Retrieving his golden pillow, he stretched out on the length of red silk. He opened his robe, presenting his body to her.

Beth opened her own robe, and knelt astride him. She let her hands drift over his chest, circling lightly around his nipples. Simon's eyes closed and he arched his back, sighing in pleasure.

She bent forward to lick and then kiss each of his nipples, then captured his hands and carried them up to her breasts. He kneaded and caressed them, then brushed his thumbs across her pebbled nipples. She shuddered, and felt an answering quake beneath her.

Gliding her hands down Simon's sides, she gently massaged the tender muscles around his thighs and the root of his manhood. His erection stiffened beneath her touch.

"When you're ready," he said.

Slowly, she inched forward, taking him into herself. She watched the almost unbearably erotic play of emotion across Simon's face as he tipped his head back, eyes closed, and let her claim him.

When she thought he was as deeply inside her as he could go, he bent his knees, sliding her forward that last little bit. They groaned together. But she knew they could be closer still.

His hands settled around her waist, and Beth leaned backwards, grabbing his ankles to brace herself. She took a deep breath, and when she exhaled, she thrust her hips forward.

Spots of red light darkened her vision. She breathed deeply again, straightening her back and slipping a little way off of him. With her next exhale, she thrust herself over him again, crying out as he filled her as deeply as she could dream.

She mimicked his earlier motions with tiny back and forth thrusts, teasing him without letting him seat his fullness within her. Simon's face contorted with effort, his breathing labored. Slowly, ever so slowly, she sank onto him, until he filled her. Again, she rose up and sank slowly onto him.

He forced his eyes open, staring up at her with passion dilated pupils. She teased him again with short, quick dips.

Groaning, he pleaded, "Beth. Beth. Beth!"

She sank onto him, her own trembling making it difficult to move as slowly as she wished. Her arms and thighs shook with restraint as she eased herself off of him, then started down again. Almost. Almost, but she didn't think she had the strength for one final thrust.

"Simon, help me."

He placed his hands around her waist and lifted her, then pulled her down. She strained for that last fraction, aching for his deepest touch. Her body shook and trembled above him, but she couldn't quite reach.

Then he arched his back, rising up to meet her as he pulled her down. He filled her, completely, once again touching her inner depths.

She screamed his name as the most powerful release yet ripped through her, leaving no cell untouched by its force. Spent, she collapsed forward, once again covering his body with her own.

Beneath her, Simon gasped and groaned, trembling, and chanted over and over, "We are one. We are one. We are one."

She felt him suddenly still and relax, going limp and sliding out of her, although she hadn't felt his release. She considered asking him about it, but the thought of speech seemed like too much effort. Instead, she closed her eyes and spread over the musky warmth of his sweat dampened body like water, poured from a bottle and finding its new level.

Later, much later, the cramps he'd warned her about finally struck, forcing Beth to roll off of him with a yelp.

"Ow! Cramp!" She beat uselessly at her calf.

Simon woke instantly, and captured her leg in his strong hands. Probing lightly with his fingertips, he quickly found the knotted muscle, and assaulted it with a deep massage. She sighed in pleasure.

"Better?" he asked.

"Yes, much. Thank you." She slipped her leg out of his grasp, and stood up.

A moment later, he joined her. Beth couldn't believe the change in attitude, from the exhausted man who had dragged himself out of the workroom, to the vibrant man before her now.

Something teased the back of her mind. Something about exhaustion.

Her eyes widened, and her hand flew up to muffle her gasp.

Simon stepped forward, his eyes darkening with concern. "Beth? What's wrong?"

"Oh my God. I can't believe I made love like that with Keith in the house."

Simon froze. "You let someone into the house? Today?"

"It's just Heather's friend Keith. And you didn't see him. The poor boy was running on the very edge of his endurance. If I'd turned him away, he wouldn't have made it to the end of the driveway. He collapsed before I could get him to the couch in the front parlor."

"What did you do with him?"

"I dragged him the rest of the way. It was easy, because he's painfully thin. I figured he'd sleep for hours, and left him a note saying there were sandwiches in the kitchen and for him to help himself."

Simon snatched up the two pillows and the length of red silk. Crossing to his other belonging piled next to the door, he dropped his current load and picked up his watch.

"It's already after four. Dusk will be coming soon, and Halloween. We have to start the final ritual now."

CHAPTER TWENTY

Simon arranged the tools he would need for his spells in the center of the room, placing his athame beside the previously prepared chalice. The arrangement reminded him of the "Blade in Chalice" protection spell he'd performed with Beth. That spell had been so much stronger than he'd anticipated. Now he understood why he and Beth together made such powerful magic. He only hoped he had enough skill to channel that power.

He directed Beth to her place by the altar and lifted his arms, ready to begin. But something felt wrong.

After a moment of thought, he retrieved the length of red silk they'd lain on to share the power of their love. He covered the altar with that, then rearranged his tools on top of it.

Beth tipped her head in confusion. "That wasn't part of the ritual we worked out."

"I know." He shrugged. "So much of magic is focusing the will. I thought the visible reminder would help you concentrate on transferring your energy to me."

She smiled. "I think you're right."

Leaving her to contemplate her crucial role in the upcoming ritual, Simon started his first protection spell. Soon, he was completely involved in the delicate mesh of will and word that molded his power into an impermeable shell of defense.

The last phrase of the spell slipped into place, completing the solid strength of his working. He blinked, coming back to the world around him.

Beth was watching him with wide eyes. When she realized he was looking at her and actually seeing her, she pointed at the athame.

"Is it time?"

"Not yet. That was only the outer protection." He stretched, rolling his muscles, and breathed deeply.

"But you're so tired! I could see the energy draining out of you."

He felt the twinges of abused muscles, and the bone-deep weariness that accompanied strong magic. After he cast the inner circle, he'd have barely enough energy left for a metaphysical tap on the shoulder, let alone a full attack. Without Beth's help, he would have been doomed.

"I know," he said. "That's why I need your strength."

She nodded, standing tall in solemn promise. "Let me know when, and it's yours."

The inner circle did not require nearly as much effort to cast. Simon would keep the entity within the charged space by defeating it. If he failed, the circle would collapse. Its only purpose was to hide the stronger, outer circle from the entity's perception, so that it could be tricked into instantiating where Simon could fight it.

Weak with exhaustion, Simon joined Beth in front of the altar. He leaned against the sturdy block of marble under the guise of straightening the tools. His fingers brushed the chalice containing his stored power, and the overflow of energy restored him enough to straighten and smile at Beth.

"You're on," he told her.

"A kiss for luck." She leaned forward and kissed him, the brief touch echoing all they had shared together. Then, she picked up the athame and held the blade poised over her wrist.

Simon began chanting the invocation. At his signal, she slashed her wrist, gasping at the fiery pain of the knife biting through her flesh. Her blood welled up, first dripping, then pouring in a stream over her clenched fist and into the waiting cup.

The veil between the planes faded, casting Simon into a milky gray mist where only the glowing chalice had any fixed form. Faster than would normally happen from loss of blood, he drew Beth's life force from her body, emptying her memories and emotions, hoarding her strength.

He could no longer see her clearly, but heard her labored breathing. The athame tumbled from her fingers, the length of silk muffling the clang of steel blade against marble slab. She slumped forward, sprawling across the altar.

With all his heart, Simon longed to use the energy filling him to wake her, to restore her spirit and rekindle her life. His fingers tightened around the stem of the chalice. Softly at first, then growing in strength, he cast the spell that invited the entity to fill the vacancy Beth's spirit had left.

Beth straightened, and turned to him with a smile like none he'd ever seen on her face. Every sense within him screamed that an abomination stood before him.

She flexed her arms, gathering power. Simon let it build as long as he dared, then threw the contents of the chalice onto her chest and face. With all of Beth's and his combined power, he fought to drive the entity out of the material plane.

The snap of transferred energy echoed just below conscious hearing, but nevertheless set his ears ringing. Beth blinked, and with shaking fingers, wiped the blood from her eyes. Simon sensed no trace of the entity remaining in the circle with them.

"Is it over?" she asked. "Did we win?"

Simon placed his hands over the chalice, draining any remaining power from it. Picking up the blood-slicked athame, he circled the altar, dispersing the inner protective spell and reabsorbing as much of its energy as he could. Only after he'd prepared himself for a surprise attack did he answer Beth's question.

"No. We were tricked."

Beth closed her eyes, an expression of pain passing over her face. Then, with a soft sigh, she crumpled to the floor.

"Beth!"

Simon bolted to her side. He pressed two fingers against the side of her neck, reassured to feel a pulse. But it was so weak!

"Of course," he muttered. "Loss of blood. Purely physical, but just as dangerous."

He stretched her out on the floor, then bent her knees to keep the blood pressure up in her heart and head. Pressing the flat of the athame against her wrist, he used the residual power of the blade to speed healing energy to her.

Her condition was stabilized, but he didn't dare use any more power to help heal her until he discovered how the entity had slipped their noose. Their attack hadn't driven it off completely, but he'd felt the spell connect. The entity was weakened. If Simon could track it down, he still had a chance to defeat it before it could cause any more trouble.

But first, he needed more power. Turning his attention to the more complex outer circle, he started unraveling it.

"Hello? Is anyone here?" a muffled male voice called.

Simon nearly lost the power he was working with. He'd forgotten about the student Beth had invited in.

He glanced around the workroom, seeing it as a stranger would—Beth lying like a corpse next to the altar, and blood everywhere.

If he could spare the power, he'd send a subtle compulsion to the boy, steering him clear of the secret door in the study. But he had no power to spare.

He had no time to spare, either. Simon needed to dissipate the protective circle as quickly as he could, to reclaim the most power possible. But he didn't dare start the process when he could so easily be interrupted. Losing his concentration would be disastrous.

With no occult solutions available, he fell back on a traditional strategy. He held his breath and didn't move, hoping Keith would pass by the silent room.

Simon could hear footsteps now, the soft squeak of sneaker treads on a hardwood floor.

"Hello? Anybody here?" Keith's voice carried clearly from the study. "Hey, what's with this bookcase?"

Simon closed his eyes briefly, offering an incoherent prayer to all the gods and beings who protected Guardians. The prayer went unanswered. The false door swung open.

Keith looked inside the workroom, doing a double take as he spotted Simon, Beth, and the results of their failed spell. His eyes widened.

"Oh my god!"

"Keith, this isn't what it looks like."

"It's not real blood?"

Okay, it was what it looked like. Damn it, Simon did not have the time to deal with the boy now. He had to find the entity before it did any more damage.

He spread his hands in a pacifying gesture. As Keith's wide-eyed gaze tracked the movement, Simon realized too late that his hands were stained with Beth's blood.

"Look, I can explain," Simon said. He quickly weighed the loss of power versus the loss of time, and decided in favor of time. Placing the smallest bit of power behind his words, he said, "Nothing happened here that needs to concern you."

"I'm not concerned." Keith smiled.

Simon's blood ran cold. He recognized that smile. He'd seen it on Beth's face, just before he blasted the entity out of her. But how had it managed to possess Keith so swiftly?

Hiding his feelings, Simon kept his expression bland as he waved Keith forward. "Come see. She's fine."

Every sense of self preservation screamed at him to keep the entity where he could see it, but Simon forced himself to turn away from the entity, and turn toward Beth. His one hope lay in convincing the entity that he didn't suspect it was inhabiting Keith's body.

Behind him, he heard Keith step forward, stopping just outside of the protective circle. Simon held his breath, convinced that he'd finally done something right. In an effort to conserve his power, he'd limited the circle as much as he could. It had the strongest magic he was capable of, to prevent anything from escaping from inside it. But there were no spells preventing things from entering the circle.

The entity apparently paused to look for protective spells. It couldn't find the circle Simon had already dissipated, and failed to notice the one-way protections still standing. No doubt thinking Simon had dissipated all of his wards, Keith entered the circle.

Keith stopped next to Simon, his confident and arrogant posture at odds with the scrawny body he wore.

"You're supposed to be such a hotshot protector," Keith taunted. "You sure as hell couldn't protect her. Unless you meant to kill her."

Simon's heart plunged. But no, Beth was not dead. He could feel her strength and love, faint but definitely alive.

He turned to face the entity. "I meant to kill you."

Keith threw his head back and laughed. "Oh, very good, professor man. But you didn't, did you? I took out both of your girlfriends, and you couldn't even scratch me. Now that I'm back, you haven't got a prayer."

The entity bent forward and picked up the discarded chalice. "This was a clever conceit, I'll give you that much. But in the end, it didn't matter. A straightforward expulsion spell? Puh-lease! I learned the counter to that when I was still in diapers."

Simon's mind was racing, trying to fit what he was learning with what Andrew had told him. Clearly, he was speaking with the human symbiote that had melded with the elemental. But rather than the elemental mining the human's memory for knowledge, the human spirit appeared to have stolen the elemental's power.

A dangerously daring plan formed in Simon's mind. If he could split the human and elemental symbiotes, they might cease to be threats. Quite likely, on its own, the elemental would have no malicious intent toward the material plane. And the human would lack the power to do anything about its hatred and fury.

The best aspect of the plan was that Simon knew just how to break them apart. It was a defensive, healing spell, the last thing the entity would be expecting. There was only one problem. He needed to know exactly who he was casting the spell upon. Somehow, he'd have to trick the entity into revealing its true name.

Simon grabbed the chalice out of Keith's grasp. "That's a lot of fancy talk. But I notice I'm still alive, so you can't be as powerful as you pretend."

Keith's face tightened in fury. "You were trying to kill me. I wasn't trying to kill you. I don't want you dead."

"What do you want?"

"I want you broken and beaten. I want to see Andrew admit his perfect protégé is nothing, that I am the better magician."

Andrew? The clues snapped into place. Simon was dealing with Andrew's former apprentice. The one Andrew had failed to protect while he confronted an elemental to prove his skill with attack magic.

The entity continued to rant, but Simon ignored him.

Carefully, Simon formed the shape of the spell he wanted, speaking the words silently in his mind. He fed all of his remaining strength into the magic. When it was ready, he faced the entity, and shouted the key words to invoke the spell.

The entity smirked, amused by Simon's efforts.

Simon bared his teeth in a primal smile, and said clearly, "Scott Hanson."

His shot struck home. The entity howled and tried to flee, but the protective circle contained it. It turned at bay, its back pressed to the flowing wall of power. Scott struggled to find a counterspell, but the Guardians didn't teach counters to healing spells. After all, why would anyone want to break a spell protecting them from elemental influences?

Simon's power beat against Scott's furious defenses. They were both weakening. But he knew from past experience how closely matched they were. Either one of them could prove triumphant.

Simon fell to his knees. The world dimmed. He wasn't going to make it. But at least he'd weakened the entity to the point where it couldn't possibly escape from the circle. Esperanza could finish it off when she arrived tomorrow.

As he was losing consciousness, Simon regretted that he hadn't been able to tell Beth he loved her one last time before he died. Although he'd be able to tell her soon enough in the afterlife, since without him to summon help, she would die as well. Then he remembered the sense of her love he'd felt before. Focusing his emotions, he projected all of his love at her.

A wave of love washed over him in return. And with it, Beth's remaining power.

Simon threw himself against the entity with renewed vigor, and felt the entity shatter.

He sensed an elemental, bereft of the malicious will that had given it focus. It lingered for only a moment before dissolving, returning to its home plane.

Scott hung on a little longer, fighting to remain in Keith's body. But without the elemental's power, his willpower was not sufficient. Howling in frustrated rage, his spirit faded from the material plane.

Barely able to focus his thoughts, Simon dissipated the protective circle as quickly as possible. Most of the energy was lost, but he recovered enough for what needed to be done. Crawling to Beth's side, he rested his palm upon her chest, and let the power flow out of him, back into her.

Beth opened her eyes and blinked.

Simon collapsed on top of her, unconscious.

* * * * *

Simon was getting far too familiar with the feeling of having been run over by a truck. Every joint ached. Every muscle throbbed. It felt wonderful.

Slowly, he cranked open his eyelids. White bed, white floor, white walls, and an ugly avocado vinyl chair. He was in a hospital.

But how had he gotten there? He remembered dispersing the protective circle and waking Beth. She must have recovered enough to call for help.

Simon groaned. What had the ambulance crew seen when they arrived? How was he going to explain his secret workroom? Beth must have told them something. But what? And where was she?

He had to find her. He hurt all over, but nothing seemed to be broken. A clear plastic tube was taped to the back of his wrist, leading to a bag hanging from the wall beside his bed, but he seemed otherwise unencumbered by wires or bandages. There was nothing to keep him from getting out of the bed and finding Beth.

He threw off his sheets, and started the slow process of sitting up. A knock on the open door interrupted him.

Detective Freemont walked into the room. "Hey, Professor. Good to see you awake. You gave me a hell of a scare when I walked into your study and saw you covered in blood. I thought you were our next victim."

"I feel like crap, but I'll live." Simon finished pulling himself into a seated position, and looked intently at the detective. "Have you seen Beth? Is she okay? Can I see her?"

The detective raised his hands to forestall any further questions. "Your girlfriend is fine. They patched her up, gave her some blood, and let her go. She's waiting outside now, and can see you as soon as I'm done getting your statement."

Simon tensed. "My statement?"

"Anytime someone calls 9-1-1, we have to file a report. I already took Ms. Graham's statement, and I've got a pretty good idea of what happened. I just need your statement to corroborate hers." Abruptly, his expression shifted from friendly concern to the mask of a disinterested professional. "Are you well enough to answer a few questions?"

Simon sighed. How could he ever explain the situation in his workroom to the police? Although, Detective Freemont had said he'd found Simon in his study. Had Beth somehow dragged the two men out of the workroom before calling 9-1-1? Whatever she'd done, she'd given the detective a plausible explanation. Simon would have to be careful, and try to pick up on whatever story she'd told.

The detective flipped open a notepad and clicked open a pen. "How well did you know Keith Whitehall?"

"Who?"

"The young man who attacked you and your girlfriend."

"Oh. Is that his name?" Simon blinked. "You said 'did' not 'do.' Is he dead?"

"Yes."

Simon closed his eyes, sparing a moment to regret the boy's death and hoping his spirit had found peace. Although that answered his earlier question, as to how the Scott Hanson entity had been able to possess Keith's body so quickly. Beth had been right all along. Keith had formed such a strong connection to the entity that banishing Scott Hanson had severed Keith's spirit as well.

Simon opened his eyes and looked at Detective Freemont. "Is this a murder investigation? Do I need to get a lawyer?"

"No. You're not being charged with anything. It seems like a pretty straight forward case of self defense. But please answer the question. How well did you know Keith Whitehall?"

"I didn't know him. But I knew of him. He was a friend of my graduate assistant, Heather Montcalm. His roommate was the one involved in that murder/suicide. Heather was trying to help Keith work through his grief."

"What was he doing at your house?"

"I think he was looking for Heather."

"Didn't you ask him?"

"I didn't see him. I was in the study, and Beth answered the door. She said he looked exhausted. She decided to let him sleep on the sofa."

"Do you often let people you don't know come into your house to take naps?"

"No, I don't," Simon snapped. He rubbed his untethered hand over his face. "I'm sorry. I know you're just doing your job. Besides I'm not the one who let him in. Beth did. I think she felt sorry for him. And she didn't tell me about it until much later."

"Ah, yes." The detective flipped back a few pages in his notebook. "According to Ms. Graham, she didn't tell you about Keith until the afternoon. About how much after his arrival would that have been?"

Simon considered. "I was in the study most of the morning, so he could have arrived at any point during that time. I can't hear the doorbell when I'm working. But it was at least several hours later."

"I thought you said you didn't know when he arrived."

"I don't."

"Then how do you know how much later it was that she told you?"

"Because she was with me, so he must have arrived before that."

"She was with you the whole time, and didn't mention the young man on your couch?"

"We were busy."

"What was so important that she couldn't find time to tell you about him?"

Simon glanced away, cleared his throat, and glanced back. "We were making love. For about four hours."

The detective stared at him. "You made love for four hours?"

"Or thereabouts."

"I guess the doctors don't need to be concerned about your heart." Freemont shook his head. "No wonder a scrawny little guy could knock you out."

"I wasn't at my best. I'd called in sick on Friday."

"Four hours wasn't your best?" The detective recalled himself to his line of investigation with a visible shake. "Okay, so after you spent the morning catching up on work you'd missed the day before, and the afternoon having sex with your girlfriend, what happened?"

"Well, he must have woken up, and came looking for us."

"Did he say anything when he saw you?"

Simon thought. "I don't really remember. Something along the lines of 'Hello, where is everybody?' I was more concerned about him finding us than with what he was saying."

"Concerned? Had he done something to make you fear him?"

Simon hadn't wanted his ritual discovered, but he could hardly tell the detective that. He settled on a simpler answer. "Beth and I were...um...not dressed for company."

The detective nodded. That detail must have jibed with Beth's version of events. "What happened when he came in?"

"It all happened so fast."

What could Beth have told the police? She was unconscious when Keith came in. But presumably her injury and the resulting blood covering everything was being blamed on Keith's attack, which Simon had been defending her against, rather than on the ritual she and Simon had performed.

Simon rubbed his temples. He really wasn't up to playing hide and seek with the truth.

"Are you okay?" Detective Freemont asked. "Do you want to stop the questioning for a bit? I can call a nurse."

"What I want is to see Beth. Let's just get this over with."

"Why don't you tell me what you can remember?"

"Mostly, I just remember being worried about Beth. I had to keep him away from Beth. She's okay, though, right? You said she was okay."

"She's fine. When did you first perceive the assailant as a threat?"

Assailant. So Keith was supposed to have started the attack. But how could he explain the entity's desire to defeat a magical rival in terms the police could understand? In a flash, Simon realized how to explain events.

"When he came in, I said something about what Beth and I were doing was no concern of his. He answered that he was very concerned. Something about the way he said it made me think he wasn't talking about our sex life."

Simon shook his head. "I wish I'd seen him earlier. Maybe I could have found a way to help him. But by the time he came to see me, it was too late. He seemed completely paranoid. He was convinced that we were enemies and out to get him. I thought he might be on drugs."

"What did he say or do to make you believe that?"

Simon paused, trying to pull together a story that would make sense. The doctors had treated Beth's injury, and would have mentioned that the cut was straight and clean, with no sign of a struggle. The only thing that could explain it was if Beth was unconscious or in shock. Simon hoped that's what Beth had said, and tried to make his version of events vague enough to match whatever answer she'd given.

"He kept saying 'You know what I'm talking about' and asking what I'd told the police. Then he said he'd fix things. And he cut Beth."

Detective Freemont leaned forward. "You saw the weapon?"

"Yes. A bone handled knife. Didn't you find it?"

"No."

Damn. Beth must have left it in the workroom when she dragged them out.

"Well, I can describe it for you. It's mine. A very valuable antique, with a carved bone handle."

"You keep a knife like that just lying around your study?"

Simon chuckled. "Detective, I'm a professor of occult studies. I have all sorts of strange things lying around my study."

"So he used your knife. He didn't have a weapon of his own."

"That's right." Simon wondered why the detective was so interested in the knife, then realized he was trying to connect the crimes. "He cut Beth's wrist, the same way he cut that waitress's wrist, but he used my knife to do it. Maybe he hadn't planned to attack her, and just took advantage of the opportunity."

"How did he subdue her to cut her wrist?"

"I don't know. One moment he was just standing there, saying we knew he was the one everyone was looking for, then he was holding the knife and Beth was bleeding. I think she might have been in shock."

Detective Freemont nodded, and Simon allowed himself to relax. His story was close enough to Beth's to be accepted.

"So then what happened?"

"I had to keep him away from Beth. And I had to get the knife out of his hand. Beth was covered in blood...."

Simon closed his eyes, remembering how pale and still she had been.

"It's all right. She's okay," the detective reassured him.

Simon swallowed and nodded. "I remember wrestling with him, and throwing the knife away where he couldn't reach it. I guess I knocked him down, because I remember trying to put pressure on Beth's wrist, to stop the bleeding, and I wouldn't have done that if he was still fighting."

"That's how the sleeves of your robe got the blood on them?"

"Yes."

"What happened next? When we arrived in response to Ms. Graham's call, you were unconscious."

Damn. He couldn't very well say he'd used up his strength on a healing spell for Beth.

"I'm not sure," Simon said slowly. "I was just thinking about Beth. But I guess he got the jump on me."

"So the two of you struggled. What then?"

"I was fading fast. I remember being terrified of leaving Beth alone with him. I managed to push him away. That's the last thing I remember." Simon hesitated, then asked, "How did he die?"

"You didn't kill him. The doctors think two weeks of near constant stimulant use weakened his heart. He had a massive heart attack."

Detective Freemont stood up, closing his notepad. "Thanks for your help, Professor. That wraps everything up."

"Are you closing the other cases as well?"

The detective nodded, once more treating Simon as an equal. "He had the method and motive. Keith Whitehall was a pre-med student, so he knew all about anatomy and had done a number of dissections for classes. He was apparently unhinged by his roommate's occult inspired suicide. We're checking on his whereabouts during the various crimes, but we expect we'll find he had the opportunity as well. After all, both you and Ms. Graham said he admitted to having perpetrated the crimes."

Indecision clouded the detective's features. "Professor, just between you and me, is that what really happened?"

Simon hesitated, the decades deep habit of silence warring with his newly learned knowledge that some people, like Beth, could be trusted with the truth. "Not exactly."

"Could I ever include what really happened in a police report?"

"No."

"That's what I thought. But we got the bad guy?"

"The bad guy is dead," Simon reassured him. The detective didn't need to know the real bad guy had been Scott Hanson. "You won't have any more attacks or mutilations."

Detective Freemont raised two fingers, brushing the brim of an imaginary police hat in salute. "Do me a favor, then. Don't ever tell me what really happened."

"If you do a favor for me. Go tell Beth it's okay for her to come see me. I want to propose to her before anything else happens."

The detective glanced through the doorway and beckoned. Beth had obviously been waiting just out of sight, and hurried into the room. The detective nodded to her in greeting, then considerately closed the door on his way out.

Beth grinned, her smile lighting up her entire face. "I heard that. Not the world's most romantic proposal, but it's good enough for me. Yes. Nothing would make me happier than to marry you."

Simon held out his hand. Her fingers closed around his. She was his lifeline, his partner, his support, and his love.

"I never would have made it without you," he whispered. "At the end, it was knowing that if I failed, I would be abandoning you to him that give me the strength to defeat him."

"I knew you wouldn't fail."

"You have more faith in me than I have in myself."

She sat carefully on the edge of his bed. "That's what makes us such a powerful team. You have the knowledge, I have the belief. We're two halves of a matched set."

"Like logic and emotion?" He lifted her hands and placed a gentle kiss at the edge of her bandaged wrist. "Except I was filled with emotion. Crazy with love for you, and terrified of losing you."

"And I wasn't exactly illogical. After all, I knew enough to drag you and Keith into the study and close the secret door before the ambulance arrived."

Simon nodded. "Beautiful, brave, and intelligent."

"And you're sexy, strong...and too darn stubborn." She shook her head. "You needed my help, and yet you kept trying to go it alone, doing your macho best to protect me. I'm glad Lydia was so nasty when we first met, or I never would have snuck in to find out what she was doing, and you never would have told me the truth about the Guardians. I might have lost you forever."

Simon stared at Beth for so long that she became alarmed.

"Simon? Don't be insulted."

"I'm not. It's just that you reminded me of the exact words of Lydia's divination. She said she needed to come here in order for me to defeat the entity, and that I couldn't fight it alone. I just assumed that meant she was the one I'd fight it with. But her role was just to get you and me together."

Beth grimaced. "So she really can tell the future?"

"She can see it. She doesn't always understand what she sees." He groaned, imagining their conversation when he saw Lydia again. "I hate it when she's right."

Beth's face transformed with an impish smile. "We'll just have to think of some way to surprise her, then. I wonder what she'd say to being my maid of honor?"

They laughed, holding hands.

About the author:

A pinch of this, a smidgen of that ... and lots and lots of anything sparkly! Whether it's cooking, decorating, or writing books, Jennifer Dunne is never one to do anything the same way twice, allowing her wide-ranging interests to lead her where they will and trusting that sooner or later, it all comes out in the writing. Her strategy has paid off, earning her three EPPIE awards, as well as a host of lesser awards, and devoted fans who eagerly wonder where her next story will take them. Her fiction spans the fantasy, erotic romance, and science fiction genres, but wherever one of her stories goes, it can always be counted on for an exciting ride.

Jennifer Dunne welcomes mail from readers. You can write to her c/o Ellora's Cave Publishing at P.O. Box 787, Hudson, Ohio 44236-0787.

Also by JENNIFER DUNNE:

- Tied With a Bow anthology with Dominique Adair &
  Madeleine Oh
- Luck of the Irish anthology with Kate Douglas & Chris
  Tanglen

Why an electronic book?

We live in the Information Age—an exciting time in the history of human civilization in which technology rules supreme and continues to progress in leaps and bounds every minute of every hour of every day. For a multitude of reasons, more and more avid literary fans are opting to purchase e-books instead of paperbacks. The question to those not yet initiated to the world of electronic reading is simply: *why?*

1. *Price.* An electronic title at Ellora's Cave Publishing runs anywhere from 40-75% less than the cover price of the <u>exact same title</u> in paperback format. Why? Cold mathematics. It is less expensive to publish an e-book than it is to publish a paperback, so the savings are passed along to the consumer.

2. *Space.* Running out of room to house your paperback books? That is one worry you will never have with electronic novels. For a low one-time cost, you can purchase a handheld computer designed specifically for e-reading purposes. Many e-readers are larger than the average handheld, giving you plenty of screen room. Better yet, hundreds of titles can be stored within your new library—a single microchip. (Please note that Ellora's Cave does not endorse any specific brands. You can check our website at www.ellorascave.com for customer recommendations we make available to new consumers.)

3. *Mobility.* Because your new library now consists of only a microchip, your entire cache of books can be taken with you wherever you go.

4. *Personal preferences are accounted for.* Are the words you are currently reading too small? Too large? Too...**ANNOYING**? Paperback books cannot be modified according to personal preferences, but e-books can.

5. *Innovation.* The way you read a book is not the only advancement the Information Age has gifted the literary community with. There is also the factor of what you can read. Ellora's Cave Publishing will be introducing a new line of interactive titles that are available in e-book format only.

6. *Instant gratification.* Is it the middle of the night and all the bookstores are closed? Are you tired of waiting days—sometimes weeks—for online and offline bookstores to ship the novels you bought? Ellora's Cave Publishing sells instantaneous downloads 24 hours a day, 7 days a week, 365 days a year. Our e-book delivery system is 100% automated, meaning your order is filled as soon as you pay for it.

Those are a few of the top reasons why electronic novels are displacing paperbacks for many an avid reader. As always, Ellora's Cave Publishing welcomes your questions and comments. We invite you to email us at service@ellorascave.com or write to us directly at: P.O. Box 787, Hudson, Ohio 44236-0787.

Printed in the United States
22514LVS00003B/49-255